COLD IN

John Harvey is the author of ten Charlie Resnick novels, th was named by *The Times* a Novels of the Century'. His first novel featuring Detective Inspector Frank Elder, *Flesh and Blood*, won the CWA Silver Dagger in 2004, and a Barry Award for the Best British Crime Novel published in the US in 2004. In 2007 John Harvey was awarded the CWA Cartier Diamond Dagger for sustained excellence.

He is also a poet, dramatist and occasional broadcaster. For more about the author please visit www.mellotone.co.uk

Praise for John Harvey

'*Cold in Hand* has sharp plotting, great characterisation and a powerful narrative; it's as good as they get.' *Observer*

'In John Harvey's sure and practised hands, police procedural novels achieve new heights in grainy reality . . . The writing is thrilling and atmospheric.' *Guardian*

'*Cold in Hand* is an impassioned, at times heartbreaking story about love and violence and the breakdown of contemporary society and it confirms Harvey as one of our most accomplished writers in any genre.' *Sunday Telegraph*

'*Cold in Hand* is classic Harvey and classic Resnick . . . [it] doesn't just pack a hefty punch from the word go, it stays with you.' *Daily Mirror*

'[*Cold in Hand*] is quite possibly Harvey's most authoritative in years: visceral, engaged and yes, unputdownable.' *Independent*

JOHN HARVEY

COLD IN HAND

arrow books

Published by Arrow Books 2009

2 4 6 8 10 9 7 5 3

Copyright © John Harvey 2008

First published in Great Britain in 2008 by William Heinemann

Arrow Books
The Random House Group Limited
20 Vauxhall Bridge Road, London, SW1V 2SA

www.rbooks.co.uk

Addresses for companies within The Random House Group Limited can be
found at: www.randomhouse.co.uk/offices.htm

The Random House Group Limited Reg. No. 954009

A CIP catalogue record for this book
is available from the British Library

ISBN 9780099505648

The Random House Group Limited supports The Forest Stewardship
Council (FSC), the leading international forest certification organisation.
All our titles that are printed on Greenpeace approved FSC certified paper
carry the FSC logo. Our paper procurement policy can be found at
www.rbooks.co.uk/environment

Typeset by SX Composing DTP, Rayleigh, Essex
Printed and bound in Great Britain by
CPI Cox & Wyman, Reading, RG1 8EX

For
Robin Gerry, Charles Gregory
David Kresh and Angus Wells

All gone too soon

PART ONE

1

It was that curious time, neither day nor night, not even properly dusk, the light beginning to shorten and fade, the headlights of a few overcautious drivers raising a quick, pale reflection from the slick surface of the road, the main route back into the city. Past Ezee-Fit Tyre Change & Exhaust. Quality Decking. Nottingham Building Supplies. Carpet World. The occasional small parade of shops set back to one side: newsagents, florists, Chinese takeaways, bookies, Bargain Booze.

Lynn Kellogg was driving an unmarked saloon that jolted slightly when she changed down from fourth to third, the force radio whispering sweet nothings through a field of static. She was wearing blue jeans and a pair of scuffed Timberlands, her bulletproof vest still fastened beneath a red-and-black ski jacket, unzipped.

There were school kids all along both sides of the street, spilling over the pavements, pushing, shoving, shirts hanging loose, rucksacks slung over their shoulders, sharing, some of them, the headphones from their MP3s and iPod nanos; a covey of girls, no older than thirteen or fourteen, skirts barely covering their skinny behinds, passing a joint between them. Another day, Lynn might have pulled over, stopped, delivered a lecture. Not today.

The fourteenth of February, Valentine's Day, a little after four p.m. and she wanted nothing as much as to get home at a reasonable time, strip off these clothes and soak in a hot bath. She'd bought a present, nothing fancy, a DVD, *Thelonious Monk, Live in '66*, but it still needed to be wrapped. The card she'd left propped up against the toaster where she thought it might get found. When she glanced in the mirror, the tiredness was all too clear in her eyes.

She had been sitting with her second cup of coffee that morning, half-listening to the early news: another fifteen-year-old had been shot in Peckham, South London, the third in almost as few days. Payback. Bravado. Respect. Some part of her thinking, at least this time it isn't here. She knew the number of senior detectives currently investigating gun-related incidents in the Nottingham area and around was such that the Homicide Unit were having to consider bringing in officers from outside.

As the newsreader moved on to the prospect of more job losses in the industrial sector and she reached for the off switch, the phone cut in.

'It's okay,' she called through to the other room. 'It's probably for me.'

It was. A man holding his wife and children prisoner in Worksop, north of the county, threatening them harm. Almost certainly armed. Lynn swallowed another mouthful of coffee, poured the remainder down the sink, and grabbed her coat from where it was hanging in the hall.

'Charlie, I've got to run.'

'I'll see you later,' he said, hurrying to the door.

'You better.' Her kiss just missed the side of his mouth.

'The table's booked for eight.'

'I know.'

A moment and she was gone.

Nine months earlier, Lynn had finished her training as a hostage negotiator, ancillary to her main role as detective inspector on the Homicide Unit, and since that time she had been called out twice, both incidents being peacefully resolved. In the first, a fifty-five-year-old man, forcibly retired, had held his previous employer captive for eighteen hours, under the threat of trepanning his skull with a sharpened scythe; Lynn had eventually talked him into setting his weapon aside and releasing his prisoner with promises of a hot meal, a probable maximum of seventy-two hours' community service and a personal interview at the local jobcentre. Her second call-out had been to a twenty-four-hour grocery store, where an attempted

5

robbery had resulted in one youth being arrested as he tried to flee the scene, leaving another inside with a Stanley knife to the throat of the terrified Somali shopkeeper. Against Lynn's advice, the incident commander had allowed the youth's mother to talk to the boy directly and her pleas for him to surrender had succeeded where Lynn's had so far failed. Bad practice but a good result, the shopkeeper unharmed, the youth walking out in tears into his mother's arms.

This particular morning it was a thirty-four-year-old engineer who'd returned from a six-month stint in Bahrain the previous evening to find his wife in bed with his ex-best mate, the three kids all downstairs, clustered round the television watching *Scooby-Doo*. The mate had legged it, leaving his trousers dangling from the bedpost and the wife to face the music. Neighbours had registered a lot of banging and shouting, but not thought too much of it, until, in the early hours, the oldest of the children, barely seven, had shinnied through the bathroom window and gone running to the nearest house. 'My dad's gonna kill my mum. He's gonna kill us all.'

By the time Lynn had arrived, the street had been cordoned off, the house surrounded, anyone with a close knowledge of the interior and the family debriefed, both the layout and the names and ages of those inside clear in their minds. Firearms officers were already in position, ambulances ready and waiting. What the boy had told them was halting and confused;

some of the time he seemed to be saying that his father had a gun and sometimes not. They weren't about to take any chances.

The incident commander was Phil Chambers, a detective superintendent Lynn had worked with once before, a murder-suicide out at Ollerton: a husband and wife who'd been together for forty-seven years and wanted it to end the same way. Ben Fowles was the senior firearms officer at the scene, a good thirty pounds heavier than when Lynn had first known him, the pair of them young CID officers working out of Canning Circus station; Fowles moonlighting most weekends, fronting a band called Splitzoid that somehow never seemed to have made the grade.

There was telephone contact with the house, but after the briefest of conversations – little more than grunts and curses – the connection had been broken and the man had so far refused to pick up again. Lynn was forced to resort to a loudhailer, self-conscious despite herself, knowing that all of the assembled officers would be hearing what she said, how she handled the situation, listening and judging.

The man had stepped into clear sight several times, once with what looked like a kitchen knife held against the side of his wife's throat, not an easy shot but possible, nine times, maybe, out of ten. Not a risk they were anxious to run. Not yet, anyway. Lynn had seen Chambers and Ben Fowles several times in close conversation, weighing up the pros and cons, the decision to shoot theirs and not hers. Neither of the remaining children, a girl of five and a three-year-old boy, had been seen for some little time.

'Let the children go,' Lynn said, her voice echoing across the late morning air; the sun up there somewhere, trapped behind a bank of cloud. 'Let them come outside. Their gran's here. She can look after them. Let them come to her.'

The grandmother was standing off to the left of the cordon with other members of the family, agitated, distraught, chain-smoking Silk Cut; a deal had already been struck with a local reporter who was a stringer for one of the nationals – *My Little Angels: a Grandmother's Anguish*. Should the worst happen.

'Let me see them,' Lynn said. 'The children. I just want to be sure they're all right.'

A short while later, he held them up awkwardly to the window, both crying, the boy squirming in his hands.

'Let them go now,' Lynn said. 'Let them out and then we can talk this over. Nobody's hurt yet. Nothing's happened. You should let them go.'

Half an hour later, the front door opened just wide enough for the girl to squeeze through; for a moment, out there on a square of cracked paving, she froze, before running towards a female officer, who scooped her up and carried her off to where her grandmother was waiting. Another minute and the little boy followed, running, falling, scrambling to his feet and then falling again.

The mother's face showed, anxious, at the upstairs

window, before she was pulled away.

'Let your wife out now,' Lynn said. 'Then you and I can talk.'

The window was thrown suddenly open. 'The only way she's coming out's in a fuckin' box!'

And the window slammed shut.

'Could've taken him then,' Ben Fowles said softly at Lynn's shoulder. 'Back home in time for a spot of lunch.'

'Not my call.'

'I know.'

'What's the thinking on the gun?' Lynn asked. 'He armed or not?'

'No sign.'

'Maybe the boy was wrong.'

'Seven, isn't he? Six or seven? Old enough to know what a gun looks like, I should say.'

'He must have been frightened out of his wits, poor kid.'

'Doesn't mean he made a mistake.'

Lynn shook her head. 'I think if he had a gun we'd have seen it by now. His situation, he'd have made sure we did.'

'And if you're wrong?'

She looked at him squarely. 'Either way, unless you and Chambers have got something cooked up between you, we carry on waiting.'

Fowles smiled. 'Till what? He sees the hopelessness of his position? Walks out with his hands above his head?'

'Something like that.'

Out of the corner of her eye, she saw Chambers checking his watch and wondered what calculations he was making.

Not so many minutes later, the man picked up the phone. Lynn was pliant but firm, letting him have something to hold on to, something that could lead to a way out. Little by little, bit by bit. She shook her head, some old song ringing like tinnitus in her ears. Retro nights at the Lizard Lounge. Some white soul singer, she couldn't remember the name. Back when she was a young DC. Before she'd met Charlie. Before everything.

It was close to two and a slow rain was starting to fall.

'Let your wife out through the front door. Once she's outside she should turn to the right where she'll see a female police officer in uniform. She should walk towards her with her hands well away from her body. Is that understood?'

Come on, come on.

The front door budged open an inch or so, then swung wide and the woman stumbled out, blinking as if emerging from the dark. As she began to walk, less than steadily, towards the waiting officer, the door behind her slammed shut.

Lynn gave the man time to get back to the phone.

'All right,' she said. 'If you have a weapon, I want you to throw it out now. Then, once that weapon is secured, you can come out yourself. Walk towards the uniformed officer with your hands in the air and follow his instructions. Lie down on the ground when you are told.'

Moments later there was the sound of a gunshot, muffled, from inside the house.

'Shit!' Lynn said beneath her breath and for a split second she closed her eyes.

Fowles looked across at Chambers and Chambers shook his head. Instead of sending the troops charging in like some SWAT squad on late-night TV, the incident commander was content to bide his time. The man was alone in the house now and a danger only to himself. Assuming he was still alive.

Time was on their side.

When the man failed to pick up the phone, Lynn used the loudhailer instead. Firm but fair. If he could hear her, this is what he had to do.

She repeated it again, unflustered and clear.

Nothing happened.

And then it did. The door opened gradually and a handgun was thrown out on to the grass.

'All right,' Lynn said, 'now step outside slowly with your hands in the air . . .'

Halfway across the patchy square of lawn he stopped. 'Couldn't even do that,' he said to no one in particular. 'Couldn't even do fucking that.'

'Pathetic,' Ben Fowles remarked.

There was a scorch mark on one side of his face; at the last moment he had pulled his head away.

One of the children tried to run towards him, but the grandmother held him back.

11

Not for the first time, Lynn caught herself wishing that she still smoked.

Chambers came over and shook her hand.

Fowles nudged her on the shoulder with his fist. 'Good job,' he said.

Lynn did her best not to smile. Dusty Springfield, she said to herself on the way back to the car, that's who it was. Dusty, the one and only.

She tried Charlie's office number but there was no reply; his mobile seemed to be switched off. No matter, she'd be home now soon enough. A table for two at Petit Paris on King's Walk. Paris, Nottingham, that is. *Moules, steak frites.* A decent bottle of wine. Try to leave room for dessert.

Lucky?

Her hands were still shaking a little when they touched the wheel.

Like a tooth you couldn't stop probing with the tip of your tongue, the song was still nagging away at her as she made a turn on to the Woodborough Road and eased into the outside lane. She heard the call over the force radio nonetheless: disturbance on Cranmer Street, near the junction with St Ann's Hill Road. Only moments away.

'Tango Golf 13 to Control.'

'Control to Tango Golf 13, go ahead.'

'Tango Golf 13 to Control. I'm on Woodborough Road, just turning into Cranmer Street now.'

Lynn swung sharp left across the traffic, cutting off a

mud-spattered four-by-four and causing it to brake sharply. Cranmer Street was only narrow, barely a two-car width, vehicles parked down the left-hand side making it narrower still. A builder's van with fading Forest stickers in its rear windows made to pull out in front of her and then thought better of it.

'Control to Tango Golf 13. Response units are attending. Advise await their arrival.'

There were several small blocks of new-build flats high on the right and beyond those an old municipal building that was now student accommodation. Behind fencing along the near side, the ground was being cleared, deep holes being dug; council housing demolished and replaced. Just opposite the intersection with St Ann's Hill Road, a crowd of youths, many of them wearing hoodies – what else? – had gathered in a rough circle that spread out across the street.

As Lynn cut the engine, she heard the sound of shouting, raucous and angry; chanting, like a soccer crowd baying for blood.

'Control, this is Tango Golf 13. I'm on Cranmer Street at the scene. A gang of fifteen or twenty youths fighting.'

Lowering her window she heard a scream, urgent and shrill, the one followed almost immediately by another.

'Control, this is Tango Golf 13. I'm on top of the incident and shall have to intervene. Immediate back-up required.'

'Control to Tango Golf 13, advise—'

But she was already out of the car and running towards the crowd.

'Police! Police, let me through.'

As she pushed her way into the circle, an elbow struck Lynn in the ribs and an outflung hand caught her high on her cheek, a signet ring breaking the skin.

A few of those standing at the front turned to see what was happening and she was able to force her way to the centre. Faces, all shades, stared at her, showing everything from indifference to pure hate. Young males mostly, wide-leg jeans slung so low it seemed as if their crotch hung somewhere down between their knees. More than a few wearing black and white, Radford colours. A gang thing, is that what this was?

'Fuck off, bitch!'

A head arched sharply back then jerked forward and the next second she was wiping a gobbet of spittle from her hair.

Jeers. Laughter.

More shouts, more threats.

The two young women – girls – who'd been at the heart of the fighting had broken apart when Lynn pushed her way through.

Fifteen, she guessed, sixteen at best.

The one closest to her – thin white face, head close-shaven like a boy's, leather jacket, black-and-white scarf, skintight black jeans – was bleeding from a cut high on her left cheek, a slow trickle of blood running down. There was another cut on her arm. Her adversary, facing Lynn, was most likely mixed race,

14

dark hair tied back, denim jacket and jeans, a short-bladed knife in her hand.

Lynn took a step forward, focusing on the girl's eyes.

'Okay, put the knife down.'

Two steps more, then three. Slow, measured, as assured as she could be. Somewhere in the middle distance, the sound of a police siren coming closer. Overhead, the street lights seemed to be getting brighter with each second.

'Put it down.'

The girl's eyes were bright, taunting, only the merest flicker of fear. Of doubt.

The crowd almost silent, scarcely moving.

'Down.'

Another half-step and the expression on the girl's face changed, her shoulders seeming to relax as she shifted her hold on the knife and lowered it to her side.

'On the ground,' Lynn said quietly. 'Put it on the ground.'

The girl began to bend as if to obey, Lynn reading too late the widening of her eyes, too slow to counter the movement, lithe, as she sprang past, the blade slashing at the right side of the other girl's face and opening it like a ripe plum.

The girl screamed.

Lynn pivoted on her left foot, seizing the attacker by the sleeve and swinging her hard round, one knee coming up into the small of her back, her fist chopping down on the girl's elbow and the knife tumbling to the kerb, the girl continuing to struggle all the same.

15

The police siren was closer still, the sound of an ambulance in its wake.

Lynn had forced the girl's right arm high behind her back when, from the corner of her vision, she saw the youth step forward from the retreating crowd, arm raised. Time enough, as she swung towards him, to note the black-and-white bandana wound tight around his head, the pistol held almost steady in his hand, the contempt in his eyes. The force of her movement took the girl round with her, propelling her forwards, the first shot striking Lynn in the chest and seeming to lift her off her feet before sending her stumbling back, legs folding beneath her, falling away even as the girl, still standing, free hand outstretched as if to ward off what was to come, took the second bullet in the neck, immediately above the gold chain she wore with her lover's name engraved, a wash of blood arcing over the mottled ground and into Lynn's mouth and eyes.

2

Early evening. A & E at the Queen's Medical Centre housed the usual miscellany: elderly ladies who had lost their footing on slippery, uneven pavements and taken a tumble, bruising a coccyx or fracturing for the second time an already pinned hip; disorientated men of uncertain years with voices like rusted industrial saws, whose clothes stank of stale urine and hostel disinfectant; distraught mothers with babies who would simply not stop crying or fractious toddlers with badly grazed heads and gashed knees; a scaffolder who had stepped, helmetless, out into the air from the roof of a four-storey building; a trainee chef with the first two joints of his middle finger safe in a plastic bag of slowly melting ice; a young Muslim girl of twelve who had just started her first period; a cyclist who had been sent somersaulting high into the road by the outflung door of a Cherokee Jeep; a charmless fourteen-year-old boy, alarmed and obese, who had been taunted into swallowing the dregs of a bottle of toilet cleaner: each and every one waiting.

Later, when the clubs had spilled out on to the streets and the pubs had finally called last orders, there would be the usual motley collection of barely walking wounded, drunk many of them, drugged, loud and angry and all too ready to strike out in frustration, bleeding from encounters with brick walls or nightclub bouncers, or injured in scuffles that had set off for no better reason than an ill-judged look, a nudged shoulder, a drink sent flying; and this being Valentine's Night there would be a slow procession of discarded lovers, for whom the occasion had led to bitter accusations, confessions of infidelity, sudden realisations, overdoses, stabbings, attempted suicides, broken relationships that would be mended tearfully, some of them, there amongst the crowded chairs with dawn approaching.

The triage nurse barely looked up as Resnick approached, tall, bulky, his shirt crumpled, jacket unfastened.

'Lynn Kellogg,' Resnick said, 'she was brought in twenty minutes ago. Half-hour at most.'

The name rang no obvious bells.

'She's a police officer,' Resnick said, persevering. 'She was shot.'

The nurse looked up then, little more than a glance, enough to read the anxiety in his eyes. 'And you're what? The father?'

Resnick bridled, reining back his anger. 'No, I'm . . . we live together.'

'Right.' She looked at him again. One of the buttons on his jacket, she noticed, was just hanging by a thread.

'Look . . .' Resnick fumbled in his wallet. 'I'm a police officer too. Detective inspector.'

The nurse handed him back his warrant card. 'Go down that corridor, third cubicle on the left.' And went back to her list.

Lynn was lying on a narrow bed, pillows at her head and back, wearing a flimsy hospital gown. Her own clothes were neatly folded on a plastic chair.

He had been standing there for some moments before she opened her eyes.

'Hello, Charlie.'

Her voice was faint, like something passing on the wind.

'How you feeling?' he asked, reaching for her hand.

She made an effort to smile. 'Like I've walked into a ten-ton truck.'

'She's a little woozy,' the doctor said, appearing at Resnick's shoulder. 'Something we've given her for the pain.'

He was young, late twenties Resnick reckoned, little more, and spoke with an Australian accent, not too strong. Australia or New Zealand, he could never be sure.

'How is she?' Resnick asked.

'I'm fine,' Lynn said from the bed.

'A lot of bruising around the point of impact,' the doctor said. 'Tender certainly. Could be a fractured rib

19

or two. We're going to run her down to X-ray, get that checked.'

'Nothing more?' Resnick asked. 'Internal?'

'Not as far as we can tell. I've had a good listen to the lungs and they seem to be functioning properly.'

Resnick was still holding Lynn's hand and he gave it a squeeze.

'Up and around in no time,' the doctor said cheerfully. 'Chasing down the bad guys.'

Lynn said something neither of them could properly hear.

'Back in two shakes,' the doctor said, leaving them alone.

Resnick lowered himself on to the edge of the bed, careful of her legs.

'I'm sorry,' Lynn said.

'What for?'

'Dinner. We were meant to be having dinner.'

'That doesn't matter.'

'Your card . . .'

'I saw the card. Thank you. It was lovely.'

There were tears at the corners of her eyes.

'What?' Resnick said.

'I should have waited, shouldn't I?'

He didn't answer.

'Back-up. I should have waited for back-up instead of going blundering in . . .'

'You didn't blunder.'

'I made a mistake.'

Resnick shook his head. 'You did what you had to do.'

'And nearly got myself killed.'

Resnick breathed out slowly. 'Yes,' he said and folded both of her hands in his.

'The girl,' Lynn said. 'The one who was shot . . .'

'I don't know. Touch and go, I think.'

'You'll find out.'

'Yes.'

'You could go now.'

He shook his head. 'I'll wait. A few minutes won't make any difference, either way.'

'What about the other one?' Lynn asked. 'The other girl. Her face was badly cut.'

'Here now, as far as I know. Getting stitched up.'

The curtain was pulled to one side and a nurse came through with a wheelchair. 'Time to take you for a little ride,' she said cheerily.

Resnick leaned over carefully and kissed Lynn on the cheek.

'Here,' she said, holding out one hand, loosely closed into a fist.

'What is it?'

When she opened her fingers, there was his loose button, snug in her palm. 'Take care of it. I'll sew it back on when I get home.'

'Promises,' Resnick said, and grinned.

The officer outside Intensive Care hastily dropped his newspaper to the floor, the crossword less than a quarter done.

'Sorry, sir. I . . . the girl, Kelly, they've taken her

21

down. She's being operated on now. I thought it best to stay here.'

'The family?'

'In the cafeteria, waiting. I said I'd contact them if there was any news.'

'Kelly, you said the girl's called?'

'Yes, sir.' He checked his notebook. 'Kelly Brent.'

Resnick nodded. The name meant nothing to him. Not until that moment.

'I'll be down in A & E,' he said. 'You hear anything specific, any change, find me, let me know.'

Lynn was sleeping, her face, devoid of any make-up, young and pale. A thin dribble of saliva ran down on to the pillow from one corner of her partly open mouth and Resnick wiped it away.

'She's lucky,' the doctor said. 'No fracture, as far as I can tell. Heavy bruising around the third and fourth ribs, close to the sternum. Breathing's going to be painful for a while, and she'll likely be tired, sleepy, but otherwise she'll be okay.'

'How long before she's up on her feet?'

'On her feet? As long as she's sensible, nothing too strenuous, a matter of days. Fully operational, though, if that's what you're asking, I'd say a couple of weeks.' He nodded back towards Lynn. 'You two, you're an item?'

An item, Resnick thought. He supposed they were, that at least.

'Yes,' he said.

22

'Word to the wise,' the doctor said, and winked. 'These next few weeks, take your weight on your elbows, okay?'

Home, she slept.

Resnick, fearful of accidentally knocking into her, dismissed himself to the spare bed, where he lay fitfully, staring at the ceiling, getting up finally at two and mooching from room to room, unable to stop his mind from playing over what might have been.

Lucky, the doctor had said.

Nearly got myself killed.

If Lynn hadn't been in too much of a hurry to get home and still wearing the bulletproof jacket, she would likely have been where Kelly Brent was now, in the operating theatre, fighting for her life.

Resnick poured himself another Scotch and looked again at the Valentine's card Lynn had given him, a simple heart, red against a pale background. Written inside, in her sloping hand: *Still here, Charlie, against all the odds. All my love.* Then kisses, a small triangle of them, pointing down.

When Lynn had first moved in with him, the best part of three years before – and this after a plethora of overnights and occasional weekends, holidays, periods when they were close and others when they pulled apart, unable to decide – a friend of hers had sent her a CD by a singer called Aimee Mann, the title of one particular track, 'Mr Harris', highlighted in green. The story of a younger woman falling in love with an older man, despite her mother's best advice. A father figure, the song goes, must be what she wants.

When they had first slept together, made love, himself and Lynn, it had been soon after her father's funeral, dead from cancer at not so much more than Resnick was now. A blessing, in a way, that he went when he did. Better than it dragging on. The pain. Death. Sooner or later, it came to us all.

I suppose, Resnick thought, we're programmed to think the oldest die first, fathers before daughters, mothers before sons. It's the way it most usually is. Anything else seems wrong. Aberrant. Yet in a split second yesterday, the time it takes to squeeze back on the trigger, propel a bullet from a gun, that could all have changed.

Lucky?

Resnick turned and looked around the room. A magazine Lynn had been reading left on the floor by where she normally sat. Her bag hung over the back of a chair. A painting that she'd bought in a charity shop – a landscape of hills, bare trees and snow – brought home and hung on the wall alongside the stereo. A photograph of her parents, leaning on a farm gate, looking out. A pair of slippers on the floor. Reading glasses. A glove. Clutter. Stuff. A life they shared.

This house he'd lived alone in for years, some of the rooms unused and thick with dust. Must rattle around in there, Charlie, like a pea in a drum. Find somewhere smaller, why don't you? Nice little flat. Take in a lodger, at least.

No, he'd say, I'm fine. Suits me just as it is.

And it did.

Until the day – the afternoon – he had heard her car, recognised the sound of the engine as it pulled up outside – the interior jam-packed, barely room for her to squeeze behind the wheel. Just a few boxes, Charlie, I'll go back later for the rest.

Now it was different: it was this.

Lucky?

At twenty-one minutes past three that morning, sixteen-year-old Kelly Brent, sixteen years and nine months, was declared dead at the Queen's Medical Centre, two operations unable to successfully repair the lacerated tissue and stem the bleeding, or to restore the flow of blood to the brain.

Lucky for some.

Resnick stood for a while at the bedroom door, listening to Lynn's breathing, before settling back into the spare bed and, against the odds, falling almost immediately to sleep.

The phone rang at twenty to seven, startling him awake: Detective Superintendent Berry from the Homicide Unit.

'Breakfast, Charlie? That Polish place up on Derby Road, still a favourite of yours? Thought we might have a little chat.'

3

Five years Resnick's junior, Bill Berry was a hard-edged Lancastrian who had settled in the Midlands some twenty or so years before, without ever losing an accent that had been honed close to the Pennines, or an abiding interest in the fortunes of Lancashire County Cricket Club and Preston North End.

Much like Resnick himself, Berry had worked his way up through the ranks, the difference being that where Resnick's career had stalled, in part through his somewhat curmudgeonly resistance to change, Berry's had elevated him to the rank of detective super-intendent.

Not without it being earned.

He was, in the old-fashioned argot of the trade, a good copper.

He had a full head of hair, a chiselled face and, since his last promotion, a taste for tailored suits that sat a touch uneasily on his rawboned, angular body. He was already at the table, leafing through the morning paper, when Resnick arrived.

'Charlie,' he said, half-rising. 'Good to see you.'

The two men shook hands.

'In the news again for all the wrong sodding reasons.'

Resnick grunted agreement. However hard the public-relations staff at Reputation Nottingham tried to put a positive spin on things, the public perception of the city these past years had changed. And not always for the better.

When it had been announced that London had won the bid for the 2012 Olympics, the joke had been that with several of the events being outsourced, the rowing would be at Henley, the horse riding at Badminton and the shooting would be in Nottingham. Robin Hood had now, it seemed, abandoned Lincoln green for upmarket sportswear, developed a taste for crack cocaine, and, instead of his trusty bow, had a 9mm automatic tucked down into the back of his jeans.

Unfair or not, mud stuck.

'How's the lass?' Berry asked.

'Lynn? Well enough. Bruised ribs, nothing worse.'

'Young bones,' Berry said with a wink. 'Soon mend, eh?'

'Something you wanted to see me about,' Resnick said.

'You didn't catch local TV this morning, any chance?'

Resnick shook his head.

'Brent family out in force, bigging it up for the cameras. Breakdown in law and order, too many guns on the streets, police failing in their duty, the usual malarkey.'

'They're angry.'

'Course they're bloody angry. And looking for someone to blame, I can see that. Schools, teachers, the courts, the council, probation, you and me – everyone except them-bloody-selves. Anything other than accept responsibility. Fathers, especially. No, easier to go off and raise a petition, start a campaign. Come Sunday there'll be a minute's silence out on Slab Square and everyone'll go off feeling better about themselves, but what flaming good does it do? By evening kids'll be back out on the streets and it starts all over.'

Resnick sighed. Education, wasn't that at the heart of it? Jobs, housing? Maybe the Brents were right to feel they deserved better.

'What was she, Charlie, this kid? Sixteen? Barely that. My kid or yours, she'd not be out there running with a gang, likely doing drugs, getting laid. Ask yourself why.'

Resnick didn't have a daughter. If he had, he'd no idea what it would be like to help her live her life without due harm. Except that it would be hard.

'Let's order,' Berry said. 'Smell from that grill's making me fair starving.'

He had bacon, sausage and fried eggs, Resnick pancakes with a couple of rashers of bacon on the side. Coffee, rye bread. Resnick exchanged with the proprietress the few Polish pleasantries that came easily to the tongue. Since he'd started living with Lynn, his visits to the Polish Club had become less and less frequent; now months could pass without him ever stepping through the door.

'Kelly Brent's murder,' Berry said. 'I've drawn the short straw.'

Resnick broke off a piece of bread and wiped it around the bacon juices that had collected at the side of his plate.

'I want you for my number two.'

Resnick stopped what he was doing and looked at Berry squarely.

'Jerry Latham for office manager,' Berry said, 'and the outside team, that'd be down to you.'

'Prentiss'd love that,' Resnick said, popping the bread into his mouth.

'Fuck him,' Berry said.

Derek Prentiss was the City Division commander, accountable for balancing budgets and hitting an array of ever-shifting targets, one of which, relating to robbery, was currently Resnick's specific area of responsibility. Since he'd taken charge of the division's robbery squad, the number of offences was down, all right marginally, but improving further, even if the clear-up rate was, as yet, lagging behind. Prentiss wasn't going to be happy with anything that put those figures under threat.

'Besides,' Resnick said, 'with Lynn involved . . .'

'Outside team, Charlie, that's where I want you, like

29

I said. No conflict of interest there. Any part she's got to play, evidence, whatever, you steer well clear.'

'I don't know.' Resnick shook his head.

'It's your patch, Charlie.'

'Used to be.'

'Youths likely involved'll be known to some of your lot, I'd not be surprised. Street robberies and the like.'

'Possible.'

'More than bloody possible.' Berry speared a piece of sausage with his fork. 'Come on, Charlie. Stop dicking me around. Bring one of your lads in with you, if it'd make you feel happier.'

Resnick leaned back, pushing away his plate as he did so. 'What you're not saying, Bill, behind all this flannel, Homicide's stripped so bare there's no bugger else. It's either me or a DI you don't know from outside.'

Berry laughed. 'Some clever bastard wheeled up from the Met. I'd love that, right enough. But no, that's not it. That's not it at all.'

'No?'

'Charlie, Charlie. A bloke with a good head on his shoulders, someone I can bloody rely on, someone I can trust. That's why I want you.'

'Is it, bollocks!'

Berry laughed even louder. 'Come on, Charlie. Kids thievin' mobile phones and MP3 players, old dears having their pensions snatched, that's not your mark. This'll get you out of the office for a bit, instead of shuffling bloody papers. Bit of real police work for a

30

change. Let me put my feet up on the desk, instead.'

Angling away, Resnick looked out through the glass at the traffic making its way up Derby Road from the city centre. For years he'd been stationed at Canning Circus, no more than a stone's throw from where they were now, his squad handling everything from petty misdemeanours to murder. Not much time in those days for Best Value Programmes or monthly Performance Scrutiny Boards, little of the pressure of constantly changing Home Office directives.

What had Berry just said? Some real police work for a change.

'Prentiss,' Resnick said, swivelling back round. 'Even if I wanted to go along. If. He'll never wear it.'

'Don't be so sure. I had a word with the ACC, before I rang you. He'd like to get this little lot sorted as soon as possible. Now what d'you say. In or out?'

Resnick hesitated, but he didn't hesitate for long. 'In,' he said.

'Good man. Now let's get out of here and get things started.'

'Over my dead fucking body!' Derek Prentiss said.

The Assistant Chief Constable smiled a corporate smile. 'I wonder, Derek, if we need to be so extreme.'

If the Divisional Commander could have breathed fire from his nostrils, the reports on the ACC's desk would be singeing at the edges, about to spark into flame. 'You know how long, sir, it's taken to get street robberies under control?'

31

'Of course, Derek, of course. And you know, from the last trimonthly report of the Performance Committee, that's not gone unnoticed. Far from it.'

'Then why the—?'

'Because there are other priorities. And because now the robbery squad's on a more even keel, it shouldn't be beyond the realms of possibility for someone else to steady the ship. For a time, at least.'

Fucking yachting metaphors, Prentiss thought. Just because you've got forty thousand pounds' worth of motor cruiser moored on the Trent.

'A month or so, Derek,' the ACC said, 'that's all. With luck and a following wind, it could be even less. Then you can have him back refreshed. Not that he'll be on board for ever, mind. There's that to consider. Can't be far off his thirty, our Mr Resnick, and then he'll draw his pension and be on his way without so much as a by-your-leave.'

'Not forced to go, sir. Just 'cause his years are in.'

'Wouldn't you?'

Too fucking right, Prentiss thought. 'Not necessarily, sir. Not if I thought there was a job I could still usefully do.'

The ACC gave him a look which suggested that was dubious at best, then glanced down at his desk. There was a meeting of the Corporate Governance Panel in a little over an hour, and before that he'd promised the head teacher of St Ann's Well Nursery and Infant School he'd drop in and present a certificate to the children who'd raised the most money towards sponsoring a police horse called Sherwood.

'All right then, Derek. Thanks for stopping by. Your cooperation, as ever, much appreciated. I know you'll do your best to ensure it all runs smoothly.'

'Yes, sir.'

Bastard, Prentiss thought as he left the room, I hope your boat fucking sinks.

When Resnick nipped home, Lynn was sitting in a wicker chair near the bay windows at the front of the house, cushions at her back, reading a book.

'Shouldn't you be in bed?' he said.

'I got bored.'

'And is that comfortable?'

'Not really.'

He kissed her cheek. 'How's it feel?'

She winced a little as she moved. 'Could be worse. Long as I keep on with the painkillers, it's bearable.'

'Get you anything?'

'Not right now.'

He kissed her again.

'What's that you're reading?'

She held it up towards him. *This Book Will Save Your Life*.

'Bit late for that.'

Lynn smiled. 'Not really that kind of book. Good, though.' She folded down the corner of a page and set the book aside. 'What did Bill Berry want?'

'The girl who was killed, he's leading the inquiry.'

33

'And what? He wants to borrow some of your squad to bump up his numbers?'

'Not exactly.'

She looked at him carefully: no mistaking the smile that was crinkling his eyes.

'He wants you,' Lynn said.

'So it seems.'

'For his number two.'

Resnick nodded.

'Handling the outside team?'

'Yes.'

'Prentiss'll go spare.'

'Over this, apparently, Prentiss has his balls in a vice.'

'I always thought it was just the way he walked.' Lynn laughed and then, as the pain lanced through her, wished she hadn't.

'Are you okay?' Resnick said, concerned.

'It'll pass.'

'You sure I can't get you anything?'

'Some peppermint tea, that would be nice.'

'Have we got any?'

'Somewhere.'

He was almost at the door when she called him back. 'I'm glad. About the inquiry. You'll do a good job.'

'I'll try.'

'I always said you were the best DI I ever worked under.'

'That's just because you were trying to get into my pants.'

'You wish!' She laughed again and grimaced at another sudden shoot of pain. 'You bastard, stop making me laugh.'

Resnick smiled. 'I'll get the tea.'

While he was in the kitchen he made coffee for himself and cut off a slice of bread to go with the nub end of cheddar that had been hiding in the back of the fridge and was just this side of edible. The trouble with big breakfasts, he thought, they made you hungry for the rest of the day.

'I suppose you'll be wanting me to make a statement,' Lynn said.

'Not me. Bill Berry'll get it sorted first thing.' He smiled. 'You're a key witness, after all.'

'He'll want me to go into the station?'

'I shouldn't think so. No sense you rushing back before you have to.'

Lynn nodded and sipped her tea. 'As long as I'm okay by the trial.'

'Your Albanian.'

'Not exactly my Albanian.'

'You know what I mean.'

Nine months before, Lynn had been largely instrumental in the arrest of an Albanian national, accused of murdering an eighteen-year-old Croatian girl at the massage parlour where she worked.

Resnick took a knife to the cheese. 'The inquiry, I was thinking of taking someone from Robbery across with me.'

'A bag man.'

35

'Sort of.'

'Someone to watch your back.'

'Something like that.'

'Mark Shepherd? He's steady.'

Resnick shook his head. 'Catherine Njoroge.'

'Really?'

'You don't think it's a good idea?'

'I don't know. You think she's ready?'

'Yes, I think so.'

Lynn went back to her tea.

Catherine Njoroge was twenty-seven and had been on the force since leaving university; it was only a matter of time before she made the move up from detective constable to detective sergeant. Her family had left Kenya in 1988, during the disturbances following the re-election of Daniel arap Moi to the presidency. Her father was a lawyer, her mother a doctor, and they had hoped she would follow in one set of footsteps or the other. Now they did their best to hide their disappointment and understand the choice their daughter had made.

'She's very lovely, I'll say that for her.'

'Is she? Can't say I'd really noticed.'

'Charlie, you're a terrible liar,' Lynn said, smiling.

The press conference was more than usually crowded, national interest as well as local, more sleek digital cameras and state-of-the-art recorders than the average car boot sale on a Sunday morning. The Assistant Chief Constable sat polishing his glasses, papers on the desk in front of him, Bill Berry to one side and a reluctant Charlie Resnick to the other.

When the press officer had got wind of Catherine Njoroge's involvement in the inquiry, she'd done her utmost to get her up on the platform.

'A young black girl murdered and we're going on national television with three middle-aged white men, how do you think that looks?'

'It looks,' the ACC told her, 'as if we're taking it seriously. Not playing to the fucking gallery.'

Sometimes, she felt like saying, that's not such a bad idea. But this time she bit her tongue and got ready to deflect the fallout as best she could.

Though they were present, no one from the Brent family would agree to join the officers on the platform, no matter the urging: her mother was too distraught, her father too angry. Instead, they sat together at the back of the room, indignation mixed with sorrow on their faces.

'Our sympathies,' the ACC was saying, reading from his prepared statement, 'are with Kelly's family, as they struggle to come to terms with the loss of their daughter. As a force, we share their abhorrence at this thoughtless crime, and their anger. The anger, indeed, of the whole community. And we would ask all members of that community to assist us in bringing Kelly's killer to justice. Someone out there knows who did this, and we would urge them, for the sake of Kelly's family, to contact the police.'

A low rumble of voices from amongst the crowd.

A few more cameras flashing.

The inevitable questions about gun crime from Sky News, Channel 4, ITV.

The ACC slid several pages of bar graphs from the folder in front of him.

'It is important,' he said, 'to see this tragic event in context and to set it against the wider picture. In the operational year to date, the figures for all recorded crime in the city are down, and although there has been a slight, but nonetheless regrettable, increase in recorded crimes against the person, there has also been a significant increase in the number of such crimes detected.

'Much of this is due to our joint initiatives with the city council and an increased emphasis on citizen-focused policing and enhanced community engagement.

'And I can tell you . . .' holding up a sheet of paper, '. . . that in February, the last month for which figures are available, there has been a clear and definite fall—'

'Why?' a voice interrupted from the back of the room. 'Why you going on about this? Statistics, that's all it is. Well, my daughter's no statistic. She's flesh and blood, my flesh and blood – this family, my family – and now she is out there, laying in a morgue somewhere . . .'

'Mr Brent . . .' the ACC said, attempting to override him. 'This is not the place . . .'

News cameras swivelled and refocused and captured Howard Brent, still shouting at the top of his lungs, being escorted out of the hall.

Lynn saw it less than an hour later, edited down, on *BBC News 24*. Read – just a quick cutaway – the acute discomfort on Resnick's face, before the cameras homed in on Brent, standing on the steps outside the building where the press conference had been held. A handsome man of West Indian descent, still comparatively young, soberly dressed in a dark suit and tie, his voice now more under control, though the anger was still evident in his eyes and his stance.

'My daughter was the innocent victim of the violence on our streets. Violence that is threatenin' to tear our community apart, but which the police do nothing about. And why? Because they don't care.

'My daughter Kelly lost her life because she was in the wrong place at the wrong time. But the bullet that took that life was not meant for her. That bullet was meant for a police officer, intent on making an arrest. An officer who, when she was under attack, used my daughter as a shield. A human shield. And if that officer is watching now, I hope she is feelin' guilty for what she has done. Sacrificed my daughter's life for her own.'

What Lynn was feeling was sick, a cold sickness that spread through her and kept her rooted in front of the screen.

4

The incident room was in the Central Police Station, with views out across the new Trinity Square development towards the Victoria Centre and the clock tower that was the last remaining sign of the old Nottingham Victoria railway station. Not that any of the twenty or so officers assembled were, at that moment, concerned with the view.

Conversations faltered as Bill Berry entered with Jerry Latham, the office manager, and then picked up again as Berry and Latham stopped to share a few final words. Resnick, who had been no more than a pace or two behind them, stood to one side, surveying the room. A number of the officers he knew in passing, a few he knew well – Michaelson, Khan, Fisher, McDaniels, Pike. Most were as new to him as he was to them.

Anil Khan, who had worked with Resnick as a young DC, and was now a sergeant in Homicide and on the

40

verge of promotion, came up and shook his hand. 'Like old times, sir.'

'More or less,' Resnick said.

'Lynn, she's all right, I understand?'

'Thanks, yes. Give her a few days, she'll be fine.'

'You'll pass on my best wishes?'

Resnick assured him that he would.

'The girl's father,' Khan said. 'That was way out of line.'

Howard Brent's angry accusation had been repeated endlessly the previous evening, channel to channel, rolling news. In response, the press officer had issued a statement, citing Lynn Kellogg's exemplary record and making reference to a commendation she had received from the Chief Constable for the skill, determination and professionalism she had shown in a recent murder inquiry. 'Detective Inspector Kellogg,' the Chief Constable had said, 'is a credit to the force and the agencies she represents. She fully deserves our gratitude and our praise.'

'We understand,' the statement continued, 'that Mr Brent's remarks were made when he was under considerable personal stress, and the Force continues to have every sympathy for him and his family at this difficult time.'

'Horseshit,' the ACC said, when it was passed by him for approval. 'But horseshit we can live with.'

Of the nationals, only the *Guardian* gave the story any particular prominence on its front page; the *Sun* offered an exclusive interview with Kelly's grieving mother on page five and the *Mirror* countered with a centre spread of colour photographs showing Kelly as Mary in a school production of *Godspell*.

'All right,' Bill Berry said, bringing the room to attention. 'Before we get down to the main business, a word or two about Mr Brent. Unless you've had your head in the sand the past twenty-four hours, you'll be aware of how he's been shooting his mouth off.'

There was enough angry muttering to suggest this was the case.

'Well,' Berry said, 'we've been taking a closer look at the righteous Mr Brent, and he's not the paragon he seems.

'For one thing, rather than being the concerned family man he's setting himself up to be, it seems he walked out on the family home when Kelly was just seven, her brothers eleven and nine. While he was AWOL, he was being chased by the Child Support Agency for nonpayment of dues over a period of almost two years.'

Positive sounds from the assembled troops: payback time. They were enjoying this.

'Brent moved back about five years ago, since which time he's got himself involved in a couple of local businesses, part shares in a Caribbean restaurant in Hyson Green and some gimcrack record shop in Hockley. Both above board as far as we can tell, but might be worth taking a look.'

Berry paused and scanned the room. 'More importantly to us, he's got something of a record. A twelve-month suspended sentence for possession of a class C drug back in '89, and a three-year stretch for ABH.'

'Explains why he's not been home much,' one of the officers at the back remarked.

Laughter all round.

'So,' Berry continued, 'if Mr Brent doesn't keep his head down and his mouth closed, I'll have the Press Office pull the rug from under him so fast he won't know if he's on his head or his arse.'

More laughter.

The DS looked towards Resnick. 'Charlie, you want to bring us up to speed?'

Resnick positioned himself in front of a diagram showing the immediate area where the incident had taken place.

'Fortunately for us,' Resnick said, 'there were three CCTV cameras in operation at the time of the murder. One, here, at the side of Gordon House; another further back along Cranmer Street, the direction from which DI Kellogg would have approached; and lastly, here, on St Ann's Hill Road, just short of the intersection.

'What seems clear is that one group of youths, a number wearing Radford colours, made their way into St Ann's along Forest Road East and Mapperley Road and entered Cranmer Street at its western end, here. They then met with a group of similar size from St Ann's – we're talking around a dozen to fifteen – some of whom came along Cranmer Street from the other end, some cutting up alongside these houses here,

43

where there's a lot of rebuilding going on, on St Ann's Hill Road.'

'Prearranged, then, sir?' Anil Khan asked.

'Looks that way.'

'Turf war,' Frank Michaelson said.

'Could be.'

'Radford and St Ann's,' Bill Berry remarked. 'Never mind the Montagues and the bloody Capulets. Not as dead set against one another as St Ann's and the Meadows, maybe, but close enough.'

'According to DI Kellogg,' Resnick said, 'the shooter was wearing a black-and-white bandana, which, as we know, are Radford gang colours.'

'Could be a Notts fan,' someone suggested, jokingly.

'Anything to do with County,' someone else called out, 'he'd have bloody missed.'

More laughter, especially from the Forest fans in the room, Resnick, despite his allegiances, smiling along with the rest.

'Tracking down the gunman,' he said, 'that's obviously our priority. DI Kellogg will be working with a sketch artist later today, to see what they can come up with. We've spoken to Joanne Dawson, the girl who was injured before the shooting, and we'll need to talk to her again.

'Beyond that, we want as full a list as possible of all those present at the scene, those names checked through the computer, connections traced. You know the drill. Which means, aside from going frame by frame through the CCTV, talking to any local residents who might have been home, along with students from the university flats.'

'Likely in bed asleep,' someone said. 'Lazy bastards.'

'Questions?' Resnick said.

'Anything yet from Forensics on the type of gun?' Steven Pike asked.

'I spoke to Huntingdon this morning,' Bill Berry said. 'They've promised something by the end of the day. Note the promised.'

He rolled an invisible pinch of salt between finger and thumb and threw it over his shoulder for good luck.

'There's one last thing,' he said. 'If this is part of a gang war, we'd best be braced for what's to follow. Radford takes out someone from St Ann's, it won't be long before St Ann's fights back. Revenge shootings, unless we're careful. Tit for tat. I'll talk to the powers that be about stepping up patrols, but they might say they're already doing what they can. So let's wrap this up fast before the proverbial hits the fan.'

Murmurs of agreement volleyed round the room.

'Okay,' Berry said, 'all of you. Off your backsides and get to work.'

By rights, Resnick thought, he should send Anil Khan off to talk to Kelly Brent's parents and keep himself back from the firing line; maybe go and see Joanne Dawson instead, see if he couldn't persuade her to be a little more cooperative. But the temptation to meet Howard Brent face to face, after the things he'd said about Lynn, was too strong.

45

After all, get you out of the office, that's what Bill Berry had promised, bit of real police work for a change. Well, the real police work, Resnick knew well enough, that was slow, laborious routine, check and double-check, two steps up, most often, and three steps back. But out and about, interviewing suspects and the like, that was, some might say, the icing on the cake.

Lynn couldn't shake it out of her mind. It didn't matter how many times she told herself to forget about it, just someone hogging the spotlight, venting his spleen.

Used my daughter as a shield. A human shield.
Sacrificed my daughter's life for her own.

She had been taken through it in the debriefing yesterday: had replayed the incident, time after time, in her mind.

Two girls facing each other at the centre of a rough circle, one of them, Kelly, armed with a knife. As Kelly jumped past her to attack Joanne, Lynn had grabbed hold of her sleeve and then her arm, applying pressure, forcing her arm upwards, Kelly all the while struggling, kicking, lashing back with her free hand – and then the youth with the gun stepping out from the crowd as Lynn, catching sight of the movement from the corner of her eye, had swivelled towards him, the movement taking Kelly with her, the gun aiming in her direction, the youth's eyes focused, at that moment, on her. Her, and not Kelly, close alongside her? She couldn't be sure.

How possible was it that the gunman had been shooting indiscriminately into the crowd? How possible that both bullets had been intended for Kelly Brent rather than for her?

It had all happened so suddenly, so fast, Kelly and herself so close together. And then the impact of the bullet sending her staggering back, falling, arms flailing, leaving Kelly standing, exposed, in her place.

Used my daughter as a shield.

Consciously, unconsciously, could that have been what she had done?

Sacrificed my daughter's life for her own.

In the bathroom, bent low over the toilet bowl, Lynn retched until her throat was dry, each movement jarring her chest with pain.

Sombre suit, dark tie, Resnick sat uneasily on the thin cushions of the settee, Catherine Njoroge in a plain black trouser suit alongside him, the jacket with three-quarter sleeves and wide lapels; her hair tied back with purple ribbon, hands clasped in her lap.

Facing them, so close in the small room they could have reached out, almost, and touched, Kelly's mother, Tina, sat pinch-faced, stiff-backed, dark lipstick smudged across her pale face, alternately toying with the small silver crucifix that hung from her neck or picking at skin around her fingernails that was already plucked raw. The father, Howard, leaned back into a leather chair, legs crossed, sleeves of his grey sweat-shirt pushed back above the elbow, a pair of ice-blue Converse All Stars, unfastened, on his feet.

No one spoke.

A framed photograph of Kelly, head and shoulders, smiling, had pride of place on the tiled shelf above the fireplace, smaller family photographs to either side. There were others on the side wall and balanced on top of the widescreen TV: Tina and the children, Kelly and her two older brothers, Michael and Marcus; Michael, the elder boy, the more prominent of the two.

Everything in the room was neat, dusted, in its place. A home.

The last time Resnick had been in such a home it had been to talk to a mother whose daughter had been killed in a drive-by shooting and one of whose sons was now in prison for avenging her murder.

Stories that repeated themselves too many times.

Tina Brent brought her finger to her mouth and bit away a piece of fraying skin.

It was quiet enough to hear the flat tick of a clock from one of the other rooms, the rattle of someone skateboarding past outside, the distant bass beat from a stereo along the street.

Contempt in his eyes, Howard Brent's gaze went from Catherine Njoroge to Resnick and back again.

'What she doin' here?' he said. 'Make us feel good, yeah? One of us. Token nigger. Token black.' He leaned sharply forward, feet to the floor. 'Girl, how that make you feel?'

Unruffled, head turning slowly on her long neck, Catherine Njoroge looked back at him calmly through dark almond eyes. 'I feel for you in your loss,' she said. 'Both of you.'

'I bet you do,' Brent said, leaning back.

Catherine's eyes flickered once.

One of Resnick's hands gripped the arm of the settee, the other, resting on his leg, had formed into a fist and he willed the finger to relax.

'Mr Brent,' he said, speaking deliberately, 'so far, apart from one brief instance, you have refused to allow the family liaison officer into the house. You declined to take part in the official press conference, choosing instead to make a statement of your own, in which you made a rash and wholly unfounded accusation against a member of this force. In fact, you've shown much more interest in talking to the press than you have to the police. And now you insult one of my officers with what could only be described as racist remarks.'

'Yeah, well . . .' Brent said.

'Well, what?' Resnick said sharply. 'You want us to find your daughter's killer or not?'

'What sort of stupid question's that?'

'The one I'm asking.'

'Fuck you,' Brent said, just beneath his breath, and, rising, quick to his feet, he turned and left the room, slamming shut the door in his wake.

Tina Brent winced and shrank even smaller into her chair. Brittle, she was close to tears, close to collapse.

Catherine Njoroge looked quickly towards Resnick, a quick nod telling her to go ahead.

'Mrs Brent,' Catherine said, 'Kelly was wearing a gold chain with the name Brandon.'

'So?'

49

'That would be Brandon Keith?'

'Yes.'

'He was her boyfriend?'

'Yeah.'

'And she was still seeing him? Brandon?'

'Far as I know, yeah.'

'She hadn't said anything about them breaking up, some kind of a row, nothing like that?'

'Not to me, no.'

'And she would have talked to you? If it had been anything serious?'

'She might.'

'Only we think Kelly might have gone to Cranmer Street because of some kind of argument over Brandon, with another girl.'

Tina Brent reached down into her bag for her cigarettes. 'I don't know nothin' 'bout that.'

'Joanne Dawson,' Resnick said, 'does that name mean anything to you?'

A quick shake of the head.

'Mrs Brent . . . ?'

'No.'

'You never heard Kelly mention her name?'

'I just said.'

Using a disposable lighter, she lit her cigarette.

'The afternoon that Kelly was killed, she and Joanne Dawson were fighting.'

'I said I don't know nothin' 'bout that.'

'Kelly attacked her with a knife.'

'Says who?'

'There are witnesses.'

'Some people, they'll say anything.' She drew the smoke down into her lungs, held it there, and then released it slowly from the corners of her mouth.

Catherine Njoroge picked up Resnick's glance. 'Mrs Brent, do you know if Kelly had a knife?'

'What knife?'

'You didn't see her, that day, with a knife in her possession?'

'Course I didn't. What would she be doin' with a knife?'

'Perhaps she thought she needed it,' Catherine said. 'For protection.'

'She didn't have no knife. How many more times?' The cigarette was trembling in her hand. 'What the fuck's it matter, anyway, she had a knife or not? My daughter, shot with a fucking gun and you're sitting there asking me about some stupid, sodding knife.'

Ash fell across her lap and she brushed it away, smearing grey across her skirt.

'What we're trying to do,' Resnick said patiently, 'is establish the reason for Kelly being there that day so that we can find out just why she was killed.'

'Why she was killed?' Tina Brent's eyes were suddenly bright. 'We know why she was killed. One of you lot, that's why. That's what got my Kelly killed.'

Angrily, she stubbed out her cigarette. There were tears at the corners of her eyes and she wiped them away with her sleeve.

'Your daughter,' Resnick said evenly, 'was killed

51

because someone that afternoon was in illegal possession of a firearm, which they discharged into the centre of a crowd of people.'

'So what? Some kind of soddin' accident, that what you're saying now?'

'What I'm saying, Mrs Brent, is we don't yet know. We don't have all the facts that will tell us exactly what happened. We don't know if your daughter was deliberately targeted or if her death was a terrible accident. But it's our business to find out – and we can do that better with your cooperation, yours and your husband's.'

Tina Brent took a quick sideways glance towards the door. 'You'll get no cooperation from him, I'll tell you that now.'

'But you can help us,' Resnick said.

She nodded and lit another cigarette. The bass sounds from down the street were louder now, more insistent.

'Brandon Keith,' Catherine Njoroge said, 'have you seen him recently?'

Tina Brent shrugged. 'Maybe.'

'Can you remember when you saw him last?'

'Yeah, matter of fact I can. Last weekend. He come round for her. Sat'day, it'd be. That motor of his. Some fancy bloody thing.'

'You saw him?'

'Like I said.'

'How about the other day? The afternoon Kelly was shot. Did you see him then?'

Tina Brent's face tightened. 'No.'

'You're sure?'

'Sure.' She wafted cigarette smoke away from her face. ''Sides, he wouldn't've had nothin' to do with this. Kelly hangin' out with her mates an' that, he don't like it. Told her so, I heard him.'

'And you don't know where he might be now?'

'Brandon? No. Sleepin', most likely. Works nights, don't he?'

'Works where?' Resnick asked.

'DJ, i'n he?'

'You know where? Where he DJs?'

Tina Brent shrugged. 'All over. Golden Fleece, maybe. The Social?'

The front door closed firmly. Howard Brent leaving or someone else coming in?

'Your boys – two, isn't it?'

'Yeah, what of it?'

'They around?'

A shake of the head. 'Michael, he's down London.'

'Working?'

'No, university, i'n he?' As if daring him to contradict. 'King's College, studying law.' For a moment, pride lifted her head and added resonance to her voice.

'The youngest boy,' Resnick said, 'Marcus, is it?'

'How 'bout him?'

'He still lives at home?'

'What of it?'

'That wouldn't have been him coming in just now?'

'No, still sleepin', i'n he? Lazy sod. Anyway, no point talkin' to him. That day, he weren't even here.'

'Oh?'

'Work experience, from the college. South Notts. Bunch of 'em. Wellingborough somewhere. Got the train down that morning. Didn't get back here till . . . till after it happened.'

'You won't mind if we have a word? Just to check?'

For a moment, it looked as if she were about to protest, but then she slumped back against her chair. 'Suit yourself. Upstairs, back.'

Marcus Brent's room was small and dark, the curtains closed. It smelt of tobacco and dope and unwashed clothes. Posters of rap stars, nude women and Premiership footballers filled the walls. A stereo, a bunch of CDs, PS3 and a small TV. Jeans across the foot of the bed, T-shirts on the floor. Several pairs of trainers, Adidas, Nike. A crumpled can of Coke.

Marcus stirred when Resnick entered the room and pulled the covers further over his head.

'Marcus,' Resnick said.

A grunt and nothing more.

With a quick movement, Resnick pulled the covers clear. 'Rise and shine.'

'What the fuck . . . ?'

'Lovely day. Time you were up and about. Besides, haven't you any classes, lectures?'

Marcus pushed himself up on to one elbow. 'What you gonna do? Arrest me? Skippin' off?'

Resnick smiled. 'You know who I am then?'

54

'Smelt you when you come through the door.'

The smile disappeared. 'The day your sister was killed, where were you?'

Wearily, Marcus told him: exactly as his mother had said.

'If I get in touch with the college, someone will confirm that?'

'Try it and see.' He lay back down and yanked the covers over his head.

'Nice meeting you,' Resnick said. He closed the door and went back downstairs.

'Satisfied?' Tina Brent said.

'Michael, where's he live when he's away?'

'Some student house in Camberwell.'

'Best let us have the address, just to keep things tidy.'

Catherine Njoroge wrote it down. Resnick thanked Tina Brent for her time.

Howard Brent was on the pavement outside, smoking a cigarette. Flowers, most, but not all, wrapped in cellophane, rested up against the low wall, along with several teddy bears and a cloth doll. Expressions of sympathy on small, decorated cards. *Never forgotten. Luv Always. Kelly – U R the Greatest. Rest in Peace.* Others, in plenty, had been left at the site of the shooting.

Brent looked at Resnick with a taunting sneer. 'Word is, you and the cop who was shot, you're like this, yeah?' And he ran the index finger of one hand slowly back and forth through the cupped palm of the other.

For a big man, Resnick moved with surprising speed, fists raised.

'Come on,' Brent said. 'Take a swing, why don't you? Here.' And he thrust out his jaw. 'Go on.'

'Boss,' Catherine Njoroge said quietly from just behind him. 'We should go.'

She turned and started to walk away and, after a moment, Resnick fell into step beside her, Brent's mocking laughter following them down the street.

5

Shortly after she'd moved in, Lynn had come home one afternoon with a pair of bird feeders and a bag of mixed seeds.

Resnick had taken one look and laughed. 'The cats'll love you,' he said.

Only a few days before, Dizzy had dragged the mangled body of a robin through the catflap and laid it at Resnick's feet, purring proudly, tail crooked and raised, for all the world as if he were still a quick young hunter and not a fading champion with a half-chewed ear and burgeoning arthritis in his hind legs.

But Lynn remembered with pleasure the birds that had gathered in her parents' garden in Norfolk – the middle of the country, admittedly – and had bided her time. Early the following spring, by dint of standing, tiptoed, on a chair, she had attached the feeders high on the trunks of two fruit trees that stood towards the back of the garden, close against the wall; an apple tree, whose fruit was small and somewhat sour, and a pear whose blossom promised more than it delivered.

For the first few mornings she saw nothing and wondered if she had sited the feeders wrongly, or if the mere presence of the cats – just three, now that one had wandered off and failed to reappear – was sufficient deterrent.

But then, suddenly, there was a blue tit on the apple tree; perching on an overhanging branch at first, before darting down to take a seed, then skittering away. Five minutes later, it was back, and this time not alone. Within the space of a week there were great tits, a pair of blackbirds, robins, a wren, and once, a goldfinch, with its red-banded head and the fierce yellow of its wings.

Occasionally, either Dizzy or Pepper would gaze wistfully upwards, attracted by the quick flutter overhead, but other than that, they seemed to pay little heed.

'Happy now?' Resnick had said one morning, stopping behind her as she stood at the kitchen window, looking out.

'Yes,' she said, twisting her head to give him a kiss. 'Reminds me of home.'

'I thought that's what this was,' Resnick said.

She turned it over in her mind now as she had then: how long did it take, living with someone, living in their house, before you felt that you belonged?

Lynn walked out into the garden, shoots already appearing here and there, fresh buds on the roses well ahead of their time, the pink flowers of the camellia scattered over the ground. New growth enough on the lawn for it to need a trim. Careful not to lean too heavily on the wall, loose bricks shifting slightly beneath her hand, she looked down on to the allotments of Hungerhill Gardens and watched for a moment as a man wearing an old, patched tweed jacket, grey trousers tied above the ankle with string, paused in his digging long enough to lift his grey herringbone cap from his head, wipe an arm across his brow then replace his cap before resuming digging. The man sufficiently like her father to make her catch her breath.

The last time she had seen him, almost five years ago now, he had been sleeping, oblivious, thankfully, to pain, to everything, his skin a murky bilious yellow, the cancer eating into his liver, kidneys failing, a mask of hard unforgiving plastic over his mouth and nose.

'No heroic measures,' the doctor had said. 'He's lived a good life. You have to let him go now, in peace.'

And she had continued to sit, holding her father's hand, talking every now and then, saying the first things that came into her head, not supposing the words mattered, if anything now did, other than the sound, perhaps, of her voice.

Once or twice, he had moved his head, as if to speak, and she had lowered her face close to his and, for a moment, lifted away the mask, but all there had been was a faint, dry gurgling deep in his throat and the smell of rot and decay: his teeth, yellow and crooked, and the parched skin flaking back from his lips.

Had he squeezed her hand before the end or had that been her imagination, her need?

They had buried him on a cold day with the wind eddying the shallow topsoil into dusty circles and the rooks loud and restless in the trees.

In the allotment below, the man had set his spade aside while he rolled a cigarette.

A good life, the doctor had said. Well, yes, good perhaps, hard certainly, but not enough. Barely scratching sixty when it was over. These days, when so many continued, relatively fit, into the eighties, it was no life at all.

And her mother, who had married him at twenty, the only man she had ever seriously been out with, had been left bereft by his death. Age claiming her, too, before its time. Her face, her body shrivelling, closing in upon themselves as her life shrank down to the few daily tasks she performed now more or less by rote.

Lynn felt guilty that she did not visit more often, that she begrudged, sometimes, her mother's regular Sunday-morning calls, the enquiries after her and Charlie's health, the regaling of news that was the same as it had been the week before.

At the sound of the doorbell, Lynn went back into the house.

The woman on the doorstep was wearing a green tabard top with the same name embroidered on one side as had been painted on the van standing at the kerb.

'Miss Kellogg, is it?'

She was holding up a large bouquet of flowers, cellophane wrapped.

'Yes,' Lynn said, her face breaking into a smile. It wasn't like Charlie to go for broke like that, but she was glad that he had.

Thanking the woman, she took the flowers back inside. Red, yellow and white roses, some barely out of bud, surrounded by wisps of decorative grass and fern. Beautiful.

Pulling off the small envelope attached to the wrapping, she ran water into the washing-up bowl and slid the stems down into it until they were well covered. They could rest there until she'd unearthed a suitable vase.

Her nail was long enough to slide under the envelope corner and tear it across.

It was the usual cream-coloured card with embossed flowers around the edge. The writing was small yet distinct. Not Charlie's at all.

Hope you're recuperating well. Next time remember to duck!
   Stuart D.
PS. Maybe you should come and work for us instead.

Stuart D.? Stuart D.? For no good reason, the skin at the back of her arms went cold. She couldn't think who it was and then she could.

Stuart Daines.

Stuart D. Tall, stepping towards her, smiling. Holding out his hand.

It had been at a SOCA conference she had attended the previous November. SOCA: the Serious and Organised Crime Agency, set up to combat various kinds of high-level national and international crime and mostly staffed by ex-police and ex-Customs and Excise. Tobacco smuggling, people trafficking, the illegal transit and sale of weapons. On paper, it had all sounded quite buzzy and attractive, but none of the speakers, with the possible exception of one, who had talked enthusiastically about the need for closer cooperation at grass-roots level, had been particularly convincing.

And speaking, in one of the breaks, to a former detective inspector from the West Midlands, who had joined up and rapidly become disenchanted, had further convinced Lynn to steer well clear. Too many training courses, too much internal wrangling, not enough practical, hard-headed investigation.

She had just finished talking to him and was heading back towards the conference room, when the speaker who'd impressed her cut across her path.

'Our friend from Sutton Coldfield bending your ear?'

'Something like that.'

'Not a happy bunny.'

'No?'

'Thought it was going to be all James Bond,' he said, smiling. 'Finds out it's hard graft instead.'

Lynn found herself smiling too.

'Stuart,' he said, holding out his hand. 'Stuart Daines.'

'Lynn Kellogg.'

He nodded. 'Notts force, right? DI. Major Crimes – or is it Homicide these days?'

'Homicide.'

'You thinking of transferring? Giving SOCA a go?'

'Not really.'

'Shame.'

Daines was close to six foot, an unstructured cotton-linen suit hanging easily from his lean body, dark hair prematurely greying at the sides. Late thirties, Lynn thought? Maybe forty. One brown eye had a chip of green at the far corner, like a flawed stone.

'I enjoyed your talk earlier,' she said.

'One of the few, then.'

'Not at all.'

'Speak about liaising with local forces, setting up viable targets in the provinces, and most of this lot don't want to know. Anything fifty miles out of London, they think everyone's going to be wearing loincloths and painting themselves with woad.'

Lynn laughed. 'Nottingham city centre on a Friday night.'

'I'll take your word for it.'

He was looking at her in a way that made her feel less than comfortable.

'You staying down?'

Lynn shook her head. 'Back up on the seven-thirty train.'

'A pity. We could've had a drink, gone for a meal.'

'I doubt it,' she said.

63

When she got to the conference-room door, she quickly turned her head and he was still standing in the same spot, looking directly at her.

Stuart Daines.

Too fond of himself by half.

She slipped the card back into its envelope and slid it between two jars on the shelf. There was a vase standing empty in the living-room fireplace that would do.

For a few moments the goose pimples returned to her arms. How had he known where to send the flowers? How had he known where she lived?

She set the kettle to boil for some tea and thought about calling Resnick at work, but realised she'd not be thanked. Earlier, she had been debriefed at length by two of Bill Berry's officers, after which she had done her best to prime a sketch artist into drawing a likeness of the young man who had shot Kelly Brent – who had shot her – but her sighting of him had been too fleeting to produce anything other than a generic stereotype. Nice try, the artist said jovially, but no cigar.

Tea made, she switched on the radio for the news.

There had been another fatal shooting, this time in Manchester.

A government minister was speaking. 'What we must remember is that incidents such as these, though they cause extraordinary grief and agony in particular communities, are, nonetheless, isolated occurrences. And what we must do, as a government, is to think again about the nature of those communities which are most affected, and how we can best intervene to tackle gang culture, and work with families and voluntary organisations so as to combat that culture and make the communities themselves more resilient.'

Lynn turned off the radio.

Her book was in the front room. After twenty or so minutes of reading, she felt her eyes beginning to droop and the pain in her chest, coincidentally, to return. She would take another couple of painkillers and lie down on the bed, maybe close her eyes. Just for a little while.

When she woke it was dark.

In the bathroom, she splashed cold water on her face, wincing as she raised her arms, cleaned her teeth and brushed her hair. She'd wanted to get dinner going before Resnick got home, a task that was more usually his. There were some chicken thighs in the fridge, onions, garlic, rice, a few carrots starting to go soft, frozen peas. She was halfway through chopping the second onion, tears pricking at her eyes, when she heard the front door.

'What's wrong?' Resnick asked, coming into the kitchen.

'Nothing, why?'

'You're standing there with your apron on, crying, that's why.'

Lynn smiled. 'Onions, that's all.' She tilted up her face to be kissed.

Resnick cast his eyes over the assembled ingredients. 'Sure you know what you're doing?'

'I dare say I'll manage.'

'Don't forget to brown—'

'I said, I'll manage.'

Resnick backed away. 'In that case, I'll have a quick shower.'

'Time enough for a bath, if you want.'

'Sounds good to me.'

Chicken sizzling away in the pan with the garlic and the onions, she took him up a glass of Scotch and set it on the edge of the bath.

'I can't see any wine,' she said.

'There's a couple of bottles of White Shield, if you fancy beer.'

'Why not?'

She took a quick glance at herself in the mirror, but it was clouded with steam.

Forty minutes later, having remembered to warm the plates, she was about to serve up when she heard Resnick's voice from the other room.

'What's all this?'

'All what?'

'Flowers. Roses.'

'Hang on a minute.'

Lynn carried the plates through to the dining table. Resnick had set a compilation of West Coast jazz he'd picked up cheaply playing on the stereo.

'Got a secret admirer then?' Resnick said, grinning.

'No secret,' she said, and showed him the card.

'Who's this?' Resnick asked, having read it. 'Stuart D.?'

'You remember that SOCA conference I went to last year?'

'Uh-hum.'

'He was one of the speakers. Stuart Daines.'

'And he sent these?'

'Yes.'

'"Maybe you should come and work for us instead"?'

'That's what it says.'

'Funny way of recruiting.'

'I don't think it's altogether serious.'

'A lot of roses for someone who isn't serious.'

Lynn's turn to grin. 'Not jealous, Charlie, are you?'

'Should I be?'

'What do you think?'

'I just don't remember you saying much about him at the time, that's all.'

Lynn cut off a piece of chicken. 'There wasn't much to say.'

'Good-looking, is he?'

'I suppose so. In a pared-down George Clooney sort of way. A bit taller, probably.'

Resnick nodded. 'Nothing special, then?'

'Not really.'

For several minutes they ate in silence. Chet Baker faded into something more sprightly, Bob Brookmeyer and Jimmy Giuffre playing 'Louisiana', an old favourite Resnick hadn't listened to in years.

The youngest of the cats was hovering hopefully beneath the table, rubbing its back from time to time against one of the legs.

'This is good,' Resnick said, indicating his plate.

'Don't sound so surprised.'

'I didn't mean—'

'Yes, you did.'

He grinned. 'I'm sorry.'

'So you should be.'

He poured what was left of the White Shield into her glass.

'Preliminary forensic report came through from Huntingdon as I was leaving. Gun was firing home-packed bullets using discarded empty rounds. Lethal enough, but they don't have the same power.' He pointed at her with his fork. 'Hence the bruised, not broken, ribs.'

'Didn't help Kelly Brent.'

'No. No, it didn't.'

'How about the make of gun?' Lynn said. 'Anything on that?'

'Converted air pistol, most likely.'

'Brocock?'

'That's what they're thinking.'

'Cheaper than chips a while back. Could well be.'

Resnick nodded. It was just such a weapon that young Bradford Faye had used to avenge his sister, a Brocock ME38 Magnum, his for a hundred and fifteen pounds, the deal set up in the back room of a pub, money changing hands there and then and the weapon handed over in the car park later that evening, by a kid who couldn't have been more than eight or nine. With a mandatory minimum sentence of three years for sixteen- and seventeen-year-olds found carrying guns, underage gun runners were being used more and more.

'Seconds?' Lynn asked, indicating Resnick's virtually empty plate.

'No, thanks, I'm fine.'

'You sure? There's another piece of chicken. Some more rice.'

'Oh, go on then.'

'How's the rest of it going?' Lynn asked, when she came back in.

'Falling out over a lad at the heart of it. DJ called Brandon Keith. According to Joanne Dawson, he'd dumped Kelly for her a week or so back and Kelly'd taken it badly. Said a few things about Joanne which were, shall we say, less than charitable, some of them finding their way on to a few walls near where Joanne lives. As a result of which – and, again, this is Joanne's version – she suggested herself and Kelly meet and have a little chat, clear the air, so to speak.'

'And brought along a few friends for company.'

'Yes. And Kelly did the same.'

'Radford versus St Ann's. Nice.'

'Still, from what Joanne said, what started out as a lot of verbals turned nasty when Kelly produced a knife. Thirteen stitches to one side of her face to prove it, to say nothing of another seven or eight in her arm.'

'And we're thinking it was one of her crew had the gun?'

'Likely. Long way from what she's saying, though, Joanne.' Resnick eased back his chair. 'Claims no one she knew was carrying a gun. Didn't really see the shooter, no idea who he was. Not one of her mates, she's certain of that.'

'You'll talk to her again?'

'Oh, yes.'

'How about this Brandon?'

'On his way down to Bristol when it happened, spot of DJing in a club down there. Really cut up about what happened to Kelly, close to tears talking about it to Anil, apparently.'

'He backed up Joanne's story, though? The row between her and Kelly.'

'After a fashion. "Joanne Dawson," he said. "That skank. I only did her 'cause she was beggin' for it." '

'Nice man.'

'Charming.'

'You want apple pie? There's some left from last night.'

'Why not?'

After washing up and clearing away, they read the paper, watched television; Resnick listened to some more music, reading for the second time a book by Bill Moody about Chet Baker, while Lynn took a bath. She was just coming back into the room in her dressing gown when the phone rang.

'Probably another of your well-wishers,' Resnick said, as Lynn lifted the receiver.

'Watch your back, bitch,' a voice said and the line went dead.

70

6

He waited till mid-morning, the first time he could really get away, anger still simmering inside him. When he arrived at the house it was empty, no one answering the door. He was just leaving when a neighbour looked up from cleaning his car and told him where they were. Resnick thanked him and went across the street, walked a little way down and waited some more.

It wasn't long till he saw them: the Brent family making their way back from a two-minute silence at the spot where Kelly had been killed.

Several dozen friends and neighbours walked behind them in a slow procession, teenage friends of Kelly's clutching soft toys and bouquets of flowers, a local councillor and the minister from the Baptist church bringing up the rear.

Howard Brent was immaculate in a black suit, black shirt, black tie, his only adornment a diamond stud in his left ear. His wife, Tina, walked beside him, head down, the spirit drained out of her. Behind them, the two sons, Michael and Marcus, stared, serious faced, ahead. Michael, with his glasses and his small goatee beard, reminded Resnick of photographs he remembered seeing of a young Malcolm X.

If Brent noticed Resnick amongst the bystanders who were standing here and there now along both sides of the street, watching the procession file past, he gave no sign.

Resnick waited until they had arrived at the house, Tina and the younger boy going immediately inside, while others stood shaking Brent's hand and offering a few last words of condolence and sympathy.

Within minutes only a dozen or so, including the Baptist minister, remained, spreading from the pavement out into the street. Most of the onlookers had drifted away.

As Resnick walked towards them, Michael Brent detached himself from the group and stood directly in front of him, blocking his path.

Automatically, Resnick reached for his warrant card. 'I'm—'

'I know who you are,' Michael said, cold contempt in his eyes.

'I need to talk to your father,' Resnick said.

'My father is busy. This is not the right time.' The young man's voice was loud and firm.

'I still need—'

Marcus pushed past his elder brother. 'What? You deaf, i'n it? Not the right fuckin' time.'

'Marcus!' Howard Brent's voice stopped the youth in his tracks. 'Get inside.'

'I—'

'Inside. Now.'

Marcus scowled and turned, slouch-shouldered, away.

'Now,' Howard Brent said, moving to stand at his elder son's shoulder. 'What seems to be the trouble?'

'I've told him,' Michael Brent said, 'he's not welcome here.'

'Two minutes,' Resnick said. 'That's all I need.'

'And I said, no.'

'Michael,' Brent said, a hand on his son's elbow. 'It's all right. Please go back into the house.'

'You know you don't have to—'

'Michael, please. Look to your mother.'

The young man stared at Resnick hard then walked away.

'This so important,' Brent said, 'you have to come here now?' He glanced round. 'My family, my friends.'

'Last night,' Resnick said, 'you made a call.'

'I what?'

'You called my house and left a message. A message for the person I live with.'

'I dunno what you talkin' about,' Brent said.

'You don't remember what you said?' The colour was rising on Resnick's face, his body tense. '"Watch your back, bitch." That's what you said.'

'You're crazy,' Brent said, beginning to turn away. 'Crazy.'

Resnick stopped him with a hand against his chest. 'Three years, wasn't it? What you went down for? Actual bodily harm. Beating some poor bastard within an inch of his life.'

A smile crossed Brent's face, as if remembering what he had done. 'He asked for it,' he said. 'And that was a long time ago. Another life, you understand?'

Resnick moved closer. 'Lynn Kellogg,' he said, 'you come near her, try to speak to her, you as much as walk down the same side of the street, I'll have you inside so fast your feet won't touch the ground.'

'What charge?'

'Any charge I like.'

'You threatening me?' Brent said. 'In front of all these people, you're threatening me?'

'A warning, that's all.'

For a long moment, Brent held his stare. 'We done here?' he said then, stepping back. ''Cause I got friends waiting. The minister, come to pay his respects.'

Smile replaced by a sneer, he turned away.

'For God's sake, Charlie, what were you thinking?'

They were facing one another in Bill Berry's office, the room untidy, impersonal, as if the detective superintendent had merely borrowed it for the afternoon.

'What the hell got into you? Accusations without a shred of proof. Threats in front of a dozen witnesses. Like some cowboy.'

Resnick shrugged heavy shoulders.

74

'Letting your feelings run amok.'

'He needed telling,' Resnick said.

'There are ways.'

'That was my way.'

'Jesus, Charlie! Conflict of interest, remember? You and Lynn.'

Berry pushed both hands up through his hair and sighed. 'Sit down, for Christ's sake.'

'If I'm on the carpet—'

'And don't box clever. Just sit the fuck down.'

Resnick sat.

Both men continued to sit, silently, directives and graphs and papers spread across the desk between them, until Berry leaned forward in his chair. 'Before seeing you, I spent an uncomfortable twenty minutes with the Assistant Chief, explaining to him why, at the present time, you shouldn't be suspended from duty.'

Resnick said nothing.

'As the ACC was at pains to remind me, I was the one who argued for you to be prised out from behind that desk of yours to be number two in this investigation. And then this.'

Resnick still said nothing.

'I mean, when you went after him like that, the way you did, what did you think was going to happen?'

'I thought it would make him think twice before doing it again.'

'The phone call?'

'Yes, the phone call.'

'You don't even know if it was him.'

'It was him.'

'She didn't recognise the voice. She didn't recognise his voice, how could she?'

'It was him.'

Berry slammed both hands down hard against the desktop, sending papers ballooning. 'And if it was. *If* it was. Supposing for a moment, in the absence of any real evidence, you're right, you think that makes it okay for you to confront him in front of the whole sodding community? Threatening him like some vigilante, Steven fucking Seagal on a white horse. Jesus Christ! You know what this man's like, you know how much he loves the sound of his own voice, how much he thrives on publicity.'

Resnick looked away.

'The first thing Brent did after you left him was contact every radio and TV station in a hundred-mile radius. The *Post* have got a picture of him on the front fucking page, serious and responsible in his best suit, alongside some old one of you they've pulled from the files, showing you on your way into court looking as if you're wearing someone else's clothes.'

'All of that—' Resnick began.

Berry ignored him, steamrollering on. 'The Chief Constable's had the chair of the Police Authority breathing down his neck, the Professional Standards Committee demanding a special meeting. To say nothing of the African Caribbean Family Support Project and the Racial Equality Council practically camping outside his door. Shall I go on?'

Resnick hoped not.

'Because this murder investigation is at a crucial stage, and only because of that, you're left clinging on to your job by the skin of your teeth. But if you step out of line once more, you're finished, washed up and hung out to dry. Clear?'

'Clear.'

'Then get the fuck out of here.'

Resnick did as he was told.

The investigation moved slowly on. Anil Khan took Catherine Njoroge with him when he went to talk to Joanne Dawson a second time, hoping Joanne would respond more readily to a woman. The house was one of the few in the street that wasn't at least partly boarded up. Joanne's father answered the door, a short, shaven-headed man in Lonsdale sportswear, a gold chain around his neck and carpet slippers on his feet.

'What's this now?' he said, looking from one officer to the other and back again. 'United fucking Nations?'

Joanne was sitting in a darkened room, curtains drawn, hiding, as best she could, the injuries to her face. Despite Catherine's presence, she didn't tell them a great deal more than she had before. It was Kelly as started it, weren't it? Going mental when she'd heard about her going with Brandon, calling her slag and whore and worse. Meeting up, like, that'd been to sort it out, not for no fight. Taken some mates with her, course she had, don't go down no St Ann's on me own,

77

no way. When they got there, everything had been cool at first, just a lot of shouting, not much more, then Kelly come out with the knife.

Whoever'd fired the gun, she didn't know who he was, never saw him, blood streaming down my fuckin' face, how could I? Just heard the noise, the shots, you know, and then everyone screaming. Kelly's laying there, blood streaming out of her. Sorry for her in a way, I s'pose, the lyin' bitch, but then, she never should have started it, should she?

'The boy who fired the gun,' Catherine said, one more try before leaving, 'someone said he was wearing Radford colours.'

'No,' Joanne said. 'I don't think so. Don't see how he could be. Ask any of them I was with and they'll tell you. Not one of our lot, no way. You ask 'em. Go on.'

Ask they did and kept on asking.

Stone wall.

Seventeen of the twenty-three shown on CCTV had been identified and all but one of those interviewed, some on two separate occasions. More than half had had run-ins with the police before, a few ASBOs, supervision orders, nothing too serious. The missing names were still being chased down. Meantime, Marcus Brent's college had confirmed that on the day of the shooting his group had been on a visit to a supermarket warehouse in Wellingborough.

Resnick sat at his desk, subdued.

He read reports, listened to officers, shuffled schedules, prowled the corridors like a wounded bear.

When he'd phoned Lynn to check how she was and given her the gist of what had happened, she thought at first he was winding her up, spinning a yarn. 'What on earth were you thinking about?' she asked, when she realised it was true.

'I don't know. I wasn't, probably. Not clearly, anyway.'

'You're telling me.'

'I just felt – I don't know – angry. Felt I had to say something.'

'But then? You shouldn't have gone anywhere near him, especially not then.'

'I know, I know.'

'And don't you ever let me hear you say you were doing it on account of me.'

Resnick rang off.

Five minutes later he called back to apologise, and then, only partly mollified, went scowling off to the canteen.

He was heading back towards the incident room, bacon sandwich and a large tea later, when he met Catherine Njoroge coming from the other direction.

'I never thanked you,' Resnick said, 'for the other day.'

She looked back at him, uncertain.

'Outside the Brent house. I might have had a go at him. You stopped me from doing something stupid.'

Catherine smiled. 'Perhaps I should have been there today?'

Resnick grinned, despite himself. 'Word gets around.'

'We're only human,' Catherine said.

'Contrary to rumour.'

Catherine smiled again and started to walk on, then stopped. 'Have you spoken to Michaelson, boss?'

'Not recently.'

'I think perhaps you should.'

Frank Michaelson was wiry and quite spectacularly tall, six seven or eight, depending on whom you believed. From an early age, when his height had become apparent, his teachers and sports coaches had tried their best to talk him into playing basketball, but running was Michaelson's thing, distance running in particular. Marathons, half-marathons, cross-country, 10K. Show Frank anything with a K at the end of it, the joke went, and he'll be stripped down to his shorts and lacing up his running shoes before you've drawn your next breath. Handy, he liked to point out, when it came to chasing little tossers through the back alleys and ginnels off the Alfreton Road.

When Resnick found him, he was crouched over one of the computer screens, his body bowed practically in two.

'Got something, Frank?'

'Could be, boss. Not sure. This lad here, Alston . . .' He pointed at the screen. 'First off, swore blind he wasn't there. Then, when he saw that wasn't going to work, he tried fobbing us off with someone else's name. Got it out of him in the end. Reason, far as I can make out, he didn't want us looking at him any closer, he's been doing a bit of dealing. Nothing major. Small-time. Bottom feeder, at best. Someone higher up the chain drops him seventy quid to make a delivery, you know the kind of thing.'

Resnick nodded.

'What is interesting,' Michaelson said, 'is the name he gave when he was trying to fob us off.'

He manoeuvred the mouse, made a couple of clicks and a new name appeared on the screen.

Ryan Gregan.

Various bits and pieces as a juvenile: theft, robbery, one instance of aggravated burglary. Arrested in Manchester when he was sixteen, along with a seventeen-year-old youth and a nineteen-year-old man, and charged with possession of a firearm with intent to cause fear of violence. The case against him was dropped for lack of evidence, the other youth and the man found guilty and sentenced to three years and five years respectively.

'I've asked around,' Michaelson said. 'He's been questioned about two gun-related incidents since.'

'Walking the line,' Michaelson said.

'Could be coincidence, of course,' Resnick said.

'I don't know,' Michaelson said. 'Gregan. Not exactly a name that eases off the tongue.'

'Unless he's someone you know well.'

'Or have got reasons, maybe, for dropping him in the shite.'

'Either way, it won't hurt to bring Gregan in for a little chat.'

'Right, boss,' Michaelson said, crooked teeth showing when he smiled.

7

Ryan Gregan's father had been born in Belfast, grown up around the Shankill, did little with his life beyond petty thieving and coming down hard on anyone smaller and weaker, which included Ryan's mother and several of his brothers and sisters. When Ryan was twelve years old, his old man smacked him round the back of the head once too often and Ryan, big for his age, hit him full in the face with a convenient piece of two-by-four which he'd set aside for just such an occasion.

His father never touched him again; never said a word to him either, civil or otherwise. When Ryan, over in England by then and living with an aunt in Salford, just outside Manchester, heard that his father had been kneecapped by the paramilitaries for dipping his hands into the wrong pockets once too often, he bought a large Bushmills to celebrate and followed it with another.

He went dutifully back over each Christmas and Easter to see his mother. In Manchester, he fell in with a gang selling crack cocaine on Moss Side, Ryan one of the youngest, but not letting anyone else push him around; as far as his aunt knew he was going off to college every afternoon, training to be a chef. When one of the Cheetham Hill gangs tried to take over a stretch of their territory, it didn't take much persuading for Ryan to step up and explain the ethics of the situation. Only instead of a primer on Aristotle or John Stuart Mill, Ryan made use of an obsolete Tokarev TT-33 pistol, a Russian copy that was the dead spit of a 1911 vintage US Colt.

It did the trick. A few shots exchanged late one night, alongside Hulme Market Hall, Ryan discharging all eight rounds and making most of them count; no fatalities, a few flesh wounds, the moral victory theirs. Ryan liked the heft of the gun in his hand. He loved it. He learned everything he could about guns.

After that things got tasty, the feud with Cheetham Hill hotted up, and following a pitched battle running either side of the A57 motorway a meeting to patch things up was called. Both sides went armed and the police were forewarned. Ryan and two others were arrested and when he was kicked free, he decided it was time to move on.

A few days after his seventeenth birthday, he followed a mate up to Glasgow, but, one way or another, he couldn't settle, too many reminders of home. He drifted for a spell after that, Newcastle,

Birmingham, Sheffield and on down to Nottingham, nineteen now and shacking up in a squat in Sneinton, out near the railway line. Just till he could find something better, which turned out to be a two-roomed flat in Radford, right around the corner from the old Raleigh factory, long since flattened to the ground.

It was midway through the afternoon when Michaelson and Pike hammered on the door and Gregan came grudgingly downstairs, wearing a Manchester City T-shirt and an old pair of jeans, nothing on his feet, looking as if he'd just crawled out of bed.

'Ryan Gregan?'

'Who wants to know?'

'We'd like you to come with us to Central Police Station.'

'A party is it?'

'Depends,' Pike said.

'I'll bring my guitar, then, should I?'

'Just shoes will do for now.'

'Oh, fine. I've this pair of new Adidas upstairs, just want wearing in.'

'Make it snappy,' Pike said.

Gregan honoured them with a smile and went back up to comply. It didn't take them long to realise he wasn't coming back down. Out through the rear window and legging it across waste land for all he was worth.

Even with a good two hundred metres' start, he didn't stand a chance against Michaelson's long, loping stride, a tackle any Rugby League forward would have been proud of bringing him to the ground.

Not so long ago, they might have shut Gregan away in an airless box-like room and left him to stew for an hour or so, the isolation preying on his mind. Now any self-respecting tearaway knew enough, if that happened, to have the duty solicitor charging false imprisonment and, if a sausage cob and a can of Ribena weren't forthcoming inside the first twenty minutes, be prepared to petition the Hague about denial of his human rights.

So, everything by the book.

Something to eat and drink.

A doctor summoned to examine and treat the injuries sustained during arrest – cuts and bruising to the side of the face, left elbow and knee, all occasioned by DS Michaelson's flying tackle – Polaroids taken, dated and signed.

And all of this done slowly, carefully, with punctilious attention to form and detail, all gaining time for a search warrant of Gregan's flat to be signed and executed, more perhaps in hope than true expectation, but one never knew . . .

As soon as he was ready, Gregan, with due representation, was ushered into an interview room with sound-recording and video facilities and invited to take a seat opposite Michaelson and Pike.

It was Michaelson, Resnick thought, who had set this whole thing in motion and now, buoyed up as he was by successful pursuit and capture, it was only right that he should be given the chance to bring it home. And Pike – well, perhaps Pike was a more than adequate companion for the occasionally loquacious Michaelson – taciturn to the edge of rudeness, flat northern vowels in tune with his wedge-shaped head and stocky body.

For now Resnick was content to leave them to it and observe the proceedings from an adjoining room.

'Not smart,' Michaelson began, 'taking off the way you did.'

Gregan shrugged.

'Guilty conscience, that's what it could make us think. Something to hide. Unless, of course, you simply fancied a run. Unquenchable thirst for exercise, that what it was?'

Gregan shrugged again, uncomfortable on his seat. Michaelson was forced to sit back from the table, unable to get his legs comfortably underneath.

'First hundred metres or so,' Michaelson said, in the same chatty tone, 'you were looking pretty good.'

'You reckon?' Gregan said.

'You've had no training? Any kind of coaching?'

Gregan squinted back at him. 'For running, you mean?'

'Running, yes.'

'Not me,' Gregan said.

'Must be natural, then. Natural ability. And practice. Plenty of that, I dare say.'

Gregan didn't reply.

'What you'd learn,' Michaelson said, 'with proper

coaching, one thing anyway, conserve your energy. Any kind of distance, that's the key. Stamina, of course, that can be developed, but pacing, fail to learn that and what happens? Into the bend on the back straight, final lap, and what you need is a strong sprint finish and there's nothing left. Well, you've seen it yourself, probably, European Games, the Olympics, on television, this tall white guy been labouring round for God knows how long in the lead, doing all the work, and then, on the bell, these three skinny Kenyans go past him as if he's standing still.'

'And that's me,' Gregan said, 'the white guy, that's what you're saying?'

'It was today.'

'And you, you and your mate here, you're the Kenyans?'

'In a manner of speaking.'

What the holy fuck, Gregan thought, is all this about? Some kind of young offenders' inclusion project? Community outreach? Some eager-eyed bloke in shorts, wanting him to sign up for midnight hikes through the Lake District, drama workshops in some scabby church hall. He'd fended off a few of them in his time.

'Bit racist, isn't it?' Gregan said, playing along. 'What you were saying, Kenyans and that.'

Michaelson appeared to give it some thought. 'Racial stereotyping,' he said, 'I know what you mean. Like saying the Irish are all thieves and tinkers. Plain wrong, wouldn't you say?'

Gregan didn't say anything at all.

'Not above a bit of thieving yourself, though,' Michaelson said. 'By all accounts.'

'Nobbin' off stuff from Woolies,' Gregan said, 'that the kind of thing you mean? Coin or two from my gran's purse?'

'That could be the start of it.'

'Kids,' Gregan said. 'Part of growing up. Rite of passage, isn't that what it's called?'

Enough, Resnick thought, watching, of the preamble, although he could see what Michaelson was doing, encouraging Gregan to feel relaxed at the same time as keeping him just that little bit disorientated, not knowing from which direction the next question was coming.

It wasn't coming from Michaelson at all.

'February fourteenth,' Pike said, his voice more jagged, harsh. 'Valentine's Day. Where were you that afternoon?'

Gregan didn't even have to think.

'Skeggy,' he said.

'What?'

'You know, Skegness.'

'I know what it is,' Pike said. 'What I want to know, what were you doing there, middle of February?'

The last time Pike had been to Skegness, three years back, it had been the middle of summer and still the wind had cut off the North Sea like a knife to your throat.

'Girlfriend, she'd asked me,' Gregan said. 'Soft cow. Instead of the usual.'

'The usual?'

'Chocolates, whatever.'

'Name?'

'What?'

'This girl's name.'

'Karen. Karen Evans.'

'Those'll be her knickers we found in your place, then, will they? 'Less they're yours, of course. Bit of cross-dressing.'

'Fuck off.'

'This Karen Evans,' Michaelson said, 'does she have an address?'

No, Gregan thought, she lives up a tree in Clumber Park. He gave them the address, mobile number too. 'Text her, why don't you? Where she works. See if she don't say she was with me that afternoon.'

'And not in St Ann's,' Pike said.

'What?'

'Corner of St Ann's Hill Road and Cranmer Street, four thirty, thereabouts.'

'I told you where I was.'

'There was a shooting,' Pike said. 'Police officer injured, a young girl killed.'

'I told you—'

'Because somebody told us you were there.'

'Fuck off.'

'You said that before.'

'I'm saying it a-fucking-gain. I was about a hundred fucking miles from there, in Skeggy with Karen, eating fish and chips and shagging her on the dunes while she got sand in her crack. Fucking ask her!'

'We will, we will. But meantime we have a witness—'

'What witness?'

'That doesn't matter.'

'Course it fuckin' matters!'

'You know someone named Billy Alston?'

'That scrote! You're relying on him? I'd have to be standing up to me knees in fucking water before I'd believe Alston telling me it was fucking raining.'

'Have you any idea,' Michaelson asked, 'why Alston might have mentioned your name?'

'Because he's a stupid twat?'

'That apart.'

Gregan could think of at least one, possibly two, neither of which he wanted to divulge. 'No,' he said. 'I can't.'

'I really think,' the duty solicitor said, speaking for the first time, 'that to take, as it seems, the uncorroborated assertion of one individual, as against an alibi which my client has provided and which he assures us—'

'Well,' Michaelson said, interrupting, 'there is always the other thing.'

'The other thing?'

'The matter of a handgun and some seven hundred and fifty rounds of ammunition, found in a holdall in Mr Gregan's bedroom.'

Gregan's face at that moment, Resnick thought, watching, was a picture of despairing realisation.

'I should like,' Gregan said, his voice just a little shaky, 'a few words with my solicitor in private.'

There was to be no denial, no passing off, no sleight of hand. No, that's not my bag, never seen it in my life, someone must have planted it there; no, I was just minding it for a friend, no idea what was inside. Gregan, as his solicitor had confirmed, was looking at a mandatory sentence of five years. Five years, minimum.

He knew enough about prison to realise it was the last place he wanted to go.

'If my client,' the solicitor said, 'can furnish you with information that is helpful in your investigation into this unfortunate recent shooting, how willing would you be to disregard the contents of the bag?'

'Disregard?'

'Yes.'

'As in pretend it was never there?'

The solicitor turned his head aside and coughed, once and then again; he hoped he wasn't coming down with a cold. 'What my client is looking for is a marked degree of leniency.'

'I'll bet he is,' said Pike.

'I shall have to take this to my superior,' said Michaelson.

'So be it,' the solicitor said, and readjusted his glasses on his nose.

'Tell him we need to check his alibi,' Resnick said, after speaking to Michaelson. 'Then we'll listen to what he has to say. But Frank, no promises, okay?'

Karen Evans scarcely looked up when Michaelson and Pike came into the shop. Time enough to register that one of them was unusually tall and that they were both police officers of one kind or another; the amount of shoplifting that went on, there were officers in and out all the time, sometimes seeming to take it seriously, sometimes not doing a whole lot more than joking around with one or other of the security staff, while pretending not to be noticing which women were taking exactly what garments into the changing rooms – fuel, she thought, for their own little fantasies when they got home. Ryan had talked her into playing that game a time or two: you're in the changing room, stripped down to your bra and panties, and the door swings open just enough . . . panties, she hated that word.

She was just finishing rearranging the sweaters on the shelf, when the manager came over and said the two policemen wanted to speak with her. As long as it didn't take too long they could use the office . . .

Michaelson would have been lying if he'd said he hadn't hoped it would be her. Small – petite, was that the word? – but not like those models they were forever getting exercised about, so stick-like, they looked as though they'd break the moment they were touched. This one looked tougher than that, her brown hair cut short with reddish streaks, a pale top that fitted nicely and then a short little skirt, brown with large white dots, over a pair of dark tights going down to ankle-length red boots.

'Your tongue,' Pike said.

'What?'

'It's mopping the floor.'

The office was small, the three of them close together, Michaelson bending forward uncomfortably, as if his head might graze the ceiling. He could smell the girl's perfume – how old was she? eighteen? nineteen? – and something else that he hoped wasn't his own sweat but probably was.

Karen looked at them expectantly. 'This is about last week,' she said, 'when those four guys steamed the shop?'

'Ryan Gregan,' Pike said.

Karen blinked.

'You know him?'

'Yes.' She nodded and blinked again.

'He's your boyfriend?'

'Yes, I suppose . . .' She glanced up at Michaelson. 'Has something happened? To Ryan?'

Michaelson shook his head. 'He's okay.'

'Really? I thought, maybe, there'd been an accident . . .'

'Nothing like that,' Michaelson said, and saw her body relax. 'Can you remember where you were on Valentine's Day?' he asked.

'Of course. Can't you?'

Michaelson blushed. On Valentine's Day evening, sitting across from his girlfriend of eighteen months in Hart's poncey restaurant – an arm and a leg that had cost him – he'd asked if she didn't think it was time, maybe, they got engaged or something, and she'd laughed, thinking he was making a joke, and Michaelson, despite himself, had laughed along too, covering his embarrassment.

'Where were you?' Pike asked Karen.

'In Skegness with Ryan, freezing my arse off.'

'All day?'

'More or less.'

'What time did you get back?'

'I don't know. Six, seven, something like that.'

'Not sooner.'

'No. Why? What's all this about?'

'And Ryan was with you the whole time?'

'Yes. I mean, not every single second. But, yes, we were there together. Valentine's, you know? I had to book it off six months in advance.'

As well as the red streaks in her hair, Michaelson realised, there were a few flecks of silver that only became noticeable when she moved her head as she did now. 'Ryan,' she said, 'he's in some kind of trouble, isn't he?'

'Yes,' Michaelson said.

Karen turned away from the pair of them, towards the rota on the wall.

'This boyfriend of yours,' Pike said, 'any idea what he does for a living?'

'Of course,' Karen said. 'He's a supervisor out at Northern Foods.'

They checked that out before returning to the station. Ryan Gregan had been temporarily employed as a

95

sandwich filler on the night shift and had jacked it in after just two weeks.

Resnick talked it through with Bill Berry, what they might legitimately offer, what they should expect in return.

'We're certain he's not in the frame for this himself?' Berry asked.

'Girlfriend could be lying, but no, looks unlikely.'

'Play him carefully then, Charlie. Talk to the CPS. If we're going to recruit him, let's have it done properly. All by the book.'

Not the same book, presumably, that Resnick had seen Bill Berry using on a suspect back at the fag end of the seventies, the local phone directory smacked hard around the back of the lad's head. 'A few more whacks like that,' Berry had joked, watching the suspect clamber shakily back to his feet, 'he'll have the bloody lot memorised, imprinted on his sad excuse for a brain.'

Happy days!

Resnick sent Pike off to check Gregan's possible contacts and took Michaelson in with him.

Gregan was sitting with his chair propped back on its rear legs, hands behind his head, and, only when Resnick had taken the seat opposite, did he let the chair come slowly forward until it was upright, hands resting now on the table edge.

'We're going to want to know about the gun,' Resnick said. 'That and the ammunition. Then about the shooting . . .'

Gregan started to say something, but a look from Resnick stopped him short.

'Billy Alston, Kelly Brent's murder, anything and everything you know.'

'And if I do?'

'If you do, and if what you tell us checks out, then, and only then, we'll see what we can do to help you.'

'That's it?'

'That's it.'

'And I'm supposed to give you everything on a plate without a single promise being made?'

'Correct.'

'In a pig's ear.'

'Okay.' Resnick was on his feet. 'Take him down to the duty sergeant. See he's charged. Illegal possession of a firearm and ammunition under section 24 of the Police and Criminal Evidence Act and the Violent Crime Reduction Act of 2006—'

'All right, all right, all fucking right!'

'Mr Gregan?'

'I said, all right.'

8

Lynn had spent the afternoon watching *Singin' in the Rain*, the DVD bought from Tesco Metro for the princely sum of £4.99. It had been one of her mother's favourites and Lynn had bought her a video copy for her birthday one year, back when videos were the thing. On visits home they would sit together watching, her mother so familiar with the lines that at key moments she would say them along with the actors, Lynn bored by then with so much of it and willing the plot along to the next manic dance number, the next small explosion of action.

Gene Kelly, whom her mother adored, Lynn found far too smarmy and self-satisfied, always cheering at the moment when the young Debbie Reynolds punctures his complacency, at least temporarily, and brings him down to earth. Until, of course, he does the dance. The dance with the umbrella, in the rain. For that, Lynn thought, he could be forgiven more or less anything.

She had managed the walk into the city centre without any great discomfort, her ribs still a little sore, but her breathing relatively easy and untroubled. At the market she'd bought six small chorizo sausages in a vacuum pack and, from another stall, onions and celery and a flourish of parsley; at Tesco, DVD aside, she'd picked up a tin of crushed tomatoes to go with the one in the cupboard back home and another of chickpeas. And a small pot of sour cream.

If she managed to carry that lot back up the hill without aggravating her injury, she was well on the way to recovery.

Early evening she stood in the kitchen, half-listening to Radio 4, chopping onions and crying, wiping the tears away with her sleeve. Run the cold water tap, that was her mother's remedy; Charlie favoured fresh air on his face from the open window; as far as Lynn was concerned there was no way round it: if you wanted onions you got tears.

She was just stirring in the pieces of sausage, the juices at the bottom of the pan slowly oozing orange, when she heard Resnick's key in the lock.

He stood for a moment inside the kitchen door, savouring the smell. 'I could get used to this, you know.'

'What's that?'

'You home here, doing the cooking.'

'Meal waiting for you after a hard day at the office.'

'That kind of thing.'

'How about everything dusted and hoovered, the ironing done, shirts on their hangers . . .'

'Bloody perfection.'

'Here,' she said, slapping the wooden spoon down into the palm of his hand. 'Get stirring. I need a wee.'

Resnick fiddled with the tuner on the radio, searching for something other than educated chatter; the only alternatives seemed to be opera, what he believed was now called urban music, or garrulous oiks in love with the sound of their own voices. He switched off and concentrated on the stew.

'How's this?' he asked when Lynn returned, offering her a liberal tasting from the end of the spoon.

'You've added something.'

'Just a little paprika.'

'Hmm . . .'

'Too much?'

'I'm not sure.'

'By the time the sour cream's stirred in, it'll be fine.'

'If you say so.'

Resnick had bought a bottle of wine, which he opened now, reaching down two large glasses from the shelf.

'Aren't you supposed to let it breathe?'

'Probably.'

They sat at the kitchen table, the cats weaving hopefully around their feet. The meal a far cry, Lynn was thinking, from what she had grown up with, her mother's scarcely varying rotation: roast chicken or a joint of lamb or beef at the weekend, cold meat or shepherd's pie on Monday; Wednesdays and Thursdays, cauliflower cheese or jacket potatoes, Fridays a nice bit of fish.

When Lynn had left home to live alone, she had existed on pasta and bought-in pizza and supermarket salads shaken straight out of the packet and on to the plate. Living with Resnick had broadened her horizons in that area, at least. That and being able to tell Billie Holiday apart from Ella Fitzgerald and Sarah Vaughan; sometimes she could even distinguish Ben Webster from Coleman Hawkins or Lester Young.

'How did it go today?' she asked. 'Any progress?'

'Some.'

She listened with interest while he told her about Ryan Gregan.

'The gun,' she said, 'it's not the same . . .'

'As was used on you and Kelly Brent? No. It's a semi-automatic. 9mm. Heavy bloody thing. Swiss, Gregan reckons. Swiss police or army. But odds are it's a Croatian copy.'

'And Gregan had it why?'

'Well . . .' Resnick speared a piece of chorizo with his fork, '. . . the trouble with people like Gregan, so much of their life is spent lying, they can make more or less anything sound plausible. But what he says, he went back up to Newcastle for New Year, see some mates, celebrate. He'd lived there for a while before moving down. New Year's Day, they were out having a quiet drink in this club, so they thought, and it all sets off. Gregan claims he doesn't know what started it, but the next minute everyone's getting stuck in. Pell-mell. One of his pals gets glassed in the face and Gregan smashes a bottle on the bar, wades in after the bloke who did it and takes out his eye. Like a softboiled egg, was how Gregan put it, right there inside an empty bottle of Newcastle Brown.'

Lynn lowered a mouthful of stew back on to the plate, uneaten.

'Next thing, the police are on their way and everyone scarpers, Gregan's back down here on the morning train. Couple of days later, one of his friends gets in touch. The blokes they clashed with know where he is and they're out to get him back. Evil bastards, his pal says. So Gregan thinks he'd better get some protection. Goes out and buys a gun.'

'Just like that?'

Resnick shrugged. 'Not difficult. As you know.'

'A gun and – what was it? – seven hundred rounds of ammunition?'

'Give or take.'

'What's he want to do? Start a small war?'

'He says that was the deal. All or nothing.'

'And this was how long ago? The beginning of the year?'

'Yes.' Resnick broke off a piece of bread to wipe round his plate, mopping up the juice. 'Gregan says he tried to trade it back to the bloke he bought it from, but he'd disappeared. Done a bunk. That was when he started putting the word out he might be willing to sell.'

'That's what he does?' Lynn said. 'Buys and sells guns?' Leaning across, she refilled their glasses.

'Not above using them, too, if his record's anything to go by. But in this case, I think selling's right. Had a

102

few people sniffing round, nothing definite, holding out for a good price, and then this Billy Alston comes to see him, all the usual haggling, but in the end it looks like they've got a deal. Hundred and fifty, cash. Comes to it, Alston's standing there with ninety quid and promises, trouble getting the rest, what if he takes delivery now, lets him have the remainder in a week's time? You can imagine what Gregan thinks of that. Tells the kid to get lost.' Bread consumed, Resnick licked his finger ends. 'Week later, Alston's back. Reckons something big's about to go down, some kind of bust-up with St Ann's, and he'll give Gregan the hundred and fifty, no problem. They arrange a meet and Alston shows up with half a dozen others and immediately starts trying to talk Gregan down in price. Gregan doesn't like being pissed around, doesn't appreciate being pressured, and gets out of there fast. Two days later he hears there's been a shooting and Kelly Brent's been killed.'

'And he thinks it's down to Alston?'

'Got to be more than coincidence, that's what he said. Reckons Alston dropped his name in it because the deal went sour.'

'Gregan could be doing the same thing.'

'I know. But with a possession charge hanging over him, he'll want some solid ground. And we do know Alston was there, at the scene.'

'You're bringing him back in?'

'Alston? First thing.'

Lynn reached across for Resnick's empty plate and

103

set it on top of her own. 'How's it been left with Gregan?'

'Police bail. He's on the spot. Agreed to ask around. If Alston wasn't the shooter, he might get an inkling of who was. And meantime we've got his statement, implicating Alston, on tape.'

'You're not afraid he'll do a runner?'

'Always a risk. But if he doesn't, if he proves reliable, we might be able to use him again. Someone that close to the local gun scene, something we haven't had in a while.' Resnick pushed back his chair. 'You wash and I'll wipe?'

As was often the case, Lynn was still sitting up in bed, reading, when Resnick switched out the light on his side, stretched out, and manoeuvred the covers up to his shoulder. He was more than half asleep when he felt Lynn snuggling down beside him, one arm reaching round to his chest, her legs pressed against his own.

'Goodnight, Charlie,' she said softly and kissed him at the base of the neck.

Some ten minutes later, awake now, he turned towards her and kissed her cheek and then her mouth, his hand moving to her breast.

'Charlie,' she said sleepily.

'Mm?'

'Let's just cuddle, eh?'

'Okay.' Trying not to sound too disappointed.

*

They were both up early, Lynn, for some reason, strangely unfocused, spending longer than usual in the bathroom and then standing, undecided, in the bedroom, uncertain what to wear. She was still dithering when Resnick put his head back round the door. 'I'm off.'

'Already?'

He glanced at his watch. 'Should be lifting Alston pretty soon.'

'Good luck with it.'

'Thanks.'

Quickly across, she kissed him on the cheek and gave his arm a squeeze. 'I'm sorry about last night.'

'That's okay.' There was a smile in his eyes.

'Just wasn't feeling like it.'

'I know.' He gave her a hug and then stood back. 'Take care.'

'You too.'

'Do my best.'

She listened to his feet, heavy on the stairs, and then the closing of the door. One more glance at the black trousers in the mirror and she changed her mind; she'd wear the brown linen skirt she'd lucked on in the Jigsaw sale instead.

9

With the strong possibility of Billy Alston being in possession of a firearm, or of there being guns and ammunition on the premises, Armed Response officers had been requested from the Tactical Firearms Unit attached to Operational Support – armed for their own safety and for the protection of members of the public, as the rubric goes.

The house where Alston lived with his three younger siblings, his aunt and mother, was close to a main road which, even at that hour of the morning, could be expected to be carrying a certain amount of traffic. Immediately before officers moved in to effect the arrest, therefore, roadblocks would be moved into place.

Resnick sat with Catherine Njoroge in an unmarked car some little way back along the Boulevard; Resnick slightly unnerved by the way in which Catherine could sit motionless, not speaking or feeling the need to speak, for quite so long.

Otherwise, he was content to be close to the action without being directly involved; the issue of rank aside, his days of charging up and down flights of stairs, yelling at the top of his voice, were, he was not unpleased to think, well past.

Thirty-one officers all told, nine vehicles, not exactly softly-softly, but as Bill Berry had pointed out, this was a young man they had good reason to believe had not only shot and killed at close range, but had also fired on a police officer in the execution of her duty.

'No risks, eh, Charlie. Either way.'

Amen to that, Resnick thought, and checked his watch.

Still a good few minutes to the off.

He leaned back in his seat and closed his eyes.

There was a pub, he remembered, back along the Boulevard from where they were now, lively even by local standards, parties most weekends in the function room above the bar. Resnick had met a woman there once, way back before Lynn, back, even, before he was married. A young PC off duty on a Friday night, most often he'd wander down to the Bell by Slab Square, in search of some jazz; either there, or out to the Dancing Slipper, where Ben Webster, one of his heroes from the Ellington band, had turned up one night too drunk to stand, never mind to play. But this particular evening a couple of pals had been going to someone's birthday party at the pub and they'd dragged him, reluctantly, along.

'Never know, Charlie, you might strike lucky.'

107

After a manner of speaking, he had.

She was tall with that kind of tightly curled permed hair that was fashionable at the time. Dark hair and blue eyes. She'd been laughing when she'd pulled him out on to the floor. Something by Geno Washington or the Foundations; Jimmy James, perhaps, and the Vagabonds.

'You can dance, can't you?' she'd said and laughed again.

Well, in those days, after a fashion, he could.

When he kissed her later, on the street outside, her mouth had been cool and quick and her hair had smelt a little of sweat and cigarettes.

'Shall I see you again?' he'd asked, as her taxi pulled in to the kerb.

'Maybe,' she'd said. And, with a pen she borrowed from the driver, had written her number on his wrist.

He'd realised then he didn't know her name.

'Linda,' she called through the cab window. 'Don't forget.'

'I don't know if you'll remember me,' he said, when three days later he phoned.

'Course I do,' she said cheerily, 'you're the dancer with two left feet.'

The first time he went round to her place, an old farm labourer's cottage she was renting out at Loscoe, they'd fooled around a little on the settee and just when he'd thought push might be coming to shove, he'd been shown the door with a hug and a swift kiss goodnight; the time after that she'd left the door on the latch and

108

was sitting up in bed with a glass of wine, the room lit by candlelight.

For the next three months, he saw her every free minute he could, every minute she'd grant him, until one evening when he called round, hopeful and unannounced, the door was answered by an ambulance driver with his shirt unbuttoned and hanging outside his uniform trousers.

'She's busy,' he said and closed the door again promptly.

His jacket had been neatly folded over one of the straight-backed chairs.

Resnick saw her a couple of times after that and then not again. He heard once that she'd moved up to Cumbria to manage one of the big hotels, stayed and got married. Resnick was married himself by then, to Elaine, and it had scarcely mattered.

Now, for some stupid reason, it did.

This damned place, he thought, I've lived here too long and the longer it goes on the more ghosts there are, beating a path to my door.

He checked his watch again.

'Okay,' he said into the radio, 'roadblocks in place.'

And then, moments before giving the order to go, he cursed softly, staring down the road ahead.

'What's wrong?' Catherine Njoroge asked.

But by then she, too, had seen the television van that had drawn up at the closest possible point.

Smack in the middle of the inner city, early though it might be, Resnick had known there was always the possibility of the arrest being something of a public event. What he hadn't counted on was a camera crew from the local television station and an eager young reporter who would doubtless soon be trailing her microphone around the neighbourhood, collecting a selection of vox pops she could edit to her advantage.

'Go,' he said into the radio. 'Go now.'

Billy Alston was a light sleeper. He was wide awake and vaulting out of bed almost the moment he heard the door going in downstairs. Wearing only the striped boxers and vest he slept in, he was out of the room while his younger brother, with whom he shared the room, was barely stirring. Heavy footsteps on the stairs below, voices shouting, 'Police. Police. Armed police.'

Alston kicked open the door to the attic room where his sisters were sleeping, both of them surrounded by dolls and soft toys, Lauren half out of the top bunk, her arm trailing down towards the floor. When he pushed at the catch, the window into the slanting roof refused to budge, and Alston picked a stool up from the floor and, one arm cradled across his head, smashed the stool against the centre of the glass.

He could hear both his mother and his aunt screaming now, shouting and screaming, and the voices of the police getting louder, their feet closer. Reaching up, he grasped the sides of the window and hauled himself through.

Behind him, Lauren cried out as an armed policeman

110

burst into the room and she ducked her head back down beneath the covers.

Alston slid down towards the guttering, scattering loose tiles in his wake, balanced for a moment, precariously, then jumped, barefoot, on to the flat roof of the rear extension. Another jump, down into the back yard, and this time he fell awkwardly, his ankle turning under him, scrambling to his feet and part-hopping, part-jumping towards the back gate, which, hanging half off its hinges, gave out into the narrow ginnel running down between the rows of houses.

There were police marksmen some fifteen metres along in both directions, weapons raised.

Fuck!

Without waiting to be asked, Alston raised both hands and placed them, fingers linked, behind his head.

'Down! Down on the ground. Now! Now! Do it, now!'

Slowly, Alston obeyed.

'A charade, Charlie, that's what it was, a fucking charade. Like something out of *Life on* fucking *Mars*.'

They had just finished watching the television news, shots of heavily armed police swarming towards an innocuous-looking terraced house, interspersed with talking heads, both black and white, speaking, almost unanimously, of police intimidation, overkill, the harassment of an entire community.

'The purpose of the raid, according to a police spokesperson, was to arrest a young male, whom the

111

police have so far declined to name, for questioning in connection with the murder of fifteen-year-old Kelly Brent. One of the reasons given for the presence of so many armed officers at the scene, was the very real possibility that there were guns and ammunition on the premises. As far as we can tell, no guns or ammunition have so far been found.'

Cut to footage, taken from a distance and slightly blurred, of an officer breaking down the door and others pushing past into the building.

'The question we must ask ourselves is to what extent police actions such as these serve to alienate the very communities they are empowered to serve.'

The camera tightened on the reporter's finely made-up face and well-groomed hair.

'This is Robyn Aspley-Jones on the streets of—'

Bill Berry silenced her with the remote, blanking the picture from the screen.

'Public-relations disaster, Charlie.'

'I didn't think,' Resnick said, 'public relations were our main concern.'

'Fuck off, Charlie! Where've you been the last fifteen fucking years?'

Resnick chose his words with care. 'With respect, sir, I think I'd consider this morning's operation a success. The man we were after was taken into custody without a shot being fired and is currently being questioned. A detailed search of the premises is still being carried out and, despite Robyn what's-her-name, it's far too early to say what we might find.'

Berry uttered a long, heartfelt sigh. 'All right, Charlie, okay. Only for God's sake don't start calling me sir. We're both of us too long in the tooth for that.'

Alston had been given a pair of jeans that were several sizes too large in the waist and an abandoned Nike top with a broken zip. His solicitor was wearing a pinstripe skirt that covered her knees and a neat little jacket over a pale pink blouse. Every now and again, she made a brisk note in the spiral-bound book open on the table before her.

'*Casino Royale*?' Michaelson said.

'What?'

'The new Bond.'

'You what?'

'You didn't see it? Daniel Craig, the new James Bond?'

Alston stared back at him, bemused.

'That's what it reminded me of,' Michaelson said. 'You jumping across rooftops and that. I thought maybe you'd seen it, wanted to give it a try.'

'Takin' the piss, i'n'it?' Alston said.

'Shame about the fall at the end, bit of a tumble, but otherwise, you ever want to apply for any stunt work . . .'

Resnick and Bill Berry were watching on a monitor in an adjoining room.

'You know who this pair remind me of?' Berry said.

'Michaelson and Pike? No, who?'

113

'Little and Large, remember them?'

'Not often,' Resnick said.

'Little and Large without the laughs.'

Hard to imagine, Resnick thought.

'Focus,' he said into Michaelson's earpiece. 'Get to the point.'

This just as Pike was saying, 'Two days before the Kelly Brent shooting, you tried to buy a gun.'

'I did?'

'Trouble with St Ann's, that's what you said.'

'Yeah?'

'You needed a gun, protection, that what it was?'

Alston shook his head.

'Two days before it happened, Billy. Trouble with St Ann's, like you said.' Pike slammed the flat of his hand down fast against the table. 'One girl dead.'

Alston blinked.

'Kelly Brent, you know her, Billy?'

'No.'

'You didn't know her?'

'I knew, like, who she was. Seen her around, yeah.'

'She was what? Fifteen, sixteen?'

'I dunno, man. Didn't really know her, like I say.'

'You got sisters, Billy, that right?'

'They got nothin' to do with this.'

'How old are they, Billy? Your sisters?'

'I don't see the relevance—' the solicitor began.

'Come on, Billy, how old?'

'Eleven an' seven, i'n'it?'

'Eleven and seven.'

114

'Yeah. But that ain't—'

'Suppose it had been one of them?' Michaelson said. 'How would you feel then?'

Alston stared back at him.

'Easy happen, Billy. Split second, someone out there with a gun.'

Alston shifted on his seat, hitched his shoulders and let his arms fall down by his side, long fingers, big hands.

'This little confrontation with St Ann's,' Pike said. 'This meeting you had. There was always going to be trouble, right?'

Alston shrugged.

'Billy, you thought there'd be trouble?'

'Nothin' we couldn't handle, i'n'it?'

'Nothing you couldn't handle.'

'Yeah, 's right.'

'Because you had a gun.'

'I never had no gun.'

'Two days before, you were out trying to buy one.'

'No.'

'Pub car park out at Carlton. Half eleven.'

'I don't know no pub out Carlton. I don't never go to no Carlton.'

'We've got a witness, Billy.'

'Yeah? Well, he's lyin'. Whoever it is, I'm tellin' you, he's lyin'.'

'You're not listening, Billy,' Michaelson said. 'We know you were there and we know why. You were there to buy a gun.'

115

'Bullshit!'

'One hundred and fifty pounds for a handgun and ammunition, that was the deal.'

Alston started to say something, then sat back, the beginnings of a smile on his face. 'Say, just say, right, I was there, like you say . . .'

His solicitor reached out a hand as if to intervene.

'An' lessay, jus' for the sake of argument, right, I was thinkin' 'bout buyin' this gun . . .'

'Billy,' the solicitor said, 'I really don't think . . .'

'Then if you got someone was there, you know I didn't buy no gun, right?'

'Billy . . .'

'Could be, I was tempted to buy a piece, but then I realise, like you all always tellin' me, that's not such a cool thing to do. So I jus' walked away. Far as I know, ain't no law 'gainst thinkin' 'bout doin' somethin' an' if that's all I'm here for you wastin' my time an' your own. Aw'right, Mr Bond?'

'Fuck's sake, Charlie,' Bill Berry said. 'Little bastard's running 'em round in circles.'

Resnick told Michaelson to suspend the interview and allow Alston to take a break. Forty-five minutes later, he went back in there himself, taking Anil Khan with him, still hoping for something positive from the Scene of Crime officers searching the house.

According to Alston, the reason he backed out of the deal over the gun was that he realised it was stupid, get caught with a firearm in your possession, you were

116

looking at serious time. And, no, he still maintained, as far as he knew, none of his crew had gone up to St Ann's that day strapped. As for the identity of the shooter, he had no idea. No more than the police did themselves.

Resnick knew the clock was ticking down.

Charge him or let him go.

Resnick had been back at his own desk for twenty minutes or so when one of the duty officers rang up from below. 'Howard Brent, sir. He's down here now. Wants to see you if he can.'

Resnick sighed and raised his eyes towards the ceiling. 'I'll come down.'

Today Brent was wearing his blue Converse with black jeans and a suede jacket, a white T-shirt with two overlapping gold chains, a gold ring in place of the stud in his ear.

'Mr Brent, what can I—?'

'You arrest someone for my daughter's murder and I have to learn this when someone phone me from the paper.'

'Mr Brent—'

'This is my daughter we talkin' about . . .'

'Mr Brent, if you hadn't been so hostile towards officers engaged in this investigation—'

'Hostile? That's good comin' from you. You callin' me hostile.'

'If you hadn't persistently refused to have anything to do with the family liaison officer appointed, then you

117

would have been informed in the proper way, using the proper channels. As it is, I can confirm, yes, a suspect has been arrested and is currently being questioned at this station.'

'Alston, right?'

'Mr Brent—'

'What everyone's sayin', Billy Alston. That's what everyone's sayin' on the street.'

'A statement—'

'Hey, man!' Brent jabbed a finger towards Resnick's face. 'Don't fuck with me. Alston, he here 'cause he killed my daughter, I got a right to know.'

Wearily, Resnick shook his head. 'Mr Brent, all I can tell you is this. We are speaking to someone in the course of our inquiries and nothing more. No charges concerning your daughter's murder have been made.'

Brent made a tight scoffing sound, somewhere between a snort and a laugh.

'If and when that happens,' Resnick continued, 'you will be informed. Now please go home. There's nothing you can do here.'

'You think? That's what you think, eh? Well, I tellin' you, this gonna get sorted. One way or another. You know that, yeah? You know?'

Resnick turned and walked away.

At four o'clock that afternoon, the report came through from the team that had been searching the Alston house: a small quantity of cannabis aside, nothing

118

illegal had been found. No firearms, no other drugs, no ammunition.

At a quarter past six that evening, Billy Alston was released.

10

The closer the trial date came, the more it played on Lynn's mind.

She'd been in court to give evidence on more occasions than she could remember: had sworn the oath and had told, despite the attempts of the defending barrister to throw her off course, the whole truth and nothing but.

She felt nervous, nevertheless.

Always had, always did.

The fear that she might trip up, throw away the case with a careless word, a slip of the tongue, some misremembered fact, let herself and everyone down. As if she were being tested: as if, somehow, she were the one on trial.

'All relative, isn't it?' a colleague had once argued, a young DC who'd taken a philosophy course as part of his criminology degree. 'Your truth, another man's falsehood. A matter of perception. Prisms. Nothing's absolute.' He'd left the force after four years and taken a lecturing post at the University of Hertfordshire.

Those who can't hack the real world, teach, Lynn thought. The rest of us dig in our heels and get on with it as best we can. But then, when she heard the stories coming out of the local schools and academies, she reckoned that kind of teaching was probably real enough.

This was real, too.

Viktor Zoukas, charged with murder.

Culpable homicide. The arcane language was imprinted on Lynn's mind: where a person of sound memory and discretion unlawfully killeth any reasonable creature in being, under the Queen's peace, with malice aforethought, either express or implied, the death following within a year and a day.

It had been a Saturday night, nine months before, an emergency call at close to half past two, the force already stretched by the usual array of running fights and mass brawls and sudden, singular acts of violence, as the clubs started to disgorge their customers and began the arduous task of counting the weekend's profits and swilling down the floors.

The call was to a sauna and massage parlour above a sex shop on one of the seedier side streets in the old Lace Market, the caller an alarmed customer who, unsurprisingly, had refused to give his name. When the two uniformed officers arrived only minutes later, dispatched from a disturbance they had been attending at an Indian restaurant on the same block, they found several young women sitting on the pavement outside, another slumped, bewildered, against the sex-shop window. A young man in a stained dress shirt and the still-smart black trousers of a dress suit, sat on the stairs with his head in his hands. At the top of the stairway, a woman with dyed reddish hair, wearing the same short pink tunic as the rest, mascara smeared across her face, was leaning back against the wall, cigarette in her shaking hand.

As the officers moved past her along the narrow corridor, one of the doors near the far end opened abruptly and a man lurched out, stumbled two paces forward and stopped. He was a little above medium height, broad-shouldered, solid, muscle turning to fat, a purple shirt unbuttoned almost to the waist, the purple at the left shoulder darkened almost to black. There were splashes of what looked like blood on his face and neck and caught in the dark hairs of his chest. In his eyes, a mixture of anger and surprise. His right hand held a knife, a short, straight blade close against his leg.

'Drop it,' the first officer said. 'Drop the knife. Now. On the floor. Put it down.'

The man's muscles tensed, and in the dim light of the single bulb overhead the officers could see the movement in his eyes as he looked beyond them towards the stairs, as if seeking a possible way out.

'Down,' the first officer said again. 'Drop the knife down now.'

The man's fingers tightened further around the handle, then gradually opened and the knife landed

122

with a quick, dull sound on the meagre carpet covering the floor.

'Kick the knife over here, towards me. Now, with your foot. Not hard. Towards me, that's it. Okay, now clasp your hands behind your head. No, clasp, clasp, fingers together, like this. Good. Now, get down on the floor. Down. Down, that's right. Now don't move. Don't move until you're told.'

The officer nodded to his companion and began to call for back-up, and the second officer moved towards the doorway from which the man had emerged.

The room was narrow, little more than a cubicle, with a high, narrow bed to one side, the kind you find in doctor's surgeries, a thin yellow sheet hanging half on, half off towards the floor. On a small circular table at the head were several pots and plastic tubes of lotion and a single transparent latex glove, pulled partly inside out. Poking out from beneath the corner of the sheet where it brushed the floor was a woman's foot with a fine-meshed gold chain above the ankle and chipped red polish on the toes.

The officer squatted down and used finger and thumb to lift away the sheet.

The woman was on her back, face turned towards the wall, and even in the dim light available, the officer could see that her throat had been cut.

Vomit hit the back of his throat and he swallowed it away.

Steadying his breathing, he let the sheet fall back into place.

Lynn was the first senior detective at the scene, anxious to ensure it was contaminated as little as possible and that vital evidence was preserved intact.

The body.

The presumed assailant.

The knife.

She could conjure up, even now, the mixture of smells in that narrow trench-like room: cheap baby lotion and stale sweat, spent jism and fresh blood.

Before the man who had been holding the knife was taken away under police guard for treatment, Lynn had established his identity. Viktor Zoukas. Originally, he said, from Albania. The premises were licensed in his name.

Of the five female workers, two were local, two recently from Croatia, their legal status doubtful, one, a student, from Romania. Mostly they were frightened, unwilling to talk, in various stages of shock. One of the local women, Sally, a sometime stripper, some ten or fifteen years older than the rest, was paid extra to take bookings, collect the cash from the customers, keep a weather eye on the girls.

Lynn quickly separated her off from the rest.

'There's not much I can tell you,' Sally said.

Lynn waited, patient, while the woman lit a cigarette.

She had heard voices raised, Sally told her, an argument between the dead girl and one of the punters – not unusual, with the dead girl, Nina, especially. She'd been about to go and see what was happening when Viktor had stopped her. He wasn't that often on the premises, not that early, usually only came around to cash up at the end of the night, but this time he was. He would go and sort things out, he said. The next thing she knew there was this awful screaming and one of the girls – Andreea Florescu, the Romanian – came running into the reception area, shouting that Nina was dead.

Pandemonium. Punters not able to get out fast enough. Which of them might have phoned the police she'd no idea. Surprised, to be honest, that anyone did.

Viktor, Lynn had asked, Viktor Zoukas, when all this was going on, people leaving, shouting and screaming, where was he?

Sally didn't know. She hadn't seen him. Still in the room with Nina perhaps? Who could say?

Lynn had talked then to the other women who worked there, several, she suspected, feigning a worse command of English than was actually the case, but she had got little from them. Andreea, who had raised the alarm, kept her eyes averted when Lynn spoke to her, head mostly angled away.

'Just tell me,' Lynn said quietly. 'Just tell me what you saw.'

Andreea did look at her for a moment then and the shadow of what she had seen passed across her eyes.

'It's okay,' Lynn said. 'Later. Not here.' And briefly, she touched the back of the young woman's hand.

They met next morning in the Old Market Square, Andreea wearing a grey short-sleeved jacket over a yellow vest, blue jeans that bagged at the knees, white

125

sneakers like old-fashioned school plimsolls, make-up heavy around her eyes.

Lynn took her to one of the few cafés in the city centre that the coffee conglomerates had yet to take over. Somewhere anonymous where she thought they were less likely to be noticed or disturbed.

There were sauce bottles on the tables and small foil containers that had previously held pies and pasties serving as ashtrays: only a few months till the smoking ban came into force and most of the customers were taking full advantage.

Lynn ordered tea, asked questions, listened.

Andreea lit one Marlboro from the butt of another.

Through the window Lynn could see the usual panoply of men and women walking past, talking into their mobile phones, some smartly, even fashionably, dressed, others in the camouflage of cheap sportswear, young women who looked as if they should still be at school pushing prams or gripping unsteady toddlers by the hand.

'You?' Andreea said, following Lynn's gaze. 'You have children?'

Lynn shook her head.

'I have little girl,' Andreea said, quietly. 'Monica. She is three.'

'Here?' Lynn asked, surprised.

'No, at home with my mother. In Romania. Constanta. It is on the sea. The Black Sea. Very beautiful.'

She took a photograph from her purse and passed it

across the table. Lynn saw a girl in a red-and-white dress with big, dark eyes and ribbons in her hair.

'She's lovely,' Lynn said. 'You must miss her a lot.'

'Yes. Of course.' Andreea wafted smoke away from her face. 'I saw her last time at Christmas. When I went home for holiday. She has grown so big.'

'It must have been hard to leave her,' Lynn said.

'Of course. But there is no life for me there. I am making life here, then I will bring her. Now I am a student.'

'A student?'

'Yes. I learn Tourism and Hospitality. And English. We have to learn English.'

'Your English is very good.'

'Thank you.'

'And the job at the sauna?'

Andreea blushed and looked at the floor. 'I have to earn money.'

'There must be other ways.'

'Yes, a few. I could work, maybe, at night in factory. Pork Farm?'

'Pork Farms, yes.'

'Some of my friends, they do this.'

'But not you.'

'No, not me.' She tipped ash from the end of her cigarette. 'I try it once.' She made a face. 'The smell. You cannot get rid of the smell.'

Lynn went to the counter and fetched a packet of biscuits and two more cups of tea. Aside from a few elderly people sitting alone, the café was more or less empty. The workmen – plasterers, electricians, labourers – who had been there when Lynn and Andreea had arrived had now gone.

'Tell me again,' Lynn said, 'what you saw when you went into the room.'

Andreea stirred one and then a second spoonful of sugar into her tea. 'Viktor, he was standing there, his hand like this . . .' she reached one hand across her chest, '. . . holding his shoulder. He was bleeding.'

'And Nina, where was she?'

'I think . . . I said . . . she was on the floor.'

'You're not sure?'

'No, I am sure.'

'She was on the floor?'

'Yes.'

'Whereabouts on the floor?'

'I don't know, beside the bed. It must have been, yes, beside the bed.'

Was she simply nervous, Lynn wondered, or lying? Something about the eyes, the way they would never focus on Lynn directly when she answered, that and the way she sat, fidgeting, restless. She was lying, Lynn thought, but she didn't know by how much or why.

'Sally says you came running into the reception area shouting that Nina was dead.'

'I don't remember.'

'You don't remember shouting, or . . .'

'I don't remember what I said.'

'But was that what you thought? That she was dead?'

'Yes.'

'How could you be sure?'

Andreea's voice was so low, Lynn had to strain to hear. 'There was so much blood,' she said.

Lynn leaned back and sipped her tea. She stripped the cellophane from around the biscuits and offered one to Andreea, who shook her head.

'Before you got to the room,' Lynn said, 'you didn't see anyone else? Someone running away?'

'A man, yes.'

'The man who had been with her?'

'Yes, I think so.'

'Can you describe him?'

'Yes. He was bald and with tattoos, here . . .' She touched her fingers against the side of her neck.

'The left side?'

'Both, I think. I'm not sure, it was so quick.'

'What was he wearing, can you remember?'

'A shirt, some kind of T-shirt, a football shirt, perhaps. And jeans.'

'No coat? No jacket?'

Andreea thought. 'No, I don't think . . . No, no.'

'The shirt, can you remember the colour?'

'White. I think that it was white.'

'An England shirt?'

'Maybe.'

Andreea stubbed out her cigarette; drank some more tea.

'When you got to the room,' Lynn said, 'Viktor apart, was there anybody else there?'

'Only Nina.'

'And the knife,' Lynn said. 'Where was the knife?'

'On the floor. Between them. On the floor.'

'You're sure of that? Absolutely positive?'

'Oh, yes.'

Lynn sat back and sighed. Earlier that morning, she had heard Viktor Zoukas's version of what happened. When he got to the room, he said, Nina and one of the customers were already fighting. A short man with a bald head, shaven. Viktor didn't think he'd seen him before. They were struggling for control of a knife. He thought Nina was already wounded, bleeding. When he tried to intervene, the man lashed out and stabbed him in the shoulder. He tried to get the knife from him, but fell and knocked his head against the wall. For a short while, seconds maybe, he must have lost consciousness. When he came to, the man had gone and at first he thought Nina had, too. Then he saw her, underneath the bed, the knife close by. He picked up the knife and went back out into the corridor and that was when the two policemen arrested him.

It wasn't only Andreea who was lying, Lynn thought, it was Viktor, too. Somewhere between them lay the truth.

'Nina,' Lynn said, 'did you know her well?'

'I know her a little,' Andreea said. 'Not well.' She had removed her jacket and hung it from the back of the chair. There were bruises on her arms, faded but still distinct.

'Had she worked there long?'

'I think, maybe, six, seven months.' Andreea lit

another cigarette and tilted back her head, letting the first shallow stream of smoke drift up towards the ceiling. 'This her first job in this country. Since she came from Croatia. Her English is not very good. She and Viktor, they argue all the time. She won't do this, won't do that. She is always telling me that she will run away, leave . . .' Andreea shook her head. 'She is frightened of him, Viktor. She owes him money, I think, for bringing her to this country.'

'She was here illegally?'

Andreea shrugged, a small, slight movement of her shoulders, barely noticeable.

'When he argued with her, Viktor, did he ever strike her?'

'Hit?'

'Yes.'

'Yes, of course. He call her names and hit her. I kill you, he says, I fucking kill you, and Nina, she cries and says to me she will leave, but next day she is there again.'

' "I'll kill you," that's what he said?'

'Yes. But this is because he is angry. He does not mean . . .' She balanced her cigarette on the table's edge. 'She make good money for him. The men like her. Why would he kill her?'

Lynn looked at her watch. 'Listen, Andreea,' she said, 'I have to go.' She took a card from her bag and placed it in front of her. 'If you think of anything else, or if you just want to talk – about Nina, or about anything – give me a call.'

She got to her feet and leaned back down. Up close, she could see, beneath the make-up, the dark violet patches of tiredness around Andreea's eyes, the faint patina of a bruise on her cheek.

'What happened to Nina, it could have happened to any one of you,' Lynn said. 'It could have happened to you.' She rested her hand for a moment on Andreea's shoulder. 'Come and talk to me. Don't let it happen again.'

When she looked back through the café window, Andreea was still sitting there, smoke rising from her cigarette, staring into space.

It would be almost two weeks before Lynn heard from her again.

11

The autopsy on Nina Simic showed that she had been killed by a single stab wound to the neck, of sufficient depth to suggest that considerable force had been used, a single-edged blade entering below the right ear and severing the common carotid artery as it moved diagonally down and round towards the central hyoid bone beneath the chin. There were defence wounds on both the upper and lower arms, as well as a number of small cuts to the hands, which suggested that she had struggled with her killer for the knife. There were also a significant number of other signs of trauma to the body, bruises and contusions, mostly on the arms and upper torso, some recent, others older.

Forensic examination of the knife found in Zoukas's possession found that it matched in most particulars the weapon used in the attack. Further, there were three sets of fingerprints on the handle of the knife, Viktor Zoukas's, Nina Simic's and the smudged finger- and thumbprint of a third person, as yet unidentified.

Zoukas himself was questioned again and again.

All of the evidence so far could be made to support his story: a struggle between Nina Simic and an unknown assailant in which he had unsuccessfully attempted to intervene. Though inconclusive, medical evidence seemed to support his assertion that he had suffered a blow to the head which could have rendered him briefly unconscious. Nor was there any faking a four-centimetre-deep stab wound to the shoulder, almost certainly caused by the same blade.

Meantime, a small number of the men who had patronised the sauna that evening had been contacted, but by no means all. According to Sally, several punters had entered at more or less the same time, ten or fifteen minutes after two, often their busiest time, and she had not been able to keep track of who had gone with whom. She did have a vague memory of seeing someone who approximated to Zoukas's equally vague description of a stocky, shaven-haired man with tattoos, but could not be certain if had been one of Nina's clients or not. 'Face it,' she said, 'short and near bald on top, between thirty and forty, you're talking about most of the blokes who come here looking for business.'

The police continued their efforts to seek him out.

Perhaps, Lynn thought, her instincts were wrong and Zoukas was telling the truth.

Perhaps . . .

It was nearing the end of the day when Andreea finally phoned, her voice hesitant and indistinct.

'Andreea,' Lynn said. 'I'm sorry, I can't hear you.'

There was a pause, and then, more clearly, 'What I told you before, it was not all true.'

Lynn felt a quick surge of adrenalin through her body.

'Where are you?'

'By the river.'

'The Trent?'

'I don't know. I suppose. My friends, they live in Meadows.'

'Trent Bridge? You're near Trent Bridge?'

'Yes, I think so.'

'A big building with a green roof, can you see that from where you are?'

'Yes, I can see.'

'Which side of the river is it? The side you're on or the other?'

'The other.'

'Okay. Wait there. I'll come to you. Five, ten minutes. No more.'

Quick as I can, Lynn thought, before she loses her nerve.

At first, she feared Andreea had changed her mind. And then she saw her, stepping out from between two slender trees. There was a fine rain in the air and it was approaching dusk. Andreea was wearing a dark anorak, several sizes too large; her red hair had been pushed up inside a black beret, a few stray strands hanging free; closer to, Lynn could see that whatever make-up she'd

135

been wearing earlier had mostly faded or been rubbed away.

Somehow she looked both older and younger than when Lynn had seen her last.

'Do you fancy a drink?' Lynn said, nodding in the direction of the pub by the bridge.

Andreea shook her head. 'No. No, thank you.'

'Then let's walk.'

They set off along the river, the bridge at their backs, Lynn content for now to listen as Andreea talked about the couple she was staying with, the man from the Republic of Moldova, here studying at the university, and the woman from her own country, from Bucharest, the capital. Andreea had been frightened to stay in the flat she'd been sharing with three others and, for now, was sleeping on the settee in her friends' front room.

'Why were you frightened?' Lynn asked.

Andreea stopped to light a cigarette. Cars passed slowly along the Embankment, headlights burnishing the rain.

'This man,' Andreea said, 'he came to see me.'

'Which man?'

'I don't know his name. He was a friend of Viktor's. I have seen him before, at the sauna. He came one night when I was sleeping. He make me put a coat over what I am wearing and go with him to his car. Somebody else was driving. They take me to this place, I don't know where it is. All . . . all rubbish, in big . . . I don't know how to say . . .' She gestured with her hands.

'Containers?'

136

'Yes, I think maybe so, containers, yes.'

'Some kind of refuse dump.'

'Refuse, yes. Rubbish. He make me get out of the car and I am sure he is going to kill me. I am certain of this. He has a knife and I think I am going to be dead like Nina, he is going to cut my throat.'

Andreea stopped and in the halting light Lynn could see the sweat beading her forehead, the shake of her hand as she held her cigarette.

'He made me tell him what I told the police, and I told him there was nothing. I had seen nothing. Except Nina on the floor. He asked me if I mention Viktor and I say no, of course not, I did not know Viktor was there. He make me get down on my knees and holds the knife against the side of my face, here.' Andreea touched her cheek, a slow line from below her ear to her neck. 'He say I am good girl. He say if I ever say anything different to the police, he will kill me and throw me in the rubbish. And then he make me . . . you know, with my mouth. And then he take me home but I am too frightened to stay there. I come here to Meadows.'

'And the sauna? You haven't been back to the sauna?'

Andreea shook her head.

'What will you do?'

'I have a good friend in London. Leyton? Leytonstone? I am not sure. Perhaps they are the same. Alexander. He comes from Constanta, like me. He is student there. He says I can stay with him. He can even get me job, he thinks, in a bar. Or if not, in hotel, cleaning I think.'

'What about your own studies? These courses you're doing?'

'Alexander thinks it may be possible to transfer somehow, I don't know. But it will be safer there, in London. Yes? You think?' She grasped Lynn's arm.

'Maybe. Yes, perhaps.'

They drew level with three men of indeterminate age, sitting on a bench, passing a can of cider back and forth. A short-haired mongrel dog lay curled on the ground between them and raised its head to growl and show its teeth as they walked past. One of the men held the can out towards them, good-naturedly, and Lynn smiled and said no thanks.

'Despite the threats this man made,' Lynn said, 'you still want to change your story about what happened?'

'Yes. Yes, I think so.'

A little way further along there was an empty bench and they sat facing the water, the traffic at their back. Andreea fumbled for a cigarette in one of the pockets of her anorak.

'Nina,' she said, 'she was nice to me. One time especially I remember, she saw that I was upset. I had a letter from home, from my mother. There was drawing Monica had made of two people. Holding hands. How do you call them? Match men?'

'Matchstick men.'

'Yes. Like that. One big and one small. It was Monica and me. My mother had written our names on the top.' There were tears in her eyes. 'Nina, she had a child, too, she told me. A boy. When she was fifteen. She had not seen him for a long time. She hold me and tell me not to cry. I will see my little girl again.'

Andreea stopped and turned her face towards Lynn, the tears now running down her cheeks.

'I want to tell the truth of how she died.'

Lynn smiled reassuringly. 'Go on,' she said. 'Tell me in your own time.'

Andreea flicked away ash and the end of her cigarette briefly sparked. 'There was a man,' she said, 'the man I spoke of, a customer, he and Nina had started to fight. I don't know what about. Something, perhaps, he had asked her to do. I don't know. I am across corridor, close, I can hear them shouting and then, I think, I hear the man leave, still shouting at her, fucking whore and things like that, and I think now it will be all right. But Viktor, I hear him go into the room and there is more shouting and Nina she starts to scream and I know he is hitting her, hitting her bad, and I am frightened for her, so I go into the corridor and the door it is open, just a little, not all the way, but I can see she has a knife, and when Viktor hits her again she stabs him in the shoulder, like this, here, and Viktor falls back against the wall and the knife falls to the floor and I am very frightened and I call her name, Nina, Nina, and she turns to look at me and starts to come towards the door and the next thing I see Viktor is on his feet and has the knife in his hand and he stabs Nina in the neck, from behind, and this time there is so much blood,

139

more blood, and I run before Viktor can see me, I go running to Sally and tell her I think Nina is dead.'

She stopped, drained, shaking, looking at the slowly darkening sky.

'Viktor,' Lynn said, 'he doesn't know what you saw?'

'No,' Andreea said. 'And he must never know.'

Lynn rested a hand on her arm. 'Thank you,' she said. 'You're very brave. And don't worry. He won't hurt you. Neither him nor his friend. I promise.' Even as she spoke, knowing how hollow the words were. Promises are like piecrusts, wasn't that what her mother used to say?

They kept Andreea under wraps, took a statement from her in an out-of-the-way police station, questioned her some more. Andreea's name would not be used when her statement was finally disclosed, as it had to be, to the defence before the trial; she would be simply Miss X, Miss Y. But from the statement, Lynn knew, it would not be too difficult for the defence team to work out her identity.

Andreea told them that a week or so before she was killed, Nina had shown her the knife. She had got it from a friend. One of the regulars, Andreea thought, she didn't know for sure. This is for Viktor, Nina had said, if he hits me once more.

'I did not think she meant it,' Andreea said. 'But she did. What she said, it was true.'

Steadily, they accumulated evidence of Zoukas terrorising the women who worked for him,

140

threatening, striking, lashing out in anger. According to one of the customers, Zoukas had once pushed past him yelling, 'That bitch. That fucking Nina! I fucking kill her!' And then, after a second television appeal, the police received a number of phone calls, including several from his ex-wife, identifying the tattooed man as Kelvin Pearce.

Officers found him in Sneinton, working on a building that had recently been gutted and was now being refurbished and restored; Pearce busy removing the old window frames while listening happily to Suggs on Virgin Radio. 'Reasons To Be Cheerful' followed by the Dexys' 'Come On, Eileen'.

Asked why he hadn't come forward of his own volition, he gave the officer a look of sheer incredulity. 'Stick my head in a fuckin' noose, right? I'm not as stupid as I might bloody look.'

Once he started telling his story, he was clear and to the point. He and the girl had started arguing. Got him all worked up, the cunt, and then asked him for another twenty quid. He'd lost it, taken a swing at her, fair enough, he'd put his hand up for that, but then she'd only pulled this knife on him and started waving it in his face. He'd been trying to get it from her when this fat bastard come in, swearing and shouting, and he'd legged it out of there as fast as he could.

Had he touched the knife?

'Yes, of course. Said so, didn't I?'

Had he at any point stabbed or cut Nina Simic with the knife?

141

'No. No way.'

'Or Viktor Zoukas?'

'That mad bastard? You're kidding, right?'

'That's a no, then?'

'Too fucking right!'

'And once you left the room, you never went back?'

'You're kidding, yeah?'

Now that there were two witnesses placing Zoukas firmly at the scene, the CPS were happy to go ahead and he was formally charged with Nina Simic's murder. Lynn was in court, when, with a very real presumption that he might flee the country, Zoukas was refused bail. Turning away before being led down to the cells, he saw her and their eyes locked. 'You!' he shouted. 'You . . . !'

Before he could say more, the duty officers hauled him none too gently away, leaving Lynn shaken by the intensity of hatred on his face.

As the trial approached, Andreea telephoned Lynn several times in tears: she was too frightened, she said, to stand up in court.

'It's all right,' Lynn said. 'I've told you before. You can give your evidence from behind a screen, or not even that. A video link. You don't have to be in the courtroom at all. He won't see you. You don't have to see him. Nobody need know who you are. It will all be fine.'

Lynn was doing the ironing on Monday morning when

the CPS phoned, Rachel Vine's voice instantly identifiable. 'I thought you ought to know,' she said. 'The Zoukas case, we're applying for an adjournment.'

'What on earth for?'

'You haven't heard? One of your witnesses has gone AWOL.'

'Andreea?'

'No, the other one. Pearce. No one's seen hide nor hair of him for two days.'

The Crown Prosecution Service offices were on King Edward Street, close to the city centre; the old Palais, remodelled and renamed, was at one end, a bingo hall and mosque at the other.

Rachel Vine was taller than Lynn, with dark hair and a figure that suggested working out in the gym three nights out of five. Either that or the pool. She was bright and smart, with a reputation for staying focused under pressure and an attitude that could, on occasion, get in the faces of friend and foe alike. When the current Chief Prosecutor moved on, she was tipped for the position.

She shook Lynn's hand and asked again how she was recovering from her injury. 'I promise not to make you laugh,' she said. 'Don't want to set those ribs off again.'

Lynn didn't think she'd be laughing.

She'd already called the DS who'd been her number two on the Zoukas investigation and given him a bollocking for not keeping her in the loop over Pearce's disappearance. So far, she'd learned, Pearce had been

143

traced to a sister in Mansfield, where he'd stayed a night before moving on. The sister didn't know where to.

'It's unfortunate,' Rachel Vine said. 'Losing Pearce so close to the trial. Quite apart from him being one of our only two witnesses who can place Zoukas in the room with Nina Simic just before she died, his disappearance now only makes the defence case, that he was the one who killed Nina, look all the stronger.'

'Someone got to him, is that what you think?'

'I really don't know. It's possible. The care officer said he'd been getting more and more jumpy as the trial date got closer, but, in a case like this, that's only normal. All we can hope is that it's just a bout of bad nerves and he'll calm down, come to his senses. Or that we'll find him. Presumably, every effort's being made to trace him?'

'So I believe.'

'Well, I don't feel we can go ahead without him.'

'But surely, with Andreea . . .'

'Andreea's evidence on its own isn't enough. And I worry she's going to get pulled to pieces on the stand. She comes apart and what's left? No, we go into court like that and I think there's a real danger of Zoukas getting acquitted.'

Lynn looked away: she didn't like what she was hearing, but couldn't think of any counter-arguments that were strong enough.

'I've talked it over with the Chief,' Rachel Vine said, 'and she's in agreement. I shall be requesting an adjournment first thing tomorrow. I imagine, in exchange for complying, the defence will do their utmost to get Zoukas released on bail.'

'Leaving him free to intimidate witnesses or skip the country altogether.'

'Don't worry,' Rachel Vine said. 'That's not going to happen.' She reached out and touched Lynn's arm. 'I know what this case means to you. I'm not about to let it slip away.'

By early afternoon of the following day, it was all agreed: passed through with surprising speed.

Rachel Vine herself had phoned Lynn with the news.

'There's one thing we had to swallow,' she said. 'We've had to agree not to oppose bail.'

'You're kidding!'

'No. Without it, the defence would never have agreed to an adjournment of more than a few days, five at most. The chances of Pearce being found in that time are too slim.'

'I don't believe it,' Lynn said, as much to herself as to Rachel Vine.

'Look, we've gained a month, that's the most important thing, and as far as Zoukas is concerned, we'll be arguing for a surety of around fifty K. Passport surrendered and a residency order imposed, plus he'll have to report to the local police once a week, if not every day. Watertight as can be.'

'I still don't like it,' Lynn said.

'Well, live with it like the rest of us.'

145

'Yes, right. What was it you said? Something about not letting it slip away?'

There was a pause at the other end of the line. 'Look,' Rachel Vine said hesitantly, 'I probably shouldn't be telling you this, but we were requested not to oppose bail.'

'By whom?'

'The DPP.'

'But for Christ's sake—'

'Lynn, Lynn, listen, I can't say any more. If you want to take it any further, I suggest you go and see your ACC.'

When Lynn tried to push her for more details, the line went dead.

After some finagling and not a little persuasion, she talked her way into an appointment with the Assistant Chief Constable (Crime) in his office at Sherwood Lodge at the end of the day, still unclear in her mind where the pressure behind the DPP's request had come from.

She got her answer when, having been kept waiting a good twenty minutes, she was ushered into the ACC's office and there was Stuart Daines from the Serious and Organised Crime Agency, smiling as he stepped towards her and offered his hand.

'Lynn, good to see you again.' The smile broadened. 'You wouldn't come and join us, so I thought we'd come and join you.'

12

'The arrogant, self-centred bastard, standing there with that smug smile stuck on his face, as if he'd just sold me several thousand pounds' worth of double bloody glazing.'

Lynn had gone straight from Sherwood Lodge to Resnick's office, interrupting a late meeting, Khan and Michaelson taking the temperature quickly and leaving.

'I thought you quite fancied him,' Resnick said lightly.

'It's no bloody joke, Charlie.'

'I know.'

'Zoukas out on the streets, no matter what sort of conditions, it sticks in my throat.'

'There must have been a reason, some kind of explanation?'

'Explanation?' She dropped her voice an octave in imitation. ' "Viktor Zoukas is a small but integral part of an ongoing major investigation, and it is important for the progress of that investigation that he remains free at this time." '

'At this time?'

'Yes.'

'That's what he said?'

'Yes.'

'Daines?'

'Principal Officer Daines.'

'That's his rank?'

'Civil Service grades in SOCA. Tells you what you need to know.'

'And he didn't give you any more details than that?'

Lynn shook her head. 'The last thing he wanted, he assured me, was for me to feel shut out from what was going on.'

'Good of him.'

'But because the investigation was at quite a delicate stage, he couldn't say a great deal more right now, though he fully intended to bring me up to speed as soon as he possibly could.'

Resnick shifted in his chair. It was a long time since he'd seen Lynn so openly angry and with such apparent cause. 'What did the ACC have to say?'

'Oh, some waffle about the importance of cooperating with a national organisation. Seeing the wider picture – you can imagine. From what I could make out at the conference I went to, SOCA have had precious little to do with forces outside London. Won't be doing the Chief Constable any harm politically if we're one of the first. Help shift attention away from

148

kids shooting themselves on the streets.'

'You're getting cynical in your old age,' Resnick said.

'And you're not?'

'Just older.'

Lynn went over to the window and looked down towards the street. A large crane was being manoeuvred towards the entrance of the adjacent building site, blocking the traffic in both directions.

'Kelly Brent,' she said, turning back into the room, 'any progress?'

Resnick sighed. 'The words "brick" and "wall" come to mind.'

'No word from Gregan about a possible shooter?'

'Not so far.'

'Something'll break sooner or later.'

'You have to hope.'

Lynn turned towards the door. 'I'd better go.'

'Okay.'

'See you at home.'

'Resnick nodded. 'If you see Frank or Anil . . .'

'I'll ask them to come back in.'

Andreea phoned Lynn the following day, her voice shaky, her accent unclear. The witness-care officer had informed her of the adjournment, thinking, perhaps, that it might put her more at ease.

'Where are you?' Lynn asked. 'Are you phoning from London?'

No. She was there, in the city, at the bus station.

'Wait where you are,' Lynn told her. 'Wait there and I'll find you.'

She was sitting on one of the benches, head covered by a patterned scarf. Since Lynn had last seen her she seemed to have lost weight; her face had become thinner, more gaunt.

As Lynn approached, she looked around anxiously, then grabbed at her arm. 'I did not want to come here, but I have to see you. I am afraid.'

'It's okay.' Lynn disengaged herself. 'It's okay. Let's go somewhere where we can talk.'

The Victoria Centre was beginning to empty, some of the shops already closing, their shutters being pulled down and locked for the night. Lynn steered Andreea along the upper level and on to the covered walkway that crossed Upper Parliament Street; down then past stalls selling electrical goods and discount batteries and cheap clothes, a few hundred metres and a few more corners and they were on Broad Street and there, across from the arts cinema, was Lee Rosey's, Lynn's little oasis in the city centre.

She'd stumbled on it by chance, a small café with no more than six or seven tables running to the back and a few stools by the front window looking out on to the street. Arranged neatly on the shelves along one wall were fifty or more different kinds of tea, everything from Assam and Ceylon through peppermint or chamomile to cinnamon and hibiscus. You could get coffee if that's what you wanted, and the coffee was okay, smoothies also, but tea was the thing, the proprietor going against the trend, not coffee but tea.

Generally, Lynn liked to keep the place to herself, not go there with anyone associated with the job. Most of the regular customers seemed to be patrons of the cinema opposite or students from one or other of the nearby colleges, but at that time of the evening there were only a few stragglers left: a young man using his laptop by the window, a young woman leafing through a book about photography while she listened to her iPod, a couple sharing a piece of coffee cake and staring into each other's eyes the way only adolescents could.

'Please,' Andreea said, 'what happened – I don't understand.'

'You mean the adjournment?'

'Yes.'

'It's difficult to explain.'

'You think he is not guilty?'

Lynn breathed out slowly. 'No, it's not that, it's . . . Look, Andreea . . .' touching her hand, '. . . I'll be honest with you. I don't fully understand everything myself. But Zoukas, in the end he'll pay for whatever he's done, I assure you.'

'And me?' Andreea said. 'What of me?'

'You'll be fine. Nothing will happen to you.'

'But now that he is free.'

'He's not free, that's not true. He has to report to the police all the time.'

'But he knows that it was me who would speak against him at the trial.'

'Look, Andreea,' Lynn leaned closer, 'you don't

know that. And even if he did, right now the last thing Zoukas is going to want to do is draw more attention to himself. He'll be going out of his way to stay clean.' She glanced up as somebody came into the café. 'Besides, he doesn't know where you are.'

'You don't think he can find out, if he wants?'

'London's a big place.'

Andreea shivered. 'I don't know.'

'Andreea, listen. Listen. Listen to me. Go back to London. Keep your head down. Stay where you are. Nothing's going to happen to you. I promise. Okay?' She squeezed Andreea's hand. 'Andreea. Okay?'

'Yes.' A smile, hesitant and quick with doubt. 'Okay.'

When Lynn got home, having seen Andreea safely back on to the express coach to London, what she had wanted most was a drink. Resnick moved the casserole he'd been reheating down to the bottom of the oven, lowered the gas, and opened a bottle of red.

Lynn downed most of the first glass as if it were water.

'Jesus, Charlie! What was I doing?'

'How d'you mean?'

'Making promises like that. Again. Promises I can't keep.'

'You really think she's in danger?'

'I think she could be. If Zoukas wants to be sure she won't speak out.'

'You think he can find out where she is?'

'It depends. If she's drifted back into the same kind

152

of work, it's more than possible. It depends how wide his connections go. Andreea's got a friend she was telling me about, from Romania, working in a hotel down in Cornwall. She might see if she can find work down there later in the year.'

'A shame she can't go now.'

'I know.'

Resnick reached across and refilled her almost empty glass. The street light was sending a dull orange glow into the room, where only the small lamp on the shelf above the stereo was burning.

'You think that's what happened to Kelvin Pearce? Someone looking out for Zoukas threatened him in some way?'

'Either that or paid him off.'

'No sign of him yet?'

Lynn shook her head.

They continued to sit there, each to their own thoughts, while the room darkened further around them.

'You ready to eat?' Resnick said eventually.

'We'd better. All this wine's going to my head.'

On his way out of the room he paused to put some music on the stereo. Laurindo Almeida and Bud Shank. One of the first jazz bossa nova sessions. 1953. Shank's alto, sinuous and precise over the intricate filigrees of Almeida's guitar. Perfect in its way.

He carried his glass out into the kitchen, turned up the temperature of the oven and set two plates to warm. How long after eating, he wondered, before they were both in bed?

13

Resnick had already left for work. Lynn, not yet fully back on official duty, had lingered over breakfast, leafing through the paper, passing time with the quick crossword, before finally casting it aside when the clue for ten across, 'shy target', ten letters, annoyed her, not with its complexity, but because she was sure the answer was simple and she couldn't for the life of her work out what it was.

That done, she contacted the detective sergeant heading up the search for Kelvin Pearce. One sighting, unconfirmed, in Retford; two calls made to his sister in Mansfield, both of which she at first denied. Kelvin, she told the officers, was scared stiff. All bluster on the outside, our Kelvin, but push a little and he's soggy inside as a Gregg's meringue. A couple of blokes had been round to his place in Sneinton, she told them, letting on to a whole lot more than she had before, put the frighteners on him something awful. Reckoned if he

154

as much as showed his face at that trial, like, they'd put a bullet through both kneecaps, make sure he never walked again.

No, she swore, she didn't know where he was, where he'd been phoning from, but wherever it was she didn't think he'd stray far. Doncaster, perhaps, used to have a good mate up in Donny, did Kelvin.

Lynn emptied the laundry basket, sorting the whites from the coloureds, pushed the latter into the machine, added liquid, selected the right programme and pressed the button. The whites she could do later.

She was contemplating a slow walk down to the corner shop for a fresh loaf of bread, fancying a slice of toast and marmalade, when the phone rang.

'The other day,' Daines said, 'I think I might have been a little unfair. Shutting you out like that.'

No intention of making things easy, she held her tongue.

'I thought maybe we should meet up. Then I could fill you in. As far as I can, at least. What do you say?'

A pause, and then: 'All right.'

'Good. Excellent. Why don't we meet for a drink this lunchtime? Somewhere quiet.'

'I don't think so.'

'Oh, come on. Surely . . .'

'They didn't give you an office?'

'Yes.' A small laugh. 'We have an office.'

'Fine. Then let's meet there.'

'Okay. Twelve o'clock? Twelve thirty?'

'How about eleven?'

'All right, eleven.'

He gave her the address. One of those streets of Georgian houses off Wellington Circus that are now mostly offices for solicitors or the better class of architect, the ones for whom kitchen extensions are a thing of the past.

Lynn dressed carefully: a dark brown trouser suit that gave little concession to shape, court shoes with a low heel, minimal make-up, her hair pulled back from her face.

Daines's office was as anonymous as a room in a Travelodge motel but better proportioned, furniture that had come flat-packed and in need of assembly, the surface of his desk empty save for a laptop computer and mobile phone. Blue and grey files were shelved at the far side of the room. The windows were double glazed to keep out the sound of traffic and the air was somehow limp and odourless, save for the faint taint of air freshener.

'Welcome. Such as it is.'

Daines was wearing grey suit trousers and a white, open-necked shirt that was turned back once above the wrist. Lynn accepted his handshake and sat on a metal folding chair facing the desk.

The indistinct sounds of other voices came from other rooms.

She wondered how many SOCA staff there were in the building, what size budget and how many personnel had been allocated to this part of the operation. Whatever the operation was.

'Until the machine arrives,' Daines said, 'the only coffee I can offer you is instant. Or I could send someone down to the Playhouse bar.'

'There's no need,' Lynn said.

'Water then, or—'

'Viktor Zoukas,' Lynn said.

Daines smiled. 'No time for pleasantries.'

'You were going to explain . . .'

'As far as I can, yes. Some things, of necessity, I'm afraid, are still under wraps.'

Lynn nodded.

'One more thing,' Daines said, 'before we start. That bag . . .' He indicated the leather shoulder bag that was resting now on the floor beside her chair. 'You wouldn't have a recorder of some kind in there?'

Lynn picked it up and held it out towards him. 'You want to check?'

She was beginning to feel as if she'd wandered into an episode of *Tinker, Tailor, Soldier, Spy*. One that she'd missed.

Daines smiled again. 'It's okay. This job, it's making me slightly paranoid. But one or two things leaking out at the wrong time . . .' He shrugged. 'Anyway, Viktor Zoukas, let me tell you a little about him you still might not know. A little background. He came over from Albania in '99 under the guise of being a Kosovar refugee, though that may not have been strictly true. He's got family here, a brother, cousins, mostly settled in North London, Wood Green. There's a whole bunch of them there, mostly from Northern Albania. One or

157

two, quite respectable. One who's a doctor, working at the Royal Free. He was the one who stood surety for Viktor's bail.

'Viktor and his cousins though, prostitution, that's their thing. A younger brother, too. Valdemar. Brothels. Massage parlours. Trafficking women from Eastern Europe and then forcing them to work in the sex trade. Girls as young as fifteen, sixteen, some of them. You probably know how that works, in principle at least. They make a lot of false promises, charge a small fortune to bring the girls into the country, often via Italy, and then keep them as virtual prisoners while they pay back what they supposedly owe.

'Either they put them to work themselves or sell them on. Someone like Nina Simic, the girl who was killed, she could have been bought and sold for a few thousand pounds and a hundred cartons of cigarettes.'

Daines paused as someone approached the door, thought better of it and walked away.

'Tobacco smuggling, that's how I first made contact with these people. When I was still working for Customs and Excise. It was a big thing, still is. Since then, the Albanians have moved on to cannabis and they'd like a chunk of the heroin trade as well, but the Turks have got that pretty much sewn up and are keeping it to themselves. So now, this last year or so, they've shown every sign of adding another string to their bow. Broadening their portfolio, I guess you could say. Guns. Guns and ammunition. Big time.'

'And that's what SOCA's interested in?'

'Principally, yes.'

'I still don't see why it was so important to have Zoukas released on bail.'

Daines sighed. 'Timing. That as much as anything.'

'I don't understand,' Lynn said.

'You know those games – I think they're supposed to be for kids. Jenga, something like that. A tower made out of little strips of wood placed diagonally across one another in sets of three. The skill is to pull one out and reposition it on the top without making the whole tower fall down. That's Zoukas, one of those little pieces.'

'And the tower?'

Daines drummed his fingers on the edge of the desk, a neat little pattern, the reverberations of which turned his mobile phone through a quarter-circle.

'Anything else I say now, it doesn't go beyond this room. Is that understood?'

'Understood,' Lynn said. If she were still a child, she might well have had her fingers crossed behind her back.

'Okay. Our information is this. Some enterprising free-marketeer in Lithuania has been buying up large quantities of relatively low-powered pistols – alarm pistols, that's what they call them over there – okay for scaring off the neighbour's pet Dobermann, but not a lot else – and remodelling the barrels so as to take regular 9mm ammo. He sells them for a few hundred quid each and by the time they reach the UK they're fetching upward of fifteen hundred a piece.

'We've intercepted several small consignments over

159

the past few years, Customs and Excise that is, most usually in vehicles that have been fitted with hidden compartments, so no more than a couple of dozen at a time. But now, according to our information, a far larger consignment is on its way. As many as seven hundred weapons, maybe, fourteen thousand rounds of ammunition. We're just not sure yet when. Nor which route they're taking. But you can imagine what it would mean if they got through, that lot get into the wrong hands and out on to the streets. After what happened, you especially.'

'Yes. Yes, of course,' Lynn said. 'But I still don't see the connection. These men, the guns, everything, you say they're Lithuanian.'

'Correct. And the guys over here are shitting themselves because they think, after that last arrest especially, we've got their number. Better, then, to sell on to somebody else and take a smaller profit than run the risk of fetching up behind bars.'

'Which is where Zoukas comes in.'

'Absolutely. Viktor and his brother, yes, we think so. We've been watching, waiting. Liaising with the Office of Organised Crime and Corruption in Lithuania. Letting them get everything into place. Our best guess, Valdemar was set to handle the London end, Viktor anything further north. Here, Leeds, Manchester, Glasgow. Once Viktor was in custody and taken out of the equation, everything was put on hold, which made the Lithuanians jumpy. According to our information, they've been threatening to take the guns elsewhere.

160

The Turks, maybe. Last thing Valdemar and his pals want. The whole deal's on the verge of falling to pieces and if that happens we're back to square one and left having to start all over again. Months of work, God knows how many man hours down the drain. But if we can keep it in play and strike at the right time, we get the buyers, the sellers, the pistols, the works. Once we heard there was a chance of Zoukas being released on bail, that gave us our chance.'

A frown set on Lynn's face. 'Heard? Heard how?'

Daines tried for what was meant to be a disarming smile. 'We've been interested in the outcome of the case, naturally enough. Frankly, it had always seemed to us there was a strong possibility of Zoukas being acquitted. But then, once one of your main witnesses opted to run for cover—'

'Is that what he's done?'

'I really wouldn't know. But it seems possible, don't you think?'

'And convenient. For you, anyway.'

Daines's smile broadened. 'A little good luck never hurt anyone.'

'Nina Simic's throat,' Lynn said, 'was cut practically from ear to ear.'

'I know. I know. And if he's found responsible, Zoukas will pay. Just later rather than sooner. What possible harm is there in that?'

'Come on,' Lynn said. 'Don't be naive. If someone managed to find one witness and put the fear of God into him, what's to stop them finding the other? A month for us to track down Pearce, but a month also for Zoukas or whoever's looking out for him to find the only other good witness we have. Result: Viktor Zoukas walks free.'

She fixed him with a look. 'Perhaps that's what you want all along.'

'Perhaps in a way it is.'

Lynn's eyes widened. 'That young woman,' she said, quick to her feet, 'was bought and sold like fresh meat. From what we can tell, she was systematically beaten, almost certainly raped, then forced to have sex with anyone and everyone, twelve, fourteen hours a day. And then she was slaughtered, butchered—'

'Whoa, whoa! Don't you think you're getting a bit emotional?'

'Butchered, that's the word I chose. Butchered, and if you have your way, she'll get no justice, no justice at all. And emotional? Yes, okay, I'm emotional. I saw her laying there dead, with her blood soaking into a rotting carpet that was sticky with men's come. Of course I'm bloody emotional.'

She turned away and headed for the door.

'Time of the month, I dare say,' Daines said. 'Probably doesn't help.'

Lynn spun round. Quite how she stopped herself from going over and slapping the supercilious smile from his face she didn't know.

'Fuck you!' she said.

'You know,' Daines said, grinning, 'you never did thank me for the flowers.'

Lynn slammed the door hard in her wake.

Furious with herself, Lynn walked – no, strode – she strode across the city centre, past the refurbishments of the Old Market Square and up Smithy Row, in the middle of which a short, wiry-haired man, stripped to the waist, was entertaining the early lunch crowd by wrapping himself, Houdini-like, in chains. Not so many months before, the same man, or one just like him, had been forced to call emergency services when he'd been unable to set himself free.

She sat in Lee Rosey's, facing the window, leafing through a local lifestyle magazine that had been left on the counter: bars, restaurants, nightclubs, fine wines, promotional drinks nights, bottled beers, a contemporary and relaxed environment, cool music for cool people.

Cool.

Well, no one had ever accused her of being that.

Cold, maybe, even though it had never really been true.

But cool . . .

Any claims she might once have pretended to cool had been jettisoned once and for all inside Daines's office. Pissed off first of all by his disregard for one woman's rights to justice if they stood counter to his master plan, and then – God! What was the matter with her? – allowing herself to get wound up by the kind of juvenile remark that, as a young officer, she had shrugged off a thousand times.

She closed her eyes and willed herself to relax, but when she opened them again the same strained face was looking back at her, faintly reflected in the glass.

Four or five years ago she tried yoga.

Maybe it was time to give it another go.

She still hadn't quite shaken her anger from her system – anger at Daines, anger at herself – when she met Resnick in the Peacock early that evening, just around the corner from the Central Police Station.

'Sounds to me,' Resnick said, after listening carefully, 'as if Mr Daines's a bit of a fool.'

'He's worse than that.'

'Maybe.'

'And I'm the fool for letting him get under my skin.'

Resnick nodded to two other plain-clothes officers who had just come into the bar.

'Happens,' he said. 'Take me with Howard Brent. So close to thumping him, I could practically feel him on the other end of my fist.'

'So what's happening?' Lynn said, finding a smile. 'Am I getting more like you or are you getting more like me?'

'Heaven forbid it's the former. Overweight and about to be put out to pasture, wouldn't suit you at all. Anyway, maybe it's the job that's changing, not the likes of us.'

'You think I should jump ship before it's too late? Retrain? My mother always thought I should be a nurse.'

Resnick sank a little more of his pint.

'You'll be fine,' he said. 'You'll adjust. As for me, the sooner I'm out of here the better.'

'Now you're talking daft.'

'Am I?'

'Where would you go, Charlie? What would you do? You'd be lost without all this.'

'No. A nice little smallholding somewhere. Up in the Dales, maybe. Couple of donkeys and a few dozen chickens for company.'

Lynn laughed at the thought. 'Donkeys! You're the donkey. Any more than a couple of weeks in the country and you come out in hives.'

'We'll see.'

'I doubt it.'

They picked up two portions of cod and chips on the way home, together with an extra portion of fish for the cats. Lynn did a necessary amount of ironing while Resnick watched part of the Monk DVD she'd bought him for Valentine's Day. After watching the ten o'clock news, they decided to call it a night.

This time it was her hand sliding across his chest, her legs pressing up against his, and he did nothing to push them away.

14

As senior investigating officer into the Kelly Brent murder, Bill Berry was both being harassed by the media and leaned on by the powers that be, and he, in turn, was leaning on Resnick hard. Resnick's troops harried and scurried, but to no great effect; their street-level informers, now including Ryan Gregan, came up with next to nothing. Pretty soon, Resnick knew, the likely course was for someone fresh to be brought in to look over his shoulder and scrutinise what had been done, decisions taken, avenues left unexplored. If the force had not still been so short of experienced officers of senior rank, this could well have happened already, sending Resnick, with a certain ignominy, back to supervising street robberies until he drew his pension.

Well, he told himself, there's nothing dishonourable about that.

In a move that smacked, almost, of desperation, they

had Billy Alston in again for questioning and again let him go.

No sooner were Alston's feet back on the pavement, it seemed, than Howard Brent was back to rant and rave and lodge another complaint on behalf of his family. At least this time Resnick avoided speaking to him directly.

The older son, Michael, was interviewed by one of the local television channels, a serious young man, sombrely dressed, talking in reasoned tones of how his sister's death had torn the family apart and how desperately they needed the closure that conviction of her murderer alone would bring.

'As it is,' he said, with a barely veiled reference to Lynn, 'the police seem more preoccupied with protecting their own than they do with unearthing my sister's killer. And let us be in no doubt, had this murder occurred, not in the inner city, but out in Edwalton or Burton Joyce, had my sister been white and not a young woman of colour, the police, the predominantly white police, would not be dragging their heels as they are.'

Impressive, Resnick thought, watching. Not just Malcolm X, but a touch of Martin Luther King too. As if Michael Brent had been listening to their speeches on tape, or watching them on DVD. He would make a good solicitor, Resnick was sure, perhaps even a barrister.

The point he neglected to make, however, Resnick thought, was that Edwalton and Burton Joyce were not so steeped in drugs and guns as the Meadows or

167

Radford or St Ann's – or if they were, it was a better quality cocaine served as an after-dinner treat, along with the brandy and the chocolate-covered mints, and licensed shotguns used for potting the occasional rabbit in the fields and not turf wars on the streets. Which didn't mean that colour wasn't a big part of the difference: colour, race, expectation, employment, education.

If there were answers, solutions, he didn't begin to know what they were.

Scrub it all out and start again?

Increasingly bored and listless, Lynn persuaded the medical officer to declare her fit to resume work and, rather than being assigned to the hunt for Kelvin Pearce, she was pulled in to help out on an investigation into a double murder that had stalled, a twenty-nine-year-old woman and her four-year-old daughter, the daughter smothered with a pillow as she slept, the mother stabbed with a kitchen knife eleven times. To the senior investigating officer it had looked straightforward, open and shut: the woman and her partner had split up acrimoniously eight months before, since which time she had started a new relationship with another man.

There was ample evidence to suggest that the father, who had moved out of the family home when the split occurred, had made several attempts at reconciliation, all of which had been rebuffed. Neighbours were aware of numerous rows between the pair, and on two occasions – once in the aisles of the local supermarket and once on the street outside – he had been heard to threaten violence. 'If I can't fucking have you, no other bastard will!'

As the SIO had said, open and shut.

Except that the father – the obvious suspect – had been on a friend's stag weekend to Barcelona when the murders had occurred. Friday night through to Sunday afternoon. Witnesses from amongst the men he had travelled with, staff at the various clubs and bars they had visited, hotel staff and airline personnel, accounted for practically every minute of his time.

As accurately as the pathologist had been able to pinpoint it, mother and daughter had been killed in the early hours of Sunday, somewhere between two and four a.m.

When the father had been informed of what had happened on his return, he had broken down, visibly shocked, and wept.

The only other person potentially involved – the new boyfriend, a fitness instructor at one of the city's health clubs – had been visiting his family in Newcastle-upon-Tyne; all of them had been out celebrating a sixtieth birthday till late on the Saturday, midnight and beyond.

Open but far from closed.

Lynn read through written statements, watched taped interviews, talked to the detectives working on the investigation. She went out to the house where the murders had taken place, a neat semi-detached within sight of Bestwood Country Park, and spent time standing silently in the girl's bedroom – an abundance of toys and Miffy posters and cards from her last birthday – and then downstairs in the neat MFI kitchen, echoes of blood high in the ceiling corner and across the slats of the window blind.

Sometimes, visiting the scene, standing there in the silence alone, walking slowly from room to room, gave a sense of what might have occurred. It was something she'd learned from Resnick when she was still a young DC and adopted as her own. But this time there was nothing aside from the obvious, the already known, no shadows stepping away from the walls.

Her next step would be to re-interview the two men, though, more and more, she was convinced someone else had been involved. A stranger, another lover, a friend.

She was on her way back to the office when she all but bumped into Stuart Daines as he was leaving the building.

At first, she thought he was going to carry on past, with scant acknowledgement at all, but instead he stopped and turned and hesitantly smiled.

'Why is it,' he said, 'whenever I see you, I always seem to be apologising?'

'Because you're such an arsehole?'

Daines laughed. 'That could be it. There's an ex-wife and two Jack Russells somewhere who'd agree. Marry in haste and repent at leisure, isn't what they say?'

'Is it?'

'You married?'

Lynn shook her head.

'But you're . . . you're with somebody, right?'

'That's right.'

'Someone here on the force. I think that's what I heard.'

'Look, I don't see—'

'How long?'

'What?'

'How long have you been together?'

'That's none of your business.'

'It's just . . . you know . . . if you've been together quite a while and still not hitched . . .' He grinned. 'I thought I might be in with a chance.'

'You are joking?'

A little self-consciously, Daines laughed. 'Yes, I suppose I am.'

'Thank God for that.'

She started to walk away.

'The girl . . .' Daines said to her back.

'Which girl?' Turning.

'The witness. Andreea?'

'Andreea Florescu, yes.'

'I'd like to talk to her sometime.'

Lynn's face tightened. 'Whatever for?'

'As I understand it, she worked for Viktor Zoukas for quite a while.'

'So?'

'So I'd like to show her some photographs, people Zoukas might have met.'

'Here? At the sauna?'

Daines shrugged. 'It's possible.'

'Seems a long shot.'

'They often are.'

'She won't be happy. She might well not even agree.'

'If you asked her . . .'

'I don't know.'

'It could be important.'

'Another piece of – what was it? – Jenga?'

'Yes, exactly.'

Lynn still hesitated.

'You do know how to get in touch with her?' Daines said.

'Yes, I know.'

'All right, then. Perhaps you'll give me a call? The next couple of days?'

Without waiting for an answer he moved off, leaving Lynn to her thoughts.

Back home that evening, she and Resnick watched as the bulk of Michael Brent's speech was repeated on *Newsnight*, followed by a discussion between the head of the Metropolitan Police's Operation Trident, which investigates gun crime within black communities in London, a representative of the Campaign for Racial Equality and the Labour Member of Parliament for Nottingham South.

'Talks a lot of sense that one,' Lynn said. 'For an MP.'

'How about Michael Brent? What did you think of him?'

'Bit different from his father. Doesn't go flying off at the handle. Much more controlled. More articulate, too. Better educated.'

Resnick nodded. 'He's articulate, certainly. More so than his brother. But then so's his old man, in his way. Michael just seems, like you say, more in control. As if maybe going off to university or wherever's made a difference.'

'Made him less black, is that what you mean?'

'No, not really, it's not that. Being black's at the heart of what he's saying.'

'Less ghetto, then? Further from the stereotype.'

'Maybe,' Resnick said. 'Maybe he's our best hope. For the future.'

'Michael Brent?'

'People like him.'

Lynn wasn't sure.

At a quarter past three both were awoken by the telephone. Bleary-eyed, Resnick answered first. The Alston house in Radford was ablaze. Two adults and one child were on their way to hospital suffering from second-degree burns and smoke inhalation. Billy Alston had sustained a suspected broken arm and broken leg after falling from a second-floor window.

173

15

Resnick knew the watch commander well. Terry Brook. They'd first encountered one another ten or twelve years before, the commander then a leading firefighter in charge of the rescue tender, Resnick the DI on call, the fire engulfing several of the old warehouse buildings along the canal – something bizarre about the ferocity and seemingly unstoppable speed of the flames so close to so much water, their reflection on the lightly moving surface of the canal a compulsive arsonist's delight.

It had been the fourth such fire in nine months, all of them amongst industrial buildings long abandoned by British Waterways or what would then have been British Rail. The first was put down to carelessness, kids most likely or dossers sleeping rough, a fire started for warmth and allowed to get out of control. After the second occasion, the fire investigation officer detected a shape and purpose, a characteristic burn pattern along the edges of the boards, the presence of petrol vapour in the air, a charred box of matches close to the point where the fire had begun.

It had been Terry Brook who had spotted the youth first, a gangly fourteen-year-old with glasses and the slightest of stutters; the lad hanging around near the tender, asking questions, telling Brook how he'd like to join the Fire and Rescue Service when he'd finished college, either that or become one of those investigators employed by the big insurance companies.

'A gas chromatograph, is that what they use to figure out what made it all go up so fast? GC/MS, is that what it's called? Something like that?'

Brook said he wasn't sure, but he could introduce the lad to someone who was.

When they'd searched the boy's room they'd found a battered history of the British Fire Service, purchased from some local charity shop or car boot sale, and a nearly new copy of *Images of Fire*, borrowed from the central library and never returned.

Brook turned now from where he was standing and shook Resnick's hand, the front of the Alston house on its way to being little more than a charred shell, residents on both sides evacuated and standing, some of them, with blankets round their shoulders, watching, as if it were all part of some reality TV show.

'Everyone got out okay?' Resnick asked.

'Far as we know.'

'Accidental, you think?'

'Always possible. Too early to tell.' He looked

Resnick in the face. 'You got reason to think other-wise?'

'I might.'

The two men had met not infrequently over the intervening years, shared a jar in this or that pub or bar. Terry Brook, originally Brok, had come over from Poland with his family in the early seventies, several decades after Resnick's own parents, who had been driven out of their homeland in the early years of the War. This back when Poles were still a relative novelty in Britain and signs on supermarket windows advertising *Polish Goods Sold Here* were yet unthinkable.

Brook supported the other one of the city's two soccer teams, couldn't stand jazz, and his ideas of adventurous cuisine didn't extend much beyond having sauce as well as mustard with his pie and chips, but somehow he and Resnick found a quiet ease in one another's occasional company, each of them still, to some small degree, strangers in a now familiar land.

Resnick told him about Billy Alston and his presumed connection to the death of Kelly Brent, about the possibility of her father or some member of the family taking the law into their own hands.

Well, I tellin' you, this gonna get sorted. One way or another. You know that, yeah? You know?

'Be a while,' Brook said, 'before we can get in there, take a proper look around.'

'Soon as you turn up anything, you'll let me know?'

'First thing.'

They shook hands again and Resnick went back to his car: at that time of the morning, not yet properly light, St Ann's was no more than minutes away. Mist hung low over the Forest Recreation Ground as he drove past, the trees along the upper edge darker shapes amidst the prevailing grey.

Howard Brent came to the door in a T-shirt and a pair of hastily pulled-on jeans.

'What the fuck now?'

'There's been a fire in Radford. Where Billy Alston lives. I thought perhaps you knew?'

Brent shook his head.

'Billy's in Queen's. Broke his leg jumping from an upstairs window to escape the blaze. Arm, too.'

'Shame.'

'Yes?'

'Shame the bastard didn't burn.'

Nice, Resnick thought. 'You can account,' he said, 'for your whereabouts between midnight and three a.m.?'

'Yeah, I was down Radford chuckin' petrol bombs,' Brent laughed. 'No, man, I was home here in my own bed.' He cupped his genitals and lightly squeezed. 'Ask Tina an' she tell you. Know what I'm sayin'?'

The news of the fire and Billy Alston's injury seemed to have improved his mood considerably.

'Got to thank you,' Brent said, as if reading Resnick's mind. 'No matter what pass between us before. Ain't every mornin' the police knock me outta bed with good news.'

This cheery, Resnick thought, no way his alibi isn't going to hold.

And so it would prove.

Anil Khan and Catherine Njoroge went round later that morning and took statements. Friends had called round at the house on their way back from the pub and had stayed, drinking and, as Brent admitted, passing round a little weed, until close to one o'clock. Later, maybe, than that. Not so long after the friends left, Brent and his wife had gone to bed, if not immediately to sleep.

The younger son, Marcus, had spent the evening with a bunch of friends from college and had ended up spending the night on the floor of one of them who lived in Sneinton.

Michael was back in London, at his shared digs in Camberwell.

Howard Brent's friends supported his story. It was Marcus's alibi that was the weakest and potentially the easiest to break; Marcus and his pals with time and opportunity, Khan thought, to torch the Alston place before getting their heads down for the night.

Just maybe.

When he put his doubts forward Resnick told him to go ahead and find out what he could.

That morning Lynn had arranged to see Tony Foley, the husband and father in the Bestwood murders, Lynn explaining that she was taking a new look at the case and Foley, concerned, wanting to know should he bring his solicitor. Up to you, Lynn had told him, if you think it would make you feel more comfortable go ahead, but, she assured him, it was just an informal conversation, filling in background, bringing herself up to speed.

In the event, Foley arrived on his own, smart after a fashion in a dark blue suit that had probably been dry-cleaned too many times, white shirt, blue-and-silver tie, shoes polished to within an inch of their lives.

Lynn asked herself if she'd have pegged him as a car salesman if she hadn't already known.

'Good of you to come in,' she said, offering her hand. 'I'll try not to take too much of your time.'

Foley's smile was practised, his grip firm and just a little overeager, holding on to her hand that few seconds too long. 'Anything I can do to help. Anything at all.'

His breath smelt freshly of peppermint, either from one of those little gizmos you sprayed in your mouth, Lynn thought, or else he'd been sucking extra-strong mints in the car.

On the way to the interview room, he chatted on about the day, the weather, the drive down from Mansfield where he was currently living – more Ravenshead than Mansfield, really, pricey that side of town, south, but nicer, bit more class, plus easier for getting into the city. As if priming her for the moment he showed her the new Audi Cabriolet TDI Sport convertible. Definitely a lady's car and for her he could see a way of shaving 5K off the price.

'Please,' Lynn said, 'take a seat.'

'Thanks.' He sat back easily enough, one leg hooked

across the other, helpful smile in place. He was quite heavily built, more than a few kilos overweight, a reddening in the cheeks which suggested, Lynn thought, high blood pressure or an overdependence on alcohol or both. Thirty-nine, but she might have placed him as older, mid-forties easily.

'The inquiry into the murder of your wife and daughter,' she said briskly, taking the smile off his face in a stroke. 'As I explained on the phone, I'm just familiarising myself with the case, the people involved. Sometimes it's useful to have someone look at things with a fresh eye.'

Foley shifted a little in his seat. 'Different perspective, that sort of thing.'

'Yes, if you like.' She shuffled a few papers on her desk. 'Susie,' she said, 'she was how old?'

Foley blinked. 'She was four.'

'And you've two other children? From a previous relationship?'

'Yes.'

'How old are they?'

'Fifteen and eleven. Jamie, he's fifteen, Ben's eleven.'

'Both boys.'

'Yes.'

'It must have been different, having a girl?'

'Yes, I suppose.' He looked away, as if there were something logged in his brain. 'I suppose it was.'

'You still see them,' Lynn asked. 'The boys?'

'Not really.'

'You not want to or . . .'

Foley shook his head. 'They're living in Essex for one thing. Colchester, just outside. Not as if you can nip across of an evening, anything like that. For another she's married to a real self-righteous prick, excuse my language, who's gone out of his way to make it clear from day one that any contact with me was definitely a bad idea. So, no, I don't see too much of them any more.'

'They're your children.'

'I know, but . . .' Foley leaned forward, one arm on the table between them. 'You've got to understand, this last five, five and half years, since I met Chris, Christine, my life . . . well, let's say my life changed. Tanya and I, when we got together, got married, and Tanya had Jamie, I was what? Twenty-four? Twenty-five? Still wet behind the ears. I was out there working all the hours God sends. Different jobs, lots of different jobs in those days. Tanya, too. Bits and pieces, you know how it goes. And the boys – it was never easy. Jamie, he was always getting into trouble at school, and Ben, Ben was . . . well, Ben was, I suppose you'd say, slow. Kind of slow. Special needs. So it wasn't easy. None of it was easy. And we'd row, Tanya and me. Fight. Argue. It was all a kind of nightmare. I don't know why we stuck with it, either of us, as long as we did.

'But then, then I met Chris and everything else, everything that had happened, it didn't seem to matter, this was it now, this was my life, and when Susie was

181

born I suppose . . . I suppose, if I'm honest, that was when I seemed to start caring less about not seeing the boys, just birthdays and Christmas and not always that.' He looked at Lynn. 'That's wrong, I know.'

'Not necessarily.'

'But that's how it was, Chris and Susie and me, the three of us, you know? Perfect.'

He brought his hand to his mouth as if to stifle a sob and turned his head aside and Lynn asked herself if he were putting it on.

'Till something went wrong,' she said.

'What?'

'Something went wrong, with the relationship. Between you and Chris.'

Foley tilted his head back and, for a long moment, closed his eyes.

'I had this stupid, this bloody stupid – I won't even call it an affair, it wasn't an affair, not anything like that, it was a fling. I suppose if you want to call it anything, that's what it was. A fling with this girl, worked in the showroom. I needed my bloody brains tested, I know. It was all stupid, like I say. She was just some kid flashing her legs, bending forward whenever I walked past the desk so I could see right down her front. I mean, she knew, she knew I was married, I think that was half the fun of it for her, to see if she could. Jesus!' He hit the edge of the table with his fist. 'We were at this sales conference, Milton Keynes, a whole bunch of us drinking in the bar after dinner, you know how it is? Having a laugh.' He shook his head. 'I'm not making excuses, it's just how it happened. One minute we're down in the lobby and the next we're getting into the lift and then we're there, in my room and, to be honest, I was too pissed to remember much about what happened, but it did, just the once, and Chris she finds out. Next day. Only texts me, doesn't she, this stupid little tart, and Chris has got my mobile because the battery on hers is flat and the cat's out of the fucking bag and I'm out the door. No explanations, no excuses, no fucking second chance.'

He pushed his hands up through his hair.

'I still don't understand it, you know, how you can throw everything away, everything we had, all because of one little . . . transgression. One half-drunken step in the wrong direction that didn't mean a thing. Not a bloody thing. You understand that? Can you?'

Lynn wasn't sure. Although, looked at coldly, it did seem a bit extreme, she thought perhaps she could. If what they'd had together had really been as full, as complete as Foley had said, then maybe all it needed was one little crack to feel the whole thing was in danger of falling apart.

'I mean, would you?' Foley persisted. 'In her situation. React like that?'

Would she, she wondered? If she found Charlie going over the side? She didn't know. She'd never really given it a thought.

'You tried to get her to change her mind,' Lynn said.

'Of course I bloody did. Only she'd met up with what's-his-face, bloody Schofield, by then, hadn't she?'

'How did you feel about that? Christine meeting somebody else?'

'How d'you think I felt? Like shit got wiped off some fucker's bloody shoe.'

'You got angry, then?'

'Of course I got bloody angry.'

'With her?'

Foley shook his head. 'First off, I thought it was, you know, tit for tat. Sauce for the goose, something like that. But then it was more. More, and I was out on my ear for bloody good.'

'You didn't like that.'

He looked at her as if it were a question not worth answering.

'You kept trying to get Christine to change her mind. Rowed in public. Shouted. Argued.'

'She wouldn't let me into the house.'

'So you shouted at her in the street.'

'It was the only way to get her to see sense.'

'Not just in the street, the shops, the supermarket.'

'Her fault for locking the door in my face.'

'She was within her rights.'

'What about my rights?'

'You threatened her.'

'Never. Shouted, maybe. Lost my temper, all right. But I never raised a hand to her. And I never threatened to, never.'

' "If I can't fucking have you, no other bastard will." '

'What?'

184

'It's what you said.'

'When? Where?'

'One evening, outside the house. Little more than a week before she was killed.'

'No.'

'"If I can't fucking have you, no other bastard will."'

'No way. No fucking way. I'd never've said that, not to her. Not in a million years.'

'You were heard.'

'Yes? Who by?'

Lynn lifted out a copy of the statement. 'A neighbour. Evelyn Byers. Lives across the street.'

'Nosy cow.'

'Thursday evening. The week preceding the murder. Says she knows it was Thursday because that's the evening her daughter always comes round. Heard the shouting and went to the window to see what was going on.'

'I'll bet she did.'

'And that's when she heard you.'

'And when was this again? Thursday? Thursday before?'

'Yes.'

'Then, no. Can't have been. She might have heard somebody, but it wasn't me. I was in Portsmouth. Gone down about a job. New job, change of scene. Living so close, driving me round the twist. I went down that morning, the Thursday morning. Drove. Interview in the afternoon, dinner that night with the sales manager

185

and a couple of the staff. Here . . .' He took a personal organiser from the inside pocket of his suit. '. . . names and numbers, you can check.'

'And it checked out?' Resnick asked.

'In detail,' Lynn said.

It was not so long after eight thirty in the evening, neither of them with time or inclination to cook, and they were sharing a takeaway from one of the Indian restaurants on the Mansfield Road. Lamb pasanda and chicken korma, saag aloo and brinjal bhajee, fried rice and naan bread, plus an assortment of pickles from the cupboard and the fridge. In the absence of any more Worthington White Shield, they split a large bottle of Hoegaarden between them.

'You have to ask,' Resnick said, 'why it never came up before?'

Lynn shrugged. 'Nobody asked the right question. I've looked at the tape of the original interview. The words the witness claims she heard being used, they were never put to him directly.'

'So what now?'

'We're checking it out. But I've been out there. It must be twenty, twenty-five metres at least between the witness's upstairs window and the Foley's front path. Plus it would have been dark. The nearest street light is a good thirty metres away.'

'And this witness,' Resnick said, helping himself to some more lamb, 'she's how old?'

'Sixty plus.'

'So her eyesight's likely not what it used to be.'

'Exactly.'

'It could have been anybody standing there having a slanging match with the victim. Anybody who fits the same basic description.'

'Which the new boyfriend does, apparently. Younger, but around the same height, same darkish hair worn quite short.'

Resnick speared a piece of chicken with his fork. 'You're talking to him, too?'

'Tomorrow.'

'You going to eat that last piece of naan?'

'No, go on.'

'It's all right, keep it. You have it.'

'For heaven's sake, take it.'

'All right. Thanks.'

'Maybe next time we should order two.'

'We tried that. Ended up with most of the second one getting thrown away.'

Lynn poured herself some more beer. 'It's an inexact science, ordering Indian takeaway.'

'Bit like police work, then.'

She smiled. 'Anything new on the fire?'

'Not as yet. Tomorrow, most like.'

Lynn nodded. Tomorrow. Another day.

16

Some of the old industrial buildings in the centre of the city had been left to slowly decay and harboured little now beyond floors thick with pigeon waste, an infestation of rats and the occasional body burned almost beyond recognition; others had been eviscerated and reborn as luxury flats and waterside bars, or health clubs with cyber cafés and solariums, personal trainers and corporate membership schemes.

The particular club where Dan Schofield worked was housed in one of the old low-level railway-station buildings close by the canal. He had hesitated only momentarily when Lynn had phoned: eleven thirty would be fine.

Several young women slicked past her on their way to an hour or so of ergonomically calibrated exercise – an aqua workout in the pool maybe, or a little holistic t'ai chi – each one fashionably dressed for the occasion, make-up perfectly in place. In her blue-black jeans, black cotton top she'd had for more years than she cared to remember, short corduroy jacket and clumpy shoes, Lynn felt just a smidgeon out of place.

Beyond the enquiry desk, a tanned individual in an official health-club vest and eye-wateringly tight shorts was flexing his muscles for all to see.

'Dan Schofield?'

He shook his head without breaking sweat.

'He's around somewhere. You'd best ask at the desk.'

She did. A quick call and Schofield appeared. Late twenties? Round about the same age Christine Foley had been when she died. And where the man she'd seen first was all overdeveloped muscle and curly dark hair, Dan Schofield was trim and athletic in his uniform tracksuit, not tall, no more than an inch more than Lynn herself, smooth-shaven with neat, short hair. Were he a soccer player, she thought – something else in which Resnick had partially schooled her – he would be a midfield play maker, not afraid to put his foot on the ball, look up, then play a probing pass upfield.

'Is there somewhere,' Lynn asked, 'we could go and talk?'

'There's the juice bar, though that tends to be busy this time of the day. Or we could go outside.'

It was only a short walk back on to London Road and the entrance to the canal.

As they went down the steps towards the water, a narrowboat puttered past, brightly painted, a brown-

and-white dog stretched out on deck, a man with heavily tattooed arms seated at the helm, contentedly reading a book. All it needed was for the sun to break through the matt grey coating of cloud or for the refuse that cluttered the far bank to disappear and it could be a perfect scene, a perfect moment in the day.

'What happened to Christine,' Lynn said, 'I'm really sorry.'

'Thank you.'

'It must have been a terrible shock.'

'Yes, it was.'

'You'd known her how long?'

'We'd been living together five months, give or take. If that's what you're asking. But I'd known her longer than that. A good year and a half.'

'And you met her where?'

'Here, at the club. She used to come for classes. Just the one at first, but more often after that.'

'Your classes?'

'Some. Not all. But mainly, yes, I suppose they were.'

'And that's when you got to know one another?'

'Yes, like I said. We used to talk after the session sometimes, just, you know, chat. Nothing special.'

They stopped and sat on a bench back from the edge of the canal path.

'She was lonely,' Schofield said, 'Christine. At least, that was how she seemed. I mean, okay, she had a busy life, with her little girl and everything, part-time job, home, but just the same you sensed that she needed something else. Someone to talk to.'

'Aside from her husband.'

Schofield half-smiled. 'You've met him? Foley?'

'Just the once.'

'Then maybe you'll know, you don't talk to Tony. He talks to you. You listen.'

The more she listened to Schofield, the more she could hear the vestiges of a Geordie accent filtering through. They were silent for a moment as a couple of swans ghosted past.

'Your friendship with Christine, then,' Lynn said, 'it had started quite a long time before she broke up with her husband.'

'Yes, I suppose so. Not that that had any bearing on what happened. That was all down to Foley, wasn't it? Screwing some bimbo from work. Christine, she was gutted. Said she could never look at him in the same way again.'

'But you helped, I dare say.'

'How d'you mean?'

'Oh, you know. Someone to talk to, a shoulder to cry on.'

'You could put it that way if you like.'

'And you weren't sorry.'

'How d'you mean?'

'When they broke up.'

'I was sorry for her.'

'It meant the field was clear.'

'That makes it sound – I don't know – wrong some-how.'

191

'Your friendship could move on. That's all I'm saying.'

'We were already close. When Foley left, we became closer. No crime in that.'

'And there was never any thought she might go back to him?'

'Foley? Not in a million years. Why would she?'

'I don't know. Because of the little girl, perhaps. Susie. She must have been really upset her dad was gone.'

'A little, maybe.' He shook his head. 'I'm not sure how much time they ever really spent together.'

'And you got on with her okay?'

'Susie? Yes, fine.'

Lynn smiled. 'A ready-made family.'

'You could look at it that way.'

'Lucky, some would say.'

'I would,' Schofield said emphatically. 'I would and no mistake. Those few months . . .' He looked away. 'What you were saying, about Susie, about us being like a family. I'd never . . . never really thought of having kids, you know? Being a dad. I was happy the way I was. Friends. Girlfriends. Working where I do, no shortage of those. Women coming on to you. Well . . . like I say, I'd not figured on settling down, but then the more time I spent with Christine the more it was what I wanted to do. What we both wanted to do.'

'And it was working out? Living together?'

'Yes. Yes, of course it was.'

'No problems?'

'Not really, no. It was great. It was fine.'

Lynn smiled. 'When something like that happens, it's only the good times you remember.'

'That's all there were.'

'You must have had arguments. The odd one or two, at least. It's only natural.'

Schofield was shaking his head. 'I don't think so.'

'Not one?'

'Not one.'

'What about the time you came home and found Foley in the house, talking to Christine?'

The expression on his face changed, his voice tightened. 'That was different.'

'How so?'

'He was the one I was angry with, not her.'

'You're sure?'

'Of course I'm sure.'

'You didn't have a bit of a shouting match out front, after he'd gone?'

'Out front? Out front of the house?'

'Yes.'

'No. Not at all.'

'You didn't threaten her?'

He laughed, incredulous. 'Christine? Absolutely not.'

'You didn't say if you couldn't have her, nobody else would?'

'No.'

'"If I can't fucking have you, no other bastard will."'

Schofield made a sharp sound of disbelief, half snort,

193

half laugh. 'Look, this is ridiculous. I don't know who you've been talking to, but whoever it was, whatever they've said, it's a lie. Okay? A lie.' He was quickly to his feet and backing one step, two steps away. 'Now, if it's all right with you, I've got to get back to work. I've got another session.'

'Of course,' Lynn said. 'Thanks for your time.'

He hesitated a moment longer before walking crisply back along the canal path, Lynn continuing to sit there, thoughtful, watching him go.

Terry Brook got in touch with Resnick ahead of the fire investigator's report. Any doubts that the fire had been started accidentally could be dismissed. Some crude kind of petrol bombs had been used, hurled through windows at both the front and back of the house, more or less simultaneously.

The youth on whose floor Marcus Brent had allegedly slept was Jason Price, currently studying entry-level Music and Sound Technology at South Notts College and with two previous brushes with the police to his credit. Both youths worked in Marcus's father's music shop on Saturdays and in whatever spare time they could scrounge. Though the shop always stocked a certain amount of rap and reggae, dub was what it specialised in, what set it apart from the big chains and the independent opposition: rare vinyl alongside remastered versions of classic King Tubby and new recordings by bands like Groundation and Bedouin Soundclash.

When Anil Khan spoke to him, Price was surly and affable by turns: he and Marcus had been out with mates, just hanging out, i'n'it? Then down to Stealth – DJ Squigley and Mista Jam. He didn't know nothin' about no fire, no Billy Alston, nothin'. Not till later, aw'right? Marcus came back and crashed at his crib like he sometimes did. Time, man? Come on, I dunno what time, but late, like, late, i'n'it? Aw'right?

As alibis went, it was all vague in the extreme. They took them in for questioning, the pair of them, applying pressure where they could. Officers, meantime, searched Price's flat for whatever they could find incriminating, hoping, if not something as obvious as an empty petrol can or a bottle of paint thinner, then clothing that had been splashed with petrol or still had a residual smell of smoke.

There was nothing.

Both Marcus and Jason stuck to their stories.

Disappointed, Khan thanked them for their co-operation, trying hard not to react to the smug grins on their faces.

Bill Berry caught Resnick on the way out and insisted on a catch-up over a pint. Make that two. By the time Resnick got home, Lynn was asleep on the front-room settee, head lolling to one side, half-drunk mug of tea grown cold on the floor alongside.

Resnick stood watching, his feelings for her such that, had she woken and seen them on his face, she might have been frightened by what they revealed.

They spoke, neither of them, about their personal emotions a great deal.

It was 'love' and 'sweetheart', a kiss in passing and a squeeze of the hand, a quick hug or cuddle, the reality of what each truly felt buried beneath the mundane and the day-to-day. A few weeks before, when the call had come through to say she had been shot, he thought he had lost her and in that moment his life had stopped, the blood refused to pump round his body.

She stirred and moved her head and, as she did, a small sliver of saliva ran from one corner of her mouth on to her cheek. Taking a handkerchief from his pocket, Resnick stooped and dabbed it away.

'Charlie?' As if from a dream, she blinked herself awake. 'I'm sorry, I must have dropped off.'

'No harm.' With a smile, he brushed the hair back from her face.

'D'you want something to eat?' he asked.

'I suppose I should.' With a small grunt of effort, she sat up straight.

'I'll see what I can find.'

Scraps. Bits and pieces of this and that. Small bowls of leftovers covered in cling film and pushed to the back of the fridge. He fried up some cooked potato with garlic and onion, added half a tin of cannellini beans and a few once-frozen peas, then sliced in some cold pork sausage from God-knows-when. In a basin, he whisked up eggs with black pepper and a good shake of Tabasco, and, when everything else was starting to sizzle, poured the mixture over the top. The result, served with hunks of bread and the last knockings of a bottle of Shiraz, was close to a small feast.

'You're a wonder, Charlie.'

'So they say.'

'In the kitchen, at least.'

'Aye.'

It was a while before either of them spoke again, just the contented sounds of two people eating, with the occasional promptings from one hungry cat and in the background the brushed sound of Lester Young's saxophone, a track Resnick had set to play, Lester with Teddy Wilson, 'Prisoner of Love'.

'I talked to Dan Schofield today,' Lynn said. 'The man Christine Foley was living with when she was killed.'

'And?'

Lynn paused, her fork partway to her mouth. 'Nice enough bloke. On the surface, anyway.'

'You think he might be involved?'

'I'm not sure. If he is I can't yet see how.'

'He's got an alibi?'

'Yes. Cast-iron, so far.' She ate a piece of sausage. 'You know what I find fascinating? There's this woman, the dead woman, Christine. Attractive in a conventional kind of way. Reasonable education, a year or so of college. Works for a building society until her daughter's born, then, when she starts nursery, gets a part-time job behind the counter in a chemist's, thinks about possibly retraining as a pharmacist. Everything about her, perfectly ordinary – and yet there are two men, about as different from one another as chalk and cheese, both of them in love with her, think she's the greatest thing since I don't know when and can't stand the thought of living without her.'

A grin came to Resnick's face.

'What?'

Still grinning, he shook his head.

'You think it's sex, don't you?' Lynn said. 'You think she was this incredibly passionate, inventive creature in the sack.'

'What I was thinking,' Resnick said, 'maybe she was a great cook. You know, the kind who can whip up astonishing dishes from almost nothing . . .'

Lynn laughed. Resnick poured the last of the wine.

'Any idea,' he said, 'what you're going to do next?'

'I don't know. Wash up? Do some ironing? Go to bed?'

'I mean about the investigation.'

'Oh, talk to a few of Christine Foley's friends, I think. People she worked with, try and get a different perspective.'

Leaning across the table, half out of his chair, Resnick kissed her on the lips.

'What was that for?' Lynn asked, surprised.

Smiling, Resnick shrugged. 'Good luck?'

17

Ryan Gregan had insisted they meet in the Arboretum, down near the pond and the bandstand. Just over the road from the cemetery, you know?

Resnick knew.

Many times, when he'd been stationed up at Canning Circus, he and his sergeant, the redoubtable Graham Millington, had eaten a quick sandwich lunch while staring at the elaborate tombstones, talking their way through whichever investigation was uppermost in their minds. Now Millington, a few years Resnick's junior, had wangled a transfer down to Devon, where his wife hailed from, and was doubtless cycling round the lanes that very moment, keeping an eye out for sheep rustlers while whistling his way through the Petula Clark songbook.

Resnick shuddered at the thought.

Not just the constant repetitions of 'Downtown' and 'Don't Sleep in the Subway', but the prospect of all those high, winding hedges and undulating hills and fields. Lynn had been right: short term apart, the country was not for him. The other man's grass, in this case, not greener at all.

Gregan was sitting on one of the benches beyond the bandstand, shoulders hunched, rolling a cigarette. He was wearing blue jeans and some kind of camouflage top, a peaked New York cap pulled down over his eyes. Tattoos, which might have been new, on the backs of both hands.

Resnick had taken Pike with him, regulations insisting that two officers were present when an informant was interviewed, and favouring Pike over Michaelson, as Pike, at least, could be relied upon to sit still and say nothing unless directly spoken to.

'Mr Resnick.'

Resnick nodded.

Gregan glanced at Pike, but nothing more.

'I thought you'd not mind the stroll,' Gregan said. 'The open air, you know.'

They sat either side of Gregan on the bench and waited while he lit up, a few stray curls of tobacco hissing briefly as they caught.

'You've got something for me,' Resnick said.

Gregan smiled.

At the far side of the pond, a tram began its slow ascent along Waverley Street towards the Forest. A boy of no more than ten or eleven, who should certainly have been in school, went past, dragging a scrawny mutt by a piece of string.

'The shooting,' Resnick said. 'You've heard something?'

Gregan shook his head. 'Only the same as before. Billy Alston's finger on the trigger, that's the word.'

'You believe it?' Resnick asked.

'Maybe. Maybe not.' Gregan's cigarette had gone out and he lit it again.

'You've got reasons to think it might have been somebody else?'

Gregan shook his head. 'Alston, I'm just not sure he's the type. Too jumpy, you know? All over the damned place. Not certain he has it in him, aside from the bragging, that is.'

'Bragging? Is that what he's been doing?'

Gregan's face showed contempt. 'All mouth and trousers, isn't that what they say? No bottle. No body. Letting people think he was the one did the shooting, good for his rep out on the street. Hard man.' Gregan laughed. 'And besides, where did he get the gun? Not from me and I've asked around and I've yet to come across anyone who sold Billy Alston as much as a fucking catapult, never mind a pistol, replica or not.'

'Any other names being mentioned?'

'Not to me.'

'You'll keep your ear to the ground?'

'Absolutely.'

Resnick waited. Gregan clearly wasn't done. At the other end of the bench, Pike shuffled his feet.

'The fire now,' Gregan said eventually. 'Alston's place. Kelly Brent's old man, can't wait for you to do

201

the business, that's most likely what you're thinking. Take the law into his own hands.'

Resnick said nothing, let him continue.

'I heard a whisper. Could be nothing to it. But Billy, he was dealing. Just kids' stuff. Five-, ten-pound deals, you know? Seems he was holding out, even so. Bulking it out, pushing the price and not passing it on. Had a warning a month or so back but paid it no mind. This was the final word, something he couldn't ignore.'

'The fire?'

'The fire.'

'It's not just talk? Someone making noises after the event?'

Gregan shook his head. 'That's always possible, of course. But I don't think so.'

'You've got names?'

'Just the one. Ritchie.'

'Spell it.'

Gregan did.

'First name?' Resnick asked. 'Second name?'

'First, I think.'

'You could find out some more?'

A smile played around Gregan's eyes. 'I could try.'

'Try harder.'

As they were walking back across the Arboretum, Resnick asked Pike what he thought.

'Is he telling the truth, boss? Is that what you mean?'

Resnick nodded.

'He could be, I don't know. I mean, if he's not, if he's making it up, what'd be the point?'

'He might think it's clever, stringing us along. Or he could be doing someone else a favour, Brent, for instance, trying to make us look elsewhere.'

'How do we know?'

'We don't. Which is why, as far as we can, we check. See just how reliable he is. You and Michaelson, find out what you can about any medium-level dealer called Ritchie. Ask around. If he wasn't Billy Alston's supplier, find out who was. Maybe, for once, we can put two and two together and make four.'

Lesley McMaster had known Christine Foley – Christine Devonish, as was – since school, since primary school, in fact. Lesley, neat and trim in her little black suit, but with worry lines starting to show around the eyes, didn't want to think exactly how long that was.

They'd worked together at the Shires Building Society, starting on the same day, nervous as anything; Christine had been the first to settle, not too long before she was being packed off on courses, tipped for promotion. Reliable, that was the thing. Not only that. Initiative, too. Manager, she'd have been by now, if she'd stayed, Lesley was certain. If she hadn't jacked it in when the baby was born. Even then they were on at her to come back, pick up where she'd left off, but Christine had said no, she wanted a change, though to Lesley's way of thinking it was more her Tony who was behind it, happier for some reason if his wife was wearing a white coat in the corner chemist's, doling out cold cures and sanitary items instead of doing something more responsible, earning more cash.

One thing Lynn would say later about Lesley McMaster, she could talk for England.

'You kept in touch with her then,' Lynn said, 'afterwards?'

'Yes. Well, not as much perhaps once she took up with Dan Schofield. In each other's pockets and no mistake, the two of them. Christine, she loved it at first, all, you know, the attention. Doing everything together. Tony, she'd probably spent as much time talking to him on his mobile, texting him and that, as she did in person.'

'You said at first,' Lynn prompted. 'She loved it at first.'

Lesley smiled. 'For all Tony's faults, he never bothered about her going out for a drink with her mates, as long as Susie was being looked after and everything. Well, it gave him a bit of leeway himself, that's what I think. But Dan, he was different. Didn't like it at all. If she wasn't out with him, he thought she should be at home, made it really difficult for her to get out on her own. In the end, she had to create a bit of a scene. Lay down the law, like. Stick up for her rights. I mean, it wasn't as if they were married or anything. And she could be quite tough, Christine, when she had to be.'

'It was a real cause of friction between them, then? That's what you're saying?'

'The last time I saw her,' Lesley said, lowering her voice as if betraying a confidence, 'she said she was wondering if she hadn't made a mistake. Not over Dan himself, not really. I think she loved him, I really do. But whether, you know, she should have let him move in as soon as he did. Instead of letting herself have a bit of freedom first. After Tony. Out of the frying pan, that's what she said. "Sometimes I think, Lesley, that's what I've done, stepped out of the frying pan and right into the fire."'

'She said that?'

'Word for word.'

'And you think she might have said it to Dan, too?' Lynn asked.

Lesley took her time before answering. 'Yes,' she said, finally. 'Yes, if that's what she felt, strongly enough, I think she might.'

Back at her desk, Lynn checked the route on the computer: Newcastle-upon-Tyne to Nottingham, A1(M), M18, M1. 158.75 miles; 255.5 kilometres. Keeping to a reasonable speed, three hours and a few minutes, but in the early hours and driving fast, that could be pegged back to two hours thirty either way.

She looked back at the reports.

Dan Schofield had travelled up by car to Newcastle earlier that day and met up with his brother and two sisters, various and sundry aunts and uncles and cousins, all congregating to help celebrate his father's sixtieth birthday. His parents' house in Heaton was too small to take even the immediate family and Dan had booked into the Holiday Inn, a room for himself and

Christine, though, as he explained, making apologies on her behalf, Christine had come down with really bad stomach pains just that morning, something she'd eaten, most likely, sends her love and best wishes.

After drinks at the house, eighteen people had sat down at eight sharp to dinner in a hotel restaurant close to the city centre. Somewhere between ten and ten thirty, some dozen or so, Dan Schofield included, had moved into the bar and carried on drinking. At around half past eleven, some of the younger ones had decided to make a real night of it and headed out clubbing. And it was at this point that accounts began to vary: according to Dan's brother, Peter, who'd been one of the prime movers, Dan had been up for it and had certainly come along, although after a while – you know what clubs are like – they'd lost sight of one another, so Peter couldn't say what time Dan might have left. Dan's younger sister, however, remembered him as being less than keen – just a quick one and I'm off back to the hotel, catch some beauty sleep, leave this clubbing to you kids.

Christine Foley and her daughter had been killed between two and four in the morning. If Dan Schofield had got back to his hotel by, say, twelve thirty, by pulling out all the stops, he could have been in Nottingham by three.

How long did it take to smother a four-year-old with a pillow, stab a grown woman to death?

He could have been back in his Newcastle hotel, back in his room, by six. Six thirty, latest. Between eight thirty and nine, he had called round at his parents' house to say his goodbyes. We'll come up and see you soon, his mother quoted him as saying, the three of us.

Lynn pushed back her chair, closed her eyes, tried to conjure back the man she'd spoken to by the canal, trim, controlled, so genuine-sounding when he spoke of his feelings for Christine Foley and her daughter. She wondered at what stage in his relationship with Christine he had begun to see the possibility of it as something else? At which point had he started thinking, scheming, undermining, possibly, a relationship that was already on its way out? Whatever was going on between himself and Christine, that had nothing to do with her breaking up with Tony, no bearing on it at all.

Lynn found that hard to believe.

But could she believe that Schofield, rather than lose what he had manoeuvred himself to gain, would commit murder? Cold, calculating murder at that?

She tried to imagine the scene in which Christine had tried to explain to him, as nicely as she could, mindful of his feelings, that maybe they'd been a bit hasty, living together so soon after she and Tony had split up. Perhaps if they took a break from one another, just for a little while, so she could get her head round things . . .

She tried to picture Dan Schofield's reaction, what he might say or do if all of his calm and reasoned arguments came to nothing.

If I can't fucking have you, no other bastard will.

Would he say that? Would he snap?

Could he act upon those words?

Luckily, it wasn't for her to decide. Enough that she could establish motive, possible cause, the logistics of opportunity. Enough to put Schofield's alibi under further scrutiny, bring him back in for questioning. The ultimate decision, guilty or not guilty, was not down to her.

Lynn passed on her findings to the SIO in charge of the case and, later that afternoon, sat down with him and four of his detectives, talking through the whys and wherefores; Lynn careful not to overplay her hand and give any of the other officers cause to be resentful. She was on her way back from this session when she saw Stuart Daines in the corridor near her office door.

'Lurking?' Lynn said.

'Not at all.'

'Hardly accidental.'

'I've been waiting for you to call.'

'What about?'

'Your witness, you remember? Andreea Florescu.'

'What about her?'

'You were arranging for us to go and see her.'

'I've been busy.'

'So I hear.'

'So you hear?'

'Some kind of break in that double murder, mother and daughter . . .'

'How did you . . . ?'

Daines treated her to his disarming smile. 'What is it? Ear to the ground? Ear to the wall? Either way, I've found it pays. Information – you never know when it's going to come in useful.'

'And that's what you're hoping to get from Andreea? Information?'

'Hopefully.'

'That might or might not be useful.'

The smile changed to something more sympathetic, caring. 'Look, I appreciate what you've told me, about her being nervous and everything. I wouldn't be pushing this if I didn't think it might lead somewhere, believe me.'

'All right,' Lynn said, 'but I can't contact her directly. It has to be through a friend. It may take a couple of days to set up.'

'That's fine. I'll keep my diary flexible and wait for your call.' He hesitated. 'Kelvin Pearce, nothing there, I suppose?'

'You know damn well there isn't,' Lynn said. 'And if there were, you'd've probably heard before me.'

Daines was chuckling as he walked away.

Back at her desk, Lynn found herself wondering exactly who Daines's contacts were, how high they ran, whom he might have spoken to in order to find out about the twist in the Bestwood investigation so soon. And why so interested in her and what she was doing? Was it because she was his conduit to Andreea and he had a vested interest in knowing where the witnesses in the Zoukas case were? Or was there something else? Some other link in the chain, another brick in the tower he was constantly building and rebuilding? And to what effect, what cause?

After only a little hesitation, she looked up the number she had for Andreea's friend, Alexander Bucur, and began to dial.

18

Two more days. The temperature rose, then fell back down. There were portents of storms, banks of cloud shouldering in from the Atlantic. Background checks into Howard Brent's business affairs led nowhere, and when his car was pulled over for the second time in three days, he made an official complaint about police intimidation. Kelvin Pearce seemed to have disappeared from the face of the earth. Brought in for questioning, Dan Schofield retreated behind a series of denials, braced by several terse no-comments and an increasing reliance on his solicitor to intervene. Staff at the hotel where he'd stayed, friends and relatives were all being questioned again. Billy Alston's low-level drug dealing had indeed, it transpired, depended on an arrangement with a Derby-based dealer named Richie – Richie not Ritchie – and there had been words exchanged between them, Richie telling Alston he'd put a bullet in his brain if he held out on him again.

Telling him in front of half a dozen witnesses, three of whom, surprisingly, were apparently willing to say so under oath. Richie himself, however, was proving difficult to find. According to one report he was in Glasgow, visiting an old girlfriend, according to another he was in the Chapeltown area of Leeds.

Investigations continued.

Pearce. Schofield. Richie.

The first arrangement Lynn had made to see Andreea clashed with a meeting Daines was due to attend at New Scotland Yard.

'How about the day after?' Daines suggested. 'Morning. I'll be down in London anyway. Staying over.'

They met at Leyton underground station, a false promise of sun behind flat grey cloud as Lynn stepped out on to the High Road, Daines already there and waiting, cup of takeout coffee in his hand.

'Here,' he said, handing it towards her. 'I've had mine.'

Lynn shook her head. 'No, thanks.'

'Wise,' he said. 'Poor as piss.' And dumped it in the first bin they passed.

The main street was a mixture of newsagents and convenience stores, fish bars and Internet cafés, hair-dressers, fashion shops and saunas; butchers advertising halal meat and four small chickens for £4.99, chemists and dry cleaners; Pound Plus discount centres and motor factors, cash-and-carry wholesalers and second-hand furniture stores; the offices of the

African and Caribbean Disablement Association and the Somali Bravenese Action Group, the Refugee Advice Centre and the Leyton Conservative Club.

Signs in shop windows were written in Urdu or Farsi, Bosnian or Serbian, Greek or Polish or poorly spelt English. A poster featuring a smiling, scantily dressed girl promised a Polish Party at one of the local pubs each and every Saturday, ten till late.

They walked for fifteen, twenty minutes, barely talking, following the route Lynn had Multimapped before leaving, until, just past Leyton Midland Road overground station, they turned into the first of several tightly packed parallel roads of small terraced houses. Two more turnings, right and left, and they stopped outside a house with a pebble-dash exterior which, some years ago, had been painted a shade of bilious, acid yellow, grimy patterned net at the downstairs windows, mismatched curtains higher up. A bicycle with a flat rear tyre was chained to what remained of the iron railing alongside the front door.

After a brief hesitation, Lynn rang the uppermost of two bells.

A pause, and then the sound of feet approaching.

Alexander Bucur was tall, willowy, fair-haired, handsome – cautious until Lynn showed him identification and Daines did the same. He smiled then as, introducing himself, he stepped back to invite them in. Free newspapers, fliers and unwanted mail leaned in ramshackle piles against the side wall. Vinyl floor covering petered out short of the stairs, which were bare save for the overlapping stains of spilt food and drink and dust which had collected at the edges in grey whorls.

The room he led them into was crowded and small: a settee which was obviously used as a bed, an improvised desk that held a computer, screen and printer, a table that was busy with books and papers and leftover breakfast things, several chairs, more books on makeshift shelves, clothes drying in front of an oil heater in the corner, a poster for a forthcoming Romanian film festival pinned to the wall above a small colour photograph of a child that Lynn had seen before – Andreea's daughter, Monica.

'If you like,' Bucur said, 'I can make tea.'

'Don't bother,' Daines said.

'Thank you,' Lynn said, 'that would be nice.'

'Very well,' Bucur said. 'I shall not be long.' The door to the small, narrow kitchen was open at his back.

'Andreea,' Daines said. 'Is she here?'

Bucur gestured towards the other, closed, door. 'She is in the bedroom. She has been sleeping. She will not be long.' His English, not strongly accented, was clipped but clear.

Lynn sat on one of the chairs; Daines went across to the window and looked down on to the street. The only sounds, those from the kitchen aside, were of a plane passing quite low overhead, on its way perhaps to London City airport, and, closer to, a Silverlink train pulling into Midland Road station.

'So what are we going to do?' Daines asked testily,

looking towards the bedroom door. 'Let her sleep all bloody day?'

'Be patient,' Lynn said.

Daines mouthed something she didn't catch.

Bucur brought in mugs of tea, milk in a carton, and an old metal container marked *SUGAR*.

'She's not joining us?' Daines said.

'I'll see.'

Bucur went into the bedroom and closed the door behind him.

'Some pantomime,' Daines said, stirring sugar into his tea.

They could hear voices, hushed but urgent, from behind the door.

'I think she is afraid to come out,' Bucur said when he returned.

'Afraid of what, for God's sake?' Daines said, letting his exasperation show. He was jittery, unusually so Lynn thought, and she wondered if this was really just about the simple question and answer he'd suggested.

'Let me talk to her,' Lynn said, getting to her feet. 'See what I can do.'

She knocked, said who it was, and went in.

Andreea was sitting on the unmade bed, her back towards the door, her face turned away. She had cut her hair short and dyed it a strange shade of almost blueish black. Each time Lynn had seen her since she had witnessed the murder, she had been less and less attractive and, Lynn thought, deliberately so.

She wondered if she and Alexander were a couple

and decided they were not. Speaking Andreea's name, she touched her gently on the shoulder.

'What's the matter?'

There were dark shadows around Andreea's eyes, the skin across her cheekbones stretched tight; her pallor was that of paper left too long in a drawer.

'I don't know,' Andreea said. 'I am tired. This job, cleaning, at night . . . I have only been home a few hours. And always it is difficult to sleep.'

'I'm sorry,' Lynn said.

'Before,' Andreea said with a weak smile, 'it was easier before.'

Lynn said nothing.

'This other man,' Andreea said. 'I have to talk to him?'

'There's nothing to be frightened of. He just wants to ask a few questions, get you to look at some photographs. That's all. And I'll be there. Come on.' She took hold of her hand. 'Come on, let's get it over and done.'

'Wait. Please. A moment.' She looked at the mirror resting on an old chest of drawers against the wall. 'You can go now. A few minutes, I will come.'

'Okay,' Lynn said, and smiled.

'She'll be right in,' she said, going back into the room.

'Good of her,' Daines said.

'She's tired,' Lynn said. 'Exhausted, by the look of her.'

'She works nights at a big hotel,' Bucur said. 'In the

West End. Near Park Lane. Twelve hours, six nights a week.'

'When she comes in,' Lynn said, speaking to Daines, 'be nice.'

With a small rattle of the handle, the bedroom door opened and Andreea stepped into the room. She had brushed her hair as best she could and put make-up on her face, the lipstick too bright, the lines around her downcast eyes too dark.

When she looked up and saw Stuart Daines by the window, she gave a small jump of recognition and, for a moment, her whole body seemed to tense.

'Andreea,' Lynn said, moving quickly, 'why don't you sit over here, at the table?'

If Daines himself had noticed, he gave no sign. Taking a seat alongside Andreea, he was charm itself. He was sorry she was tired, understood how hard she'd been working, it was good of her to make the time to help. He was interested, he told her, in any men she might have seen with Viktor Zoukas at the sauna in Nottingham and proceeded to show her a series of photographs.

Bucur went into the kitchen to make fresh tea.

At the tenth photograph, Andreea told him to stop.

'This man here . . .' she said.

'You know him?'

'Yes.'

In the picture, black and white, grainy, he was standing in a club doorway, the light from the neon sign illuminating his face, the scar that ran from close by his

217

left eye down into the dark shadow of his beard. He seemed quite tall, though it was difficult to tell for sure, strong looking, with a broad, thick neck and large, broad hands. He was dark haired, wearing a dark suit with a pale shirt and dark tie.

'You saw him with Zoukas?' Daines said.

Andreea shook her head.

'I thought you just said . . .'

'My house. Where I lived in Nottingham. Before. He came there.' She looked at Lynn. 'I told you about him.'

'The man with the knife.'

'Yes. He make me get into his car, drive me somewhere, make me tell him what I have told the police about Nina. And Viktor. He tell me he will kill me if I say anything bad about Viktor. Anything more than I tell police already . . .' She looked towards Lynn again. 'Now he will know. He will know . . .'

'Andreea,' Lynn said. 'I keep telling you, it's all right. You're safe here.'

'This man,' Daines said, 'did you see him with Viktor Zoukas?'

'No. No, never.'

'You're sure?'

'Yes, of course.'

'Not at the sauna or anywhere?'

'No.'

'And when he threatened you, was he on his own?'

'No. There was someone else. In the car, driving the car.'

'Describe him. What did he look like?'

218

'I didn't see.'

'You must have seen something.'

'No. He was in the car. Driving the car. It was dark.'

'Okay. All right. Let's look at the rest of these.'

There was nobody else that Andreea recognised; not definitely. One or two about whom she was uncertain, but so much so as to be of little use. Daines asked her more questions about Zoukas, but there was little she could tell him. Little that she knew.

After just over half an hour, he was through. 'Thank you,' he said. 'Thank you for your cooperation. It's appreciated.'

A few minutes more, words of thanks to Alexander Bucur for the tea, a quick exchange of glances between Lynn and Andreea, an assurance from Daines that the man in the photograph wouldn't be troubling her again and they were back out on the street.

'Worth the time and trouble?' Lynn asked, as they walked towards the High Road.

'Depends. Not as fruitful as I'd have hoped, but interesting nonetheless.'

'The man she recognised, what's his name?'

'Ivan Lazic. He's a Serb. He was a member of the Serbian security forces between '96 and '98, when he was captured by the KLA, the Kosovo Liberation Army. Instead of standing him up against a wall and shooting him they seem to have cut him some kind of deal. He turned up on our radar in '99, Customs and Excise, that is. Seems to have been in cahoots with the Albanians ever since.'

219

'But now he's back out of the country, like you said?'

Daines gave her a look. 'I've no idea. But I didn't want your pal Andreea throwing another wobbly.'

Lynn gave it a few seconds. 'Andreea,' she said, 'had you seen her before?'

'No. Never. Why d'you ask?'

She didn't reply.

They both took the Central line as far as Bank and changed; Daines was taking the train from St Pancras, Lynn catching the other branch of the Northern line as far as Kentish Town. She had a friend, she told him, a detective inspector stationed at Holmes Road, and they were going to have lunch before Lynn, herself, took the train back to Nottingham.

'Thanks for all your help,' Daines said, as passengers pushed round them on the Bank platform.

'No problem,' Lynn said, and moved off into the crowd.

At Camden Town, she switched platforms and reversed her journey; Tottenham Court Road to Leyton, less than ten stops. She'd called her friend, Jackie Ferris, feeling paranoid for doing so, but wanting to cover her tracks, and then Alexander Bucur also, needing to make certain Andreea would still be there.

Bucur was outside when she arrived, one leg cocked over his bicycle. 'I have to go. Andreea is upstairs.'

A smile and he was away.

Andreea had changed into a different top and

reapplied her make-up; anxiously, she looked past Lynn to make sure no one was following.

'Daines,' Lynn said, 'the man I was with earlier. You knew him, didn't you? You'd seen him before.'

Andreea hesitated. 'Yes,' she said eventually. 'Yes, yes.'

'Okay.' Lynn took a seat beside her on the settee. 'Tell me where.'

'Wait, please.' Andreea reached for a pack of cigarettes, went across to the window and opened it quite wide. 'Alexander, he does not like me to smoke here,' she explained, taking a lighter from the pocket of her jeans.

'It was in London,' she said, after the first drag. 'Two, yes, two years ago.'

'But how?'

'When I came to this country first, I was staying with some friends in Wembley. That was when I first met Viktor. One of the girls, she was working at a club that was run by one of Viktor's friends. Lap dancing, you know? She said she would see if she could get me a job there too. The owner, he told me I had to dance for his friend, Viktor. He said it was my . . . the word is audition?'

'Yes.'

'Afterwards, he laugh in my face and tell me there is no job, but Viktor say if I do not want to stay in London, I can work for him. First I have to show him what I can do. I said I thought I had done this, but he said no, this was something different.' Andreea blew smoke in the vague direction of the open window. 'It was sauna, massage parlour, belong to his brother, Valdemar. I was . . . I was not shocked, I know these things go on, and I did not want to do this. But Viktor, he tells me if I work for his brother a short time and learn business he will make me manager of place he has somewhere else, all I have to do look after girls, clients, take money.' She shook her head. 'This is not what happens.'

'And that was when you saw Daines,' Lynn said, 'when you were working for Viktor's brother?'

'At Valdemar's, yes.'

'And Daines was there in what connection?'

Andreea looked at her as if she didn't quite understand the question.

'Daines. What was he doing there?'

'Oh, at first I thought, him and Valdemar, it was business between them. But then I think, no, they are friends. They drink together and Valdemar takes him round, shows him girls. There is one, Marta, she is no younger than me, but small, you know? Small features, small bones. She can look like schoolgirl. Your friend . . .'

'Daines.'

'Yes, Daines, he goes with her. More than one time while I am there.'

'He comes back?'

'Yes. I think, twice more. I see him twice more. He does not see me, I am nothing to him. Just Marta.' She paused, as if uncertain whether to continue. 'Once, I think he hurt her. I hear her cry out, scream, and later Valdemar is angry. He and your Daines they shout a lot and I think they will fight, but later I hear them laugh and Valdemar say next time it will cost him more and they laugh again.'

Lynn looked away, towards the window.

Andreea drew hard on her cigarette and held the smoke inside. 'I did not see him again until today.'

'Never in Nottingham, with Viktor?'

'No. Never. Not till today.'

Lynn patted her hand. 'Thank you, Andreea. Thank you very much.'

'What does it mean? That this has happened?'

'I'm not sure. I expect he was working undercover. You know? Pretending to be someone else. Sometimes it's the only way.'

'Then there is nothing wrong?'

'No. No, I don't think so.'

Back out on the street, Lynn called Jackie Ferris on her mobile. 'Look, Jackie, I'm sorry I had to put you off earlier, but you couldn't manage a quick drink early evening, could you? Say around six. Six thirty. Something I want to ask. You can? Fantastic. Great. Just tell me where.'

19

It was Resnick who'd known Jackie Ferris first, when she was a young sergeant in the Yard's Arts and Antiques Squad, Resnick on the track of a burglar with a nicely developed taste for the works of the lesser British Impressionists. They had met again in the search for a serial seducer who specialised in picking up lonely women, bedding them and then stripping them bare of everything they possessed; somehow – and Lynn couldn't remember the exact circumstances – Resnick's arcane and near-encyclopedic knowledge of jazzmen of the forties and fifties had helped find the suspect. Difficult to believe, but true.

Lynn had first met her briefly in the line of duty, and then, after she and Resnick had started living together, Jackie had come up to Nottingham on a couple of occasions and stayed, once for a conference on community policing, and once for a meeting of the Lesbian and Gay Police Association, of which Jackie was a member.

Although she would have been loath to admit it, it had unsettled Lynn when she'd found out Jackie was gay, picturing someone who would be either outlandishly butch or femme the minute she was off duty. Butch, most likely, Lynn thought – she couldn't picture Jackie in pink frocks and lots of girlie make-up. But when she realised neither to be the case – and found – her other fear – that Jackie was not in the least bit predatory, she'd been able to relax and enjoy her company.

At Jackie's suggestion, they met in the Assembly House, a large old-fashioned boozer in the north end of Kentish Town, which, like so many, but with less disastrous results, had modishly reinvented itself by virtue of knocking down a few internal walls and sanding the floors, then adding a decent kitchen where the chef laboured in full view of the clientele.

At shortly after six, the place was still uncrowded and they sat at a corner table with their backs to the tall, broad windows and the slow-moving rush-hour traffic.

'Sorry about earlier,' Lynn said, as soon as they were settled. 'Overtaken by events.'

Jackie waved a hand dismissively. 'It happens.'

'Too often.'

'Tell me about it.' Jackie took a good pull from her glass. 'So,' she said. 'How's Charlie?'

'Oh, you know . . . Charlie's Charlie.'

'Looking forward to retirement?'

'He keeps watching those documentaries about elephants, the ones who, when they know their days are numbered, lumber off into the jungle to die.'

Jackie laughed. 'Get out of it, he'll be fine.'

'You think? I'm not so sure. I can't see him taking one of those security jobs, like so many do – but I can't see him being happy just sitting around either. Mind you, with our staffing levels the way they are, they'll be begging him to stay on.'

'No, get out while the going's good. Reinvent yourself. That's what I'm going to do when my turn comes.'

'Oh, yes? What as?'

'A trapeze artist. You know, high wire. Get a job with one of those little touring circuses. Hampstead Heath, Clapham Common, that sort of thing.'

'You are kidding?'

'No, I'm not. In fact, I've already started taking lessons.'

'Come on!'

'Yes, from this Hungarian woman who used be in a circus in Russia. She and her partner, they were the Flying Karamazovs. Until he fell and broke his back.'

'Terrific.'

'She's sixty if she's a day but still got an amazing body.'

'You sure this is about learning the trapeze?'

'Very funny.'

'Nothing wrong with the older, more experienced lover.'

'You should know.'

'Bitch.'

Jackie laughed again. 'So,' she said, lifting her glass,

'what was this business you wanted to see me about?'

Without going into too much detail, Lynn explained as best she could.

'You don't think there's any doubt the girl – Andreea? – could be mistaken?' Jackie asked.

'She seemed pretty certain.'

'And the reason you gave her for his being there, the Customs and Excise guy, that he was simply working undercover – you don't think that's right?'

'If the rest of what she says is true, it's difficult to swallow.'

'I don't know. If he is undercover and in the place as some kind of punter, he's got to play along. He can hardly – what did they used to say in the papers in the old days? – make his excuses and leave.'

'I suppose not. But what Andreea said about the girl . . .'

'Hurting her?'

'Yes.'

Jackie sighed. 'Maybe he let himself get carried away, it could happen. Especially if you had leanings that way in the first place. Or maybe she had her own reasons for exaggerating, not telling strictly the truth.'

'It's possible.'

'But not what you want to believe?'

With a wry smile, Lynn shook her head. 'I don't know.'

Jackie finished her drink and held up the empty glass. 'Your shout.'

Lynn made her way to the bar. The pub was busier

now, a mixture of people dropping in on their way home from work, old fogeys for whom the place was still a home from home, albeit with new decor, and women who looked as if they'd spent the bulk of the day getting their legs waxed and their highlights retouched, to say nothing of taking on an extra few degrees of tan. Music – there must be, she thought, some kind of ska revival – meshed with the increasingly dizzy conversation.

The barman who served her was Mediterranean-looking, with dark hair only a touch too long and eyes which brought butterscotch disconcertingly to mind: white T-shirt and blue jeans, neither of which, as far as she could see, left a great deal to the imagination. Fit, wasn't that the modern term for it? Tasty, some would say.

'Lust at first sight?' Jackie Ferris said, with a nod towards the bar, when Lynn returned.

'A girl can dream, can't she?'

'Long as you don't talk in your sleep.'

Lynn laughed and spilt beer from her glass as she set it down. She was enjoying Jackie's company. Enjoying, for a change, being out of the confines of Nottingham and in the big city. The Smoke, did anyone still call it that? Charlie aside.

'So what are you going to do?' Jackie asked.

'About Daines?'

'That's his name?'

'Yes, Stuart Daines. And I just don't know. If I come out and face him with it, he'll simply deny it, brazen it

228

out, her word against his. Maybe I'll ask around. On the quiet.'

'You don't trust him, that's pretty clear.'

'He makes me uneasy.'

'Like the guy behind the bar.'

'No, definitely *not* like the guy behind the bar.'

Jackie was smiling. 'I'll ask around, too. If anything, it's easier for me than you. Anything I get, I'll let you know.'

'Thanks, Jackie.'

'Now, what exactly can we do to get you off with this feller . . . ?'

20

On the Monday of that week, a few days before, at approximately fifteen minutes after nine in the morning, a black Vauxhall Astra swung into the lay-by outside the post office on the Loughborough Road and two men – Garry Britton and Lee Williams – jumped out, leaving a third behind the wheel. Britton was black, Williams white; both were carrying guns, a shotgun with sawn-off barrels and a pistol, which they pointed at the line of ten or so mostly elderly customers, ordering them to the floor.

Britton, wielding the shotgun, shouldered his way through the narrow shop towards the counter, where one of the two staff on duty had already pushed the panic button linking them with the police station less than half a mile away on Rectory Road. Pressing the gun up against the strengthened glass, he ordered both clerks to hand over the money from the cash drawers where they were standing.

A man in workman's overalls started to push open the door from the street, saw what was happening, and ducked away.

'Quick! Quick! Be fucking quick!'

The shotgun smacked against the glass and one of the clerks screamed. Outside, the Astra's driver was sounding his horn.

Several of the customers, huddled between the floor and the side wall, were crying; one, a woman in an old-fashioned tweed suit, her grey hair tied back in a bun, was praying loudly.

'Shut it!' Williams yelled in her face. 'Fuckin' shut it!'

She began to sing instead, a hymn.

Williams drew back his arm and swung the pistol towards her face.

The car horn was louder now, more insistent, and beneath it the first sounds of police sirens could be heard.

'Out! Out! Get the fuck out!' Britton snatched an envelope containing some couple of hundred pounds and ran towards the door. Turning to follow him, Williams tripped and half-fell, stumbling out on to the street as the Asian proprietor of the newsagent's several doors away made a grab at his arm.

'Fuckin' hero!' Williams said and fired his pistol from close range, before jumping into the back of the already moving car.

The Asian collapsed back against the post-office window, blood already staining his white shirt where the bullet had torn through the flesh at his side.

The exit at the end of the parade of shops was partially blocked and the Astra jumped across a swathe of pavement, narrowly missing a group of children straggling late to school, and skidded out on to the Loughborough Road as a police car approached fast from the opposite direction. The driver threw the Astra into reverse, swerved and, panicking, headed into a side road that would only lead into the Asda car park, the police car following close behind.

At that hour of the morning, less than a quarter of the places in the car park were taken and the Astra accelerated hard towards the green plate glass of the supermarket front, tyres squealing as it made a tight right turn, hoping to swing back round towards the exit, but now there was a second police car blocking its path and the driver braked again, yanked hard at the wheel and lost control, the side of the Astra bouncing off a parked delivery van and then burying itself, bonnet first, into the side of a lorry loaded with frozen foods.

Automatic air bags saved the lives of the two men in the front, but held them fast. The third man – Williams – was thrown forwards against the driver, his head striking the side window as he rebounded, jolting the pistol from his hand. He was half out of the door when two police officers grasped his arms and pulled him free, spinning him round and pushing him flat against the side of the car, legs kicked apart and arms stretched wide.

Nicked, as the saying goes.

It was Catherine Njoroge who first spotted that the gun used in the raid was similar to that responsible for Kelly Brent's shooting – a Brocock ME38 Magnum – and alerted Resnick; Resnick who got in touch with the Forensic Science Services lab at Huntingdon and, leaning on past favours, requested that comparisons with the marks on the bullets and cartridge cases from the murder scene be pushed through with all possible speed.

Meantime, Catherine went meticulously back through the CCTV footage from St Ann's. There was Lee Williams, clearly visible in one frame, at the inner edge of the crowd just before the shooting started. Williams, beyond a doubt, wearing Radford colours. Together with Anil Khan, she went back to their original sources: Williams was confirmed by three different witnesses as having been in Cranmer Street at the time of the shooting.

The FSS checks, when they finally came through, late on Friday, showed that the striation marks on the sides of both sets of bullets, the scratches made when the spent cartridges were ejected and the dents in the metal cover caused by the firing pin, were all identical. The weapon used in Kelly Brent's murder and the post-office raid was one and the same.

Not only that, a comparison against outstanding marks showed that the gun had been used in two previous incidents: a drive-by shooting in Birmingham the previous year and a post-office robbery in Mansfield just eight weeks before.

Williams himself had minor juvenile offences against his name; one charge of possessing a firearm that was dismissed. He would have a hard time, Resnick thought, walking away from this.

Resnick went to the Brent house on Saturday morning, just shy of eleven. This time he had left Catherine Njoroge behind and come on his own. Even with just the three of them there, the room still felt small. The low ceiling and the single, small window didn't help, nor the furniture, crowded close together.

The photograph of Kelly Brent on the mantelpiece had been reframed and a piece of dark purple ribbon fastened across one corner; the other family photographs had been placed elsewhere and some of the many cards the family had received stood on either side of Kelly's picture. There were flowers, slightly faded now, in two tall vases in the empty hearth. Messages of condolence had been pasted in a large, fake-leather bound scrapbook which rested, open, on the low table in front of the TV.

Despite signs of normal wear and tear, there were no special markers of poverty here, nor affluence either. Normal people, normal lives: one son away at university, one at college, one daughter dead.

The shadows were dark around Tina Brent's eyes and her fingers plucked at a stray thread that had come loose from the arm of the chair where she sat.

Howard Brent – silver-grey sweatshirt, loose-fitting, wide-bottomed trousers, new silver-grey trainers with the distinctive red Nike marking at the sides and a black band around the upper sole – looked at Resnick and then his daughter's photograph and then the floor.

It was several minutes since anyone had spoken; since Resnick had said what he had come to say. Brent, for once, not quick with words, taken aback perhaps, surprised, uncertain what response to make, the anger, the wind, knocked out of him by the news, incomplete as it still was.

'I just wanted you to know,' Resnick said, 'because of what may have happened, because of what you may have thought before, that Billy Alston was not directly involved in Kelly's death. We're confident of that.'

'And this youth now,' Brent said, 'in custody. He confess?'

'No,' Resnick shook his head. 'Not yet.'

'But he's been charged, yeah?'

'Oh, yes.'

'With murder?'

'Yes.'

'Murderin' our daughter.'

'Yes.'

Tina Brent let out a sob and her hands went to her face.

'He say why, you know why, Kelly, why he shot her? Why? Why her?'

Resnick shook his head again. 'No.'

'But he is guilty, yeah? No doubt?'

'That's for the courts to decide.'

'Court! Decide!' Pushing back his chair hard against

235

the wall, Brent rocked to his feet. 'Some time this year, next year, yeah, we go, me and Tina, each day, listen to some fancy barrister talkin' 'bout this an' that extenuating circumstance, and all the while he sittin' there, the one who shot her, fired the gun, not sayin' nothing, smilin' 'cause he know the worst can happen he go to prison for what? Fifteen years? Fifteen years and he's out on parole after ten. Ask you, man, what's that? Ten years? He what? Not twenty yet? Out here, on the street, free again, not thirty. Twenty-eight, twenty-nine, and our daughter she ten years dead. Ten years in the cold, hard fuckin' ground!'

Fingers in her mouth, Tina Brent made a strangled cry.

'You know how that feel, Mr Resnick? Mr Policeman. You know how that feel?'

'No,' Resnick said. 'No.'

'Then hope to Christ you never do!'

Resnick levered himself up from the settee. 'An officer will keep in touch. You will be informed of developments, the arrangements for the trial and so on as they occur.'

He held out his hand and Brent turned away.

Tina Brent was staring at the wall, tears drying on her face.

'Goodbye, Mrs Brent,' Resnick said, and headed for the door.

Brent followed him outside. Two kids were kicking a ball back and forth along the pavement, making it cannon every now and then off the tightly parked cars.

'You know,' Brent said, 'that's only half of it.'

Resnick turned.

'Whoever pulled the trigger – Williams, Alston – there was only one person grabbed hold of my Kelly and used her as a shield.'

Colour showed on Resnick's face. 'That's not . . .'

'Not what?'

'Not worth the time of day.'

'She's still gonna pay.'

'She what?'

'You heard. One way or another, she's gonna pay for what she's done.'

'Threats against a police officer, that's a serious business.'

Brent held out both his arms, underside of his wrists uppermost. 'Okay, arrest me, why don't you? Take me in.'

He laughed as Resnick walked away.

21

After a slow start, for Lynn at least, Monday was turning out to be a good day. One of the night staff at the Holiday Inn in Newcastle-upon-Tyne had remembered something he had failed to mention when first questioned: he had seen Dan Schofield – or someone very like Dan Schofield – driving his car back into the hotel garage as he himself was leaving work. Somewhere between six fifteen and six thirty. While he couldn't be one hundred per cent positive about Schofield, he was certain about the car. One door panel, front offside, a slightly different shade of green than the rest, where at some point it had either been resprayed or replaced.

'Course, by rights,' the SIO running the investigation told Lynn Kellogg later, 'I should be more than a bit pissed off at you for making my team look like a bunch of rank amateurs. Not seeing what was under their bloody noses.'

'Just luck,' Lynn said, though they both knew it wasn't that.

'Any road, let me buy you a drink after work. If you're not driving, that is.'

'Schofield's still to put his hand up. You sure you don't want to wait till he does?'

'No. He will and when he does we'll throw a proper party. This is just you and me, quiet, my way of saying thanks.'

Resnick was at the other end of the bar, standing with Pike and Michaelson and Anil Khan; Anil, Lynn noticed, sticking to his usual lime and soda. She sat with a half of lager, making it last, while the SIO's conversation moved from speculation as to what might have pushed Schofield over the edge on to considerations of his daughter's coming wedding, the state of his allotment, and matters in between. When he asked her, nodding towards the bar, what Resnick thought about his impending retirement, she said, 'Ask him, why don't you? Ask him yourself.'

'Best not,' the SIO said with a grin. 'Might not want to be reminded.'

Lynn smiled, suggesting that was probably the case.

'You'll have another?' he asked.

'Thanks, but no.' Glass empty, she got to her feet.

'Back home to get the old man's supper?'

'Something like that.'

Seeing her moving, Resnick held up his own glass, recently refreshed, signalling he'd be a short while yet.

239

Lynn raised a hand to show she understood and pushed her way through the door and out on to the street. As soon as she was outside, she sensed someone at her back.

'Leaving early?' Daines said, moving closer as she turned.

'What's it to you?' Lynn said. She could feel his breath on her face.

'Thought I might join you . . . but then I thought, no, relaxing with her mates, friends, her – what would you call him? – common-law husband.'

'You've been following me?' Lynn asked.

'Maybe,' Daines said, the street light picking out the chip of green in his eye when he smiled. 'Though I thought it was more a case of you following me.'

'I don't think so.'

'Really? Asking questions behind my back. Checking up on me. Amounts to more or less the same thing.'

Lynn took a step away. 'Is that what I've been doing?'

'So I hear.'

Lynn said nothing.

'Anything you wanted to ask, why not come out and ask it yourself. Straight out. Or maybe that's not your way.'

'I already did,' Lynn said.

'Sorry?'

'You know her,' Lynn said.

'Her?'

'Andreea Florescu, you know her. You'd seen her before.'

'No.'

'You're sure?'

'Positive.'

'Well, she knows you.'

'She's lying.'

'I don't think so.'

'That foreign tart, you believe her rather than me?' Daines made a scoffing sound in his throat. 'She's probably been lying about Zoukas as well. About seeing him stab the girl.'

'Why would she do that?'

'Who knows?' A smile slipped across his face and disappeared. 'A word of advice. One professional to another.' Reaching out quickly, he took hold of her arm. 'Don't make me your enemy.'

'Is that a threat?'

'If need be.'

Shaking him off, she stepped away and as she did so the pub door was pushed open and Resnick stepped outside. Daines nodded curtly in his direction, gave Lynn one final look, and walked briskly away.

'What was all that about?' Resnick asked.

She gave him the gist of the conversation as they were walking home, north from the city centre and then cutting right on to the Woodborough Road.

'You have to wonder,' Resnick said, after listening, 'what it is he has to hide.'

'Something personal? You think that's what it is?'

'I don't know. This operation, it's pretty big. International. If he can help pull it off, his career'll be made. Maybe he thinks anything that makes that possible is justified. And the last thing he'll want is for things to come out in the open before he's good and ready.'

'I don't like it,' Lynn said.

'You don't like him.'

'They're not the same.'

'I know.'

They walked on, past the mosque and up towards Gorseyclose Gardens and Alexandra Park.

'You could always report it,' Resnick said. 'Take it to the ACC if necessary.'

Lynn shook her head. 'He'd just deny every word.'

One of the cats ran along the pavement to greet them, the others were waiting on the mat beside the door. Resnick turned first one key in the lock and then the other. It struck cold when they stepped inside, the heating turned off too soon. Even so, it was good to be home.

It was a quarter to three on the following afternoon, Tuesday, before Dan Schofield confessed to killing both Christine and Susan Foley, admitting through his solicitor to manslaughter while the balance of his mind was disturbed.

'Guts enough to stab a woman to death with a bloody kitchen knife and smother a little kiddie while she slept,' as the SIO put it, 'but not man enough to own up

242

to what he's done without hiding behind the skirts of some bloody shrink.'

It had still to be seen if that ploy would succeed.

Lynn was barely back at her desk when the phone rang. It was Alexander Bucur calling from London, his voice quick and nervous, words skidding together: two men had come to the flat on the previous evening looking for Andreea. He had told them she wasn't there, but they had forced their way in nevertheless and searched. When they asked him where she was he had told them she was working but that he didn't know where. They would be back, they told him. They would be back.

'And Andreea?'

'When I told her, she panicked. It was all I could do to stop her grabbing her things and running there and then. She's terrified.'

'I'll come down,' Lynn said, impulsively. 'Talk to her.'

'You're sure?'

'Yes, of course.'

She looked at her watch. If she hurried, she could catch the 15.38 London train. Just time enough to poke her head round Resnick's office door before legging it to the station.

'Charlie, I'm off down to London. Something's come up.'

'What d'you mean, come up?'

'Alexander Bucur – the guy Andreea's been living with. In Leyton. He just called me. Someone's been round looking for Andreea. Sounds like the same guy who threatened her before. She's frightened out of her wits.'

'I don't see—'

'Charlie. I've got to run. Be back this evening, okay?'

Resnick raised his hand. 'Ring me.'

'I'll call you from the train.'

A moment and she was gone.

Bucur met her at the front door. A black eye, in the process of turning from mauve to yellow, marred his otherwise perfect face.

'What happened?' Lynn asked.

'This? Last night. When I told them I didn't know where Andreea was working, I don't think they believed me.' It made him wince to smile. 'Come in.'

She followed him upstairs and into the flat. The look on his face told her before he said the words. 'She's gone.'

'Where?'

'I don't know. Cornwall, perhaps. I don't know.'

'Tell me what happened.'

'I went out not long after I phoned you. Just to buy milk, a few other things, that was all. She seemed to have calmed down. When I got back, she'd gone. Her rucksack, too. I tried her mobile, but it was switched off.' He sighed. 'I'm sorry.'

'It's not your fault. Don't blame yourself.'

Bucur cleared a bundle of papers from one of the

chairs and set them on the table amongst all the books and other paraphernalia.

'Please. Sit. I'll make some tea.'

While she waited, Lynn cast her eye over the formidable piles of books. *The Image of the City* by Kevin Lynch. *Towards a New Architecture* by Le Corbusier. Aldo Rossi. Jane Jacobs. Mies van der Rohe.

'Architecture,' Lynn said, when he came back into the room. 'That's what you're studying?'

'Yes. Architecture. Urban design.'

'Sounds interesting.'

'Interesting, yes. But studying as I am, many years.'

The tea was hot and strong.

'I hope you don't think I am wasting your time, worrying for nothing.'

'Not at all.'

'The first time I phoned you, you were engaged, so I called the man who was here with you . . .'

'Daines.'

'Yes, his number was in the room where Andreea had been sleeping. A card. But he was not there either. So I made a call to you again and you answered. I hope it is all right.'

Lynn assured him that it was. 'When you came back,' she said, 'and Andreea wasn't here, were there any signs of a struggle? Anything to suggest she'd been taken against her will?'

'No. It was just like this. The bedroom – a few things here and there, but, really, nothing.'

'She left of her own accord, then?'

'It's what I want to believe. But I am not sure.'

'And Cornwall, if she did go off on her own, you think that's where she went?'

'Yes, perhaps. She had spoken of going there later in the year, perhaps to work.'

'Which part of Cornwall? Do you know that?'

'Yes, I think . . . Sennen . . . Sennen something . . .'

'Sennen Cove?'

'Yes, that's it.'

Lynn knew it from childhood holidays, the north coast close to Land's End. Journeys they had made all the way across country from East Anglia, Lynn sitting squashed in the rear seat beside mounds of luggage, staring out at scenery that scarcely seemed to change, hour upon hour, unable to read for more than twenty minutes at a time lest it make her sick.

Mum, Dad, how much longer?

Don't ask.

'This friend,' Lynn said, 'do you know her name?'

'Nadia. That's all. I don't know her other name.'

Unless it had changed a great deal in the intervening years, Lynn didn't think it should prove too hard to track down someone of that name working in one of the relatively few hotels.

'If that isn't where she's gone,' Lynn said, 'you've no idea where else she might be?'

'No. I'm sorry. None at all.'

'No other friends she spoke of? At the hotel, say, where she worked?'

Bucur shook his head.

246

'These men,' Lynn said, 'the ones who came here looking for her. Can you describe them?'

'Of course. They were both quite tall, leather jackets, jeans. One, the one who did most of the talking, he was older – I don't know, thirty, thirty-five – and he had a beard, dark, almost black, and a scar, here . . .' Bucur ran his hand down the left side of his face.

'What nationality would you say he was?'

Bucur thought before answering, trying to recall the man's voice. 'Not Romanian. Slovakian, maybe.'

'Serbian?'

'Yes, that is possible. You know him?' he added, seeing the expression change on Lynn's face.

'He might be a man named Lazic,' Lynn said. 'Ivan Lazic. The description sounds similar to the man who threatened Andreea with a knife.'

Bucur had not been in the room when Andreea had identified him in the photograph.

'What about the other man?' Lynn asked.

'I didn't notice him as much. Except when he hit me, of course.' He gave a quick, self-deprecating smile. 'He was young, my age, I suppose. Tall, like I say. I didn't hear his voice. I don't think he spoke at all.'

Lynn nodded.

'If you know him,' Bucur said, 'this man, surely you can arrest him?'

'Not without good reason. And always assuming we knew where he was.'

Bucur sat back, tasted the tea and frowned. 'It is too strong.'

'It's fine.'

He added more sugar to his own. 'If they come back, what shall I do?'

'If they come back,' Lynn said, 'it's a good sign. It means they still don't know where Andreea is.'

'But not so good for me,' Bucur suggested with a smile.

'Keep the door locked, don't let them in. Phone the police and tell them these men have attacked you before. I'll have a word with the neighbours while I'm here, knock on a few doors. Someone may have seen something, strangers hanging round. I might call in at the local police station, too. It's just back along the High Road somewhere, is that right?'

'Yes. Past the sports ground and on the left. Francis Road. The bike I had before was stolen and I had to go there then.'

Lynn took a quick look at her watch and gulped down a last mouthful of tea. 'I'd better move. You'll let me know the minute you hear anything?'

'Of course.'

'Likewise.' She shook his hand. 'We'll find her, don't worry. She's probably on a National Express coach even now, heading west.'

'I hope so.'

After the comparative warmth of the small flat, it struck cold when Lynn stepped out on to the street. There were lights behind most sets of curtains, but not everyone came to the door, and those who did had little useful to say. A stout woman with her hair wrapped in

248

a towel and the residue of an Irish accent thought she might have seen two men earlier in the day, not doing anything, just standing there, looking up at the house opposite. But if one of them had had a beard, never mind a scar, she hadn't noticed. Next time she looked, they'd gone.

The sergeant she spoke to at the police station listened without giving her story the fullest attention; it was all a bit vague and besides, trying to keep tracks on a transient population like theirs . . .

Lynn thanked him, left her number and headed back for the High Road and the walk to the tube; with any luck she'd be at St Pancras in time for the 20.55.

She phoned Resnick from the train, the sound of some jazz or other in the background as he spoke. She pictured him sitting there, perhaps with one or other of the cats on his lap, a glass of whisky close at hand.

'If you ask me,' Resnick said, after listening, 'she's in Cornwall even now. Coach just pulling into Falmouth or Penzance.'

'I hope you're right.'

'It's not all down to you, you know. The situation she finds herself in.'

'Isn't it? I can't help feeling it is. I put her in danger, Charlie.'

'You asked her to help put a dangerous man behind bars. Not the same thing.'

'That was a right fiasco, too.'

'No fault of yours.'

'I know.'

'You want me to meet you at the station?'

'No need. I'll get a cab.'

'You're sure?'

'Sure.'

When the CD finished he set aside the book he'd been pretending to read, recharged his glass and searched for a Bob Brookmeyer reissue he'd picked up a month or so before. Brookmeyer on valve trombone with a couple of different rhythm sections back in '54, the instrument's sound less sinuous than brittle, a slight rasp to his tone. Nothing too surprising here, pleasant, relaxed, moving with an easy swing, comforting; the trombone releasing the melody to the piano before working its way through a series of variations and then restating the final theme. 'Body and Soul'. 'Last Chance'. Four minutes and twenty-two seconds of 'There Will Never Be Another You'.

Through the music he heard the sound of a cab approaching along the narrow, poorly made-up road that led towards the house and a smile came to his face. In his mind's eye, he saw Lynn leaning forward to pay the driver, exchanging, perhaps, a few words, before getting out and, as the cab drew away again, crossing towards the house. In a moment he would hear the faint clicking of the gate. The cat jumped down from his lap as he rose and moved towards the door.

At first he thought what he heard as he stepped into the hall was the sound of a car backfiring, then knew, in the same breath, that it was not.

PART TWO

22

Waking, Karen Shields found herself reaching, automatically, for the glass of water beside the bed. Her head, as she lifted it off the pillow, felt like a medicine ball that had been thrown once too often around the gym. The water was stale and warm and she swilled it around her mouth and spat it back into the glass. Then, with a sudden jerk of memory, she reached her hand into the space beside her and, to her relief, touched nothing but tousled, empty sheets. Thank Christ for that!

Slowly, with extravagant care, she lowered herself back down against the damp pillow, damp and rank from her own sweat. Seven minutes past five. Traffic sounds were already beginning to build up two streets away on the Essex Road. In a little over twenty minutes more, the boiler would kick in and she would push back the sheets with her long legs and swing them to the floor. For now, she closed her eyes and tried to ignore the painful reverberations inside her head, which felt as if it were being bounced against a hardwood floor.

It had started harmlessly enough, as many such evenings do: a couple of drinks with colleagues after work; a couple which had somehow, almost without noticing, become a couple more. Someone had suggested moving on to this club she knew, down at the opposite end of Upper Street from where they were, not really a club, more of a bar, but with a members policy at the door. Karen well into it by now, cocktails and beer, that good buzzy feeling you get when you're with mates and the pavements are crowded with people out having a good time and every other place you pass is a busy restaurant or bar; sharing a laugh and a joke and letting the tension of the job, the day, float off in a haze of flashing lights and loud voices, the music from a dozen open doorways mingling with the strident sounds of car horns and sirens and amongst the laughter, the occasional scream or angry shout, the sharpened sound of breaking glass.

He had been watching her, she knew, almost from the minute they entered the bar, the place already full to the gills, each trip to the bar the equivalent of a full body search or more; Karen's thong – the fashionable undergarment redesigned as medieval torture instrument – already cutting into her where it hurt.

'Hi.' His voice was just the honeyed-brown of his skin. 'What happened to your friends?'

'You mean you weren't watching them too?'

'Uh-uh.' And then the smile.

Too practised, Karen thought, too smooth by half.

'Taylor,' he said.

'Karen.'

'Hi, Karen.'

'Hi, yourself.'

'What're you drinking?'

'Too much?'

He laughed and ran his hand lightly down her arm as he passed through to the bar. 'Don't go 'way.'

Outside on the street, he took hold of her hand. 'You're what? Six foot, right?'

'Five ten.'

'That's all?'

'Uh-hum.'

'Bare feet?'

'Bare feet.'

'I'd like to see that.'

He kissed her then and she leaned into it, kissing him back, her head already a blur, his hand, clear and strong, on her hip.

It took her three attempts to locate the key in the door to her flat.

'Here,' he said, 'let me.' But she shook her head and pushed his hand away.

There were books on the floor, magazines and newspapers on one of the chairs, the new Amerie CD resting up against the stereo; the top she was planning to wear next day was hanging from the door frame between there and the bathroom.

'You want coffee?' she asked.

'You got anything else?'

There was a third of a bottle of workaday Scotch and they drank it on the settee, her feet, bare, in his lap, his arm stretched between her thighs.

'You picked me out early,' he said with a grin – cat not far short of the cream – 'that what it was?'

'You were the one, staring at me,' Karen said.

He laughed. 'Hell, girl. Six-foot-high black woman walks into a bar this side of the river, ain't Hackney, ain't Dalston, what d'you expect?'

What was that Bessie Smith song her mother used to play? A cracked old vinyl album of Bessie's greatest hits that was forever on the record player at home when she'd been growing up.

'Do Your Duty?'

Well, he did his duty that night, Taylor, Karen would say that for him.

Taylor Coombes.

'You're throwing me out?' he asked, sweat still making his body shine in the dim light from the lamp beside the bed. 'After that?'

'You can usually pick up a cab,' Karen said, raising her head, 'from the end of the street.'

'Why not let me stay?' He edged into a sly smile. 'Who knows? Come morning . . .'

'Come morning I have to be up early.'

'That's okay.'

'No, I mean really early.'

'Yeah? What d'you do, anyway?'

256

'Come on, Taylor. We've had a nice time. Don't make me pissed off, okay?'

'Okay, okay.' An elaborate sigh. 'Can I take a shower first, at least?'

'Help yourself.'

She was dozing, half-asleep, when he bent, fully dressed and smelling of her deodorant, and kissed her lightly on the mouth.

'Will I be seeing you again?' he asked.

'Not if I see you first.'

The door clicked back into place with a satisfactory snap and Karen rolled on to her side and closed her eyes.

Too many bad movies, he'd written his mobile number with one of her lipsticks on the bathroom mirror and, stepping out of the shower, she took a damp flannel and wiped it away. One-night stand, number whatever. Counting didn't make her feel any better. Or worse.

'When you goin' to settle down, girl?' her grandmother habitually asked, when she made her Christmas visits home to Spanish Town in Jamaica. 'Have some babies of your own?'

'You not gettin' any younger,' she had added lately.

Karen looked at herself in the mirror, breasts still high and firm enough for their size, and her belly, considering all she'd had to drink last night, all but disappeared when she stood straight and sucked in her breath.

Even so, Grandma was right, thirty seemed a long time ago.

She dried herself with the towel, rubbing as briskly as she dared, then used the drier on her hair, more manageable since she'd had it cut short a few years back and had the sense to keep it that way. Clean underwear, coffee on the stove. No bread for toast and the empty cereal packet had found its way into the recycling box three days before. As her sister said – the one in Southend with the twins – 'It's a good job you're a sight more organised at work than you are at home, girl. At least, I hope you are.'

So did she.

Just a dribble of milk left for the coffee and this morning, faced with drinking it virtually black, she needed sugar too. She'd pick up a muffin at the Caffè Nero on Camden Parkway on her way in. SCD1. Homicide and Serious Crime Command.

Two days ago they'd wrapped up a murder investigation with pleasing speed. An argument that had started in a Euston pub had spilled out on to the road outside and from there into the forecourt of the neighbouring mainline station. A chance remark about the Sunderland football team in general and its manager, Roy Keane, in particular, had been overheard by a trio of supporters from Wearside, who had taken exception. Fists, bottles, boots and shattered glass. The man who'd voiced his opinions less than wisely had legged it across the street and into the station, Wearsiders in pursuit, scattering passengers in all directions as they chased and harried. Trapped against the wall between Burger King and Upper Crust, the man had pulled a Swiss Army knife from his pocket, levered opened the longest blade and stuck it high in the chest of one of his attackers. Despite the best efforts of station staff and the paramedics, the nineteen-year-old was pronounced dead two hours later at the nearby University College Hospital and the man who killed him had gone on the lam.

A little judicious questioning by Karen Shields's team soon determined that the man they were looking for was a fairly frequent user of the pub where the incident had started, a frequent traveller, too, up and back to Birmingham and Manchester in the course of his work: a wholesale supplier of stationery to both chains and independent stores. Quite often, he would stop off at the pub for a pint or two before catching the Northern line south to Collier's Wood. The Swiss Army knife had been given to him by his fourteen-year-old son, a present for his last birthday.

When Karen's number two, Mike Ramsden, and a couple of other detectives, went to the house, the man at first started to talk his way out of any involvement, then panicked and, against all the odds, attempted a runner, which ended when Ramsden stopped him short with an elbow immediately below the breast bone, winding him completely.

Provocation, self-defence, a good solicitor would encourage him to plead to manslaughter and, if the CPS agreed to that, a sympathetic judge would likely sentence him leniently and he'd be back in the family home before his eldest set off for university.

All of which was of little more than academic interest to Karen and her team. A result was a result.

No sign of Mike Ramsden when she entered the office that morning, nor many others: Alan Sheridan, the DS who functioned as office manager, was sitting, owl-like, behind his computer, for all the world as if he'd been there from the night before.

'A message for you,' Sheridan called out. 'Urgent.'

'Where from?'

'On high.'

'Harkin?'

'The very same.'

'What now?'

'Another promotion, I wouldn't be surprised.' He grinned. 'You know how you ethnic-minority types prosper.'

'Fuck off, Sherry!'

'Yes, ma'am.'

When Karen had been appointed detective chief inspector three, almost four years ago, the accusations of favouritism, of positive discrimination, had flown thick and fast. She's a woman, she's black, she earned it on her knees. It took Ramsden to stand up in the canteen and say she'd been promoted because she was a fucking good copper – only don't anyone tell her I said so.

Assistant Commissioner Harkin's office, Karen thought – not that she'd been there that often – always smelt of air freshener and aftershave. Like a sales rep's car. She half-expected to hear Celine Dion or Chris de Burgh coming from speakers discreetly placed beneath his desk.

'Karen.' He looked at her with a sort of brisk surprise, as if she were the last person he'd expected to see and he might just be able to find her five minutes of his time.

'Sir.'

His hand was dry, so much so that for a moment Karen imagined tiny flakes of skin rubbing off against her fingers.

'That Euston business, good result.'

'Thank you, sir.'

'Much outstanding?'

'Not too much, sir.'

A father of three, stabbed to death on the upper deck of the 24 bus, when he sought to intervene between two warring groups of Somali youths; an elderly man, yet to be identified, whose partly decomposed body had been found in an abandoned Electricity Board building down by the canal; a young Asian woman, whose fall to her death from the seventh floor of a block of flats in Gospel Oak might not be suicide as first suspected.

'Nothing that couldn't be shuffled off to somebody else?'

Warning bells sounded inside Karen's head. 'Probably not, sir. Only . . .'

'Good. Good. Something interesting's come up. Nottingham. You know Nottingham at all?'

'Robin Hood, sir?'

'Queen of the Midlands. Little raddled nowadays, but even so. Three women for every man, or so they used to say.'

Get to it, Karen thought.

'Female officer, detective inspector. Homicide Unit. Shot and killed outside her home, yesterday evening.'

A jolt ran through her – sympathy, surprise, there but for the grace of God . . .

'They want someone to go up there, take charge of the investigation.'

'But surely they've got . . .'

'Right now they're seriously understaffed, too many high-profile cases . . .'

'Even so.'

'There are complications. The victim, she was in a relationship with another officer. Serious, long-term. DI. Lifetime on the force. They need someone from outside. No connection. Easier all round.'

'You said complications. Plural.'

Harkin blanked her with a smile. 'Best from the horse's mouth. You've a meeting with their ACC, Crime. 13.30. Just time for you to get home, pack a bag. Trains leave from St Pancras, pretty much two an hour.' He glanced at his watch. 'You'll not want to hang around.'

23

Resnick had been kneeling beside her when the ambulance arrived. Blood on his shirt, his face, his mouth, his tongue. The first shot had struck Lynn in the chest, the second, fired from closer range, had torn away part of her face, exposing her jaw. Already there were no signs of breathing, no response. After calling emergency services, his voice cracked, wavering, unrecognisable, Resnick had knelt and tilted back her head, pinched her nose and covered her mouth with his own. Breathed in twice, two seconds, watching for some movement; breathed again, harder, seeing the faintest rising of the chest, another breath and her head jerked once against his hands and she coughed blood into his mouth.

'Come on,' he said. 'Come on!'

Her eyes were open, staring, registering nothing.

Shifting his position and interlacing his fingers, Resnick pressed down on the centre of her chest and blood oozed out over his hands as if he were leaning on a sponge.

Thirty compressions and then two breaths.

Thirty compressions more and the sound of sirens.

Keep going, keep going.

Sirens loud and louder in his ears, lights that flashed and circled like a fairground around his head; thirty compressions and two breaths and they had to prise his hands away; half-drag, half-pull him to his feet and lever him aside so that they could move in with their equipment, begin their work. One of the paramedics – Resnick would always remember this – was young with a freckled face, freckled around the nose and cheeks even at that time of year, a freckled face and sandy, almost ginger hair – why did he notice that and not the light going from Lynn's eyes as they rolled back in her head?

More people now, more cars; someone pushed a glass of water towards him and it slipped and shattered on the path; someone else put a hand kindly on his arm and he brushed it away. Several people spoke words he didn't understand. The paramedics were lifting her up and carrying her towards the ambulance and, stumbling once, Resnick hurried forward, calling after her, calling her name.

One of the paramedics helped him into the back of the ambulance and, breathing ragged and harsh, he sat beside her, leaning forward, her cold hand growing colder in his own.

He couldn't remember, later, leaving the ambulance or entering the hospital, just that he was suddenly there and in the corridor and a doctor was standing in front of him, putting out both hands as if to restrain him, and speaking all the time, explaining, while behind him they were wheeling her away, not walking, hurrying, almost running.

A nurse led him to a place where he was supposed to wait.

Another brought a cup of hot, sweet tea and the smell and taste of the tea and the taste and smell of blood made him retch, and the nurse helped him to the men's room where he threw up into the lavatory bowl and then knelt there on the damp floor, his forehead resting against the cold, spattered edge of porcelain, listening to his own breathing as it slowed and slowed until he felt he could push himself to his feet, just, and turn, steadying himself for a moment against the cubicle door, before walking the four long paces to the sink and splashing cold water again and again in his face, a face that, in the mirror, looked more like a mask than it did his own.

'Lynn,' he said. And again, 'Lynn, Lynn.'

The nurse was waiting outside, anxious, and she led him back to where there were others, also waiting, faces he knew and vaguely recognised, faces showing sympathy, concern, and then the doctor stepped between them and Resnick knew what he had known ever since he had seen her body, one arm flung out, one leg folded beneath her on the path; ever since he had forced his breath into the cold, bloodied void of her mouth.

Lynn Alice Kellogg, pronounced dead, 23.35.

24

The sun came out and went back in. Somewhere south of Leicester and still some thirty minutes from her destination, a brief flurry of rain washed across the train window and when it faltered to nothing and a smidgeon of sun reappeared, Karen looked in vain for a rainbow. Some kind of a sign. She'd led an investigation into the death of a fellow officer before. Also a woman, a detective sergeant in SO7, Organised and Serious Crime. Her body had been found amongst the tangled undergrowth beside a disused railway line. Multiple stab wounds: forty-odd years old and half her life still ahead of her.

Now this.

Karen leafed again through the wodge of papers Sherry had downloaded from the web and thrust into her hands as she was leaving. Alongside basic information about the structure of the Nottinghamshire force and the two most recent Police Authority reports,

266

more encouraging words about the county extolled a heritage which spread from Byron and Robin Hood to Paul Smith and Brian Clough, and which had spawned, amongst other notable items, HP sauce, ibuprofen and the Bramley apple. Well, Karen thought, just watch out for the worm.

At Radcliffe, just a few miles short of the city, the Trent had overflowed its banks into the neighbouring fields, leaving cattle to wander, disconsolately, through edges of cold grey water, while, close alongside the train tracks, the power station leached smoke up into the already grey sky.

Taking first a mirror from her bag, Karen used a brush to apply a few last touches to her make-up. Silk shirt, black suit from Max Mara which had sent her credit limit hovering perilously close to red, boots with enough of a heel to lift her above most men she'd be likely to meet and level with the rest, she was ready for whatever the remainder of the day would bring.

At the AMT in the station forecourt, she bought an espresso and drank it swiftly down.

There was a car waiting to take her to the force head-quarters at Sherwood Lodge. Karen let the young PC place her bags in the boot, sat back and snapped her seat belt into place.

Another officer waited at the entrance to escort her to the office of the Assistant Chief Constable. *Assistant Chief Constable (Crime)*, as it said on the door. Flanking him were Bill Berry, wearing a pale grey three-piece suit that might have looked good on a younger

267

man, and the Chief Superintendent responsible for the Nottingham City division. The ACC held out his hand with a few words of welcome and the hope that she'd had a pleasant enough journey. Karen nodded, it had been fine; she said no to coffee, but yes to water. Sat and waited.

'Bill,' the ACC said, 'why don't you fill in the details?'

Berry cleared his throat and set his cup aside. The facts, such as they were known, were brutal and sparse. One officer dead, another in mourning: one bullet to the upper body, another to the head. Two cartridge cases had been found at the scene. The neighbours had been canvassed, the taxi driver who had driven DI Kellogg from the railway station had been questioned; a vehicle found abandoned some three-quarters of a mile away was being examined in the supposition that it might have been used in the killer's getaway. A post-mortem had been arranged for the following morning.

'Any suspects?' Karen asked, addressing the ACC directly.

'Not immediately.'

'Except . . .' Bill Berry began.

'Except?'

After a nod from the ACC, Berry cleared his throat again. 'There was a shooting a week or so back, a teenage girl killed. DI Kellogg was wounded in the same incident. The girl's father blamed Kellogg for his daughter's death. Publicly. He and DI Resnick had a

268

couple of run-ins on the subject afterwards. One of which was also public. Quite a bit of bad feeling between them echoed in the local press.'

'This Resnick,' Karen asked, 'what's his involvement here?'

'He was my number two on the investigation,' Berry said.

'Into the girl's death?'

'Yes.'

'He was also,' the Chief Superintendent added, speaking for the first time, 'Lynn Kellogg's partner.'

'Partner, as in living together?'

'Yes.'

'Ah,' Karen nodded, understanding. Complications, wasn't that what Harkin had said? Her Assistant Commissioner back in the Met, not a man to use words lightly.

'The father,' Karen said. 'The one you mentioned. He's been questioned?'

'Gone AWOL, apparently,' Berry said. 'No one in the family claims to know where.'

'Convenient,' Karen said tartly.

'Absolutely. Though this wouldn't be the first time he's just walked out without notice, apparently. Last occasion, he didn't come back for several years.'

'But we are looking?'

'Oh, yes, we're looking.'

Great start, Karen was thinking, number one suspect does a runner and no one knows where to find him.

'I understand,' she said, 'there's a team assembled?'

'Yes. The same one, give or take, as was working the girl's murder.'

'That's sorted?'

'CPS're still a tad leery, but yes, bar the shouting. Lad called Lee Williams. Picked him up for armed robbery, post office out on the edge of the city. Fell into our lap, really.' He grinned. 'Way it happens sometimes, if you're lucky.' He waited a couple of beats. 'I dare say you'll want your own bagman.'

'Yes, sir. I might feel a bit marooned, otherwise.'

'It is a man?' Berry asked, holding back a smile.

'Oh, yes,' Karen said. Mike Ramsden would have been quick to take a swing at anyone who called him anything else.

'There's a press conference in forty minutes,' the ACC said, 'and I'll want you there. Any problems?'

'None at all, sir,' Karen said.

Media interest was widespread. The killing of a police officer, a woman officer especially, was still rare enough to be big news. The nationals were there in force, print and TV news. The room was packed, close to overflowing. After giving the bare details of the shooting, the Assistant Chief Constable spoke of the determination of his officers to bring the perpetrators to justice.

'To this end,' he said, 'Detective Chief Inspector Shields, from the Homicide and Serious Crime Command of the Metropolitan Police, will be assisting in the investigation.'

270

Karen looked up with a half-smile which was captured by a dozen cameras and reproduced by sources as diverse as the EuroNews television channel and the local *Ilkeston Advertiser*.

The ACC spoke of the great sense of loss felt by the Force at Detective Inspector Kellogg's death, and went on to outline the qualities and characteristics she had brought to the job.

'Lynn Kellogg,' he said, 'worked her way up through the ranks, always exhibiting a combination of resourcefulness and intelligence, leavened by good humour and common sense. She was, as she proved on numerous occasions, an extraordinarily brave officer, second to none in her dedication and commitment to the highest standards of the force, and it was an honour to have served with her as a member of my command.'

As Karen watched, a bulky, broad-shouldered man, quite dishevelled, clothing awry, lurched up from one of the rows near the back of the room and, shouldering bystanders aside, pushed his way out through the rear doors.

'It is the firm determination,' the Assistant Chief concluded, 'of every one of us on this platform, and of every officer in this force, to bring those responsible for this heinous crime – the shooting of an unarmed officer in cold blood – to justice as soon as possible.'

When Resnick had finally returned from the hospital in the early hours of the morning, he had stumbled around the house blindly, throwing open doors to rooms he barely recognised. Once, in the bathroom, he caught sight of himself in the mirror, shaggy haired, unshaven and hollow eyed, without knowing who he was. In the kitchen, he found the sections of the stove-top coffee pot on the drainer and started to reassemble them before giving up, the task too great.

Lynn.

Lynn.

The word stuck, like something vast and indigestible, in his throat, and he thought that he might choke.

Without his knowledge, time passed.

The cats, who would normally have fussed around his feet, steered clear, as if aware of his distress.

Marooned in the living room, he found his way falteringly to the shelves holding the stereo and pulled a CD out from the rack, but left it unplayed.

'You want me to meet you at the station?' he had asked.

And then her voice, jarred out of focus by the background noise of the train. 'No need. I'll get a cab.'

No need. No need.

'You're sure?'

'Sure.'

Oh, Christ! It came to him like a knife blade slipped cold against the heart. If he had gone, if he had gone . . . if, instead of listening and accepting what she'd said – pleased to hear it really, if he were honest, half-pleased at least, no need to get up from his easy chair and venture out into the relatively cold night air, no call to stop listening to Brookmeyer's sour trombone relishing the chords, the melodies of 'There Will Never Be Another You' – if instead what he had done – as in the first flush of their relationship he would have without fail – was to have hurried from the house to the car and made sure he was at the station well before the train arrived, waiting at the head of the stairs and gazing into the mass of passengers as they bustled towards him, seeking out her face, the smile that his presence would produce when she saw that he was there after all, the look of pleasure that would become a kiss, an embrace, her arms, her body, clinging to his – if he had done all that, Lynn would most likely be alive now.

But . . .

No need. I'll get a cab.

You're sure?

Sure.

Oh, Jesus! Sweet, sweet fuck! What had he done? What had he failed to do?

He stood there, numb and shivering, lost in the centre of the room, while grief shocked through him like cold waves breaking over his battered heart.

Karen had spent the afternoon and early evening taking soundings, getting her bearings. She spoke briefly to the SIO in charge of the case Lynn Kellogg had been working on immediately before her death, the double murder out at Bestwood, wondering if there might be any connection, then pulled together as many as she could of the team which had investigated Kelly Brent's

273

death – Anil Khan, Catherine Njoroge, Frank Michaelson, Steven Pike. She had them take her through the events of the shooting, the accusations made by the victim's family, the circumstances leading, haphazardly, up to Lee Williams's arrest.

After reviewing what was so far known about Lynn Kellogg's murder, she sat in the canteen with the young PC who had been the first officer to arrive at the scene, still shaken by what he had found. Then, on a borrowed computer, she studied a map of the specific area, the narrow, winding road – little more than a lane – which led off the main Woodborough Road towards the house where Kellogg and Resnick had lived – and where she had died.

Two shots.

Head and heart.

A professional hit, Karen thought. Paid for, organised, preordained. Either that, or blind luck. That close, she reasoned, and given a steady hand, it would have been difficult to miss.

Time would tell.

She resisted several offers of dinner in this restaurant or that in favour of room service at the hotel, amazed as ever how it can take the best part of an hour for most self-respecting kitchens to rustle up a toasted cheese sandwich. Her room was small and neat and clearly not designed with a near-six-foot woman in mind; no way her feet weren't going to stick over the end of the bed and she had to bend almost double to get her head under the shower. And whoever had decided a bright raspberry bedspread adorned with cream squiggles went with bright purple curtains, biscuit-coloured walls and a ruby-red carpet, needed, she thought, to resit her NVQ in interior design. But at least, as the hotel literature proudly proclaimed, it was only two minutes' walk from the railway station. Handy, if she changed her mind.

From tomorrow she had been promised a serviced apartment with a fully equipped kitchen, an LCD digital television, wireless broadband and breathtaking views across the city.

She could scarcely wait.

She'd phoned Mike Ramsden earlier and given him the good news: there was a train out of St Pancras at 6.35 that would get him into Nottingham at 8.29. The first meeting with the inquiry team was set for 9.00 a.m.

'You know what you are, don't you?' Ramsden growled.

'Aside from your boss?'

'Yeah, aside from that.'

Karen laughed. 'See you tomorrow, Mike. Best have breakfast on the train.'

All those thoughts rolling round in her head, she didn't reckon on getting to sleep easily, and she was right. After fifteen minutes of restless rolling and turning, she threw back the covers, splashed cold water on her face, rinsed her mouth, pulled a stiff comb through her hair and put on a sweater, jeans and padded jacket. New Balance trainers on her feet. Two minutes to the railway station was just about right.

275

The driver at the front of the short line of cabs was sitting with his door open, reading through the paper for perhaps the fourth or fifth time and listening to the local radio station.

Karen gave him the address and climbed into the back. Just time to adjust her seat belt before they pulled out on to Carrington Street and the bridge over the canal. The same journey Lynn Kellogg would have taken the night she died.

Tape was still stretched across in front of the house, preserving the scene. The house itself was dark, the curtains partly drawn across, the faintest of lights showing through from one of the rooms at the rear.

The taxi had disappeared from sight.

There were few signs of life from higher up the street.

The sound of traffic from the main road seemed more distant than it was.

Karen zipped her jacket tighter and started to walk slowly towards the house, then stopped. Someone was standing at one of the upstairs windows, looking down. A man's shape in silhouette, bulking large against the glass. She could just see the outline of the face, the faint pale blur of skin. She stood there for a moment, looking up, then raised a hand, as if in salute, and turned away.

She picked up another taxi easily enough on its way back into the city. In her room up on the fifth floor, she sat on the bed, slowly drinking a vodka and tonic from the minibar, and thought about the man in that house alone, trying and failing to feel her way into his mind, what he must be thinking, going through.

When her head finally touched the pillow, she fell, almost immediately, to sleep.

25

Mike Ramsden's train was on time. He arrived at the Central Police Station with anger still buzzing inside him after reading the newspaper account of the fatal stabbing of a young PC, who had been called to an incident early the previous morning and attempted to restrain a man who had already attacked two members of the public with a knife. Stabbed in the neck and the shoulder, his protective vest had been to no avail; less than three years in the service, he left a young widow and baby behind. All this at seven in the morning, a nondescript shopping centre in a nondescript town. What the fuck, Ramsden thought, was this fucking world coming to? His bit of the world. It was enough to make you weep.

Not that Ramsden was the weeping kind.

Dark eyed, full mouthed, the bridge of his nose angled sharply and tilted to one side from having been broken too many times.

Today, as most days, he was wearing jeans and rarely polished black shoes, a scuffed leather jacket over a grey T-shirt, iron-grey hair in need of a comb. With Karen standing alongside him, smart if slightly dressed down in a plain navy trouser suit and blue cotton top, they looked like some strange combination of Beauty and the Beast.

Karen had been up since before six, going over the notes she had made the day before, making sure the details of the murder scene, the known facts, were clear in her mind. Later that morning she would have to set up the policy log for the investigation, meticulously recording all the lines of inquiry and what she hoped they would achieve. But before that she had to address the team, gee them up and get them on her side. One of Ramsden's main tasks would be to make sure they stayed there; and if there were any rumblings of discontent to let Karen know so they could be dealt with before they got out of hand.

'Right,' she said, stepping forward once everyone was gathered and introducing herself, 'let's get down to business. I think I've got a pretty good grasp of the basic situation now, but if I'm missing anything, if I get something not quite right, I'm relying on one of you to put me straight. Okay? Preferably in such a way it seems I knew it all along.'

A few smiles, no laughter.

'So – Detective Inspector Kellogg returned from London on the 20.55 train, which arrived here on time at thirty-nine minutes past ten. She took a taxi from the station to the house where she lived with Detective Inspector Resnick, arriving there between ten and fifteen minutes later which puts it at ten fifty, ten fifty-five. She pays the driver and crosses towards the house, goes through the front gate and starts along the path towards the front door and that's when she's hit twice from close range, both shots almost certainly fired by someone who had been waiting at the side of the house.

'Alerted by the sounds of gunfire, Resnick runs out, calls emergency services, administers CPR. DI Kellogg is taken to hospital by ambulance and pronounced dead, without regaining consciousness, soon after arrival.'

There was silence in the room.

'All right,' Karen said, 'Anil, you've been liaising with Scene of Crime.'

A little self-consciously, Khan got to his feet. 'There's not a great deal, ma'am, I'm afraid. Not so far. Two cartridge cases were recovered from close to the corner of the building. One of the bullets, presumably the one which struck DI Kellogg in the head, was found on the grassed area at the front of the house. It seems to have ricocheted back from the low brick wall between the front garden and pavement. They've all been passed on to the Forensic Science lab at Huntingdon.'

'Any idea when we might get anything back?'

'No, ma'am.'

'Okay, chase it up, will you?'

280

'Yes, ma'am.'

'And Anil . . .'

'Ma'am?'

'Less of the ma'am, if you don't mind. It makes me feel like your granny. Boss, will do.'

Khan nodded, his blush evident, no matter the natural shade of his skin.

'Anyone have anything else?' Karen asked, looking round the room.

'Cigarette ends,' Pike said, 'three of them. Further back down the side entry. There's no way of knowing if they were left there by the gunman or not.'

'They've not been left by either Resnick or Kellogg?'

Pike shook his head. 'Neither of them smoked, boss.'

'How about footprints?' Ramsden asked. 'Anything there?'

'One partial, that's all. The entry's gravelled over, and anyway there'd been hardly any rain that day, just a shower, so the soil was pretty dry. Scientific Support said not to hold our breath.'

Karen glanced down at her notes. 'What's this about an abandoned car?'

'Peugeot 307 hatchback, boss,' Khan said. 'Stolen from a car park out at Arnold earlier that evening. By the leisure centre. The tax disc missing when it was found, plus there were a lot of scratches down the near side, as if it'd taken a turn too sharp and maybe run up against a wall. It could have been used as a getaway car, exchanged for another that had been stashed in

281

advance. Quick out of the city from there, M1's not so far away.'

'And this was where?'

'Old Basford. A little less than a mile away from where the shooting took place. The whole place is a regular warren. Narrow streets, back entries, old works and warehouses, factories, some in use, some not. The car's being checked for prints, DNA.'

'Any chance it was caught on CCTV?' Karen asked.

'Out by the leisure centre, where it was stolen, yes, pretty good, I'd say. But at Basford, less likely. Patchy at best.'

'How about closer to the scene?'

'That's better,' Khan said. 'In the road leading directly to the house there's nothing. But back on the main road, Traffic have got quite a few cameras.'

'Okay, let's check what we can. I know it's a slow business. Like watching some too-clever-by-half foreign movie without the subtitles. But it has to be done.'

'Who spoke to the taxi driver?' Ramsden asked. 'The one who dropped Kellogg off?'

Michaelson raised a hand.

'Anything useful?'

'Not really, no. Some suggestion that he saw a car parked further along from where he dropped DI Kellogg off, but he was unclear. All over the place, really.'

'Then let's have him in again. See if we can't straighten him out. Jog his memory.'

'Right.'

'And let me know when it's happening, I might sit in.'

Michaelson didn't know whether to be pleased or concerned.

'The same with the neighbours,' Karen said. 'Let's double back, take a second crack. It's not as if, as I understand it, there are that many along that particular stretch of road and they can't all be tucked up in bed early. Someone must have heard or seen something.'

Murmurs of agreement, the small sounds of officers restlessly shifting position; they were tired of just sitting, anxious to be getting on.

'All right,' Karen said. 'One thing seems clear. This was no random shooting, no robbery. This was cold-blooded murder. Assassination, if you will. Lynn Kellogg was deliberately targeted and what we have to find out is why.'

'Too bloody right,' somebody said.

'The answer might be found in the cases she's been involved in, recent or in the past. Someone bearing a grudge. Which brings us – I know, I know – to the death of Kelly Brent, whose father, apparently, made various wild threats and accused DI Kellogg of being instrumental in his daughter's death. Obviously we need to talk to him as soon as possible, and the fact that he's dropped out of sight makes that all the more urgent still. So let's redouble our efforts to bring him in. Check all his contacts, relations, whatever you can. But . . . but . . . while that's going on, let's not get carried away into

283

thinking if we find him we get a result. Let's look at those other cases DI Kellogg had been working, dig around, find out what we can.'

There was a palpable rise in sound, as some of the team took that as a signal to move away.

'Another thing, important. Could be vital. DI Kellogg's movements the evening she was killed. She'd been returning from London. Why? What was she doing there? Was it work or personal? Who did she see? Who knew she was travelling back when she did? Anil, that's down to you. I'm hoping to speak to DI Resnick later today and anything useful I learn I'll pass along. Okay?'

'Yes, boss.'

'And the rest of you, there's another question. Why did the murder take place where it did? Why elect to kill her outside her own home?'

She gave them a few moments to think before carrying on.

'That short walk from the far side of the street to the front door, that's the only point in the journey that evening when Lynn Kellogg would have been alone and not surrounded by other people. Not only that, but the street itself is quiet, it's narrow, rarely used except for access, and there are no buildings at all to the rear, so the killer could have waited unobserved.' She looked up, looked around the room. 'Reasons enough? What do you think?'

Coughing, low-level murmuring, uncertain glances. Catherine Njoroge took a hesitant step forward.

284

'Yes, Catherine?'

'I'm not sure how relevant this is, boss, but I was just thinking, whoever it was shot Lynn, they would probably have known that DI Resnick was there, in the house. If they knew that, then they must have known that he'd be the first to find her.'

'Go on.'

'Well, maybe what happened, it was meant for him as well. To hurt him. And maybe – I don't know, this might be taking things too far – but couldn't it, at the same time, have been some kind of warning? Nowhere's safe, we can reach you anywhere, even at home, where you feel safest.'

'We, Catherine,' Karen said. 'Who's the we?'

Catherine shook her head. 'I don't know, boss. It could be Howard Brent, after what he said, but I don't know.'

'All right. And thank you, Catherine, good point. So we might have to look back through DI Resnick's cases as well, beyond the most recent, I mean. Villains he's put away . . .'

'Hundreds,' someone said.

'Anyone recently released from prison who might be bearing a grudge. Let's check. And good luck, okay? Sharp eyes, hard graft and good luck, we'll get it sorted.'

With the team dismissed, Karen went off into a huddle with Mike Ramsden, Anil Khan and the office manager to firm up rotas and schedules and make sure that

285

procedures were in place to prioritise and process information as it came in.

Once that was settled, she had to retrace her steps from the night before.

26

Resnick had been awake since a quarter past five, when he had first stirred, shivering, in his bed. Both the pillow and undersheet were soaked through with sweat and his hair was matted to his scalp. The youngest of the cats had been sleeping on the bed, just as it had before Lynn had moved in, and when Resnick slowly straightened and swung his legs round towards the floor, it shrilled a protest and jumped reluctantly down.

Lynn's reading glasses, the ones she had had prescribed but rarely used, were on the cabinet at her side of the bed, along with several hairbands in different colours, an empty water glass, the hand lotion she applied each night last thing and the book she had been reading but would never finish.

This Book Will Save Your Life.

Not now it wouldn't.

Resnick swept it away with one hand and sent it skittering across the floor.

It was still dark outside and for a moment he had to ask himself how much time had passed since Lynn had died. How many hours? How many days?

Through the window he could see shadows from a distant street light and the shapes of trees and, below, the stone wall and gravelled path and the stubbled grass of the front garden all marked off with tape.

Let her go.

The young paramedic with his earnest, freckled face, kneeling beside him, Resnick's hands still interlocked across Lynn's chest.

You have to let her go now. Let her go.

In the bathroom, he stood beneath the shower and turned it to full, letting the water beat over him; he stood there until it began to run cold, then stepped out and towelled himself down, grateful for the steam that hid his reflection in the mirror.

Back in the bedroom, he slowly dressed, the same clothes as the day before. When Lynn had first moved in, he had teased her about the amount of clothing she had brought with her, enough, he had said, to fill the wardrobe on her own and demand her own chest of drawers.

'What on earth are you going to do with all this lot?' he had asked. 'Start a shop?'

And then, later, after she had been living there for a while – 'Why don't you sort through this stuff and chuck some out? It's not as if you ever wear most of it, anyway. Give it to Oxfam or something. It's just taking up space.'

As if that mattered.

As if space were what they were short of.

He hadn't realised it was time.

The material of the blue cotton dress she had worn on holiday burned like silk against his hand.

Despite the fact that he had pulled on a thick sweater over his shirt and a worn old cardigan over that, he was still cold. The kitchen window, which, save for the fiercest weather, he was wont to open the moment he arrived downstairs, was still locked shut. The central heating thermostat was set high. It had been like this the previous day, too, a coldness that chafed his bones: save for those moments when he could feel his face begin to flush, his skin prickle and, for no reason, he broke out in a sweat.

This morning he managed the coffee pot but not the toaster.

The card she had given him was still there, corners bent and a little grease-marked now, tucked between the sugar and the flour.

Still here, Charlie, against all the odds.

Well, no . . .

Tears sprang to his eyes and he had to grab hold of the worktop to stop himself from shaking.

The cup, when he lifted it from the shelf, slipped through his hand to the floor and broke.

He couldn't go on like that.

He couldn't go on.

Cold or not, he pushed open the back door and went

out into the garden, the sky striped with purple, red and grey. Traffic sounds merging with the close call of birds; a dog barking, sharp and insistent, at the far side of the allotments; from somewhere, faint and troubled, the cry of a child.

There were things he needed to do, decisions to be taken, calls to be made. He pressed his thumb against the rough wall at the garden edge until it began to bleed.

It had developed into a fine early spring morning, blue sky scattered here and there with wisps of cloud, pale sun. The weather forecasters had been talking of storm clouds coming in off the Atlantic, quickly changing weather patterns, but today there was no sign. Not this far inland.

Karen had toyed with the idea of taking somebody else with her, but in the end she had gone alone. Uncertain if the bell were working, she had knocked several times, called through the letter box, tried the bell again. Turning away, she had reached the gate when the front door opened and Resnick, cardigan wrongly buttoned, stepped outside, blinking at the light.

'Hello,' she said, approaching, 'I'm Karen . . .'

'You're Karen Shields.'

'Yes.'

'DCI.'

'Yes.'

They shook hands.

'Bill Berry gave me a heads up.'

'Of course.'

'You were here last night,' Resnick said.

Karen nodded.

'Walking the ground.'

'Yes.' It was all she could do to stop herself glancing sideways at the patch of grass where Lynn Kellogg had died.

'You took a taxi from the station. The same journey Lynn made that night.'

'Yes.'

Resnick nodded. 'It's what she would have done.'

'What you taught her.'

'You think so?'

'You were her DI when she first went into CID.'

Resnick's face showed mild surprise.

'I was talking to Anil yesterday,' Karen said. 'Anil Khan. He worked with you, too. Canning Circus, I think he said.'

Resnick nodded. 'You'd best come inside. There'll be things you want to know.'

The furniture in the front room was heavy looking, the upholstery fussy and starting to fade. The gate-legged table seemed to Karen to come from another age. She wondered how much Lynn had felt the need to change things after she'd moved in and what resistance she'd met, if any.

'You lived here long?' she asked.

'Too bloody long,' Resnick said, but he said it with a smile.

Some women, Karen thought, would find that attractive, that quick self-deprecating smile, and would feel drawn to him, sympathetically. Would go over and rebutton his cardigan correctly. Pat him on the arm.

Not me.

'I can make coffee,' Resnick offered. 'Just no milk.'

'Black's fine.'

While he was out of the room, she glanced at the books on his shelves – *Looking for Chet Baker*, *The Sound of the Trumpet*, *Straight Life*, several books about Thelonious Monk; clustered together, a batch of paperback novels by Alice Hoffman and Helen Dunmore, which she assumed had been Lynn's; a couple of books she'd read herself, *Beloved* and *The Lovely Bones*. *Beloved* she'd read twice.

Alongside the books were several rows of CDs, jazz for the most part, with a leavening of Prince and Madonna and Magazine, which had come into the house with Lynn, she guessed. Part of her dowry. Amongst several box sets, she noticed one of Bessie Smith, and she was looking at this, just trying and failing to free the little booklet with her fingernail and thumb, when Resnick returned, coffee mugs in hand.

'Four CDs,' she said. 'You must be keen.'

'Tell the truth,' Resnick said, 'I bought it a couple of months back and I don't think I've listened to it more than once. And then not all the way through.' He handed one of the mugs to Karen and set down his own. 'It's a bad habit of mine. I see something like that – ninety tracks for twelve pounds or whatever – and it seems too much of a bargain to resist. Lynn reckons . . .' He caught himself and stopped. 'Lynn used to say,

292

where jazz was concerned, I had more money than sense.'

He lowered himself heavily into his usual chair and Karen sat in another, her back to the window.

'What happened to Lynn,' Karen said, 'I'm really sorry. I should have said right off, but . . . I don't know, words, they seem so . . . inadequate.' She drew air in sharply through her nose. 'We'll catch him, you know. Whoever was responsible.'

'I know.'

The coffee was strong and slightly bitter, too hot to drink quickly.

'My mother loved Bessie Smith,' Karen said. 'Other singers, too. Dinah Washington. Aretha. But it was Bessie she loved best.' She smiled. 'I must have known the words to "A Good Man is Hard to Find" before I could recite "Humpty Dumpty" or "Little Bo-Peep". Not that it ever did me a lot of good. As advice, I mean.'

'Take it,' Resnick said. 'Borrow it. Let me have it back whenever.'

'I might,' Karen said. 'Thanks. I just might.' If this new apartment she was moving into had an up-to-date TV, it would surely have a CD player, too.

'You'll be wanting to know how far we've got,' she said. 'Unless someone's brought you up to speed already.'

Resnick shook his head.

She gave him a summary of what little they knew so far and the main areas the investigation would be moving into. 'Is there anything,' she said, when she'd finished, 'that you think we might be missing?'

'Not that I can think of.'

'You know we'll be running an eye over old cases of yours?'

'Someone after payback? Getting at me through Lynn?'

'It's possible, isn't it?'

'Stretching it a little, I'd have thought. And besides, why go after her? Why not me instead?'

'Maybe whoever it was wanted to see you suffer. Cause you pain.'

'Like Howard Brent?'

'You think that's where we should be looking first?'

'Him or someone close to him, yes. Aside from whatever grudge he holds against me, he felt Lynn was responsible for his daughter's death.'

'This call he was alleged to have made . . .'

'"Watch your back, bitch."'

'That's what was said?'

'Yes.'

'As I understand it, Lynn didn't recognise the voice. She couldn't say definitely it was Brent.'

'Not definitely, no.'

'And we still don't have proof. We don't know for a fact it was him.'

Resnick leaned forward abruptly. 'Look, he was convinced Lynn had used his daughter as a shield. He's on record as saying so. "One way or another, she's gonna pay for what she's done." His words. One way or another, she's going to pay.'

'When they're angry people say a lot of things. You know that. More often than not it's just hot air, letting off steam.'

'Lynn's dead. That's not just words. That's fact.'

'And you think Howard Brent was responsible? Directly? I just want to be clear.'

'Directly? Personally responsible?' Resnick shook his head. 'It's not impossible, but no, I doubt if he actually stood there and squeezed the trigger himself.'

'You think he set her up, then? Paid someone to have her killed.'

'Paid, bribed, cajoled. Then put some distance between himself and what he knew was going to happen. Gave himself an alibi.'

Karen leaned back in her chair. Howard Brent was how old? Late forties? Fifty? He had a record for violence, she knew. Drugs, also, though only possession, not supply, and that in '89. Right when the first serious spate of crack cocaine in the UK was at its height and gangs were moving in from Jamaica in large numbers. No matter how straight he might be now, if he had commissioned the shooting of Lynn Kellogg, it was likely he'd used whatever contacts he'd made in the past. And there were instances she knew, well documented, where a gunman had been brought into the country on a false passport, carried out two shootings and been back on the plane twenty-four hours later.

'More coffee?' Resnick asked.

'No, thanks. I'm fine.'

'You're sure?' Resnick was half out of his chair.

'All right then, go on. But if I start climbing walls later, you're to blame.'

The moment Karen, following Resnick, walked into the kitchen, both of the cats who'd been waiting hopefully by their bowls turned and fled.

'A clear case of colour prejudice if ever I saw one,' Karen said, amused.

'Tall, authoritarian women, they're not used to it.'

She laughed. 'Authoritarian, is that what I am?'

'You've got an air about you.'

'God knows, some days I need it. There's still enough men out there who don't like taking orders from a woman. And a black woman especially. Though some of them might not admit it.'

Resnick nodded, rinsing the coffee pot under the tap.

'How about Lynn?' Karen said. 'How did she cope, being a woman in charge?'

'Okay, I think. People liked her, she earned their respect.'

'She'd got her promotion quickly.'

'It was deserved.'

'There wasn't any tension between the two of you? Professionally?'

Resnick put the base of the pot aside. 'Was I jealous, do you mean?'

'I suppose so, yes. I mean – and correct me if I'm wrong – but you were already a DI when she started out . . .'

'And here I am, still a DI, and she's . . .' The words stuck in his throat. 'She was the same rank and likely to have been promoted higher.'

'Yes.'

'And you want to know how that made me feel?'

'Yes.'

'It made me feel proud. It didn't make me jealous, or angry. It didn't even make me feel bad about myself, as if somehow I was washed up or left behind. Okay? It didn't make me feel as if my masculinity was threatened, and it didn't mean I couldn't any longer get it up.'

He stared at her hard, just this side of losing his temper.

'That's what you wanted to know, isn't it? One of the things you've come to ask? How things were between us? Had I been taking the Viagra? Keeping her satisfied? Or had she been going over the side, having an affair? Had I? Maybe she was going to leave me, walk out? The second time in my life. How would that make me feel? Enough to push me over the edge? Enough to take her life?'

The blood had risen to his face and his voice was loud and unsteady. His fists were still clenched, but down by his side.

'You're right,' Karen said. 'I have to know. I have to ask. In my position, you'd do the same.'

Resnick pushed his hands up through his hair. 'I know.'

'And things between you, they were okay?'

'I think we were happy enough, yes. Not ecstatic, not any more. That doesn't last. And we both worked hard at what we did – Lynn especially. Long hours, stress, not much time to yourselves. You don't need me to tell you how that is. But there were no big traumas. Any little niggles, we ironed them out. An ordinary couple, I guess you'd say, just like lots of others.'

'Ordinary couples,' Karen smiled ruefully. 'I wonder if they really exist.'

'Well, if they do, that's what we were.'

The coffee was ready. Resnick dug out two folding chairs and carried them into the garden. There was more warmth in the sun now and only the flimsiest of clouds remained. Somewhere within earshot, someone was using an electric mower, having an early go at his lawn.

'This trip Lynn made to London,' Karen said, 'the afternoon before she was killed . . .'

Resnick told her the reason, filling in as much background as he felt she needed to know.

'You say she felt responsible,' Karen said, after listening. 'For this Andreea.'

'She thought she'd made promises she couldn't keep, yes. She felt guilty.'

'You don't know what happened when she was down there? With the girl?'

Resnick looked at her briefly and then at the floor. 'We didn't get the chance to discuss it.'

'I'm sorry.'

'No.'

298

'Every time I open my mouth . . .'

'It's okay. I think it even helps in a way. Talking about her as if . . .' He glanced away. 'I don't want to accept it. That she's gone. I want to believe any minute the phone's going to ring and it'll be her, saying she's sorry she's late, but something's come up and she'll be home soon.'

He turned his head sharply away and Karen sat there, knowing that he was crying and not knowing what to do or say, except that there was probably nothing, not then, and so she continued to sit there, waiting for him to pull himself together, wondering if there'd been any joy from ballistics or if any progress had been made with the prints from the abandoned car and if anyone had succeeded in tracking down Howard Brent.

'Where she went in London – Leyton, I think you said – d'you have an address?'

'There'll be one somewhere, in her notebook, most likely.'

'I've asked Anil Khan to check her movements.'

'He's a good man. Thorough.'

They both got to their feet.

'Cases she'd been working on,' Karen said, 'people she's helped put away, you can't think of anyone who might be harbouring a grudge, looking for some kind of payback?'

'No.'

'This business over the trial, the one that was abandoned – the SOCA officer involved, you don't know if he's still around?'

299

'Daines – it's possible. Likely.' A wry smile crossed Resnick's face. 'He sent her flowers. Lynn. When she came out of hospital. The Kelly Brent business.'

'He knew her well, then?'

'They'd met, some conference or other.'

Karen looked at him, another question on her lips, but let it ride.

'I had better go,' she said.

'You'll keep in touch,' Resnick said. 'Let me know . . .'

'Of course.'

Her mobile rang as she was getting into the car. Howard Brent had caught a Virgin Atlantic flight from London Gatwick to Jamaica on Sunday the fourth of March, two days before Lynn Kellogg was murdered.

27

Karen had called Catherine Njoroge over that afternoon, Catherine one of several detectives who had been reviewing the CCTV footage and pleased at any excuse to take a break.

'Howard Brent, you've been to the house, right?'

'Once, yes. With DI Resnick.'

'Good. This time you can come with me.'

Tina Brent took her time coming to the door and when she did she took one look and shook her head. 'If you're selling Bibles, I've got one already.'

Tina wearing loose sweat pants with a broad stripe down the sides and a V-necked short-sleeved top. If she recognised Catherine, she gave no sign.

'We're here to talk about your husband,' Karen said, identifying herself.

'Again? I told one of your lot already. I got no idea where he is.'

'Fine,' Karen said. 'Now you can tell me.'

They followed her inside. From the look of things, Tina had taken it into her head to give the house a bit of a spring clean and run out of steam partway through. The room into which she led them was airless and smelt of too many cigarettes. Karen noticed the photograph of the dead girl on the mantelpiece and flowers close by it that were starting to droop and fade, petals in the hearth.

'This is all about that policewoman who was shot, yeah?' Tina said, a definite edge to her voice.

Karen said that yes, it was.

'All I can say, it's a shame you never took as much trouble when my Kelly was killed. Didn't put yourself out then, did you?'

'Mrs Brent,' Catherine Njoroge said, 'I don't think that's true.'

Tina looked at her as if she were beneath contempt.

'Your husband,' Karen said, 'according to what you've said, he just left, no excuse or explanation, no note, nothing?'

'Yeah. Right.'

'He didn't give you any indication—?'

'Jesus! How many more times? That's Howard, right? The way he is. He's done it before and he'll do it again.' She reached for the packet of cigarettes resting on the arm of the nearest chair. 'One time he didn't come back for five fucking years.'

'You're not worried, then? About where he might be?'

Tina sneered. 'If I worried about everything that

302

bastard got up to I'd've topped myself long since.'

She lit up and drew hard on the cigarette, holding the smoke down in her lungs.

'Your husband, he's originally from Jamaica?' Karen asked.

Tina gave her a look. 'What of it?'

'He's still got contacts there, then? Friends? Family?'

'Friends, yes, course he has. Family, but I don't think they've spoke in years.'

'And you think that's where he might be? Visiting these friends in Jamaica?'

'Visiting friends in bloody Timbuktu, for all I know.'

'According to our information,' Karen said, 'your husband boarded a flight to Jamaica the Sunday just gone. Montego Bay.'

'Then you already know, don't you? Why keep pesterin' me about it?'

'We thought you might be able to tell us exactly where he was. Where he might be staying. So that we could make contact.'

'You're joking, right?'

'A number where he could be reached.'

Tina's laugh splintered into a brittle cough. 'I'm the last person he'd give any bloody number to. Out there with some sodding baby mother, most likely, never mind his own kids back here. Spent more time with Kelly, brought her up proper, set some kind of example, she might not be fuckin' dead.'

Anger twisted her tight little face.

Karen thought she wasn't going to get any further; aside from maybe jolting Tina Brent a little, she wasn't sure if she'd got anywhere at all.

'If, by any chance,' she said, 'you do speak to him – if, for whatever reason, he gets in touch, please tell him we want to talk to him. If he wasn't involved in any way in DI Kellogg's death, then we can eliminate him from our inquiries and move on. Okay?'

Tina sucked in her cheeks still further.

'Tina, okay?'

'Yeah, okay.'

They were on their way to the front door when Catherine thought to ask Tina whether or not Marcus was at college that day.

'Not this afternoon,' Tina said. 'He's filling in at his dad's shop in Hockley. But you'll be wastin' your time askin' him anything. He knows even less'n I do.'

'Catherine, you go and talk to him,' Karen said once they were outside. 'I ought to get back to the office.'

The shop was in one of the narrow streets leading off Goose Gate, not far from the sauna and massage parlour where Nina Simic had been murdered the year before. The door was open out on to the pavement and Catherine recognised the music that was playing: Augustus Pablo's *King Tubby Meets the Rockers Uptown*. A few years back, she had gone out with a teacher on a graduate training programme who had played it all the time.

304

The interior was dark and crowded: row after row of albums and twelve-inch singles along both side walls, CDs racked at the centre. Posters on the walls. Marcus stood behind the counter wearing an oversize T-shirt with the logo *Will Fuck for Drugs* writ large in white letters.

Appealing, thought Catherine.

There were no other customers.

Marcus looked at her with the beginnings of a smile.

A moment later he cut the volume on the stereo enough to hear the sound of his own voice.

'Like this, yeah? King Tubby? How 'bout this? You seen this?' He lifted a CD from where it lay on the counter. 'New. *Essential Dub*. Fourteen tracks, i'n'it? Traditional, fusion, hardcore. Virgin, HMV, cost £6.99. Minimum. Yours for a fiver. Okay?'

Head cocked a little to one side, he held it towards her.

'I don't think so,' Catherine said. 'But thank you.'

'No? What you lookin' for then?'

'Benga, you have any of that?'

'Bangra?'

'No, no. Benga. It's from East Africa, where I come from. Kenya. Suzzana Owiyo, she's one of my favourites. Jane Nyambura, too – Queen Jane.'

Marcus looked at her, uncertain.

'Your father,' Catherine said, 'we'd like to get in touch with him.'

Marcus's face screwed up into a frown.

Catherine held out her warrant card, but he scarcely

gave it a glance. 'Your father,' she said, 'we thought you might know where he was.'

'What's this all about then? This about Kelly gettin' shot?'

'In a way.'

'Thought that was all sorted,' Marcus said.

'It is. Mostly.'

She looked at him and he looked away, turning the stereo down then up again so that the sound filled the shop, the bass reverberating off the walls.

Catherine continued to stare at him, unperturbed, until he turned the music back down.

'Thank you,' she said.

Marcus shuffled nervously behind the counter.

'Do you know where he is?' Catherine said. 'Your father? It's quite important that we speak to him.'

'Jamaica, i'n he?' Marcus said.

'You know where? Where he might he staying?'

'Jokin', right? How should I know?'

'You're his son.'

Marcus snorted. 'Ask Michael, why don't you? Tell anyone, that's who he's gonna tell. Not me. He don't trust me with anythin'.'

'I'm sure that's not true.'

'No?'

Catherine looked around. 'He trusts you with this.'

'Yeah? I'll tell you how much he trusts me. End of the day, weekend say, I've been workin' here, he'll come in, ask if I've cashed up and when I say yeah an' tell him what it is, the total, right, he opens the cash desk, this in front of me, right in front of my mates, shamin' me, and counts it all again himself, every one fuckin' p. And you think he's gonna tell me where he is when he don't want no one to know?'

'I'm sorry,' Catherine said.

Marcus gave her a hard stare. 'What you got to be sorry about?'

Early evening, Karen went to the pub with Michaelson and a few more of the team, stood a round, left some money behind the bar and set off with Mike Ramsden to get something to eat. Someone had recommended an Indian restaurant close to the square, unprepossessing enough from the outside for Ramsden to compare it to the Wimpy Bars of his pimply youth. 'Fat plastic tomatoes full of dodgy sauce on all the tables, you'll see.'

Thankfully he was wrong in just about every respect.

True, the setting was plain, the walls largely unadorned, no fuss or furbelows, the service without pretension, but the food . . . the food, they both agreed, was excellent.

'Best Indian,' Ramsden said, waving a poppadom, 'since I was last down Brick Lane.'

She eyed him sceptically. 'When were you ever down Brick Lane?'

Ramsden grinned. 'You don't know, do you? The kind of cosmopolitan life I lead. Hobnobbing with our Muslim brothers.'

Sometimes, when he and Karen were together, he

would adopt the tones and prejudices of a dyed-in-the-wool cockney oik. It was a tricky line to tread and there had been times, one or two, when he had veered dangerously close to overstepping the mark.

'Shut up,' Karen said, 'and pass me the spinach.'

Earlier in the day, Ramsden had joined Frank Michaelson in re-interviewing the taxi driver who had driven Lynn Kellogg home from the station.

There had been no one else on the street when he had dropped Lynn Kellogg off, he was certain of that. No one outside the house. As soon as she was out of the cab he'd driven off. A fare waiting, Mapperley Plains.

'Time's money,' he said. 'You know what I mean?'

'What about the shots?' Ramsden had asked. 'Two shots, close together. Surely you heard those?'

The cab driver shook his head. 'If I did, I thought it was a car backfiring. Didn't give it any mind.'

Pressed, he confirmed there had been a car parked down on the right, dark, he thought. Dark blue or black. Sierra? So many cars nowadays, they all look the same. But he thought it was a Sierra.

'You think?' Ramsden had pushed him. 'You think or you're sure?'

'It was dark.'

'I know. We know.'

'I couldn't swear to it . . .'

'You don't have to swear. All you have to do is be certain. Certain about what you saw.'

'All right, then, it was a Sierra.'

'You're sure?'

The danger was, as Karen reminded Ramsden later, push too hard and what the witness gives you is what they think you want to hear. But, in the absence of a great deal else, they would go with the Sierra. The new number-plate-recognition software that was linked to Traffic would help them to trace any such vehicles that had been in the vicinity thirty minutes either side of the murder.

Re-canvassing the neighbours had yielded little new.

The Peugeot had been struck off their list as a possible getaway car when one of the youths who'd borrowed it for a little joyriding came reluctantly forward after watching the news, anxious to clear himself of any involvement in a fatal shooting.

The partial shoe print that had been lifted had a quite distinctive studded sole – an Adidas trainer, almost certainly, the oddly named ZX 500 Animal – but knowing that and having nothing yet to match it to, didn't get them very far at all.

FSS were still running tests on the bullets and cartridge cases and the promised report had yet to arrive.

Progress was slow.

'Brent's old lady,' Ramsden asked, tearing off a piece of naan to wipe round his plate, 'that kid of hers – you believe them about not knowing where he is?'

Karen sighed. 'Who knows?'

They had tried contacting Michael Brent in London, but so far to no avail.

'But on balance?' Ramsden persevered.

'I don't know, Mike, I really don't.'

'You haven't got any contacts out there yourself?'

'Not the kind that'd be useful, no. Operation Trident, though, back in the Met, their intelligence section's got pretty good contacts with the Jamaican police. I can pull a couple of favours from this DS I know on—'

'I'll bet.'

'Shut it!'

Ramsden laughed and raised his hands in surrender. 'Wouldn't hurt to ask if they've flagged anyone likely coming into the country round about the time of the shooting.' He winked. 'Always assuming your favours go that far.'

'Your mouth's going to get you in a lot of trouble one day.'

Ramsden winked. 'I wish.'

Treading the line, treading the line . . .

Karen's serviced apartment was in a converted hospital building on the Ropewalk, overlooking the centre of the city, and not much more than a five-minute walk from where she and Mike Ramsden had had dinner. Sand-coloured walls, neutral carpeting, everything just this side of pristine. In the living room there was a pair of wicker chairs that seemed, oddly, to have strayed in from a conservatory, and a two-seater settee, upholstered in black, that looked smart rather than comfortable. On a low table in front of the settee, the management had left a bottle of red wine and two glasses, the second glass in case, presumably, she struck lucky. The bed, she was pleased to see, was a decent size and furnished with white linen; a single, deep-red cushion to match the twin lamps at either side. The bathroom was serviceable but small, the kitchen area likewise.

Karen found a corkscrew and opened the wine, an Aussie Shiraz rich enough to live with the aftertaste of her Indian meal. For some little time she stood at the window, glass in hand, looking out, letting the thoughts of the day jostle for space in her mind, the faint hum of the city pierced every now and again by the urgency of a police siren or the sound of an ambulance hurrying to an emergency. She wondered about Resnick and whether he were alone and assumed that he was, picturing him wandering heavily, lost, from room to room. She tried to imagine what it would be like to have the person you loved shot down more or less in front of your eyes, and failed. What was that song Bessie Smith used to sing? Something about waking up lonely, cold in hand.

Slipping one of the CDs Resnick had lent her on to the stereo, she topped up her glass. 'Downhearted Blues'. Bessie Smith's first recording, 1923. Bessie proclaiming trouble was going to follow her to her grave.

Tell the truth, girl, Karen thought, tell the truth. Trouble from being black, trouble with love, trouble with men. Once, her mother had told her, when Bessie discovered that her husband was having an affair with one of the chorus girls who worked in her show, she beat the girl up and threw her off the train on which they'd been travelling, then went after her husband with a gun, chasing him down the tracks and taking potshots as she ran. Not that Bessie was averse to the occasional chorus girl herself.

Almost the last thought Karen had before falling asleep echoed that of Catherine Njoroge the day before: nowhere's safe, we can reach you anywhere, even at home, where you feel safest. Nowhere's safe, Karen thought, not any more. As her eyes closed, the night was rent by the rising wail of sirens once more.

28

Resnick woke rimed in sweat. He thought it was Lynn's voice that had woken him and then, almost immediately after, something had brushed against his face. It was a little past four in the morning, nine years before, her voice, nervous and uncertain on the telephone: 'Sir, it's DC Kellogg. Sorry to disturb you, but I think you'd better come out.'

The house had been on Devonshire Promenade, overlooking the park. Close to a full moon and cold. Lynn and another officer had been first to the scene and it was Lynn who had noticed the door out into the garden was not quite closed. She who had found one of the woman's shoes, high-heeled and black, tainted with mud, and then the woman herself, half-naked, one arm stretching out towards a mound of recently turned earth, the other reaching up in a graceful curve behind her head. Dark lines of blood like ribbons through her hair.

By the time Resnick had arrived, other officers and an ambulance crew were already at the scene. In the kitchen, someone had made tea. He spooned two sugars into the offered cup and carried it through to the front of the house.

Lynn had been standing close to the window, shoulders tensed.

'Here,' he'd said, and she'd taken the cup, unsteadily, in both hands.

Her face, normally ruddy, had seemed unnaturally pale.

There had just been time for Resnick to ask how she was feeling before the cup fell through her hands and she had pitched forward, his arms reaching out automatically to catch her, her face pressed against his chest, the fingers of one outflung hand snagged for a moment inside the corner of his mouth.

Outside, beyond the curtains, only the blue light of a police car had pierced the dark. Lynn's hand against his face. The first time they had really touched.

He woke again later, cold, to a cold room. Another day. A member of the force's Occupational Health Unit had been round to see him the previous afternoon. Help and counselling. Stress management. A brisk little chat and a cup of tea, that seemed to be the idea. Bereavement, he was told, affected different people in different ways: sometimes it resulted in a loss of identity, a sense that you could no longer function, that somehow you were the one who had ceased to exist; more commonly, there

314

was a refusal to believe the truth of what had happened and accept the reality of death. Insomnia, agitation, different kinds of anxiety, those were all to be expected. Sudden changes of temperature and mood.

'Think,' the visitor said cheerily, 'of all the bits and pieces of your nervous system being placed into a sack and given such a shaking that they don't know where they are. For a while, some of them may even cease to function at all. That's what you're going through.

'It's only natural,' he continued, 'that this sense of loss you're experiencing will leave you feeling depressed. Absolutely natural. And the closer you were to the deceased, the more dependent you might have been on one another day to day, the stronger this depression might be.' He smiled helpfully. 'Talk to your GP, he'll prescribe something to get you through the worst. And if you think it will help to talk some more, either to me or someone else, a counsellor, don't hesitate, let me know.'

He put a card down on the table, next to his cup.

A neat little man in a neat blue suit.

Somehow his visit had given Resnick the impetus to make the call he'd been dreading, Lynn's mother slow to pick up the phone and then when she did, disintegrating into tears at the mention of her daughter's name.

At least he had not been the one whose task it had been to break the news, some family liaison officer deputed to do that and doing it well, Resnick didn't doubt, properly trained, the right balance of clarity and care.

Not quite trusting himself to drive, he took the mid-morning train, an apparently endless journey across country – flat fields for the most part, deep drainage ditches in the dark soil of the Fens – through Ely and Cambridge and on to Norwich, where he would change to the small local train to Diss.

He bought a cup of lukewarm coffee and a sandwich from the trolley and glanced at the Nottingham paper he'd picked up before leaving.

POLICE IN SEARCH FOR MISSING FATHER.
Officers investigating the death of their colleague,
Detective Inspector Lynn Kellogg, who was slain
by an unknown gunman outside her Alexandra
Park home, were last night seeking the where-
abouts of Howard Brent, whose sixteen-year-old
daughter, Kelly, was shot and killed in St Ann's on
Valentine's Day. It is believed that Mr Brent may
have left the country . . .

He cast the paper aside.

At the opposite side of the aisle, a middle-aged woman glanced across at him for a moment and then looked away.

He had made a similar journey some years before, though by car; out towards the coast by the most circuitous route possible, never wanting to arrive. The girl's body had been found inside black bin bags on the floor of a disused building, close by the line he was now travelling. She had been missing for sixty-three days.

316

One of the first such investigations he and Lynn had worked as part of a team. When the girl's mother had been told a body had been discovered that might be that of her daughter, all she had said was, 'About fucking time!'

Not much bereavement there.

Mostly, the girl had been brought up by her grandmother, who, after the child had disappeared – had been taken – had left the city and moved to a thirties bungalow on the coast in Mablethorpe, cut herself off from everyone, shut herself away with her guilt. She was the one who had left the girl in the park, playing on the swings, for just five minutes while she ran to the corner shop. Resnick had promised, early on, that he would break the news to her himself.

'Listen,' he told her, 'what happened, it wasn't your fault.'

'No? Then who was it who ran off and left her there? Off round the corner for a packet of fags? Who?'

There must be days, Resnick had thought, when it was all she could do to stop herself walking out across the expanse of greying sand and on into the cold waters of the North Sea.

The first time Resnick had visited, Lynn's father had proudly walked him round the hen houses, sucking away at the pipe which served to keep the worst of the stench at bay. Resnick, polite and wanting, if not to impress, then, for Lynn's sake, not to antagonise, had kept his counsel, held his breath for as long as he could.

317

Back indoors, Lynn's mother could not bring herself to address him directly. 'Does he take sugar?' she had asked of Lynn, even though Resnick had been sitting there at the kitchen table, fully able to answer for himself. Only when her husband had been dying, his cancer unstoppable, had she softened towards him. 'Look after her,' she'd said, clutching at his hands. 'She's all I've got now.'

The chicken farm had been sold, swallowed up by some giant conglomerate, and Mrs Kellogg had bought a small flat in the market town of Diss and shored herself up with the Methodist Church and the Women's Institute, book talks in the local library once a month and, in June, two local choirs in 'A Celebration of English Song'.

She had bought a lemon cake against Resnick's coming, made sandwiches with ham and cucumber, put on a clean pinafore, set the kettle to boil the minute she heard his footsteps approach the door.

She had made up her mind: she wasn't going to cry. She was not. The moment she saw his face, her own broke apart. Resnick held her while she sobbed, small bones hard and brittle against his hands, the front of his shirt damp with her tears.

He finished making the tea and carried everything through from the kitchen, best plates on a tray, the size of the rooms making him feel awkward and over-large.

'She told me,' she said, cup and saucer unsteady in her hand, 'the young woman who came, she said it was all very sudden. That Lynn . . . that she wouldn't really have known what was happening.'

'No,' Resnick said, 'that's right.'

'She wouldn't have suffered then?'

He saw again the bottom half of Lynn's face, torn open to the bare bone of her jaw, and smelt again the blood. 'No. I don't think so,' he said.

'That's a blessing, then, at least.'

They sat with their tea and cake and sandwiches, a clock somewhere striking the quarter-hour and then the half.

'I've been trying to think about the funeral,' she said, abruptly. 'I just don't know what's for the best.'

Resnick nodded, non-committally. He knew it would be a while, at best, before the body would be released. Having opened the inquest and established the cause of death, the coroner would adjourn it again while the investigation continued. If there were an arrest reasonably soon, the accused's defence team would have the option of a second post-mortem; failing that, and with no arrest in sight, the coroner could arrange for a second, independent post-mortem himself and then release the body, but with a burial certificate only, barring cremation.

'I'd like her to be lain next to her dad,' Lynn's mother said. 'I think she'd have wanted that, don't you?'

'I'm sure,' Resnick said, 'that would be fine.'

'Please,' she said, reaching towards the table, 'have a piece more cake. I bought it specially for you.'

319

It was like ashes in his mouth.

On the way home, he dozed fitfully, the dark coming in to meet him across the fields. Crossing from the station, he walked into the nearest pub, an old travellers' hotel, ordered a large Scotch and carried it to a table, delaying the moment when he would turn the key in the lock and step back through the door.

'You ought to sell that place of yours,' Lynn's mother had said as he was leaving. 'Get yourself some- where like this. It'll be easier to manage, now you're on your own.' Her kiss, dry and quick on his cheek.

He bought a second whisky and stood drinking it at the bar. A large television screen, high in one corner, was showing a soccer match from the Spanish *Liga*, with a commentary running across the bottom of the screen in Arabic. Seated at a table immediately below it, but not watching, unconcerned, a grey-haired man in an ageing three-piece suit sat nursing a pint of Guinness and speaking, at intervals, to someone opposite who was no longer there.

The bank of fruit machines on the far wall was going full swing.

Further along the bar, two coach drivers, still in their uniform, were conducting an earnest conversation in Polish, not close enough for Resnick to understand every word, but it seemed to revolve around the poor facilities on the Autobahn east of Hanover.

'Another?' the barman asked.

Resnick shook his head. 'Best not.'

He walked past the bus station and along the underpass that would take him on to Lister Gate and from there up towards the Old Market Square.

A *Big Issue* seller Resnick had once arrested for breaking and entering accosted him as he was crossing Upper Parliament Street, close by the restaurant where he and Lynn were to have celebrated Valentine's Day. A city this size, she was everywhere.

'*Big Issue*?' The man smiled broadly through broken teeth. 'Help the homeless. Just these left.'

Resnick bought all three.

A dozen young women in varying stages of undress came cavorting down the street towards him, blowing kisses and shrieking loudly, someone's hen night off to an early start.

'I don't fancy yours much,' one of them shouted with a laugh, as a blonde in a silk top and skintight pants collided with Resnick and caught hold of his arm so as not to lose her balance altogether and go sprawling.

When she'd gone, stumbling after her mates, there was powder on his sleeve.

As he turned off the main road and into the narrow, poorly made-up road that led to his house, a chill settled over his bones. When he was no more than thirty metres off, he thought he saw something move in the shadow at the side of the building, just a few paces from the front door, exactly where Lynn's killer would have stood. Resnick stopped, the backs of his legs and arms like ice, his breath caught in his throat. Imagination, he thought, like so much else? Two, three steps and then he quickened his pace, breaking almost into a run, slowing again when he reached the gate.

'Charlie . . .'

He recognised Graham Millington's voice before he saw him, his former sergeant stepping forward to greet him, hand outstretched. 'Charlie . . . Thought I'd best come by, see how you were getting on.'

29

That Friday morning, the day Resnick was making his reluctant journey east to visit Lynn's mother, Karen had an appointment to see Stuart Daines.

It was an easy walk from her apartment, down towards Wellington Circus, the building anonymous, only the number to mark it out. Daines had assured Karen he would be at his desk by eight thirty, nine at the latest, and he was true to his word, busy at his laptop when she arrived, and begging a moment before saving whatever was on the screen. He was quick then to shake her hand, pull out a chair and make her welcome, Karen briefly returning his smile, noting the crisp pink shirt with the cuffs turned back, the Tag Heuer watch, the fleck of green in the corner of one eye.

'DI Kellogg's murder,' Daines said pleasantly, 'there was something you wanted to ask.'

'Just one or two things,' Karen said, almost casual. 'Background really.'

'Of course, anything I can do you think might help. What happened, it was terrible. I mean, I didn't know her that well, but she seemed committed to what she was doing. Efficient. A good officer.' He leaned forward a little in his chair. 'Like I say, I didn't really know her well at all.'

'You didn't send her flowers?'

'I'm sorry?'

'Flowers. You sent her flowers.'

'Oh, yes, of course. I'd forgotten. There was this incident, not so many weeks back, a girl was killed.'

'Kelly Brent?'

'Yes. Kellogg had somehow got involved, ended up stopping a bullet herself, but, thank God, she'd been wearing a vest. Nothing too serious in the end.'

'You said you didn't know her well,' Karen persisted.

'That's right.'

'Then . . . ?'

Daines smiled. 'We'd met on a SOCA course I'd helped to organise. I'd been kidding her about jumping ship, throwing in with us. A new challenge, I suppose. She hadn't been keen. The flowers, they were just a way of – I don't know – building bridges. Then we met again over this Zoukas business, the trial – you know about that?'

Karen nodded.

'After the trial was adjourned, you went down with her to London, I understand? To talk to one of the witnesses?'

'Andreea Florescu, yes. I thought she might have

324

been able to identify one or two people we're interested in.'

'In what connection?'

'A long-term investigation. Ongoing. Just looking for confirmation, really.' Another smile, there and then gone.

'And could she help?'

'She said not.'

'Which sounds as if you didn't believe her.'

'She was frightened. She might have thought keeping quiet the best policy.'

'But you didn't take it any further?'

Daines crossed his legs, one ankle over the other. 'Like I said, it wasn't crucial, more a case of dotting the "i"s, crossing the "t"s.'

'Did you know,' Karen asked, 'about this last visit DI Kellogg made, the evening she was killed?'

Daines looked puzzled. 'Visit where?'

'To London. To where this Andreea had been staying. The man whose flat she'd been living in was worried about her. Seems to have thought she might take off, disappear.'

'These people,' Daines said, 'they do.'

'These people?'

'You know. Migrants. Asylum seekers. Keeping one step ahead of the authorities if they can.'

'It's my understanding she was here legally, a student visa.'

'Even so.'

'You don't sound too concerned.'

Daines shrugged. 'Bigger fish to fry, I'm afraid.'

'And, just to be clear, you had no idea that's where DI Kellogg had been the evening she was killed?'

Daines shook his head, impatiently. 'I can't see it matters, but no. I thought I said.'

Karen got to her feet. 'There's nothing else you can think of that might be relevant?'

'No, I don't think so. Nothing. I'm sorry. If anything does occur to me, then of course . . .'

Karen gave him a perfunctory smile and turned towards the door.

'The investigation,' Daines said, 'you're making progress?'

'Oh, you know,' Karen said, 'slow but sure.'

'Good luck with it, anyway.' He was back to his computer before she'd left the room.

Outside, it was promising a better day. Karen walked on down the hill and took a seat outside the Playhouse café, opposite a large concave sculpture in shiny metal that shimmered back large sections of sun and cloud. Other than a woman in an expensive-looking black suit, busily working her BlackBerry, she had the place to herself. When the waiter came out, she ordered an Americano with a little cold milk on the side, considered some kind of muffin or maybe a chocolate brownie – to die for, the waiter said, just this side of over-friendly and ever so slightly camp – but finally rejected both. The sight of herself in the mirror that morning, the beginnings of a tummy more obvious

326

than she liked, enough to bring about restraint.

When the coffee came she wished, as she sat there gazing at the metal sheen of sky, that she still smoked. A good few years now since she'd given up and yet, on occasions like this, there was the same faint but insistent need, niggling away. The woman with the BlackBerry – some kind of marketing whizz from the conversation she'd just been having – chose that moment to light up and the nicotiney smell floated across, insidious, on the air.

Karen poured a little milk into her cup. No one, she thought, no man, at least, sent flowers to a woman who wasn't a close relative without there being some kind of sexual or, at least, romantic undertone. And Daines would be the kind of man who would have reckoned himself quite a player where women were concerned – the way he'd looked her over when she'd entered his office, not lecherous exactly, but not disguising it either, his eyes gliding down from her breasts and back again, the beginnings of a smile playing at the edges of his mouth.

So had there been anything between himself and Lynn Kellogg? Not impossible, Lynn some little time into a relationship with a somewhat older, staider man. And, if so, did it matter? Matter as far as the investigation was concerned?

She couldn't immediately see how. Unless Resnick had found out and, jealous, taken matters into his own hands. Othello and Desdemona. Somehow she couldn't believe it.

327

She had the number of the DS she knew from the Met's Operation Trident on her mobile and by some small miracle he answered straight off. 'Karen,' he said, cheerily, 'long time no see.'

'I wonder,' she said, 'if you could find your way to doing me a small favour.'

'One good turn, why not?'

She told him what she wanted.

'Yeah,' the DS said. 'I can do that. Make a few calls. We've got someone stationed out there more or less permanently. But how urgent we talkin' here?'

'Soon as you can?'

'Okay. I'll get back to you.'

Karen thanked him, promised to meet for a drink when she was back in London, and broke the connection.

'Can I get you anything else?' the waiter asked, appearing at her shoulder.

Karen shook her head. 'Just the bill, thanks.'

She left the coins on the table.

If she remembered the layout correctly, it would only take her ten minutes or so to get to the Central Police Station on foot from where she was, a thought nagging her every inch of the way – two shootings, two attempts on the same person's life within what? A month? How much of a coincidence was that?

She bumped into Khan as she was entering the building. 'Anil, thought you were down in London?'

'So I was, boss. Drew a blank.'

'How d'you mean?'

328

'Went to the address, nobody there. Talked to the neighbours, one of them said they saw the man who lived there leaving two days back, some kind of duffel bag over his shoulder. Haven't seen him since.'

'And the woman?'

Khan shook his head.

'You don't think . . .'

'Inside the flat? I went round the local nick, one of the lads came back with me and forced a window. Nobody inside. A few signs the woman had been living there, but not much to say she still was. The man – Bucur – he left a pile of books, clothes – shaving gear, though, toothbrush, that had all gone.'

Karen breathed out slowly. 'All right, get what descriptions you can. Have them circulated – witnesses wanted for questioning – you know the drill.'

'Right, boss.'

'Oh, and Anil, the man charged with Kelly Brent's murder, Williams, is it?'

'Lee Williams, yes.'

'Who interrogated him?'

'DI Resnick, I think. Catherine was with him part of the time. And Michaelson – or maybe it was Pike.'

'Thanks.'

It took the office manager scarcely any time to locate the tapes of the interview and a pair of headphones so that she could listen uninterrupted. Resnick had been thorough and methodical, forceful when necessary. Williams was adamant the only reason he'd gone armed was his own protection, the word having come down that several of the St Ann's gang would be carrying. What else was he supposed to do? And Kelly Brent? The bitch, she got what was coming to her, didn't she? Like all them black bitches. Got no respect. Not a hint of regret in his voice, not even any real sense of what he had done.

'The police officer,' Resnick said. 'She was shot too.'

'Should've kept her nose out of it, shouldn't she?' Williams replied. 'That way she wouldn't've got hurt.'

Resnick had pressed the point a little, but it was obvious that Kelly Brent had been Williams's sole target and that Lynn Kellogg had simply paid the price for doing her job and putting herself in harm's way.

Karen listened to the tape through to the end: other than the fact that Kellogg was the victim in both instances, she could find nothing to link the two shootings.

She had only just returned the tapes when Mike Ramsden came looking for her, flourishing the morning paper, his face set in a scowl.

'You seen this?' he demanded, slapping his hand against the offending page. 'Kid stabbed to death in South London. Lewisham. Running fight along the high street with thirty or more involved. Kicked this one kid in the head and then stabbed him fourteen times. Fourteen fucking times.'

He dropped the paper down on to the nearest desk.

'That girl who was shot a few days back, outside some bar in Leeds. Chatting up the wrong feller. Died last night. Never regained consciousness. It's in there, same paper, couple of lines at the bottom of page nine. Fucking country! Going out of fucking control.'

'Take a deep breath, Mike,' Karen said. 'Count to ten.'

'Okay, okay. It's just sometimes . . .'

'I know.'

'The whole bloody world seems to be going to hell in a handcart.'

'Meantime . . .'

'Meantime what, exactly?'

'Meantime we do our job as best we can.'

'You think it makes one scrap of difference?'

'I think maybe it keeps hell at bay just that bit longer.'

Ramsden cocked his head. 'Know your trouble, don't you?'

'I'm sure you're going to tell me.'

'You're just a hopeless bloody optimist. Fucking great storm, thunder and lightning, pitch bloody dark and you'll be standing there under this pathetic little umbrella – it's okay, it's okay, it's just a shower.'

Karen laughed. 'All right then, give me something to be optimistic about.'

'Not easy.'

'But try.'

Ramsden perched on the edge of a desk. 'We've been going back through investigations Kellogg was involved in, a couple worth looking at twice, but nothing that leaps out and hits you. Otherwise, the shoe, the make of trainer, that's confirmed, but it gets us exactly bloody nowhere. Cigarette ends, the same, probably been there several days before the shooting, thrown from a car, blown in off the road, whatever.'

Karen made a face. 'Anything yet back from Forensics?'

Ramsden shook his head. 'Backed up.'

'Still?'

'They're saying tomorrow.'

'Without fail?'

'Just tomorrow.'

'And the missing Sierra?'

'Possible Sierra.'

'All right, possible Sierra.'

'Still missing.'

'But we're checking?'

'Oh, yes.'

Karen uttered a deep sigh. 'Jesus, Mike. Where are we?'

Ramsden shrugged, smiling. 'Nottingham?'

30

Graham Millington had brought a bottle of good Scotch with him, a Springbank single malt, not cheap. After an awkward quarter of an hour or so, he and Resnick sat and chatted easily enough about old times and how things were going now down in Devon, Millington enjoying the police work, but quite vociferous about the perils of living so close to his in-laws, Madeleine's mother at full throttle, as he put it, being more dangerous than a Kawasaki and sidecar coming at you the wrong way down a one-way street. A jibe based on old-fashioned prejudice and out-of-date mother-in-law clichés, Resnick might have thought, had he not once met the good lady in question, the very thought of it now causing him to duck.

'When she first came to us, you know,' Millington said, 'Lynn . . .' the bottle far enough down for him to broach the subject without embarrassment, '. . . I'll be honest, I was never sure she was going to make it. Not in CID. Bright, certainly, she was always that. Keen, too. Never one to shirk. But quiet, turned in on herself. Country girl, of course, up from the sticks. And the way the squad room was in those days, before this political-correctness bollocks really took hold, not easy for a woman back then – only one in the team especially, which she was. But then there was that time she stood up to Divine, you remember?'

Resnick remembered well enough. Mark Divine, now no longer on the force, had been a thickset rugby-playing DC of the unreconstructed kind, never shy when it came to shooting off his mouth, and on this occasion he had been airing his views on the wife of a colleague who'd been suffering badly from post-natal depression. Divine's callous lack of understanding had reached the point where Lynn had felt compelled to intervene, whereupon he had upped the stakes with a few badly chosen remarks about her love life or the lack of it, the implication being the only way any bloke would fancy her would be if it were pitch dark or if she pulled the proverbial bag down over her head.

Without hesitation, she had slapped him round the side of the face with force enough to rock him back on his heels, the marks of her fingers standing out clearly on his cheek.

It had taken Resnick and one of the other officers to stop Divine from retaliating and a strong lecture afterwards to keep him in line. But Lynn had made her point. And more. Maybe it shouldn't have taken that for her to be accepted, but it had.

'You were a lucky man, Charlie,' Millington said, 'you know that, don't you? Not now, of course, I'd not wish what happened to you on a worst enemy, but back when she took up with you first. A lucky man.'

Resnick nodded, knowing it for the truth.

'You were a miserable old bugger sometimes,' Millington said. 'All those years of living on your own after that wife of yours pulled up sticks and left. Not at work, true, not so much then, but after, standing sour-faced over a pint and then off home with your tail between your legs to feed the bloody cats and listen to some old crone moaning on, one of them jazz singers you're so fond of, Billie what's-her-name.'

He laughed. 'I could never tell what Lynn saw in you, but she did, and that put something of a smile back on your cheeks, a bit of snap in your walk. Gave you a second chance, Charlie, that's what she did. Second chance at a bit of happiness. So be grateful. Not now, it's all too close, too raw, but later. When you can, when you're able. She was a grand lass and she loved you something rotten, though I'm still buggered if I can see why.'

He tipped a little more Scotch into Resnick's glass and then his own.

'There's a match tomorrow, you know. Thought you might fancy it, 'fore I go back. Be a bit like old times, me and you at Meadow Lane, watching the buggers lose.'

Maybe, Resnick thought, maybe. Football had been

far from his mind. And he was still thinking about what Millington had said – lucky, is that what he was?

Well, yes, he thought, taking a sip from his glass. Lucky and unlucky both.

After Elaine had left him for that slippery bastard of an estate agent and argued her way to a divorce, there'd been a couple of short-lived relationships but nothing more and he'd none too fondly imagined keeping his own company for the rest of his life. Cats aside. But then there was Lynn, looking at him now in a different way, and like Millington, he'd wondered what it was she saw in him that was so special. Marvelled at it. Gloried. Spent the first six months in a kind of daze, half-terrified that one morning she would wake up with a start and realise the mistake she'd made, pack her bags and be out the door. And when that didn't happen, he'd allowed himself to relax, to accept that it was all right, it was real, she was here to stay.

In seconds everything had changed.

A moment and she was gone.

He felt cold again and then warm. At least he hadn't burst into tears without warning, not in the last few hours he hadn't. With a sigh, he lifted and drained his glass. Good Scotch or not, he'd have a head like nobody's business come the morning.

Out in the kitchen, he made them both cheese on toast with mustard and Worcester sauce, feeding offcuts of the cheese to the cats. Millington insisted on having his with a pot of tea, strong enough to stand a spoon upright in the cup. The spare bed was already made up. He shunted Millington up ahead of him and pottered around the kitchen for a while, clearing up. He entertained the thought of sitting a while longer on his own, listening to – what had Millington called them, one of those old crones? But, finally, he went upstairs instead. If he slept much past four he'd be thankful.

For the first time in a long while, Resnick's heart failed to lift as he neared the ground, Graham Millington and himself part of the small crowd turning off London Road and crossing the canal, a bright sky but the air suddenly cold enough to catch their breath. Once inside, Millington, more a creature of habit even than Resnick himself, stood in line for cups of Bovril and a brace of meat-and-potato pies. Their seats were close to the halfway line, some ten or twelve rows back, the grass an almost luminous green, promising something special, almost magical.

The first fifteen minutes of mistimed tackles and misplaced passes soon gave a lie to that, the crowd saving most of their invective – officials aside – for the perceived shortcomings of their own team. Never bad enough to occasion a chorus of 'You're Not Fit to Wear the Shirt', but close. Not that the visitors were a whole lot better, a mixture of superannuated cloggers and earnest youngsters, none of them showing much wit or ambition, until, the interval not far off, they went close with a twenty-five-yard volley which the Notts goalkeeper did well to tip over the bar.

'Bloody hell!' Millington said. 'That was a near thing.' And then, glancing sideways, 'Come on, Charlie, they're not playing that badly.'

Resnick was sitting there, shoulders hunched, tears running soundlessly down his face.

The second half was better, the team talk seemed to have worked. Instead of being endlessly booted high up into the heart of the defence, the ball was played out wide to the wings and then whipped across, Jason Lee making his presence felt in the goal mouth, elbows and experience counting equally. It seemed as if they must score – a Lee header bounced back off the post, a shot just cleared by an outstretched boot – and then, with less than five minutes to go, there was a melee in the home-goal mouth following a corner, and the ball squeezed over the line.

Visiting supporters, collected behind the far goal, chanted and jeered. A few of the home fans jeered and gesticulated back, while others, heads down, started to leave. Resnick and Millington, stoics both, waited till the bitter end.

'Nice to know some things don't change,' Millington said, as they were walking away from the ground. 'Still know how to throw three points away just this side of the final whistle.'

At the station they shook hands. Millington was catching a train down to Leicester, meeting up with another old colleague before travelling back to Devon the following day.

'Look after yourself,' he said.

338

Resnick nodded, forcing a smile. 'Do my best.'

Instead of taking one of the waiting taxis, he opted to walk.

31

Resnick couldn't understand the volume of traffic noise drifting off the main road, nor the fact that the light making its way through the curtains was so bright – not until he checked the bedside clock and found it was a few minutes short of eleven o'clock. The first decent sleep he'd had in ages.

And he was hungry, too.

After a brisk shower he laid strips of bacon along the grill, whisked eggs in a basin with pepper and salt and a couple of shakes of Tabasco, and while the omelette pan was heating, set the coffee pot on the stove.

Breakfast over – or had that been lunch? – he called to ask about the release of Lynn's body for burial. Given the circumstances and the fact that the cause of death was scarcely open to question, the coroner said he would be happy to arrange for a second post-mortem himself, after which the burial could go ahead. All he needed was an okay from the senior investigating officer, confirming that no arrest was imminent.

Resnick thanked him and dialled the Central Police Station to speak to Karen Shields, but had to content himself with leaving a message. Bill Berry took his call next, but sounded so awkward and ill at ease that Resnick made an excuse and rang off.

Nothing for it but to walk into town.

The indoor market in the Victoria Centre had been in danger of being closed down several times, half of the stalls having fallen empty or changed hands, until a last-minute effort and a lick of paint had just prevented the whole enterprise from collapsing completely. The coffee stall which Resnick had patronised for more years than he cared to remember had an air now of being abandoned and the few customers sitting disconsolately around it looked like passengers stranded at an airport from which flights no longer departed.

He drank his espresso slowly and read the report of the match in yesterday evening's paper. *Notts' misery at the last*. He could remember when it hadn't always been like that, but that memory was fading fast.

His mobile rang so rarely that he failed to realise at first that it was his. Karen Shields was returning his call: if he wasn't doing anything special why didn't he come in to the station and she'd bring him up to speed?

Walking into the building, he felt like a man with the plague. Officers he knew by sight and who knew him at least by name, turned their backs when they saw him approaching and busied themselves elsewhere; others shook his hand and offered condolences without ever

341

once looking him in the eye. Only Catherine Njoroge made a point of seeking him out and asking how he was coping, then listening to the answer as if she cared.

Karen Shields, he noticed, had pinned a photograph above her desk of a woman he took, from the resemblance, to be her mother, alongside a grainy picture of Bessie Smith downloaded from the computer.

'How was it?' she asked. 'Coming in?'

Resnick shrugged heavy shoulders. 'I hadn't realised being in mourning was a contagious disease.'

'People are embarrassed. They don't know what to say so they end up saying nothing at all.'

He pulled out a chair and sat opposite her and she noted the deep shadows around his eyes.

'You've not been sleeping.'

'Not till today.'

'It'll pass.'

With time, he imagined, she'd be right: what was extraordinary would become normal and he would carry on.

'I was speaking to the coroner earlier,' he said. 'It needs your say-so before arrangements can be made for the funeral.'

Karen nodded. 'We're still some way off making an arrest. And besides, I can't see there's anything for any defence to get specially exercised about. I'll call him first thing.'

'Thanks.'

'You must find it frustrating, knowing the

investigation is going on and not being able to be a part of it.'

'I didn't at first. I don't think I was able to concentrate on anything. Didn't seem to be able to think clearly at all.'

'And now?'

'You could try me.'

She reached for a file and slid it across the desk. 'This came through last thing yesterday.'

It was a printout of the report from Huntingdon. The markings identified the weapon used as a 9mm Baikal IZH-79 pistol and confirmed that both bullets had been fired from the same gun.

'The reason for keeping the report back an extra day,' Karen said, 'they were double-checking the markings against the database. A batch of the same guns was seized in a raid last spring.'

'Seized by the Met?'

'Met and Customs both.'

'SOCA, then?'

'Not exactly. At least, I don't think so. SOCA wasn't launched until April and this operation went down in May and would have been set up a long time before that.'

'You're following it up?'

Karen nodded. 'I've spoken to one of the officers involved and he's passed on a message to the DCI who was running the Met end of things. He's on a course somewhere but he's promised to give me a call back. From what I understand, there've been several small batches of these weapons making their way into the country for eighteen months or more. Some have been intercepted, but not all.'

'And the ones that weren't could be anywhere by now.'

'Absolutely.'

'There's no word about the shooter coming in off the street?' Resnick asked.

'Not so far.'

'If anybody knew anything, you'd have thought there'd be a whisper by now.'

'One of the local firms has offered to put up a reward for information.'

'It might help. Difficult to say. Danger is, you'll get people clogging up the lines who know next to nothing, but'll make stuff up in the hope of getting their hands on the money.'

'I know.'

Resnick shifted in his chair. 'Still no sign of Brent, I presume?'

'Nothing. As far as we know, he's still in Jamaica. We're liaising with the police there as much as we can, but it's not easy. And he's not the only one missing.'

'How d'you mean?'

'Alexander Bucur and Andreea Florescu. They seem to have been missing since the day after the murder.'

'You think there's a connection?'

Karen smiled. 'Depends how much faith you put in coincidence.'

'The reason Lynn went down, Andreea was

frightened. I know from what Lynn told me, she'd been threatened before.'

'This was over the Zoukas case?'

'Yes. They warned her with what might happen if she agreed to give evidence.'

'Which she did.'

Resnick nodded.

'There's every sign,' Karen said, 'she and Alexander have both done a runner.'

'Together?'

'Not as far as we know.'

Karen's phone rang suddenly. 'I'll be right down,' she said, and then, to Resnick, 'Howard Brent's just walked into the station under his own steam.'

The reception area was busy: a couple of youths sitting morosely, one nursing a bloodied nose; a man in camouflage trousers and a Forest shirt, half his hair shaven away where a wound had been stitched; another man, older, with greying dreadlocks, reciting from the Bible, and a young woman, skinny and pale, holding a four- or five-month-old baby against her chest, while another child, barely a year older, alternately wailed and grizzled from the buggy by her side.

In the midst of all this stood Howard Brent. Black leather jacket, white T-shirt, dark wide-legged trousers, black-and-white leather shoes; diamond stud in his left ear, gold chain round his neck. Handsome. Tall. As Karen entered, Resnick close behind her, he stood taller still.

Seeing Resnick, his eyes gleamed.

'I hear your woman died,' he said. 'Shot dead, ain't it? Shot through the head. An' you know how that make me feel?' His face broke into a smile. 'That makes me feel good, you know? Good inside. 'Cause now you know. You know what it's like. To have someone you love—'

Resnick charged at him, head down, fists raised.

At the last moment, Brent sidestepped and stuck out a leg, tripping Resnick so that he went headlong, all balance gone, one arm twisting beneath him, his face slamming into the wall where it met the floor.

Two uniformed officers seized Brent by the arms and pulled him back.

Karen went to where Resnick lay, barely moving, on the ground.

Brent still smiling, shaking his head.

'Ambulance,' Karen shouted. 'Now.'

When she and another officer helped Resnick to sit up, there was a cut above his right eye which was closing fast and blood from his broken nose had splattered all down the front of his shirt.

32

One of the paramedics reset Resnick's nose before leading him to the ambulance. 'There,' he said, as Resnick screamed. 'Better than new.'

At the hospital, seven stitches were inserted over his cut eye and an X-ray determined that his left elbow, though extremely painful, was badly bruised and not broken; a precautionary CT scan revealed no intracranial haemorrhaging. Patched up and armed with a healthy dose of ibuprofen, he was sent on his way. Medical expertise could do nothing for his injured pride, the overwhelming sense of his own stupidity.

With unwonted speed, the force's Professional Standards Unit rolled into action. At a little after ten the following morning, the police surgeon deemed Resnick, somewhat conveniently, to be suffering from post-traumatic stress syndrome and registered him as officially unfit for duty.

*

'Fine welcome,' Brent had said, when Resnick was being led off towards the waiting ambulance. 'Come in of my own volition, hear you wantin' to speak to me, and what happen? This feller come chargin' at me like a wild bull, no cause, no reason.'

'There was cause,' Karen said sharply.

'You think?'

'You deliberately provoked him, wound him up on purpose.'

'What I did,' Brent said, a smile playing in his eyes, 'express my sympathy. For his loss, you know?'

'His injuries are as bad as they might be, you could be facing some serious charges.'

Brent scoffed. 'Anyone bring charges here, it's me. Assault, yeah? Actual bodily harm.' He pronounced each syllable lovingly. 'Like I say, he the one come chargin' at me, all I did, step out the way. Ask anyone.' He swept his arm in a circle. 'Go ahead. Ask these people here. Take witness statements, yeah? Ask these people what they see.'

Karen knew Brent was right. Provoked or not, Resnick had lost it completely. In many ways it was fortunate that Brent had swerved out of Resnick's path as adroitly as he did. Had he sustained anything approaching a serious injury, then not only Resnick but the force itself could be facing charges of misconduct and a battery of claims for compensation.

She asked one of the uniformed officers to fetch Brent a glass of water, asked Brent whether he would like to take a seat while she found out which interview room was most readily available. Ramsden could sit in with her during the questioning, but Ramsden on a short leash.

'You've been out of the country,' Karen said.

There were no cameras switched on, no recordings being made, no lawyer present; Brent was there, as he'd said, of his own volition, and could leave, unhindered, at any time. Unless, of course, anything he admitted to gave sufficient cause for him to be restrained.

'A few days, yeah.'

'Jamaica.'

'After what happened, a break, you know?'

'Visiting family?'

Brent made a sound midway between a snort and a laugh. 'My family back home, they fell out with me long time back. We don't speak, don't text, don't telephone.' He shrugged. 'Their loss, okay? Not mine.'

'Then why . . . ?' Karen began.

'Friends. I got friends there.'

'Girlfriends?'

Brent smiled. 'Just friends, let's say.'

'Colleagues? Business acquaintances?'

'Business acquaintances, sure.'

'What business, exactly, might that be?'

'My business.'

'Your catering business or your music business?'

Brent smiled. 'I come back with a few new recipes, somethin' to try, maybe, at the restaurant, make some changes. Keep the chef on his toes. And some new

349

recordin's, too. DaVille. Jovi Rockwell. Business an' pleasure, you know?'

'Your wife,' Karen said, 'Tina. She claimed not to know where you were.'

'Tina, she know what she need to know, that's all.'

'There was no contact between you while you were away?'

The smile, quick and lascivious, was back on his face. 'I expect she dream of me a bit, you know.'

Ramsden would have liked to knock the smile, cocky bastard, off his face once and for all. 'How did you hear about DI Kellogg's death?' he asked.

'We have newspapers over there, you know. Television. The Internet.'

'That's how you heard about it, on the Internet?'

Brent sat straighter. 'My son, Michael, he told me. Called me on his mobile as soon as he heard.'

'And what did you do?' Karen asked. 'What went through your mind?'

'Be honest, I feel sorry for her, that my first thought. Sorry she lose her life in such a violent act. Still a young woman, eh? Then I go out and buy champagne. Drink a toast with my friends.'

'You were glad.'

Brent inclined his head, not answering.

'You wished her dead.'

'What I wish, my daughter's life back. But that I cannot have. But now that Resnick he knows what it is to lose the one person you love in the world most of all. An' yes, that make me feel glad. Here.'

He laid his fist over his heart.

'How much?' Mike Ramsden said suddenly, leaning close towards him.

Karen looked at him sharply, but he carried on.

'Enough to arrange for it to be done?' Ramsden continued, bearing down. 'Bought and paid for, while you're sunning yourself a few thousand miles away, drinking rum and Coke with your friends?'

'That's what you think?' Brent said, voice raised. 'That's what you want me to come here for, to accuse me of that?' He stared at Ramsden hard. 'What you gonna do now? Get out the handcuffs? Make me confess? Or you gonna let me go an' follow me? Stop me in the street and throw me up against the wall, huh? Search my clothes? Harass my family, harass my friends? Each time I go out in the car, someone pull me over, something wrong with your brake light, mister, or book me for speedin', thirty-two mile an hour in a thirty-mile zone? Maybe I find my post opened? My telephone tapped?' He snorted dismissively and rose to his feet. 'Do what you want till doomsday, try all you can, I'm tellin' you, you never gonna lay this at my door.'

Karen took a breath. 'Thank you for your cooperation, Mr Brent,' she said. 'If we want to talk to you again, we'll let you know.'

Ten minutes later, Brent escorted from the building, they were standing in Karen's temporary office.

'Nice going, Mike.'

351

'What?'

'Subtle, the way you went about finessing things out of him.'

'Got under my skin, didn't he?'

'Really? I'd never have noticed.'

'Bollocks,' Ramsden said.

'What did you think?' Karen asked. 'That you could shake it out of him? Ruffle his feathers and he'd fall to pieces at your feet?'

'He's a prick.'

'Doubtless. Two pricks going at it together. Mine's bigger than yours.'

Ramsden put up a hand as if to ward her off. 'Okay, okay.'

Karen turned towards the window and saw her reflection, featureless against a greying sky.

'So,' Karen said, 'what did you think?'

'Seriously?'

'Seriously.'

'I wish Resnick had hit him where it hurts and done some serious damage, instead of wallowing in like some overfed water buffalo and letting Brent take the piss. But that's not what you want to know.'

'No.'

'You want to know, do I think he was responsible for Kellogg's death?'

'Yes.'

Ramsden gave himself a moment. 'Did he want her dead? Yes, think so, beyond a fragment of doubt. Longed for it. With every bone of his jumped-up, miserable body. But did he have the balls, the nous, the wherewithal to set it up, then give himself a nice alibi by being out of the country, I don't know.' He ran his hand down across his mouth. 'There's doers and talkers, you know what I mean? And up to yet, I'm not too sure which Brent is.'

'He could be both.'

'He could. And he's some talker, I'll give him that. Gift of the fucking gab. But the rest . . .' Ramsden shook his head, uncertain.

'What's the feeling amongst the troops?'

'Before today? They'd like to pin it on him, all the stuff he's been coming out with especially. And, yes, I'd say some of them like him for it, but that might just be lazy thinking, you know?'

'So we should forget about him? Cross him off the list?'

'In a pig's ear!'

'What then?'

'We keep chasing down all the other lines of inquiry. By the book. You know that better than me. But, mean-time, let's double-check Brent's contacts, ask around. Have the troops keep their ears to the ground, get every informant working overtime.'

Karen nodded. 'I can chase up that guy I know from Trident, see if we can't find out a little more about who Brent was seeing when he was in Jamaica.'

'And then, of course,' Ramsden said, face breaking into a grin, 'there's always stopping him in the street and throwing him up against the wall . . .'

Karen phoned the hospital later that evening to be told that Resnick had been treated and allowed home. When she phoned his house there was no answer. She rang him at nine the following morning and then again at ten: still no reply. She could understand, she thought, why he might not want to be speaking to anyone, least of all her.

33

'My God!' Jackie Ferris exclaimed. 'What happened to you?'

'Don't ask,' Resnick said. The skin around his swollen left eye was a dramatic purple tinged with yellow and green; the centre of his face, all around the nose, was blue shading into black. An artist's palette run amok.

They were in the Assembly House, Kentish Town, Ferris's pub of choice. Monday lunchtime, quiet, only a few tables occupied. A lone drinker at the bar. The sound of traffic accelerating away from the lights outside enough to muffle what conversation there was. Among the cards and letters Resnick had received after Lynn's death, expressing sympathy, Jackie Ferris's had been one of the most heartfelt and to the point.

'I take it,' Jackie said, 'you didn't fall off your bike?'

'Not exactly.'

355

'The other feller, then? How does he look?'

'Not a scratch.'

Jackie lifted her glass. Coke with ice and lemon, hours to go still till the end of her day. 'How've you been, Charlie?' she asked.

'You know, okay.'

'Don't fob me off, Charlie.'

'All right. At first I could hardly sleep, a few hours at most. I wandered round as if I were in some kind of daze. Didn't know where I was, when it was. And cold, a lot of the time I was cold. Shivering cold. And Lynn, she was everywhere . . .'

'Oh, Charlie . . .'

'Everywhere I looked. Not just at home, but out in the city. I'd see her on the bus or just across the street, the back of her head just turning a corner. I still do. Once today, coming here. And I can't . . .' He shook his head. 'I keep bursting into tears, no warning, no reason.'

'You've got reason.'

'Standing at the counter waiting to buy a loaf of bread and suddenly these tears were running down my face. I felt . . . ridiculous.'

'You're grieving. What do you expect?'

'Going crazy, that's what I'm doing. A little bit crazy.'

Jackie smiled. 'It's not crazy. It's normal. Perfectly natural.'

'That's what he said, the bereavement counsellor. Absolutely natural.'

356

'Well, he's right.'

'I suppose so.'

'How long is it, Charlie? How long's it been? Not long.'

He held her gaze. 'You want the hours, the minutes, or just the days?'

She placed her hand over his. 'I'm sorry.'

'I know.'

'And I need a real drink.' Pushing her Coke aside, she got to her feet. 'You want anything?'

Resnick's pint was barely touched. 'I'm fine.'

Jackie Ferris came back from the bar with a large Scotch, just a little water. She could pick up some mints on the way back to the station.

'You saw her not so long before it happened,' Resnick said, 'one evening, before she caught the train back to Nottingham.'

Jackie nodded.

'How was she?'

'She was . . . she was good. It was great to see her. I was teasing her about this bloke behind the bar, I remember. We had a laugh.'

'Did she say anything?'

'How d'you mean?'

'Anything that might have some bearing on what happened.'

'I don't think so. She'd been to see this woman over in Leyton. Andreea something? Herself and someone called Daines . . .'

'From SOCA.'

'That's right. The two of them went together and then Lynn nipped back later alone. She wanted to talk to this Andreea on her own. Apparently she claimed to have seen Daines getting his rocks off in some dodgy sauna where she was working, being pally with the owner. But when they'd been at the flat earlier, Daines had looked right through her, as if he'd never seen her before at all.'

'She challenged him about it later. She told me.'

'What did he say?'

'Denied it. Said the girl was lying. Told Lynn to mind her own business in no uncertain terms.'

Jackie raised an eyebrow. 'She didn't trust him, that was obvious. Said she was going to ask around, I don't know where. I said I'd do the same.'

'And did you?'

Jackie took a sip from her glass. 'There was a joint operation, came to a head round here, about a year ago now. Customs and Excise and the Met. Illegal firearms. Four arrests.'

'You were involved?'

'Not directly. But I know a couple of people who were. Not that they were exactly forthcoming. Daines was with Customs and Excise then – this was before SOCA really got going – part of the team. A lot of the information they were using came from him.'

'It worked out?'

'Spot on, apparently. Kept surveillance on this café where it was all due to go down. Made the exchange between lattes. Red-handed didn't come into it. Semi-automatics and ammo packed into a rucksack with an old peace sign on the back.' She smiled. 'Someone with a sense of humour, at least.'

'Four arrests, that's what you said?'

'Yes. And three sent for trial. Found guilty, all of them. Ten years apiece.'

'The one who walked, he was what? Someone's informant.'

'Looks that way. And not just to me. He was found three months later. Over in Ireland. County Wexford. Nailed to a tree.'

Resnick winced at the thought.

Jackie drank a little more of her Scotch.

'These people you spoke to,' Resnick said, 'there wasn't any suggestion about Daines being, I don't know, dodgy in one way or another?'

Jackie shook her head. 'Not really. I meant to dig a little deeper, get back to Lynn and pass on what little I'd heard, but then . . .'

'Yes.'

Resnick's beer tasted sour; his palate, not the pub's cellar. 'These guns, the ones that were seized . . .'

'Semi-automatics.'

'Baikals?'

'I think so, yes.'

'The gun that killed Lynn was a Baikal 9mm semi-automatic.'

For some moments, neither of them spoke. The few customers who had been there had mostly drifted away.

'You think there's a connection?' Jackie Ferris asked.

Resnick shrugged his shoulders. 'I don't see how.'

'Coincidence, then?'

'Probably.'

Jackie looked round at the clock on the wall. 'Charlie, I should really be getting back.'

'Of course.'

'Here,' she said, sliding the whisky glass towards him. 'Stay and finish this for me.'

'Sure.'

'The funeral,' Jackie Ferris said, 'you'll let me know?'

'Of course.'

'I'll get there if I possibly can.'

When she had gone, he eschewed his pint for her whisky and water, drinking it slowly as he sat thinking.

Daines was just leaving his office as Resnick arrived. A darker grey suit today, the colour of slate; white shirt with the top two buttons undone, no tie.

'A minute,' Resnick said.

Daines looked at him as if not immediately knowing who he was.

'Resnick, isn't it?' he said. 'I'm sorry, but your face . . .'

'A couple of minutes,' Resnick said, 'that's all it will take.'

Daines slid back his cuff and looked at his watch. 'It's really not the best time. Perhaps tomorrow?'

'Now's fine,' Resnick said.

Daines started to say something but swallowed back the words and opened his office door instead.

'Come on in,' he said. 'Take a seat.'

Resnick stood.

Daines was standing also, close alongside his desk. It was almost dusk out, the evenings still closing in.

'What happened . . .' Daines said. 'I'm sorry for your loss.'

Resnick nodded an acknowledgement. 'This operation you're working on, illegal arms sales, is that right?'

Daines's turn to nod.

'These arms, they're Lithuanian?'

Daines nodded. 'I don't understand,' he said, 'why you're interested in all this?'

'The weapon that killed her, killed Lynn, it was manufactured in Lithuania.'

'A Baikal IZH?'

'Exactly.'

Daines sat back on one corner of his desk, automatically tugging at his suit trousers as he did so. 'We managed to intercept a number of small batches over the last year or so, but not all. Some will have got through.' He shrugged. 'Without the resources we really need, it's inevitable, I'm afraid.'

'And this operation now, that's the same weapons, the same source?'

Daines didn't answer immediately. 'The initial source is the same, yes. According to the Office of

361

Organised Crime and Corruption in Lithuania, it's a factory in Kėdainiai, north of Vilnius, the capital. That accounts for the majority of them, at least. They're transported through a variety of routes to this country, via Italy and up through France, or Frankfurt and then Amsterdam, those seem to be the most popular.'

'And it's the Albanians, if I've got this right, who are making the deal here and selling them on.'

'Pillow talk,' Daines said with a sly smile.

'Lynn was at liberty to say what she wanted. You didn't exactly get her to sign the Official Secrets Act.'

'I assumed she'd use her discretion.'

'She did.'

Sceptical, Daines angled his head a little to one side.

'One thing I don't understand,' Resnick said. 'Why go to the trouble of bringing the guns here? Surely they could sell them in Europe without running the extra risk of getting them into the UK?'

'Simple,' Daines said. 'Supply and demand. As the demand for guns here grows, so does the price.'

Resnick snorted dismissively. 'The free market economy at work.'

'Precisely. And the Albanians, for a relatively small outlay, can expand their business into a new and highly profitable area, using networks that've already been established.'

'By Viktor Zoukas and his ilk.'

'Viktor and his brother Valdemar, exactly.'

'Which is why you were so keen, when the

opportunity came along, to keep Viktor Zoukas out of jail.'

Daines smiled. 'Let's say we didn't want Valdemar to be distracted by the prospect of his brother being sent down for murder. Nor did we want to wait while a whole new network was set up which we'd then have to track down. Especially not with the deal, as we believe, being so close to going ahead.'

'Convenient, then, that the Crown's witness disappeared when he did.'

'Wasn't it?' Daines said flatly, choosing to ignore the implication in Resnick's tone.

'Pearce. He hasn't surfaced anywhere as far as you know?'

'I'm afraid I've no idea.' Daines looked again at his watch. 'You know, I really do have to go.'

Resnick walked down past the Playhouse and turned left on to Derby Road, then up past the Roman Catholic cathedral towards Canning Circus, his old stamping ground. The Warsaw Diner was near the top, on the left-hand side.

After exchanging pleasantries, he settled into a corner table with a bottle of Polish beer and browsed through the *Evening Post* while he waited for his meal. When it arrived – a plateful of pierogi with sauerkraut and two large pickled dill cucumbers – he set aside the newspaper to eat and as he ate, he tried to organise his thoughts.

Lynn had been murdered after returning from

363

London, where she'd been asking about the disappearance of one of the two principal witnesses in the case against Viktor Zoukas, who was currently out on bail following the adjournment of the trial.

Coincidence?

The gun she was shot with was the same make as Viktor and his brother, Valdemar, were allegedly trafficking.

Another coincidence?

And this . . .

One of the SOCA personnel heading the operation against this arms trade, Stuart Daines, was known to have applied pressure on the CPS to have Viktor Zoukas's trial adjourned and Zoukas himself released on bail. He was also – if hearsay evidence were to be believed – on friendly terms with Viktor's brother, Valdemar, and had visited the brothel Valdemar ran under the guise of it being a massage parlour and sauna.

Resnick ordered a second bottle of beer.

He could see the Zoukas entourage threatening both witnesses and putting pressure on them to the point where they were too frightened to give evidence and went into hiding. He could even imagine Daines being involved in that process in one way or other, either out of some friendship with or indebtedness to members of the Zoukas family, or because, as he had explained to Resnick earlier, it suited his plans to bring the gun traffickers to justice.

He thought he might just have room for a couple of sweet pancakes. After which a brisk walk home in the chilling air and – hopefully – a good night's sleep would encourage things to fall into place more clearly in his mind.

It was raining when he left the diner, raining hard.

34

The market was no more than five or so minutes' walk from the Central Police Station, and Resnick guessed that at that time, not long past opening, there would be fewer customers at the Italian coffee stall than usual. In the event, there would initially be just two, Karen Shields and himself.

Karen was wearing a black jacket with deep, pouched pockets, black jeans and a kingfisher-blue satin shirt and as she strode between stalls piled high with fruit and vegetables and on past the various flower stalls and the stall selling everything from vacuum-cleaner bags and electrical odds and ends to *Jim Reeves's Greatest Hits*, the sight of her had been enough to turn most heads, female and male, and to draw forth a couple of old-fashioned wolf whistles to which she gave a prompt single-digit response.

Resnick had watched her approach, far from blind, despite everything, to the striking nature of her appearance.

'Cappuccino?' he said, once she'd settled on to the stool beside him.

'Espresso.'

'Single?'

'Double.'

She waited until it was in front of her before turning towards him and asking, 'Exactly which part of "unfit for duty" is it you don't understand?'

'Daines?'

'What do you think?'

'I never said it was anything official.'

'Nor that it wasn't.'

'Just asking a few questions. No law against that, last I heard.'

'What I heard, you did more than ask questions.'

'Not really.'

'Practically accused him of conspiring to suborn witnesses.'

'Suborn? That was his word?'

'Intimidate, is that better? Threaten?'

'The word doesn't matter.'

'You really think that's what he did? You think he'd go that far?'

'Don't you?'

Karen didn't answer.

'Daines,' Resnick said, 'how many times have you met him?'

'Just the once.'

'And what did you think?'

Karen gave it due consideration. 'He was sure of

himself – not cocky, but sure of himself nonetheless. Polite. Maybe a little offhand.' She set down her cup. 'He certainly wasn't going to give anything away.'

'Did you trust him?'

She sipped her espresso. 'I don't know.' She paused, thinking back. 'He didn't give me any reason not to.'

'But your gut feeling?'

'I'm not sure I had one.'

Resnick wasn't sure if he quite believed that. 'Lynn didn't trust him. He made her feel uneasy.'

'Maybe that's because he was coming on to her.'

Resnick's eyes narrowed sharply.

'The flowers,' Karen said. 'He sent her flowers.'

'A get-well thing. After she was injured.'

'Come on, Charlie. It's okay to call you Charlie?'

Resnick nodded.

'You think that's all it was? You think if you were the one who'd ended up in hospital he'd have done the same? Sent flowers?'

'You suggesting there was something between them?' Resnick's voice was tight, just this side of angry.

'No, no. Not for a moment. But if there were flowers, there might well have been other things. Not tangible, necessarily. I don't mean boxes of chocolates, things like that. But looks, suggestions, the odd remark. The occasional invitation. Drink after work, something of that sort. Enough to get under her skin.'

Resnick's face was like stone.

'She didn't mention anything?' Karen said.

'Nothing like that, no.'

'Then she would have dealt with it herself.' A wry smile came to her face. 'It's something you learn, something you get used to, men hitting on you. Learning how to cope. Usually somewhere around year six of primary school.'

Resnick had finished his coffee and he ordered another. A man with a long, horse-shaped face, a regular, took a seat at the far side of the stall and, settled, nodded at Resnick who nodded back.

'I loved her,' Resnick said quietly. 'More than I would have thought possible. And to me . . . to me, she was beautiful. I could sit, just sit, and look at her and that's all . . . all I needed. But she wasn't . . . what she wasn't . . .' He turned his head aside and Karen thought he was going to cry, but he sniffed and straightened and carried on. 'She wasn't the kind men set their caps at. Hit on, as you put it.'

'You did.'

'Not really.' He managed a smile. 'More the other way round. Though God knows why.'

Karen laughed. 'Women don't get hung up on the superficial, that's why. The way a guy looks, what he wears. We see beyond that, you know, right down into the soul.'

'You're kidding, right?'

'Absolutely.' She laughed again. When she took up with the Taylor Coombeses of this world, just about the last thing she was looking for was soul. Well, maybe soul of the Stax and Motown kind. 'Besides,' she said, 'the woman men won't hit on in the right situation hasn't yet been invented.'

Resnick shook his head. 'If Daines were interested in Lynn, and I'm not saying he was, I think it would have been for some other reason.'

'Such as?'

'I'm not sure. But from what little I know about him, and that's mostly from Lynn, admittedly, the impression I've got is of someone who uses people whenever he can. Cultivates them, if you like. For whatever he can get out of them. Favours. Information. Anything as long as he keeps the upper hand. When he found out – and God knows how, his connections must be pretty wide – that she'd been getting a friend to ask a few questions about him, his whole attitude towards her changed.'

'Changed how?'

'He went out of his way to warn her to keep out of his business. Threatened her, I suppose you could say.'

'Threatened? How?'

'Appeared one night, outside the pub. Don't make me your enemy, that's what he said.'

'And she took it seriously?'

'It made her angry. More than that, I'm not sure.'

Karen swung round on her stool. 'It's a long way from making a threat to . . . to being involved in taking someone's life.'

'Agreed.'

'But that's what you're suggesting.'

'I think . . . I think there could be a connection. I don't know. Daines. The whole Zoukas business. Andreea Florescu.'

Karen tossed back her head. 'We're looking at it, Charlie. Believe me. But not so long ago you were positive Howard Brent was responsible for Lynn's death. Absolutely adamant.'

'Yes, I know.'

'And now, suddenly . . .'

'It's not sudden.'

'Now, suddenly, you've changed your tune.'

Resnick sighed and swivelled towards her on his stool. 'It looks like that, I know, but . . .'

'What it looks like,' Karen said, 'you're so desperate to find Lynn's killer that you're lurching around all over the place, first one suspect, then another. And all this about Daines being somehow involved, too much of it is conjecture. Supposition. Even his threatening Lynn, it's just hearsay.'

'She didn't make it up.'

'Charlie, come on, that's not the point. The point is proof, evidence, something that might stand up.'

Karen's eyes were bright and alert, her voice urgent without being loud. Probably the last thing she needed was another large espresso, but she ordered one anyway.

'We've talked to Howard Brent again,' Karen said, once the coffee had arrived. 'And we've spoken with one or two of his associates. Not that any of that's got us anywhere. I've had a few feelers out back in Jamaica,

371

but so far they've come back empty. And there's still nothing coming back off the street. Anil's been talking to the people at the hotel where Andreea Florescu was working, but aside from some vague mention of her heading down to Cornwall, there's nothing. Same with the staff at the place where Bucur's studying.'

'Nothing else?'

Karen shrugged. 'We're still chasing down the Sierras, but so far, apart from inadvertently stepping on someone with a nice line in heroin in his wheel base, there's nothing. Nothing pertaining.'

'How many still outstanding?'

'A dozen? And we're still trawling back through your and Lynn's old cases without too much luck. Except for one of yours, maybe. I was going to ask you. Barry Fitzpatrick. Ring any bells?'

Resnick smiled, remembering. Not that it was all that pleasant a memory. Barry Edward Fitzpatrick was a doper and a part-time drunk who trawled the back streets looking for a front door that had been left unwisely open – someone who'd nipped down to the corner shop and left it on the latch, or who was just across the street, nattering with one of the neighbours. Fitzpatrick would duck in and lay his hands on whatever he could. Anyone saw him, it'd be, sorry, missus, thought it was my pal's place, lives round here somewhere, and he'd be off before they realised he'd nabbed their purse or pension book or the cash for the tallyman from under one of the ornaments on the mantelpiece.

'It was nine or ten years back,' Resnick said. 'The case you're referring to. Fitzpatrick was up to his tricks one day, Sherwood, I think it was. Lady of the house comes back in from the yard at the rear, she's been seeing to her window boxes, front and back, and there's Fitzpatrick, china candlestick in one hand, two ten-pound notes that had been resting underneath it in the other. She's well the wrong side of seventy, an inch or two maybe over five foot. Sprightly, though. Grabs ahold of Fitzpatrick and starts to lay about him with the trowel she's got in her hand. He panics and hits back with the candlestick. Breaks it over her head and keeps on hitting. Old skulls are brittle. Thin. He kills her. Doesn't mean to, but there it is. I brought him in, I remember. Went down, if my memory serves me, for fourteen years.'

Karen nodded. 'He was released early February.'

'And you think . . .'

'Convicted murderer, possibly bearing a grudge.'

Resnick shook his head. 'Barry Fitzpatrick was a coward who wouldn't say boo to the proverbial goose unless he was in drink, and even then he was never really violent. Doubt if he's ever held a gun in his life, never mind fired one. What happened to that old lady, that was out of fear, nothing else. And to think of him going after Lynn to get at me, well, prison might have changed him, sharpened him up even, but not that much. Not ever.'

'Tick that one off, then.'

'I think so.'

373

Karen looked at her watch.

'What are you going to do about Daines?' Resnick asked.

'Am I going to do something?'

'I don't know.'

'Let me think about it, Charlie.'

'Okay.'

She reached for her bag, but he raised a hand. 'Coffee's on me.'

'Thanks.' She took a step away. 'Words of advice?'

'Yes?'

'Go home. Paint the house, inside and out. Take a holiday. Give yourself time. Unfit for duty, it means what it says.'

In the short distance between the Victoria Centre and the police station, the heavens opened, and by the time Karen was safe inside she was half-drenched, her hair in rats' tails.

'Turned out nice,' Ramsden said, amused.

'Fuck off, Mike.'

'Now or later?'

'Later.'

She gave him the gist of her conversation with Resnick and he listened attentively, nodding here and there, frowning at others.

'What do you think?' she asked when she'd finished.

He jutted his head to one side. 'It's not as if we're not following that line already.'

'What we've been doing is looking for Bucur and the woman and getting nowhere.'

'You've got a better idea?'

Karen nodded. 'We might try getting at it from a different angle. Dixon, DCI, ring any bells?'

'Dixon? Dock Green? Bit long in the tooth by now, isn't he?'

'Very funny.'

'Used to watch that, you know,' Ramsden said. 'As a kid. Saturdays, wasn't it? *Dixon of Dock Green.* Saturday tea time.' He laughed. 'Now there's a real old-fashioned copper for you.'

'Your inspiration, was he, Mike?' Karen asked, amused. 'What made you want to join the force?'

'Get out of it! *Sweeney*, that's what did it for me. Jump in the motor, chase some villain halfway 'cross London, bang him up against the wall, get a couple of good whacks in when he tries to do a runner. Right, son, you're nicked.'

'I can just see it. But just for now, if you could see your way to doing something more pedestrian, why not get on to Dixon for me. Central Task Force. See if he'll agree to a meeting?'

Ramsden whistled. 'Playing with the big boys.'

'They handle most firearms trafficking. Won't hurt to see what he's got to say, even if it means Daines finding out we're going behind his back. If he has got anything to hide, it even might shake him up a little. Gets panicky, he might always do something foolish, give something away. And if not – well,

375

a few bruised feelings, soon smooth over.'

'Okay,' Ramsden said, 'I'll get to it.' At the door, he paused. 'Resnick,' he said, 'now he's passed this latest brainstorm of his along, you really think he's going to sit back and let us get on with it?'

Karen didn't answer.

35

Resnick met Ryan Gregan at the same spot in the Arboretum as before, but the continuing downpour soon drove them into the bandstand, and then, with the wind whipping the rain almost horizontally against their legs, further downhill to stand huddled up against the wall, taking what shelter they could from the over-hanging trees.

'Some old weather, eh?' Gregan said, something of a gleam in his eye. 'Reminds me of Belfast, when I was a kid. Manchester, too. Followin' me round, d'you think?'

Resnick had already asked him if he'd picked up any scuttlebutt about Brent, anything that tied him into Lynn's death, but Gregan had heard nothing. Rumours, sure. There were always those. There was one, for instance, going round that Howard Brent had put a price on Lynn's head, five K according to one, ten another, but all that, Gregan assured him, was nothing more than fanciful talk.

'You're sure of that? Positive?'

Solemnly, Gregan made the sign of the cross over his heart.

Resnick asked him about the gun.

'Baikal, is it? Baltic somewhere. Lithuania? Gas pistols, that's all they are. Till some bright spark does a bit of remodelling. Lethal then.'

'Any around on the street?'

'Here? I don't think so. Manchester, before I left, a few on sale there. Not cheap. Six, seven hundred each. Be more now.' He grinned. 'Natural rise in inflation. Like the bloody rain.'

'You're certain you've not seen any here, in the city?'

'Said so, didn't I?'

'Nor talk of any?'

Gregan gave him a look. 'Is this the gun that . . .' He let the question dribble free.

'Yes,' Resnick said.

'I'll do what I can, Mr Resnick. There's one or two people owe me favours. I'll see if I can't call them in.'

'You've got my number?'

'Mobile, is it?'

Resnick nodded.

'Then I have.' Gregan pulled his coat collar up higher against his neck and stepped out into the full force of the rain.

Resnick turned and walked back along the path that would take him to the Mansfield Road; his trousers were sticking, cold, to his legs and his coat was sodden:

getting wetter wasn't going to make any difference. There was a slender band of light on the horizon, but, as yet, the rain showed little sign of slackening. Not for the first time, he was grateful he lived on higher ground. Those with houses down close by the Trent would already have their cellars full of water and be taking their best pieces of furniture to the upper floors.

Out on the main road, he saw a taxi approaching and raised a hand and the driver, after a hasty glance, swerved to a stop at the kerb, sending a wash of water spraying up around Resnick's legs.

Home, he stripped off all his clothes and stood a good five minutes under a hot shower before drying himself briskly down and dressing. Some of his wet things he draped over the bath, others he hung inside the airing cupboard; his shoes he stuffed with old newspaper. For once, he fancied tea not coffee. From the shelves, he fished out an album of Kansas City jazz, upbeat and bluesy, his friend Ben Riley had once sent him from the States. Between the cupboard and the fridge, there were the makings of a serious sandwich.

Howard Brent putting out a contract on Lynn, a price on her head, did he believe that? No more than Ryan Gregan did, he thought. Aside from anything else, if it were true then news of it would have got back to Karen Shields and she would surely have told him.

Then again, perhaps not.

He rang Anil Khan's number, but the line was busy; the same with Michaelson. Catherine Njoroge answered promptly. If she had any doubts about talking to Resnick concerning the investigation, they didn't show. He told her what Gregan had said about Howard Brent and she said, no, no rumours of any kind of contract had come her way; she could ask some of the squad to check with their informants, but, like Resnick, she thought if there were anything to it, it would have surfaced before now. Perhaps Gregan had pulled it out of thin air, she suggested, something to keep Resnick interested.

'Yes,' Resnick said, 'I expect you're right.'

There was a small silence and then Catherine asked if he had a date yet for the funeral.

'Three days' time,' Resnick said. 'Friday.'

'I'd like to come if I could. If I can arrange the time. I didn't know her well, Lynn, but . . .'

'Of course,' Resnick said. 'That'd be fine. She'd have been pleased.'

Air caught in his throat and he swallowed hard.

'I'll be in touch,' Catherine said and rang off.

Resnick found another topcoat and a dry pair of shoes.

The rain had petered to a slow drizzle, little more than a misting in the air, and there was a vestige of a rainbow, faint over the city. The gutters were awash with running water, the pavements slick underfoot. By the time he'd reached the centre he was ready for coffee and bought one from Atlas in a takeout cup. In the music shop, Marcus stood chatting to two black youths sporting ear studs and gold chains who took one look at

Resnick and, sussing him for what he was, left without another word.

Marcus recognised Resnick right off from the time he'd interrupted the procession and mumbled something barely audible as he moved back behind the counter.

Resnick rested his coffee cup on a stack of CDs and flipped through one of the adjoining racks, lifting a CD out with finger and thumb, glancing at it and letting it slip back down.

'There's a sign,' Marcus said abruptly, coating his nervousness with belligerence. 'There. On the door. No food or drink.'

'I'm sorry,' Resnick said. 'I'll be careful.'

'Spill something there and stuff'll get ruined. You'll have to pay.'

'Detective Inspector Kellogg,' Resnick said, 'the police officer who was shot, I heard something interesting today. Your father offering a large sum of money to have her killed.'

'That's stupid,' Marcus scoffed. 'That's a stupid fuckin' lie. Why'd he do somethin' like that?'

'He blamed her for your sister's death.'

'Yeah, right. Still don't mean he'd go'n do that. That's like *The Sopranos* or somethin', i'n'it? 'Sides . . .' he looked at Resnick full on for the first time, '. . . wanted her dead, he'd've done it himself.'

'And did he?'

'Yeah. 'Cept he was in Jamaica, i'n'it?'

'And Michael?'

381

Marcus jumped. 'What about Michael?'

'Where was he?'

'I dunno. Down London, isn't he? Learning to be this hotshot lawyer an' shit.'

'Only when the police tried to get in touch with him, to ask about your father, they couldn't find him. Left a note at his college, went round to where he lives. No one seemed to know where he was.'

'Off somewhere, i'n'it, being too clever for fuckin' words. Anyway, you don't reckon he'd have nothin' to do with somethin' like that. Mister high-an'-fuckin'-mighty.'

'You don't like him.'

Marcus shrugged, 'He's my brother, i'n he?'

'You're close?'

'What d'you think?'

'How about your father, is Michael close to your father?'

'My old man,' Marcus said scornfully, 'he reckons the sun shines out of Michael's black arse.'

Resnick nodded and looked around. 'Blues, you got any blues? I was listening to this singer earlier. Joe Turner? I don't suppose you've got anything like that?'

Marcus looked at him questioningly, not certain if he were having him on.

'There's a few things over there.' He pointed towards the corner, close to the wall. 'Took 'em in part exchange.'

There were no more than a dozen CDs and Resnick looked through them quickly. Muddy Waters. Johnny

Winter. At the back, propping up the rest, was a DVD: *Warming by the Devil's Fire*, a film by Charles Burnett. Lightnin' Hopkins, Big Bill Broonzy, Dinah Washington, Bessie Smith.

'How much for this?' Resnick asked.

'Ten.'

Resnick raised an eyebrow.

'Okay,' Marcus said. 'Eight. Make it eight. Eight quid, okay?'

Resnick handed over a ten-pound note and waited for his change, Marcus still not able, quite, to look him in the eye.

'You want a bag?'

Resnick shook his head. 'Thanks,' he said, careful to pick up his coffee as he made for the door.

Mid-evening. Karen and Mike Ramsden were in the pub. They had been there a while. After no little difficulty and some heavy-duty interference from Assistant Commissioner Harkin, Graeme Dixon of the Met's Central Task Force had agreed to a meeting the following afternoon.

Karen had been thinking about Resnick's doubts and assertions off and on throughout the day. Even if there were anything in what Andreea Florescu had told Lynn about Daines and the Zoukas brothers, he could have been using them, playing a clever game, leading them on until the trap clamped shut when they were snug inside it. Then again, Daines might have got too close and somehow been drawn in beyond his depth. It wasn't impossible: such things had happened before. If that were the case, Karen thought, he could conceivably have assisted in the intimidation of witnesses, though without evidence that was asking a lot to believe.

But did it go beyond that?

And how?

The fact that the gun which had killed Lynn Kellogg was of the same type the Zoukas brothers were supposedly trafficking was an interesting coincidence but no more; making any kind of stronger link was way too much of a stretch. And besides – big question – what had Viktor Zoukas or his brother, or Daines for that matter, to gain from Lynn's death?

Some private satisfaction?

Petty revenge?

She didn't know: right now, she didn't know very much.

Ramsden was drinking pints of bitter with whisky chasers, a slightly glazed look coming to his eyes. 'You know what we were talking about before?' he said. 'All that *Dixon of Dock Green* stuff?'

Karen waited for what was coming.

'I saw the film a month or so back, where it all started. Dixon. Before the telly. *The Blue Lamp*? Some afternoon I was off duty. There's this scene, right? He walks right up to this young tearaway with a gun, Dixon, calm as you like, uniform, helmet, telling him, you know, put it down. Kid's losing it, practically pissing himself. "Drop it, I say," Dixon says. "Don't be a fool." Kid panics and pulls the trigger. Dixon, he

384

doesn't believe it. Next minute he stops breathing.'
Ramsden shook his head. 'When was that? Fifties some
time. Copper getting shot, back then, practically
unheard of. And now the bastards don't panic. They
take fucking aim.'

He shuddered with exasperation.

'You're a doom merchant, Mike,' Karen said.
'Victor Meldrew in spades. Why look on the bright
side, when you can be bloody miserable?'

'Okay, okay,' Ramsden said, animated. 'I'll tell you
this. I'd been a kid back then, I'd likely've been living
in some crummy two-up, two-down with no bathroom
and an outside khazi, running round with the arse out
me trousers. Left school at what? Fourteen, fifteen?
Some boring fart-arse job, if I was lucky, for sod-all
money.'

'Yes,' Karen said, laughing. 'But you weren't, were
you? Your gran might have had a toilet out in the back
yard, but I bet you didn't. And you didn't leave school
at fourteen either.'

'No, all right. You're right, you're right. I went to
the local comprehensive, okay? Scraped an education,
waltzed into the Met, got promotion, good job, decent
money – could be more, but it's decent – nice house,
grade one motor, wife and kid – least I did, before they
buggered off to bloody Hartlepool – and everything's
better, right? Better than it was. Yeah?'

'Yes.'

'Then why's it like this?'

'Like what?'

'Up shit creek without a paddle.' He walked across to the window and stared out. 'Whole fuckin' country. Doesn't even rain like it used to. Bloody deluge, that's what that is. Fucking flood.'

Karen laughed. 'That's it. Exaggerate a bit, why don't you?'

'What? You think I'm kidding? Flood warnings on the radio this morning. Seventeen of them.'

'You're right, Mike. The whole world's coming to an end. Just not before you've got time to buy me another drink, okay?'

Ramsden groaned and headed for the bar.

36

At first glance, Detective Chief Inspector Graeme Dixon was as anonymous as the concrete-and-glass building in which his office was housed. Dark suit, pale shirt, plain tie, hair neither too long nor too short, no beard, no moustache, no tattoos or other distinguishing marks, his only adornment the gold band on the third finger of his left hand. The kind of man, seen up close on the tube, or behind the wheel of the car alongside at the traffic lights, who would be briefly noticed and then immediately forgotten. One of the reasons, perhaps, when he had spent more time on the streets, he'd been so effective at his job.

Karen had come down to London on her own, leaving Mike Ramsden with the squad; her meeting at the Central Task Force aside, it had given her the chance to go back to her flat and check her mail, pick up some new clothes.

'Karen,' Dixon said, holding out a hand. 'Graeme.

Come on in. Sorry to keep you kicking your heels.'

There was a recognisable Essex edge to his voice, a brisk professionalism in his manner; his handshake quick and firm and dry.

He waited until she'd settled into a chair.

'Out on loan, aren't you? Wild and woolly provinces?'

'Something like that.'

'Going okay?'

'Not too bad.'

'Did that once,' Dixon said. 'When I was a DI. Manchester. Spent as much time watching my back as anything else.'

Karen smiled. 'This lot aren't too bad.'

'Murder investigation, isn't it? One of ours?'

'Yes.'

'Nasty.'

Karen nodded.

Dixon said. 'Anyway, what can I do for you? Something to do with that North London operation, your bagman said.'

'Stuart Daines, he was one of the Customs and Excise people involved?'

'Stuart, yes. SOCA now. Why d'you ask?'

Karen smiled again, almost apologetically this time. 'I'm fishing around a bit here, and of course you don't have to answer, but was there ever any suggestion he was less than kosher? Anything about him that gave you any doubts, made you stop and think?'

'Whoa!' Dixon said, and raised both hands. 'Wait

up, wait up. Just what are we getting into here? This isn't the time or the place.'

'Bear with me,' Karen said. 'Let me try and explain.'

Dixon listened patiently and, for a moment, when she'd finished, he was quiet.

'Seems to me whatever you've got linking Daines to your inquiry is limited at best. In fact, I'd say you had jackshit and were pretty frantically flailing around trying to stop yourself from drowning.'

'As I understand it,' Karen said, continuing regardless, 'one of the traffickers arrested walked free without charge.'

'That's right.'

'One of Daines's informants?'

Dixon ventured a quick smile. 'You don't expect me to answer that.'

'So, what then? Daines put in a word on his behalf? Maybe something more than that? Some piece of evidence against him getting contaminated, lost?'

'It happens.'

'Doesn't make it right.'

'Look,' Dixon pushed his chair back from the desk. 'Don't get sanctimonious with me, okay? We got a good result. Several dozen weapons taken out of commission, practically a thousand rounds of ammunition. The men arrested went down for a good thirty years between them.'

'And that justifies—'

'You know it fucking does!'

Karen slowly released a breath before rising to her

389

feet. 'Thanks for your time. Anything I've said – implied – about any impropriety – I know it won't leave this room.'

She stood away from her chair.

Dixon hesitated before he spoke. 'You may know this or not. From your questions I'll assume that you do. There's an operation SOCA and ourselves are currently running together, down here and up in Nottingham. Daines is involved. The whole thing's on a bit of a knife edge at the moment. Eighteen months watching and waiting, keeping the lines open between ourselves and our colleagues in the Baltic. We think there might be as many as three hundred, three hundred and fifty weapons, several thousand rounds of ammunition. Move at the right time and we get the goods, the suppliers, the middlemen, the whole kit and caboodle. Get it wrong and we stand to lose pretty much everything. All those hours of police work down the drain and another batch of guns out on the open market. A month from now and they could be in the hands of some serious villain taking down a security van on the Ruislip by-pass or a pumped-up fifteen-year-old in South London or Manchester who wants to earn a little respect by putting a bullet in some other kid's head. You know what I'm saying?'

'Yes, I think so.'

'It seems to me, as far as your murder investigation's concerned, anything regarding Daines is just so much whistling in the wind. But if things change, if you feel impelled to act in any way that might throw this current operation off course, I'd ask you to let me know first. Give us fair warning.'

'And after?'

'After's a different matter.' He held out his hand. 'You know where to find me.'

As soon as she'd left the building she called Ramsden on her mobile phone. 'Mike? Any luck, I'll be back around seven. Meet me, okay? The office will be fine.'

37

The television news was showing pictures of rivers in flood further north, and in South Yorkshire and out along the Humber estuary people were trapped in their homes. In East Anglia, the small market town of Louth was nearly swept out past Saltfleet and into the sea. Helicopters rescued the aged and infirm, winching them precariously to hospital. Row boats, many extemporised from containers or plastic baths, ferried people to safety. Families camped out on roofs. Cats were drowned. Cars abandoned. Houses and shops looted. An off-duty ambulance man, by all accounts a strong swimmer, lost his footing, fell into a normally placid river that had burst its banks and was swept helplessly away. A bemused toddler celebrated turning three with his parents and two hundred others in a leisure centre, water lapping up the walls as, en masse, they sang 'Happy Birthday'. The bloated body of Kelvin Pearce was found floating in a flooded used-car lot on the A1 south of Doncaster and went unidentified for three days.

The morning of Lynn's funeral was marked by more heavy rain, relentless from a leaden sky. The procession of cars heading east from Nottingham was slowed by winds that gusted across open fields and lifted standing water from the surface of the road. Detours, caused by flooding, slowed them further still.

Some twenty miles short of their destination, the rain was replaced by sudden, blinding sun, so that the church, when they first saw it, stood out like some kind of beacon on the hill, its flint-fronted walls reflecting a kaleidoscope of greys and whites and browns.

A low wooden gate with a single iron arch opened on to a gravelled path which led to the church entrance in the west wall of the nave.

Inside, the walls were surprisingly plain, painted a flat greyish white beneath the hammer-beam roof. A pointed arch, the shape and size of the whale's jawbone that Resnick knew well from Whitby's west cliff, separated the body of the church from the choir stalls and the simplest of altars: light filtering through the high window beyond.

Opposite the pulpit, Resnick sat ill at ease in black: black suit, black shoes, black tie, the collar of his white shirt straining against his neck. The wood of the pews had been polished smooth by use and was properly hard and unforgiving against his bones as he sat, cramped and uncomfortable. Across the aisle, Lynn's mother leaned against an elder sister for support, the extended family ranged behind her: a brother scarcely seen in years, aunts and uncles, nephews and cousins – great glowering lads with large feet and hands and awkward eyes – nieces in hand-me-down frocks and borrowed cardigans worn against the cold.

Behind Resnick, the Divisional Commander for Nottingham City and the head of the Homicide Unit talked in low tones, and the Assistant Chief Constable (Crime), present as the representative of the Chief Constable, forbore from looking at his watch. Behind them, filling the pews, sat men and women with whom Lynn had worked – Anil Khan, Carl Vincent, Kevin Naylor – now a detective sergeant in Hertfordshire and recently divorced – Sharon Garnett, Ben Fowles. Graham Millington had sent sincere regrets and a wreath of lilies. Catherine Njoroge sat a little to one side, hands folded one over the other, a black shawl covering her head. Jackie Ferris had phoned at the last minute with her apologies.

The vicar was new to the parish, young and earnest and possessed of a slight stammer. He spoke of a life of dedication and service cut short too soon. He spoke of God's untrammelled love. Resnick's eyes wandered to the stained-glass angels, red and green and purple, perched in small lozenges above the east window. Lynn's mother cried. Two officers – Khan and Naylor – along with two of the family, shouldered the coffin, Resnick walking behind.

The ground was sodden underfoot.

As they reached the open grave the first drops of new rain began to fall.

The vicar's stumbling words were torn by the wind.

Lynn's mother clasped Resnick's hand and wept.

The open sides of the grave began, here and there, to slip away.

More words and then the coffin was lowered into place.

Unprompted, one of the women began to sing a hymn which was taken up by a few cracked voices before petering to uneasy silence.

When Resnick was given the trowel of fresh earth to throw down upon the coffin, he turned away, blinded by tears.

The family had arranged for a wake in the parish hall, more often used by Cubs and Brownies. Curled sandwiches and cold commiserations, warm beer. He couldn't wait to get away. That night the police would hold a wake back on their own turf and Resnick would show his face, accept sympathy, shake hands, leave as soon as decency allowed.

The first time they had made love, himself and Lynn, it had been the day after her father's funeral, a collision of need that had taken them, clumsily at first, from settee to floor and floor to bed, finishing joyful and surprised beneath a pale-blue patterned quilt. After making love again they had slept and when Resnick had finally woken Lynn had been standing by the window in the gathering light, holding one of her father's old white shirts against her face.

Now, father and daughter were buried side by side.

The house struck cold when he entered; the sound, as the door closed behind him, unnaturally loud. There was perhaps a third remaining of the Springbank Millington had brought, and Resnick poured himself a healthy shot then carried both bottle and glass into the front room, set them down and crossed to the stereo.

'What Shall I Say?': Teddy Wilson and his Orchestra with vocal refrain by Billie Holiday. He had fought shy of playing this before but now he thought he could.

The song starts with a flourish of saxophone, after which a muted trumpet plays the tune, Roy Eldridge at his most restrained; tenor saxophone takes the middle eight and then it's Eldridge again, Teddy Wilson bridging the space jauntily before Billie's entry, her voice slightly piping, resigned, full of false bravado. The ordinariness, the banality of the words only serving to increase the hurt. The clarinet noodling prettily, emptily, behind.

As the music ended, tears stinging his eyes, Resnick hurled his whisky glass against the facing wall, threw back his head and howled her name.

38

At first, the assumption, natural enough, was that Kelvin Pearce had drowned, another victim of the floods. But the pathologist found no trace of water in his air passages or his stomach and the lungs did not appear to have become unduly swollen, and so he concluded that Pearce had almost certainly been dead when his body entered the water. The swelling and the badly wrinkled skin that came from prolonged immersion had disguised at first the gunshot wound at the base of the skull. Though much of the area around the wound had been washed clean, there were enough stippled burn marks around the point of entry to suggest Pearce had been shot with a small-calibre bullet at close range.

His sister from Mansfield carried out the formal identification.

The friend with whom Pearce had been hiding out, in a mid-terrace former council house in Doncaster, told

South Yorkshire police that Pearce had seemed almost permanently frightened, forever looking over his shoulder. On one occasion he had ducked out of a nearby pub when two men had entered, legging it across the car park and shinning over a wall to get away.

The men?

One of them had been bearded, he was certain of that; not a big beard, not long, but full, dark. He might have had some kind of scar on his face, but it had all been so quick it was difficult to be certain.

Which side was the scar? Left or right? No, sorry, he couldn't say.

It was Thursday, almost a week after Kelvin Pearce's body had first been found, face down, butting up against the side of a partly submerged Nissan Bluebird, before the news of his death filtered down to Karen Shields.

'The Zoukas trial, Mike,' she said, herself and Ramsden in conversation as they walked towards the incident room. 'More and more it seems to revolve around that. First Kellogg and now one of the key witnesses dead and the other witness missing.'

'Right,' Ramsden said. 'And from everything we know this Zoukas family, they're not just crooks, they're fully fledged gangsters. Bandits. Not so long back, they were shooting up the hills of Northern bloody Albania like Wild Bill Hickock.' He laughed. 'So much for the benefits of the multicultural society.'

'What's that got to do with it?'

Ramsden scoffed. 'Wholesale bloody immigration. Thought the economy of this poor benighted country depended on it. Making us richer all round.'

'For God's sake, Mike!'

'Well, it's not the bloody Krays out there, is it?'

'No, but it could be.'

'Christ!' Ramsden shook his head angrily. 'You just don't see it, do you? Or rather, you do see it but you don't want to admit it.'

Karen started to walk away.

'No, wait,' Ramsden said. 'Come on. Look at the facts.'

She stopped again and turned. 'Mike, save me the lecture, okay?'

Ramsden would not be deterred. 'Who's running heroin in this country? London anyway? Turks. Turkish Kurds. Ninety per cent.'

'Oh, Mike . . .'

'Crack cocaine, Hackney, Peckham, it's your brothers from Jamaica. Extortion, people smuggling, gambling, mostly down to the Chinese. Hong Kong Chinese. And prostitution, trafficking in girls, it's the bloody Albanians. There. That's your multicultural fucking society.'

Karen was furious, blazing. 'So what's wrong, Mike? Your poor average white British villain can't get a proper look-in?'

'Yeah, right.'

'Bloody asylum seekers, come over here, take our

houses, take our jobs and now they're preventing us from making a decent criminal living. That the picture, as you see it.'

'You got it,' Ramsden said, grinning broadly. 'On the button.'

Karen whirled away, through the incident room and into her office. A few moments later, he was there, leaning forward across her desk.

'Fuck off, Mike.'

'You've said that before.'

'And I'll say it again.'

'Just had a call from Leyton nick. Alexander Bucur, Esquire, back in residence. They think most probably since yesterday, but they're not sure.'

Karen's eyes brightened. 'You've told Anil?'

Ramsden straightened. 'He's on his way.'

Alexander Bucur opened the front door of the house nervously and then only after Khan had identified himself; he had a tube of glue in his left hand and glasses on the end of his nose, which he adjusted to examine Khan's warrant card.

'Please,' Bucur said, 'come in. Come upstairs.'

At the centre of the table was a model Bucur was in the early stages of making: the framework of a building with a long, sloping roof. Around the table edge were several cutting tools and pieces of balsa wood, with matchsticks, pipe cleaners, cellophane and tissue paper in open boxes.

'What's all this?' Khan asked pleasantly.

Bucur smiled. 'My architecture project. It should have been finished weeks ago.'

'You've been away.'

'Yes.'

'We've been trying to find you.'

'Yes, I'm sorry. I was afraid. I . . .' He shook his head, as if it were difficult to explain.

'Why don't you sit down?' Khan said. 'Tell me what happened.'

'All right.' Bucur pulled round a chair and Khan followed suit.

'I'm not sure where to start,' Bucur said.

'Detective Inspector Kellogg,' Khan said, 'she came here on the afternoon of Tuesday, the sixth of March.'

'Yes. I telephoned her. Two men had been to the flat looking for Andreea. Andreea Florescu. I think they were the same men who'd threatened her before. She panicked when I told her and she was going to run away without really knowing where and that's why I called the inspector. To talk to her, make her see reason. But by the time she arrived, Andreea had gone.'

'I see.' Khan made a note. 'So DI Kellogg never got to speak to her?'

'No. But she took it seriously, I could tell. She was worried about what these men might do. She made me promise to call her if I saw them again . . .' Bucur broke off and looked at Khan. 'The next thing I knew she had been killed. Shot. I was sitting there, where you are now, early the next morning, watching the television news. I couldn't believe it. I didn't know what to do.

401

Andreea was missing and the inspector was dead. I was frightened for my own life. I should have gone to college as usual, but instead I just packed some things and left. As soon as I could.'

'Where did you go?'

Sweat was beading Bucur's forehead. 'To stay with some friends first, in North London. Kilburn. But then I went to Cornwall. Andreea has a friend there, you see, from our country, Nadia. She works in a hotel. Andreea had spoken of working there also. I thought that was where she might have gone.'

'And had she?'

'No. Nadia had heard from her, though. A phone call. The same day she left here. Saying she was coming to see her.'

'When? Did she say when?'

'Soon. She said soon. In a day or two. But she never arrived. And when Nadia tried her mobile there was no reply.'

He shrugged. 'With me it is the same ever since she left. No signal. Nothing.'

'And you've no idea where else she might have gone? No other friends?'

Bucur shook his head. 'I have asked – people at the hotel where she worked, a few others. No one knows anything.'

'Could she have gone home?'

'Home to Romania?'

'Yes.'

'I don't think so. Her mother telephoned here three,

no, four days ago. Her little girl – she has a daughter, Monica – she wanted to speak to her. I said Andreea had gone away for a short while with a friend. A holiday. I did not know what else to say.'

'Her mother hadn't heard from her either?'

'Not for some time.' Bucur pushed back his chair. 'I am worried something terrible has happened to her. One of the men who came looking for her, the Serb, he had threatened to kill her. That's why she was so afraid.'

'You said the Serb?'

'Yes.'

'Why do you call him that? How do you know that's what he was?'

Bucur leaned forward. 'When I was describing him to Inspector Kellogg, she knew him. I don't know where from, of course, but she knew him. I think she said he was Serbian. Lazic. Ivan Lazic. I'm sure that was the name.'

'Lazic? L-A-Z-I-C?'

'Yes. He has a beard. Dark. And a scar on his face. Here.' With his finger, Bucur drew a line slowly down the left side of his face.

Khan made a quick sketch in his book.

'If we want to get in touch with you again . . . ?'

'I shall be here.' He smiled. 'Running, it is no good.'

Let's hope you're right, Khan thought. He offered Bucur his hand. 'Thank you for all your help. If Andreea does get in touch, or if you hear anything, you'll let us know?'

'Of course.'

Khan gave him a card. 'Good luck with the model.'

Bucur smiled, more readily this time. 'Yes, thank you.' He shrugged. 'I'm afraid I am not very good with my hands. All – what do you say? – thumbs and fingers?'

'Fingers and thumbs.'

Khan was barely back on the street before he was talking to the incident room on his mobile.

39

Outside, the wind was whistling tunelessly around street corners, whipping up last night's debris and throwing it into the faces of passers-by. Karen sat in her office, Mike Ramsden and Anil Khan standing at either side of her chair, all three of them looking at the computer screen on Karen's desk. The South Yorkshire force had just put out a description of someone they wanted to interview in connection with the murder of Kelvin Pearce. No name, but it fitted what they now knew of Ivan Lazic to a T.

'Get in touch with Euan Guest, Anil,' Karen said. 'He's the SIO up there. Tell him we think we know his suspect's identity. Fill him in as best you can. And while you're on to him, find out if anything more's come through on the gun that killed Pearce.'

'This Lazic,' Ramsden asked when Khan had gone. 'He's what? Czech? Russian?'

'Serbian, apparently.'

'Tough bastards, the Serbs.'

Karen raised an eyebrow. 'You'd know, I suppose.'

'Saw this programme the other night, the History Channel. Fall of Berlin.'

'Your trouble, Mike, one of many, too much television.'

'What else'm I going to do, two in the morning?'

Karen didn't want to go there.

'If the Zoukas crew are using Lazic as an enforcer, as looks likely,' Ramsden said, perching on the edge of Karen's desk, 'keeping Viktor Zoukas's sorry arse out of jail, it's got to be a good bet his finger was on the trigger when Kellogg was gunned down.'

Karen swung round in her chair, rose swiftly to her feet and pushed open the door to the incident room. Michaelson was just on the way back to his desk from the coffee machine.

'Frank . . .'

'Yes, boss?'

'The sauna Viktor Zoukas used to manage, somewhere in the city centre . . .'

'Hockley. Closed down for a time and then reopened. Fresh coat of paint, same business.'

'Get yourself down there, ask about an Ivan Lazic. Mike'll fill you in.'

'Right, boss.'

If it turned out Lazic was in Nottingham at the time of Lynn Kellogg's death, the odds on Ramsden's wager would be shortened considerably.

*

406

Michaelson had never been into a sauna before; at least, not the kind that were more generally found on seedier streets and offered sensual and relaxing full-body massage, though he knew of several colleagues who were not above paying unofficial visits and availing themselves of the occasional freebie. Neither had he been in the sex shop that occupied the ground floor of the building, offering sex toys and marital aids, adult videos and DVDs, saucy T-shirts and, as the poster put it, dildos to fit every purse. But then, as his sometime girlfriend had pointed out when he'd expressed distaste at the prominence of 35p-a-minute chat lines on which young women promised to help you unzip and unload, in some situations he could be a prude of the first magnitude – especially when he was in training for a big race. Conservation of bodily fluids, as he had tried to explain.

How much this had to do with her breaking off their relationship, he had never been sure.

He pressed the bell and, walking in, climbed the stairs.

Neither of the two young women sitting on a dilapidated settee in the first room paid him more than scant attention. To the left, seated behind an L-shaped counter, an older woman with a head of brittle curls and the reddest lipstick Michaelson could recall seeing outside of an advertisement hoarding, treated him to a professional smile.

A word from her and the couple on the settee livened themselves up and showed interest: one, darker skinned, had longish hair held back with a broad red band; her companion was petite and blonde and showed ragged teeth when she smiled. They were both wearing slightly grubby button-through tunics with, as best as Michaelson could judge, little else underneath. Without wishing it, he could feel himself becoming aroused.

Turning quickly back to the counter, he took out his warrant card.

'I'm Sally,' the lipsticked woman said. 'Can I help?'

'It's just a few questions,' Michaelson said.

The young women sat back down and resumed thumbing through old copies of *Grazia* and *Hello!*.

Sally lit a cigarette and offered one to Michaelson, who shook his head.

'Ivan, yes,' she said, in answer to his question. 'He comes up once in a while. From London. Ever since Viktor . . . you know. Hangs around for a day or so. Checking I'm not fiddling the books.' She shivered involuntarily. 'Nasty bastard. I don't like him. Gives me the creeps.'

'He's not here now? Nottingham, I mean?'

'Not as far as I know. No, haven't seen him in a while, tell the truth. Good couple of weeks it must be.'

'You remember when? I mean when exactly?'

Sally gave it some thought. 'No, but two weeks is about right. That was when Amira arrived.' She gestured towards one of the women on the settee. 'Brought her up with him in the car. Two weeks, can't be more. I tell you what, around the time that

408

policewoman was shot, that's when. All over the news, weren't it?'

'You're positive that's when he was here?' Khan asked.

'Yes, pretty much.' Sally flicked ash from the end of her cigarette. 'You ever catch anyone for that?'

'Not yet.'

Sally leaned back in her chair. 'She was in here, you know. The night that Nina was killed. Sat talking to her, just like I am to you now. Terrible, something happening like that. Only young, weren't she?'

Michaelson placed his card on the counter. 'If you do see him, Lazic, if he comes back, I'd like you to phone me.'

Sally glanced down at the card. 'All right,' she said.

Michaelson told himself not to look over towards the settee on his way out and almost succeeded.

'He'll be back,' Sally said with a grin and taking his card she pushed it down into the top of her bra.

As soon as Karen heard that Lazic had probably been in the city at the time of Lynn Kellogg's murder, she phoned Euan Guest in Doncaster to pass on the news. Guest sounded somewhat hassled, a rough throaty voice that lost some of its impatience when he heard what Karen had to offer.

'I was talking to Rachel Vine earlier,' Guest said, 'Notts CPS. She told me there was another witness . . .'

'Andreea Florescu. She was in London. No one's seen hide nor hair of her for a couple of weeks now.'

'Not good.'

'No.'

'We'll keep in touch, yes?'

'Absolutely.'

It was no more than an hour after her conversation with Guest that Karen's phone rang again. Not Doncaster this time, but Leyton . . . news she'd anticipated but didn't want to hear.

40

It was not the police who found her, but kids playing chase, a couple of eleven-year-old boys running from six or seven more, mostly older – something that had started off as a game and was on the verge of becoming altogether more vicious, less controlled. They'd raced full pelt down the main street, weaving in and out between adults as best they could, barging into others and forcing them from the pavement, ricocheting off shop windows and doors, swerving away into the entrance to the overground station and running hard up the narrow stairs towards the platform, only to realise once they were there that they were trapped, and, turning fast, bounding down again three steps at a time, knocking an old lady almost off her feet, spinning her round, and jumping, one of them, at the last moment, over the head of a startled toddler clinging to his mother's hand.

At the bottom of the steps they hesitated, caught their

breath, no more than seconds when they heard, above the squall and grind of traffic on the main road, the sounds of their pursuers, raised voices chanting, angry and shrill, and they doubled back, clambering over on to a piece of fenced-off open land beside the railway that had long since become a dumping ground, a favourite place for fly-tippers to disgorge their load.

One boy gripped the iron railings and bent his back, making a platform for the other to climb on to, then clamber over, catching his jeans on one of the blunted spikes and swearing as they tore. Once there, he balanced less than safely and grabbed his companion's hands as he scaled upwards, then hauling him precariously over, the pair of them rolling and stumbling over an accumulation of garden waste and broken furniture, stained mattresses and shattered glass, diving finally down between a long-discarded washing machine, the front ripped off, and an old chest freezer angled sharply down into the compressed debris.

Their hearts were racing.

Just out of sight, two or more of the gang ran sticks in a clanging carillon along the railings.

Others shouted their names.

Shouts that drew closer, then faded only to come closer again. They were up on the platform now, some of them, looking down.

The boys flattened themselves as best they could, burrowing down alongside washing machine and freezer into what was dank and festering.

'It stinks,' one boy whispered.

'Shut up,' hissed the other.

'It does, it stinks.'

'Shut the fuck up!'

A rat, curious, showed itself in the space between them then sprang sideways, its feet taking purchase for a moment on one boy's shoulder, before scuttling from sight.

The shouting seemed to have stopped. Cautiously raising their heads, they could see the backs of people strung along the platform above them, waiting for the next train. The heads and shoulders of others, in silhouette, were visible inside the small covered shelter. No boys, save for a solitary primary-school kid astride the low wall.

'Come on,' one said. 'They've gone.'

'No, wait.'

'It stinks here.'

'You said.'

'Well, I'm not stoppin'. You comin' or what?'

The second boy had pushed his body so far down beside the freezer that it was almost resting on top of him and in his effort to free himself it leaned even further against him, so that he had to ask for help, and it took the pair of them to lever it back and send it rolling over, the door at the top swinging open.

'Fuck!' the first boy cried. 'What the fuck is that?'

But they knew, they both knew and they ran, heedless, scrambling over the mounds of waste, scrambling and falling, losing their footing, so desperate to get away that once they'd vaulted the railings they ran, blind, regardless of one another, just running, until the first of them collided with an ambulance driver, going off duty, still wearing his uniform, who seized the lad by the collar and held fast on to him and asked him what the hell he thought he was doing and the boy pointed back towards the railway, wide eyed, and stumbled out the words, 'A body. There's a body.'

Andreea Florescu had been folded, concertina-like, into three, before her dead body had been jammed into the freezer, head pushed down hard between her knees. She was still wearing the same clothes she had on when she had left Alexander Bucur's flat sixteen days before. Her skin, where it was visible, had taken on the aspect of greenish marble; the veins in the backs of her hands and at the side of her neck stood out like dark twists of thickish wire. Blood had congealed in a black treacly film across her chest and along her thighs, sealing those parts of her together.

The smell was close to overpowering.

The area was cordoned off and ladders brought in to give easier access to the site, boards being laid across the surface of the waste, creating a single route for the crime scene manager and his team and for the Home Office pathologist to make his initial examination. Photographs were taken, measurements noted, detailed sketches drawn.

Scores of people, travellers and non-travellers both, stood on the railway platform above, gazing down.

The two boys were taken to the local police station, their parents raised, social workers summoned. Chris Butcher, one of the more experienced detectives in Homicide and Serious Crime Command, was designated senior investigating officer and an incident room was established at the Francis Road police station.

It was from there that one of the officers thought to phone Karen Shields. 'That woman you were enquiring about, I think maybe we've found her.'

Alexander Bucur was summoned for the purposes of identification.

It was nine o'clock that night before Karen got to talk to Butcher, a detective she knew by more than reputation, having worked with him on a previous investigation. Decisive, thorough, given to occasional flashes of temper, twice divorced and somehow, with the help of grandparents and a succession of European au pairs, bringing up two teenage daughters in Tufnell Park.

'Karen,' he said, the vestiges of a Scottish accent that came out more strongly after a drink or three now barely noticeable, 'apologies for not getting back to you sooner.'

'No problem.'

'What exactly's your interest here?'

Succinctly as she could, she told him.

'Maybe you, me and what's-his-name up in Yorkshire . . .'

'Guest.'

'Aye, Guest. Maybe the three of us should get

together, see what there is, if anything, by way of common ground.'

Karen agreed. 'One thing,' she said, 'the victim, Andreea, how did she die?'

'Her throat was cut,' Butcher said, 'practically from ear to ear.'

Resnick was sitting in semi-darkness when Karen called, listening to some recordings Thelonious Monk had made for Prestige in the fifties, his piano accompanied by bass and drums; Monk as ever going his own way, sounding, Resnick thought, like a cantankerous old man who, every now and then, surprised himself and those around him with flashes of good humour.

Would he mind, Karen had asked, if she popped round? She wouldn't disturb him for long.

He would not.

Earlier in the day, he read again the few cards and letters he'd had from members of Lynn's family, stilted most of them, tripping over themselves not to give offence, to find the right words. Taking a pad, he had begun to draft replies but time and again he had been overcome and, finally, he had pushed pad and pen aside, another task left for another day.

He had promised Lynn's mother that he would go through her things, some bits and pieces of jewellery Lynn had had since a teenager, a watch her father had given her for her twenty-first, a box she kept crammed with old photographs: Lynn as a chubby thirteen-year-old in school uniform, smiling self-consciously at the camera; Lynn, a little younger, on the bike she'd been given when she started secondary school; younger still, with her parents on holiday in Cornwall – one especially he remembered her showing him with pride, a girl of no more than eight or nine, hair in bunches, triumphantly holding up a pair of crabs she had caught off the quay, one in each hand.

Some of these her mother wanted, others he would keep.

Karen Shields was at the door, a bottle of whisky wrapped in white tissue in her hand.

'I didn't know what you liked,' she said, pulling away the tissue and holding up the bottle.

Resnick found a smile. 'That's fine.'

Johnny Walker Black Label: not Springbank, but good enough. He found a pair of glasses and she followed him through into the front room. Monk was still playing: 'Bemsha Swing'.

Karen listened for a few moments, head cocked towards the speakers. 'Who's this?'

He told her.

'Not exactly restful.'

'No. I can turn it off if you want.'

'No, leave it. It's good.' She grinned. 'At least, I think it is.' She cast her eye along the lines of albums and CDs. 'Always been into jazz?'

'Pretty much. One of the things that keeps me sane. Least, it used to.'

'Lynn was another.'

'Oh, yes.'

'You must be finding it hard.'

'No, not really.'

'Lying bastard.'

Resnick sniffed and smiled and poured two good measures of Scotch.

'My grandfather, you know,' Karen said, 'he was a bit of a jazz musician. Calypso, too. Trumpet, that's what he played. Trumpet and piano. When he came over to England from Jamaica it was to join this band, King Tim's Calypso Boys. It didn't work out too well, I don't know why. He did go on one tour, I know, to New Zealand, with a band called the Sepia Aces.' Karen shook her head and gave a wry smile. 'The All-Black Sepia Aces – that's how they were advertised. But after that, I think he more or less gave it up, the trumpet. He worked as a carpenter, a joiner, that was his trade. I only ever remember hearing him play a few times.'

She caught Resnick with a look.

'Andreea Florescu, they found her body.'

'Oh, shit.'

'Leyton, not so far from where she'd been staying. Her throat had been cut.'

Resnick hung his head. 'It doesn't get better, does it?'

'No, I'm afraid not.'

Resnick got up and walked to the window, whisky glass in his hand. So far he hadn't bothered to pull the curtains across and his reflection stared back at him dumbly from the darkness.

A jerky ascending phrase from Monk's piano, a rapid tumbling arpeggio and then two quick final notes stabbed out from the keyboard. 'Sweet and Lovely'. There and gone.

'Lynn used to talk about it,' Resnick said, turning back into the room. 'The danger Andreea was putting herself in by coming forward, agreeing to be a witness. She'd promised her that nothing would happen, that she'd be all right. It got to her, the fact she'd been lying.'

'She shouldn't have felt guilty.'

Resnick hunched his shoulders. 'Maybe yes, maybe no. But she did.'

'I've spoken to the guy who's handling the investigation, someone I know. Butcher. Chris Butcher. He's good. I'm going to meet with him and the SIO from the Pearce shooting. Sometime in the next couple of days.'

'When's the post-mortem?'

'Tomorrow sometime, I think. Early, probably.'

'I'd like to go down.'

'Charlie . . .'

'Oh, not to interfere. Nothing official.'

'I seem to have heard that before.'

'No, I mean it. I'd just like to see her. See the body.'

'What for?'

'I don't know . . . I'm probably not going to be able to explain it very well, but . . . it's for Lynn, somehow, what she would have wanted. What she would have done.'

The distrust, the disbelief were clear on Karen's face.

'Look . . .' He moved back and sat down, facing her. 'I won't say anything, I won't interfere. The only other thing I might do when I'm down is go and see Bucur, just to see how he's bearing up, express my sympathy. But that's all. You have my word.'

'Your word?' Karen raised an eyebrow appropriately.

'Yes.'

She tasted a little more Scotch. 'All right, I'll see what I can do.'

For a while, they managed to talk about other things, but after not too long they'd run out of what to say.

Resnick walked her to the door. When would he ever be able to open it without seeing what he had seen before, the night Lynn had died?

'This operation Daines is involved in,' Karen said, 'what I hear – what my bagman hears – I reckon it's coming to a head any day. Rumours flying round all over the place apparently. Officers in Operational Support have had their leave cancelled, armed response teams, too.'

'Likely read about the rest in the papers.'

Karen smiled. 'I dare say.'

She turned her head at the end of the path. 'I'll get back to you about viewing the body.'

'Okay.' He raised a hand and hesitated momentarily before going back into the house.

41

What was the phrase? He had read it somewhere: a cask once used for storing living things. Andreea Florescu – what had once been Andreea Florescu – lay on the stainless-steel table, cold and open eyed. The places where her body had been opened up had been meticulously sewn back, neat stitches, a mother would have been proud. First, she would have been photographed fully clothed, then photographed again as each layer was removed, a slow striptease till she was ready for the pathologist's loving care, the bone cutters, the scalpel, the saw. All external marks and stains would have been noted, samples taken from her hair, scrapings from beneath the fingernails before they were carefully clipped, swabs from here and there, all this labelled and stored. Before opening the chest cavity, the pathologist would have followed the track of the killer's knife blade across her neck with his scalpel, centimetre by centimetre, inch by inch.

Resnick looked down and saw all of this: saw nothing.

How many such bodies had he seen? How many lives rubbed out?

Another expression floated past, not quite right: somebody's mother, somebody's child.

Andreea's daughter, how old had Lynn said she was? Three? Four?

Jesus, Charlie! What was I doing? Making promises like that. Promises I can't keep.

Lynn's voice, a burr inside his head.

I put her in danger, Charlie.

He turned away.

Alexander Bucur had hardly been able to stay inside the flat since he had heard what had happened. Not that that was where he imagined Andreea had been killed, but, in staying there, he saw her everywhere. Resnick knew how this felt.

They walked, scarcely talking at first, along the High Road and then down towards the River Lea and Hackney Marshes, an expanse of flat open land where goalposts grew like trees and, on bad days, the wind razored sharp into your eyes. Today, despite the water levels being high, the wind had dropped and what few clouds there were hung immovable, like barrage balloons in the greying sky.

A group of lads, eight or ten of them, young enough they should have been in school, were playing an impromptu game around one of the goal mouths, shouting, arms raised, as they ran. 'Here! Here! Give it! Give it now! Oh, fuckin' hell!'

As the ball was booted back from behind the goal, a kid wearing knee-length shorts and a claret-and-blue shirt with the name Tevez on the back went on a mazey run that ended only when two of the others clattered into him and he went sprawling, the ball running free and across to where Resnick and Bucur were walking, and Bucur, with nice economy of movement, flicked it up on to his instep and kicked it precisely back.

'Could do with you in Notts,' Resnick said, impressed. 'Control like that.'

Bucur smiled. 'I had a trial once. Back in Romania.'

'Dynamo Bucharest?' It was the only Romanian team Resnick knew.

'No. Farul. From my home town, Constanta. FC Farul. They are in Liga 1. Not so great. Finish thirteen, fourteen.' He smiled again. 'The Sharks, that's what we call them. The Sharks. Constanta, it is by the sea.'

They walked on a little further.

'You've spoken to Andreea's family?' Resnick asked.

Bucur's expression changed. 'Yes. Her mother. The police, they had told her already what happened, but she did not understand. "How can this be?" she kept saying to me. "How can this be?" I did not know what to say. She only knows Andreea was studying here, working in her spare time as a cleaner. She did not know about this other . . . this other work she did, how

423

she would meet such people. It was too difficult to explain.'

Resnick nodded. They walked on, crossing paths with several people out with their dogs, for the most part bull terriers or similar, short-haired and muscular with flattish heads and broad shoulders, much like their owners.

'Andreea's body,' Bucur asked, 'what will happen?'

'It will be held on to for a while at least, while the investigation continues. Once a suspect has been arrested and his defence team have had the chance to examine the body, then it can be released.'

'Back to Constanta?'

'I imagine so, yes.'

The ground here was damp and gave easily to the tread. The river wound in front of them, making its way down from Tottenham Hale and the Cook's Ferry Inn, a famous jazz pub of the fifties and sixties, home for years to a fiery trumpeter called Freddy Randall. Resnick had never been.

'She told me,' Bucur said suddenly, 'this man Lazic, what he did. Why she was always so afraid. He took her, with another man, by night to this . . . this place full of rubbish. Refuse – is that the word?'

'Yes.'

'He took her there and made her kneel and then he put a knife against her throat and told her what he will do. He will cut her from here to here.' Bucur made the gesture with the forefinger of his right hand. 'He came once to the flat, you know, I told your colleague, your friend, he came asking for her and we fought. Andreea was not there. I tried to be there as much as I could after that, you know, in case, but I could not always and . . .'

'It's okay,' Resnick said. 'You did what you could.'

'No, no. I should have done more, I . . .'

'If their minds were made up,' Resnick said, 'you couldn't protect her all the time.'

'But you, the police, your friend, the inspector, she knew his name and the other policeman also. I told him, that evening . . .'

'Wait. Which other policeman?'

'The one Inspector Kellogg came with the first time.'

'Daines?'

'Yes, Daines.'

'Why did you tell him?'

'Because . . . because when I was worried about Andreea and called Inspector Kellogg on my phone there was no reply, so then I call this Daines – Andreea had his number, both numbers in her room. From Daines there is no answer also, so I leave a message for him to ring back and then when I try Inspector Kellogg's number again she is there and she agreed to come.'

'But you said you gave Daines the man's name?'

'Yes. But later. He called back not long after the inspector has gone. I tell him about Lazic then.'

'What did he say?'

'He says not to worry. He knows this Lazic, he is watching him. And Andreea, he thinks she will be fine.'

'Did you tell him anything else?'

425

Bucur gave a slow, uncertain shake of the head. 'I don't think so.'

'Nothing about Inspector Kellogg?'

'Only that she had been here, of course. And that he had just missed her, but she had left to catch her train.'

'Her train, you mentioned that?'

For a moment, Bucur looked puzzled. 'Yes, her train home.'

The three detectives met at a service station on the motorway, Leicester Forest East: a small accommodation this for Euan Guest, travelling down from Doncaster, and almost in Karen's current back yard, but Butcher happy to go the extra yard as long as it was clear the primacy of roles in the investigation was his. Guest was prepared to accept this for now and argue later, whereas Karen, a transplanted Met officer herself and aware of the Met's resources, thought it was fine.

Chris Butcher had put on a few pounds since she'd last seen him, faded blue shirt straining just a little over his chinos, jacket buttons left undone. His hair, always dark, seemed to have taken on the first few strands of grey and could have done with a trim; whenever he'd shaved last, it hadn't been that morning, maybe not even the morning before. Going for the swarthy, Mediterranean look, Karen thought: Italian waiter slash Premier League footballer. For a man of what? – forty? forty-one or -two? – he wasn't in bad condition.

His smile when he saw her was quick and, she thought, genuine; quickly in place and quickly gone.

Euan Guest in the flesh was something of a surprise: younger than she'd imagined from his voice and tall, four or five inches above six foot, a willowy build with a stooped head topped by a thatch of fair hair.

All three had coffee; Guest a Danish pastry, Butcher burger and chips, Karen abstained.

'Watching your figure?' Butcher suggested.

'No,' Karen said. 'That's you.'

Butcher laughed, caught out. He hadn't been meaning to stare, but the top Karen was wearing acted as a powerful tool to the imagination, and, he would have had to admit, she'd crossed the lascivious part of his mind more than once in the eighteen months or so since they'd worked together on a double murder in Rotherhithe – a father and son shot down in the rear car park of a pub, payback for some back-street philandering, first the father, then the son, then both together, tupping the wife of a former boxing club owner turned scrap merchant and making the mistake of posting their endeavours on YouTube.

Messy business.

'So,' Butcher said emphatically, 'what've we got?'

Guest swallowed down a piece of Danish pastry. 'The ballistics came in at last on the gun that killed Kelvin Pearce. Same model as the one used in the Kellogg shooting, similar ammo, but definitely not the same weapon. Sorry.'

'Shit!' Karen said.

'Both shootings,' Butcher added. 'Different MO altogether. Not that that rules out other connections.'

427

'To Zoukas, you mean?'

Butcher reached into the worn leather briefcase he'd carried in with him and extracted a grey card file; from this he drew four photographs, ten by eights, and laid them on the table.

'Ivan Lazic. One was taken almost eight years back now, the others are more recent. This one here . . .' he pointed to a slightly blurry shot of two men on a pavement in conversation, probably taken from a passing car, '. . . Lazic and Valdemar Zoukas, Wood Green, North London, a year ago.'

'Where d'you get this?' Karen asked.

'SOCA. Their Intelligence Directorate. Most obliging. At least, an ex-colleague was. Apparently Customs got interested in Lazic when he first came into the country in '99, claiming asylum, another refugee of the war in Kosovo. Whatever the truth of that is, God knows. There was some supposition, according to the officer I spoke to, that he'd been a member of the Serbian security services, though he claimed to have been with the Kosovo Liberation Army. Who knows? Since being here he seems to have nailed his cloth to the Albanians, so maybe he was telling the truth.'

'Wait up,' Guest said, raising a hand, 'this Liberation Army, they're Albanian?'

'Correct. Fighting for independence from the Serbs.'

'And they were what? The good guys in all this?'

Butcher made a face. 'Depends. Both sides accused the other of atrocities, ethnic cleansing, the whole bit. If the KLA was any better or worse than the Serbs who's to say?'

'And Lazic could have been either.'

'Or both. Exactly.'

'But his connection to these Zoukas characters, that's confirmed?'

'According to SOCA, he's been doing their dirty work for some little time. Not that they're above a bit of nasty themselves, but Lazic, it seems, enjoys it more than most.'

'Then why not lift him?' Guest said.

Butcher shrugged. 'Evidence, probably. Lack of.'

'What we know,' Guest said, 'he threatened both Pearce and Florescu before they died. The link to your shooting,' he added, looking at Karen, 'seems to me it's less clear.'

'Agreed.'

'What we don't yet have, though,' Guest continued, 'any more than, presumably, SOCA do, is enough evidence to be certain if we arrested him we could make it stick.'

'Ah,' said Butcher loudly, with the air of a magician about to pull a rabbit from the hat, 'perhaps we do.'

Karen smiled ruefully. What was it with men, this need to stage a grandstand finish, wait until the last minute of injury time to slot the ball into the net?

'Skin,' Butcher said, 'under the fingernails. Andreea Florescu, she put up a fight.'

'We know it's Lazic's?'

'Not yet we don't. But if we bring him in now and

429

there's a DNA match, that's Ivan Lazic looking at life inside.'

'Perhaps one of us should go to Wood Green,' Karen said, 'wherever it is he hangs out. Excuse me, Mr Lazic, but could you oblige me with a sample?'

'You ask him,' Butcher said, 'he probably would.'

All three dissolved into laughter, Karen as much as the others.

On the way back down to the car park, Butcher steered her a little to one side. 'When you've finished up in Nottingham, maybe you and me could get together? Drink, something to eat? What d'you think?'

Karen shot him a look that said, in your dreams, which, as far as Chris Butcher was concerned, was probably true.

42

By the time Resnick got back to Nottingham it was dark. Not late, but dark. The last commuters had been travelling with him on the London train, using their mobiles to let their spouses know they would be back within the next half-hour. All journey he'd been tugging at it in his mind, pulling and knuckling it into shape. Daines – Zoukas – Andreea – Lynn. Each time he pushed, some piece would slip out of place and he would worry at it again. In the end it was still imperfect, conjecture not proof, but the basic shape now held.

A lone busker was still hopefully plying his trade on Lister Gate, a song Resnick barely recognised – Bob Dylan? they often were – sung harshly over the rough chords of a guitar. A couple in a doorway, hip to hip. On the edge of the square, a woman was waiting, pacing slowly up and down in front of the left lion; as Resnick approached, she glanced up at him expectantly then disappointedly looked away. He turned left to walk through the centre of the square and a group of men, laughing loudly, crossed ahead of him between Yates's and the Bell, shirt tails to the wind.

There was only one light showing, faint beyond the front door, in the building where SOCA had their offices. Resnick was on the point of walking away when a woman came out and closed the door behind her, standing on the top step long enough to reach into her bag and light a cigarette. In the flare of the lighter he saw a roundish face with narrowed eyes. Thirty? Thirty-five?

'Damn,' Resnick said, moving briskly forward. 'Don't tell me I've missed him.'

Startled, the woman backed away.

'Detective Inspector Resnick,' he said, taking out his wallet and holding it towards her without ever really letting it fall open. 'London bloody train. Signal failure outside Loughborough. Sat there the best part of forty minutes.' He smiled. 'Shouldn't have been late otherwise.' He nodded towards the first-floor window. 'Stuart. Stuart Daines. We had a meeting. I tried phoning, somehow couldn't get through. You haven't had trouble with the line? Nothing like that?'

'No,' the woman said. 'No, not as far as I know. I'm only temping, though. Secretarial, like.' Her accent was local.

'Shame,' Resnick said. 'I tried his mobile, too. Switched off, apparently.'

'There's nobody there now,' she said. 'I was the last. Just finishing off this report. Last minute.' She smiled a little nervously and drew on her cigarette.

'It was important, too. Something we needed to discuss before the morning.'

'Daines, you said? He'll be here first thing, always is.'

'You don't know where he's staying, I suppose? This mobile number – maybe it's the wrong one.'

'No, no idea. I'm sorry.' A quick smile. 'My bus. Got to go.'

Level with him, she stopped. 'I did hear one of them say they were going for a drink. That place over Maid Marian Way. China China, I think that's what it's called. Down on Chapel Bar.' Her laugh was almost a giggle. 'Dead posh, that's what I've been told.'

Resnick waited them out. Daines and three others, sitting over towards a small corner stage that was empty save for a black glitter drumkit and a small electronic keyboard. No signs of a band. The interior was busy and dark, with minimal lighting recessed into the ceiling and, near where Resnick was standing, a cluster of small green lights hanging down amidst a nest of wires. Daines and one of the others were drinking cocktails of some kind, the other men bottled beer – Sol it might have been, Resnick thought, though he couldn't be sure. The music coming through the sound system was rhythmic and just loud enough not to get lost in the rise and fall of conversation. Cuban, he wondered? Brazilian? Most of the men were smartly turned out – smart-casual, was that what it was called?

– anything less would have been turned back at the door; the women sleek and sophisticated until they opened their mouths.

One of the quartet Resnick was watching left quite soon after he arrived, and another shortly after that, leaving Daines and one other, short with reddish hair, in close conversation.

Twenty minutes or so later, their glasses empty, Daines began to make his way towards the bar. Midway there, he stopped suddenly, his head swinging round towards the far, deep corner, left of the door, where Resnick was standing and Resnick held his breath, fearful that he'd been spotted, but then Daines excused himself past someone and continued on his way.

The music rose in volume and the conversation in the room grew louder, as if in compensation. Back at his table, Daines leaned closer towards his colleague and said something that made them both laugh out loud. A few minutes later and they were heading for the exit.

Resnick turned aside, waited, and then followed.

At the end of Angel Row they separated, the redhead walking up Market Street towards the Theatre Royal, while Daines carried on along the upper edge of the Old Market Square. Heading for one of the Lace Market hotels, perhaps, Resnick thought, or the Travelodge, just past the roundabout on London Road. A quick right and left, however, and they were out on to Belward Street opposite the National Ice Centre and Daines was veering towards the tall block of serviced apartments on the left.

Resnick lengthened his stride, moved quickly across the foyer and into the lift before the doors had closed.

'What the fuck?'

Daines had already pressed one of the buttons to set the lift in progress and now Resnick pressed another, halting it mid-floor.

Seeing who it was, Daines laughed, as much out of relief, perhaps, as anything else. 'Took you for some bastard mugger, after my wallet. Never can tell.'

Resnick positioned himself with his back towards the door.

'I thought I saw you earlier, in the bar,' Daines said. 'Couldn't be sure.'

Resnick looked back at him, impassive.

'So,' Daines said. 'I have to guess what this is all about?'

Resnick still said nothing, taking his time.

'Let's go on up,' Daines said. 'We can talk in the flat. Or go back out on to the street at least. Get another drink, maybe. Not too late.'

'This is fine,' Resnick said.

Daines shrugged. 'Suit yourself.'

'The night Lynn Kellogg was killed,' Resnick said, 'she'd been down to London, the house where Andreea Florescu had been living. The same place the two of you visited a few days before.'

'So? Why are you telling me this?'

'She thought, Lynn, that whole business, that you were in too deep.'

435

Daines scoffed and shook his head.

'Something between yourself and the Zoukas brothers that she didn't trust. She started to ask questions and you warned her off.'

'She was way off limits.'

'You threatened her.'

'That's ridiculous.'

'That evening, outside the Peacock. "Don't make me your enemy." She told me, less than twenty minutes later.'

'She was exaggerating.'

'I don't think so.'

'I don't recall saying any such thing.'

' "Don't make me your enemy." '

'That's what I'm supposed to have said?'

'Word for word.'

Daines's expression changed. 'Maybe you should take heed too.'

'Now you're threatening me?'

A hint of a smile crossed Daines's face. 'Look,' he said, 'I can understand why you're so wound up about this. You and her. It's personal, I can see that. I can sympathise. But the last I heard, unless it's been rescinded, you've been invalided out. Unfit for duty, isn't that the phrase? And for what you're doing here, keeping me against my will, you could be in deep, deep shit. I could press charges. That incident at Central Station, an unprovoked attack on a civilian, and now this, you'd be lucky to hang on to your pension. So let's both take a deep breath, okay?' Daines gestured with

436

his hands. 'I know you've been under a strain and I'm prepared to forget any of this ever happened. What do you say?'

'Alexander Bucur,' Resnick said, 'you phoned him that evening, the same day Lynn went down on her own . . .'

'Jesus! You don't let go, do you?'

'You called him back that evening after she'd gone.'

Daines's tone changed again. 'Who says? Is that what he says? Bucur?'

Resnick nodded.

'His word against mine.'

'Yes? Which phone did you use? Office phone or mobile? It shouldn't be too difficult to check.'

'Okay, that's it,' Daines said. 'I've had it with this.'

He reached for the controls and Resnick blocked him off.

'You knew which train she'd be catching,' Resnick said. 'What time she'd be getting in. Not difficult to calculate how long it would take from the station.'

'Meaning what? What difference would it make if I did?'

As soon as the words were out, he read the answer in Resnick's face.

'You think I killed her,' Daines said, incredulous. 'That's what you're saying? It is, isn't it? You think I killed her.'

'No, you'd be too careful for that. But you could finger her to somebody else who would.'

'You're crazy.'

Daines pushed past him and pressed the button and the lift slipped into motion.

'Someone,' Resnick said, 'who'd feel safer if she were out of the picture and not starting to dig around. Someone, maybe, who was bearing a grudge.'

The lift stopped on the fourth floor and as the door slid open, Daines stepped out.

'You are crazy,' he said. 'Absolutely off your fucking head.'

The door began to close and as Resnick jammed his foot in its path, he had a sudden urge, a near-blind impulse to throw himself at Daines, seize him by the shoulders and slam him back against the wall, then beat him with his fists.

'We'll see,' Resnick said instead and pulled his foot away so that the lift door closed and Daines was lost to sight.

43

Instead of reading about it first in the papers, as Resnick had suggested might be the case, Karen heard about it on the radio when she stepped out of the shower, and then, pulling on her robe, a towel wrapped round her hair, she switched on the television to catch what was still being billed as breaking news. In the early hours of the morning, officers from SOCA, the Serious and Organised Crime Agency, assisted by officers from the Metropolitan Police's Central Task Force and the Operational Support Department of the Nottinghamshire Police, had carried out raids on a number of addresses in north London and Nottingham. It was understood that firearms officers from the Nottinghamshire force and from CO19, the Met's Specialist Firearm Command, had also been deployed.

Pictures of armed police in all their gear, cars wellying along city streets and flashing lights were screened behind the newsreader's head, all stock footage, Karen was sure.

By the time she had dressed, more details had been released. Raids had been carried out on several shops and homes in the Wood Green and South Tottenham areas of London, in addition to warehouses in Paddington and Finsbury Park. In Nottingham, police and SOCA teams had targeted buildings on an industrial estate in Colwick, east of the city, as well as in the Lace Market area of the city centre itself. A number of arrests had been made and items seized were believed to include a considerable quantity of weapons and ammunition. There were reports, as yet unconfirmed, of shots being fired.

The pictures this time were real.

Video quickly released by the Met's public relations team were mixed on screen with poorly focused images emailed in by members of the public who had been awake enough to capture some of what had happened on their mobile phones. For a few unclear moments, the building housing the sauna where Nina Simic had been killed came into view, the front door hanging off, a police officer standing guard.

Karen rang Dixon and then Daines, but, perhaps not surprisingly, neither was answering his phone. When she rang Chris Butcher he spoke through a mouthful of toast.

'You watching this?'

'You bet,' Karen said.

'Any idea what's going on up there?' Butcher asked.

'Only what you see on screen. How 'bout you?'

'Give me an hour.'

'Will do.'

Wandering into the kitchen area, she made coffee, switching from national news to local and back again as she waited for it to brew. Firearms officers in Nottingham had fired eleven rounds and in London an unconfirmed number. It was not yet known if any of that gunfire had been returned. Estimates as to the items taken varied, but sources close to the Serious and Organised Crime Agency were suggesting that as many as six hundred illegal weapons had been seized, together with several thousand rounds of ammunition. The weapons, in the main, were Baikal IZH-79 pistols which were believed to have originated in Lithuania. According to the Reuters News Agency, the Lithuanian Police Bureau, in a carefully coordinated operation, had carried out a number of arrests in different parts of the country, including Rauba and the capital, Vilnius.

Karen finished her coffee while she was fixing her make-up.

She was on the point of leaving the apartment when Chris Butcher phoned. A total of fourteen individuals had been arrested in London, seven more, he thought, in Nottingham. She could check that herself. No Viktor Zoukas, no Valdemar. The police had gone to the house where Viktor was meant to be residing, but he wasn't there.

'Somebody tipped them off,' Karen said.

'Looks like.'

'How about Lazic?'

'No sign.'

'Jesus Christ!'

'My thoughts, exactly.'

'I'll be in touch.'

'Do that.'

A brush through her hair and Karen was on her way.

At Central Police Station, rumours were ripe as flies fastening on a dead dog. The number of firearms officers who had discharged their weapons varied from seven to two; shots on target from four to none. That a brief exchange of fire had taken place seemed certain, only the scale was so far open to question. One man who had taken a flesh wound to the back of the thigh was currently under police guard at Queen's Medical Centre; claims that a second man had been hit when he himself had opened fire on the police were so far unsubstantiated; none of the accident and emergency departments in the area had reported anyone else suffering from gunshot wounds. No officer had been hit.

The SOCA office in the city had, as far as Karen could tell, failed to open that day and calls to its London HQ were put on hold. Graeme Dixon's line at the Central Task Force was permanently busy; whoever he was talking to, Karen thought, it wasn't her.

She and Euan Guest shared some minutes of mutual regret that Ivan Lazic had so far avoided capture.

After that, Karen tried to occupy herself with the

small mountain of paperwork she'd been studiously avoiding, but it proved no antidote to her sense of annoyance and frustration. She was about to go and prowl the corridors in search of someone to berate when her phone sounded. Resnick at home.

'I'd like you to tell me,' he said, 'if Lazic was involved that he's in an interrogation room somewhere right now spilling his guts.'

'Not quite as much,' Karen said, 'as I would myself.'

'Got away?'

'We don't even know if he was around.'

Resnick was silent for several seconds. 'You've talked to London?'

'I'd talk to the devil if I thought it would help.'

Certainly did a lot for Robert Johnson, Resnick thought, but he kept it to himself; however keen she might be on Bessie Smith, he didn't think Karen would be up to exchanging small talk about blues singers right now.

'Could do worse,' he said.

'So they say.'

After Resnick had rung off, Karen had another brief conversation with Chris Butcher, but he had little to add to what he had told her before. She fought with a few forms, checked in with Mike Ramsden and told him to hell with it, she was going out to get some lunch.

'As long as you're buying,' Ramsden said, 'I'll string along.'

'Not this time, Mike, okay?'

If he was disappointed, he hid it well.

Karen walked down past the Victoria Centre, along Bridlesmith Gate and turned left towards the site of the new centre for contemporary art on Weekday Cross. Just along High Pavement, there was a large converted church which was now a Pitcher and Piano and, on the opposite side, further down, a pub called the Cock and Hoop – not too crowded, not too large and with a menu that looked promising. She was two bites into her rib-eye steak, and enjoying it, when Frank Michaelson called on her mobile. She even hesitated a moment before taking the call.

'Sally, boss,' Michaelson said. 'From the sauna? She's this minute rung. Ivan Lazic, she says she knows where he is.'

'Knows?'

'That's what she said.'

'Nothing more?'

'She said I have to go in, talk to her in person.'

Karen cut off another piece of tender, reddish meat. 'Where are you now?'

'That's the thing, I'm up at HQ.'

'Out at Sherwood?'

'Yes.'

'All right. I'm just round the corner. I'll go along.'

'Okay.'

'And Frank . . . ?'

'Yes, boss?'

'Phone Mike, let him know.'

Karen popped the piece of steak into her mouth and pushed the plate regretfully aside.

There were stone steps, worn down at the centre, leading up towards the front door, which was still attached by only one hinge and sagged against the frame. A hastily written sign had been fixed inside the sex-shop window, *Closed until further notice*. On the floor above, curtains had been pulled tight across. The sign above the door had been switched off. Karen pressed the bell and waited. Pressed the bell again and identified herself into the small mouthpiece alongside. Glancing up, she thought she saw a small movement at the right-hand window, the fold of a curtain falling back into place. She wasn't sure.

A car went slowly past along the street behind her, looking for somewhere to park.

Karen manoeuvred the door open carefully, closed it behind her and walked towards the stairs; dust had gathered in the corners of each tread and the carpet running up the centre was well worn. There was a light ahead.

On the landing, she stopped and called Sally's name. No response.

Opening another door, she went along a short, narrow corridor and then out into what she imagined was some kind of reception area, a counter to one side, settee and chairs to the other, a few magazines strewn around, posters showing naked girls with unlikely breasts on the walls. At the back of the counter was another door, a small sign reading *Office* between two panes of frosted glass.

'Sally?'

She thought she heard a noise from behind the office door.

'Sally. This is Detective Chief Inspector Karen Shields.'

Another sound, muffled and small. Moving quickly around the counter, Karen turned the office door handle and stepped inside. Sally was sitting pressed back against the side wall, legs folded beneath her, arms tied, a wide band of tape across her mouth.

Even as Karen registered a movement at her back, the hard small circle of a pistol barrel pressed cold against the nape of her neck.

'Don't move.'

The gun slid upwards until it was resting under the base of her skull.

'Now slowly lift your arms. Slowly! Slowly! Slow.'

Sally's eyes, watching, were wide with fear.

'Now step away, into the centre of the room. Stop. That's all. Good. Now turn around.'

Ivan Lazic's pale face contrasted sharply with his dark eyes, the dark brown, almost black, of his short-cropped hair and beard. The scar that zigzagged his cheek stood out like a lightning flash.

'Identification. Show me.'

Carefully, Karen opened her wallet and held it out towards him.

Lazic smiled thinly. 'Detective Chief Inspector, that is good.'

His accent, to Karen, sounded Russian. Russian,

Serbian, she couldn't tell the difference.

'Now sit,' Lazic said, gesturing with the gun. 'Behind the desk, there. Sit on your hands.'

When she was in position, he dragged a second chair across and sat facing her at the other side of the desk.

'What do you want?' Karen asked. The room was small and windowless and she could already smell her own sweat.

'I want,' Lazic said, 'to give myself up.'

'There's a police station in the centre of town. All you had to do was walk in.'

'And get myself shot.'

'That wouldn't happen.'

'No?'

'If you went in waving that gun, perhaps.'

'And still, if not?'

'Police in England don't shoot unarmed men.'

'No? Like they didn't shoot this Brazilian, on the train in London. How many shots? Five times to the head?'

'That was different.'

Lazic laughed. 'Different, yes.' He caught his breath. 'You know, when I was growing up, in my country, I read about the British police, how they never carry guns, and I think, how stupid, how brave. But now . . . this morning, for instance, here . . .' He looked at her. 'That was different too.'

He laughed and when he laughed he gasped and when he gasped a small sliver of blood appeared at one corner of his mouth. Between the lapels of his coat, the wool of the sweater he was wearing was stained, Karen could see now, pinkish red.

'You need a doctor,' Karen said. 'Hospital.'

Lazic smiled. 'Sally, she was my nurse.'

There were beads of sweat visible on his forehead now and Karen wondered just how badly hurt he was, how long he could hold on. She looked down at the gun in his hand and instinctively he tightened his grip.

'I want to make deal,' Lazic said.

'What kind of deal?'

'I tell everything I know, everything.'

'It may be too late for that.'

Lazic winced and bit his lower lip. 'No. Valdemar, Viktor, they have run, I know. I am sure. Leave me . . . leave me . . . what is expression? Holding baby. I do not think so. You take me. I go with you. We make deal.'

Karen shook her head. 'Even if I wanted to, it's not as easy as that.'

'Easy, yes. And only with police, not Customs.' A smile lifted for a moment the edges of his mouth. 'One of officers, customs officers, he and Valdemar, they are friends. Valdemar give him money, girls. I know. I have tape. We make deal.'

For a moment, he leaned back against the chair and closed his eyes. Long enough for Karen to think about going for the gun but no more.

'You will arrange,' Lazic said, 'doctor for me. Soon.'

The stain on his chest was darkening, spreading.

'The gun,' Karen said. 'First you must give me the gun.'

He looked into her eyes. Then slowly, very slowly, he leaned forward and placed the pistol on the desk.

'I must use my phone,' Karen said, reaching towards her pocket.

But Lazic was no longer really listening.

44

'Christ!' Butcher's voice reverberated in her ear. 'You did what? What're you after, some medal for valour? The George fucking Cross?'

Karen smiled, enjoying his indignant surprise. 'All in a day's work.'

'Give me the gun, you said, and instead of letting you have one between the eyes he just puts it down? Here, help yourself.'

'More or less.'

'More or less? This is the guy who's killed two as far as we know . . .'

'As far as we think.'

'Who's killed two, possibly three in the last month and God knows how many in the past. The scourge of fucking Serbia and you get him to surrender, nicely nicely.'

'He was pretty badly wounded in this morning's raid.'

'Not badly enough.'

'And he wanted to do a deal.'

'The only deal he'll get, parole after twenty years instead of twenty-five.'

'Maybe.'

'When're you shipping him down to London? We're the primaries on this, remember? Agreed.'

'Yes, but look, I don't think he's going anywhere right now. Not for a good few days, at least.'

'While you interrogate him, you mean?'

'Chris, he's not talking. Not to anyone. Too doped up with painkillers to think.'

'No problem getting a sample, though. Have a word with one of the docs. I want to check his DNA against what we found under that girl's fingernails.'

'Will do.'

'And, hotshot . . .'

'Yes?'

'Keep me up to speed, okay?'

'You got my word.'

There'd been prolonged applause when Karen had walked back into the CID office that afternoon and a note of congratulation had already come down from the Assistant Chief. Mike Ramsden had been busy organising a right royal piss-up for that evening.

'If there's a male stripper, Mike,' Karen told him, 'that's it, I'm leaving.'

'One?' Ramsden said. 'For you we've got a whole bloody chorus line.'

She was filling in a report when the phone interrupted her thoughts.

'Principal Officer Daines?' the switchboard operator said.

Karen looked at her watch. It hadn't taken long. 'Put him through.'

'Chief Inspector, I hear congratulations are in order.' His voice smooth as shit on the underside of a shoe.

'News travels fast.'

'Lazic, I thought we had him this morning, but somehow he slipped away.'

Karen didn't reply.

'Of course, we've had our eye on him for some time, just waiting for the right moment to haul him in. A file on him that stretches all the way back to Kosovo and beyond. But most recently he was near the heart of this gun-trafficking deal, more or less Zoukas's right-hand man.' He paused. 'I guess, with his injuries, we'll have to wait a day or so before you can hand him over.'

'I think,' Karen said, 'if any handing over's to be done, it'll be to the Met. SCD1, Homicide and Serious Crime Command.'

Daines's voice tightened. 'I don't think so.'

'I'm not sure what exactly you were considering charging him with,' Karen said, 'but whatever it is, I think you'll find murder takes precedence.'

'Murder? What murder?'

'Take your pick.' Karen was still smiling when she broke the connection and immediately dialled Ramsden's number. 'Mike, the guard on Lazic's room at the hospital, I want it doubled. And clear instructions, nobody gets to talk to Lazic, wish him well, grapes, flowers, anything. Understood? And that does mean anyone. SOCA especially. Got it?'

'Got it,' Ramsden said. 'I'm on my way.'

It was Catherine Njoroge who phoned Resnick eventually. Unfit for duty, she told him, doesn't mean you can't socialise. Join us in a drink. Still he hesitated, and it was mid-evening by the time he showed his face, no one yet seriously the wrong side of sober, but a lot of beer and whisky under the bridge and the decibel level around twice as high as normal.

So far, much to Karen's relief, no strippers had arrived, a bunch of local bodybuilders, all greased up and G-stringed and anxious to give it the full monty, though there were signs of karaoke breaking out later and Karen was already wondering whether she would have drunk enough by then to give them her best Aretha, stomping through 'Respect'.

When she saw Resnick hovering just inside the door, she beckoned him over and they found a little space close to one of the windows looking down into the street.

'You must be getting fed up,' Resnick said, 'with people saying well done.'

'Makes a change from stupid cow. Thinking it, even if they don't come right out and say it.'

'Not too often, I shouldn't think.'

'I don't know,' Karen said and smiled.

'Anyway,' Resnick said, raising his glass, 'well done.'

'Luck, Charlie. Fell right into my lap.'

'Maybe.'

A roar of laughter went up from a group in the centre of the room, ribald and raucous.

'What's the state of play?' Resnick asked.

'They've operated on Lazic to take out the bullet. Should make a good enough recovery, apparently, though by the time they got him to the hospital, he'd shipped quite a lot of blood. I doubt if the doctors will agree to him being moved for a few days and until then, my best guess, we'll keep him under wraps. Soon as we get the sign he's fit to travel, drive him down to London, somewhere high security like Paddington Green, let the Met have first crack at him.'

'Hardly seems fair, after what you've done.'

Karen shrugged bare shoulders. The dress she was wearing had been chosen with care: attractive, yes, but for an evening celebrating with a bunch of fellow officers, mostly male, she didn't want to be sending out any signals that suggested she might be available. Though by the end of the evening, she didn't doubt one or two of them would try.

'The Florescu murder,' she said, 'that's looking the strongest by far. But I know the lead officer pretty well. He'll play it straight. Let me have a crack when the time's right.'

Michaelson and Pike came over to talk to Resnick and guide him back in the direction of the bar. The

454

ACC, who'd just dropped in for a moment, pressed a large Scotch into Karen's hand, along with the Chief Constable's congratulations and apologies for not being there in person. This rate, Karen thought, they'll be offering me the freedom of the city. On a small stage off to the side of the room, Mike Ramsden was preparing to get things going with a quick burst of Carl Perkins's 'Blue Suede Shoes' delivered à la King.

Daines was sitting on the stairs outside Karen's apartment. Though it was far from a cold night and certainly not cold inside the building, the collar of his suit jacket was turned up against his neck. His tie was loose, the top button of his shirt unfastened.

'Good night?' he asked.

'Lively,' Karen said.

'I'll bet. Somehow my invitation got lost in transit.'

'From what you said earlier, I didn't think you were exactly cheering.'

'About Lazic getting arrested? We did out best earlier. Bastard tried to shoot his way out. That's how he stopped one himself.'

'A good result for you, though. All those weapons seized. Arrests aplenty. Though I hear both Zoukas brothers somehow slipped the net.'

Daines gave a small shrug. 'It happens.'

'Doesn't it though?' She was looking at him hard.

Daines smiled. 'You wouldn't want to invite me in?' he asked, with a nod towards her apartment door. 'Nightcap. One for the road.'

455

'That's right,' Karen said, 'I wouldn't.'

'Too bad.' He got to his feet and, when he did, because of the stairs, he was a good head taller. 'I tried to see Lazic at the hospital. Couple of guys sitting there with sub-machine guns in their laps wouldn't let me in. Acting on instructions, they said.'

'We wouldn't want to risk losing him now. Not any of us, I'm sure.'

'Did he say anything about me?'

'About you? No, why? Should he?'

He moved in closer and Karen readied herself; if he tried anything he was just at the right height for a quick elbow in the balls.

'You're playing games with me, aren't you?' Daines said.

'Not at all. If you want a report of Lazic's medical condition, that can be arranged. As soon as he's fit enough to be moved down to London, you'll be informed. You've got my assurance he won't be questioned while he's here and I'm sure you can liaise with SCD once he's in their care.' She took a step up and moved to go round him. 'Now that about sorts it, don't you think?'

He stepped across into her path and his face was pressed close to hers; his breath warm on her face. Even in the subdued light of the stairs, she could see the green glimmer at the corner of his eye.

'If I thought you were fucking with me . . .'

'Yes?' She held his gaze. Not for the first time, she wondered if he was armed.

'If you are . . .'

'Then what?'

He stared at her and then, as if making a sudden decision, he stepped away. 'Just wanted to add my congratulations,' he said, with a quick, almost apologetic shrug. 'Job well done.'

'Thank you,' Karen said.

She waited until he was out of sight, his footsteps fading down the stairs, before letting herself into the apartment and securing the door behind her.

When Resnick had got home, some time earlier, he had made himself a sandwich – all that beer, more than he was used to, making him hungry – and put a pot of coffee on the stove. Chet Baker somehow suited the mood. It was a while before he thought to check his phone: three messages from Ryan Gregan, the most recent an hour before.

45

After meeting Gregan, Resnick had made himself take a long, slow walk, back through the Arboretum and along Mansfield Road as far as the Forest Recreation Ground before cutting through to St Ann's. The manner in which he'd confronted Daines had been foolish. Juvenile. Sufficiently out of character for him to take the judgement unfit for duty to heart. Unfit? Unfit was too bloody right.

Not now.

Howard Brent was outside his house, touching up the offside front wing of his car where someone had scraped it driving past. He had barely paused to look up as Resnick approached, but when Resnick spoke he had listened. Listened and replied, his normal hostility tempered by something he would have been hard put to explain. Slowly, he straightened and watched Resnick as he walked away.

Jason Price lived in the upper two rooms of a

terraced house in one of the short streets that narrowed out either side of Sneinton Dale; one room had a narrow bed and a spare mattress on the floor, the other an old two-seater settee that had been dragged in from a nearby skip, a couple of wooden chairs and a third-hand stereo along with, Price's pride and joy, a large-screen plasma TV he had traded for ten grammes of amphetamines and fifty tabs of LSD. There was a microwave in one corner, next to a sink with a small hot-water heater alongside. The lavatory was on the floor below.

When Resnick arrived, Price was in T-shirt and boxer shorts, having not long got out of bed. It was a few minutes past eleven, Sunday morning. Church bells all over the city were ringing, calling the people to shopping centres and supermarkets, Homebase and B & Q.

'What the fuck . . . ?' Price said, opening the downstairs door.

'Marcus here?' Resnick asked.

Price nodded. 'Snorin' upstairs, i'n'it?'

'Get on some clothes and get lost. And don't wake him. Let him sleep.'

'What's this all about?'

'Just do it.'

Price knew the law when he saw it; knew better than to argue. Thank Christ him and Marcus had smoked the last of his stash before turning in. Five minutes and he was gone.

The upstairs room smelt of dope and tobacco and the

slightly sweet, not unfamiliar stink of two young men who slept with the window firmly closed. Resnick flicked back the catch and levered the top half of the window down and Marcus, angled across the mattress, one bare foot touching the floor, stirred at the sound. Stirred and rolled on to one side and resumed sleeping.

What was he, Resnick asked himself? Eighteen at most? Asleep, he looked younger, his face smooth and his skin the colour of copper. Fragile. Vulnerable. Somebody's son.

'Marcus.' Resnick pushed at the side of the mattress with his shoe. 'Marcus, wake up.'

Another push and the youth spluttered awake, twisting his head towards Resnick and gasping as if seeing something in a dream, except that this, he realised seconds later, was worse.

No nightmare: this was real.

'Get up,' Resnick said. 'Put something on.'

Marcus rolled sideways and pushed himself to his feet. Bollock naked, he reached for his jeans and a V-necked top.

'What the fuck is this? Where's Jason? What's goin' on?'

'I've been trying to figure it out, Marcus,' Resnick said, 'and I'm still not sure. Which was it? Greed or plain stupidity?'

'What? What the fuck you talkin' about?'

'Selling the gun.'

'What? What the . . . ? I dunno what you're on about. What fuckin' gun? I dunno nothin' 'bout no fuckin' gun.'

But the shiver in his eyes said that he did.

'A Baikal semi-automatic, Marcus, remember? I don't know who you bought it from, haven't been able to find that out yet, but I know who you sold it to. A man named Steven Burchill, round the back of the Sands in Gainsborough . . .'

Marcus made a bolt for the door and Resnick grabbed his arm and swung him hard round, so that he landed on the floor with a loud thump then rolled hard against the wall and caught the edge of the skirting board with enough force to open a cut above his left eye.

'Waste of effort,' Resnick said, dismissively. 'You didn't think I'd come here without back-up? There's men downstairs, front and back. Cars at the end of the street.'

Marcus shivered, believing Resnick's lie, and wiped the back of his hand across his forehead, smearing blood.

'Here,' Resnick said, taking a handkerchief from his pocket. 'Use this.'

He had thought, when he finally found Lynn's killer, when he confronted him face to face, that he would be unable to control his anger, that it would need others to hold him back, to stop him from trying to take vengeance into his own hands; but now, in that small sad room, looking down at that skinny youth, not yet twenty, not too bright, not so very different from the scores of similar young men he'd had to deal with over the years, he found the anger draining out of him – the anger at this individual at least.

461

'A couple of hundred, that's all you got for it. That's what Burchill said. Not a good price, but then, you weren't in much of a position to bargain.'

'There's no prints . . .' Marcus blurted. 'You can't prove . . .'

Resnick shook his head. 'Science, Marcus. Forensic science. What's that programme that's so popular? You've probably seen it? *CSI*? Of course, it's nothing like that, not in real life. Not over here, at least. But one thing is the same. What they can do, match a recovered bullet to a particular gun. And we have the bullet, two in fact. And now, since the early hours of this morning, we have the gun.'

Not the brightest apple in the box, Steven Burchill had kept it double-wrapped in plastic inside the cistern of the backyard toilet where he lived. Something he'd seen in a film once somewhere, Resnick didn't doubt, something on the box.

It had not taken Ryan Gregan long to persuade Burchill to say where it was, Resnick waiting not quite out of earshot till the job was done.

'I don't think I really understood at first why you did it,' Resnick said, 'the specifics. But now I think I do.'

Marcus was sitting on the floor with his legs drawn up towards him, head down, one hand holding Resnick's once white handkerchief against the wound.

'You and your father had a big row just before he left for Jamaica. The same sort of row you'd had before, I dare say, but this was worse. All you wanted from him, I think, was respect. A little more respect. But it ended up, as it often did, with him telling you you were useless, stupid, not worth the time of day. And all the time there was Michael in the background, Michael being held up in comparison, Michael the perfect son.

'And you knew all the things your father had said about Lynn Kellogg, how she was to blame for your sister's death. How he hated her. How much he'd told you all to hate her. How she had to pay. And you thought that would show him, once and for all. Prove to him not just that you were Michael's equal, but that you were better. Braver. So you bought the gun. And you waited. I don't know how many nights you waited. Two? Three? And then there she was.'

He could hear his voice starting to choke, but he made himself carry on.

'There she was walking towards you and from that range you didn't even have to be especially skilled with a gun. From that range it would have been difficult to miss.'

Resnick turned away and willed back tears.

Marcus was crying now, enough tears for both of them: not tears of sorrow for what he'd done, but out of his own fear of what would happen.

'You told him,' Resnick said, 'your father. When he came back to England you told him what you'd done and, of course, he didn't believe you. You wouldn't have the guts, he said. You wouldn't have the balls. So you told him you didn't care, didn't care what he thought, told him you never wanted to speak to him again and walked out, came here.'

'I don't,' Marcus cried, sobbing, rocking himself back and forth. 'I don't care what he fuckin' thinks. I hate him, I hate him, I hate him . . .'

Resnick stood back and reached into his pocket for his mobile phone.

'Karen, sorry to disturb your Sunday. But you'd better get yourself out here. Rustle up your bagman. One or two others.'

He gave her the address.

46

It was high summer. Resnick had left London in what was, to him, almost sweltering heat, twenty-eight degrees Celsius, the low eighties Fahrenheit, his shirt sticking to his back as he stood in one seemingly interminable line after another, waiting first at the check-in and then, finally, the slow zigzag shuffling towards the X-ray machines and the officials with their wands and blank expressions. In between, there were the protracted dealings with Customs, the careful scrutinising of the death certificate and the certificate of embalming, the necessary authorisation to remove the deceased's body from the country for burial overseas.

A clear and definite DNA match linking Ivan Lazic with the skin sample found under Andreea's fingernails had resulted in his being charged with her murder, and once a second post-mortem had been carried out for the benefit of his defence, Andreea's body had been released. On the evidence so far available, the CPS had opted not to charge Lazic with the murder of Kelvin Pearce.

After several conversations with Andreea Florescu's parents, using Alexander Bucur as mediator, Resnick had arranged to accompany Andreea's coffin on its journey, knowing that it was what Lynn would have wanted, what she would have done herself had she been able.

Three hours and a little more to Bucharest and then a change of plane on to a smaller Russian-made aircraft that would take him the relatively short distance to Constanta.

As he stepped out on to the tarmac at Mihail Kogalniceanu airport, the heat hit him again like a slap across the face.

Andreea's parents were waiting to greet him: her mother, small and fair haired, her face dissolving into tears the moment she saw him; her father, stocky and dark as his wife was fair, crushing Resnick's hand in both of his and then kissing him on both cheeks.

'Thank you,' he said in heavily accented English. 'Thank you, thank you, thank you.'

Behind them, Andreea's zinc-lined coffin was being slowly unloaded from the hold.

The journey south from the airport took them first along a motorway, which led to the beginnings of the town itself and a wide boulevard which swept, rather incongruously, past a succession of flat-fronted houses, small shops and garages, several crumbling apartment blocks, and then a large park busy with families picnicking and chasing brightly coloured footballs, many of them – the younger ones – in swimming costumes, the older men with their shirtsleeves rolled back and the women with summer dresses raised up along pale thighs.

'A lake,' Andreea's father informed him, jabbing his finger. In the middle of the park there was a lake. Also, if Resnick had understood correctly, a dolphinarium. Even with the windows wound down, inside the car it was uncomfortably hot.

Not so much further along, they turned left, leaving the Bulevard Tomis – Resnick had read the sign – and drove a short distance down a narrow, dusty road and then turned again, into a rundown housing estate of the kind Resnick knew only too well from his years on the beat in Nottingham. Low-rise blocks joined by a succession of walkways and arranged around central areas that on the architect's plans had doubtless been enticingly green open spaces bordered by trees, where mothers could sit nursing their babies and children could safely play. Except that the grass had soon turned to mud and was festooned with dog shit, broken glass and discarded needles, and the trees had been uprooted while they were still saplings and not replaced. A brave new world.

In Nottingham, places like this had been knocked down, demolished and replaced by social housing that was more thoughtful, more appropriate to people's needs.

Here in Constanta, some – this estate, at least – remained.

A pack of dogs, some ten or a dozen strong, came running towards them, snarling, and the father chased them off with kicks and shouts and pieces of rubble picked up from the ground and hurled into their midst.

The Florescus' flat was on the fourth floor, reached, the lift being out of order, after climbing heavily graffitied stairs and walking along a balcony with numerous cracks of several centimetres' width.

Both living room and kitchen were overrun by an extended family of cousins, uncles and aunts, all anxious to shake his hand and offer thanks.

'Our Andreea's murderer,' said one man with a white streak running up through his hair, 'you have brought him to justice.'

'Not me,' Resnick said. 'Somebody else.'

But that was not what they wanted to hear and they chose not to understand. Someone thrust a mug of sweet tea into his hand, while someone else plied him with plum brandy. Soon the room, despite the windows being open, was thick with cigarette smoke. Everyone, save for the youngest, seemed to be smoking. In one corner of the room, the television was tuned to CNN, the volume turned down low. There seemed to be forest fires in parts of Spain and Portugal, floods in South-East Asia with thousands losing their homes; several European aid workers had been kidnapped in Baghdad, and in Islamabad a suicide bomber had detonated the explosives taped to his stomach in a local market, killing fourteen and wounding more than thirty, some of them children.

After much coaxing by her grandmother, Andreea's three-year-old daughter, Monica, rising four, came out from behind the settee and stood before Resnick, head down, hands clasped, wearing a green dress with a white sash which was kept for special occasions.

Resnick fetched from his bag the presents he had brought her: a picture book on stiff board with bright illustrations of animals in strong colours, a T-shirt in blue, white and orange stripes and a teddy bear with a large red bow at his neck.

She took each from him solemnly, thanked him haltingly, and then ran to her grandmother and stood clutching her legs with one hand, while hanging on tightly to the teddy bear with the other.

A plate was passed round with slices of sponge cake filled with jam. More tea. More brandy. Wine. The wake, Resnick thought, before the funeral. One of the cousins, sixteen, quizzed him in near-perfect English about the Premiership and Tottenham Hotspur's chances of breaking into the top four. Ever since Spurs had bought both Ilie Dumitrescu and Gica Popescu following Romania's successes in the 1994 World Cup, they had been a team of special interest.

Resnick's subsequent confession that the team he himself supported was not even Nottingham Forest, formerly winners of the European Cup, but lowly Notts County was met with bafflement.

After an hour or more, towards the end of which

Resnick's eyes kept involuntarily closing, Andreea's father took pity on him and drove him to his hotel, the Intim, which dated back to the late nineteenth century and had previously been called the Hotel d'Angleterre. Someone had thought he would feel at home.

His room looked out past the cathedral towards the Black Sea, which from there looked not black but grey, the kind of grey he was used to seeing when he gazed east from Mablethorpe or Whitby.

He stripped off his clothes and showered and, after drying himself, stretched out on the clean, slightly worn sheets and fell, almost immediately, asleep.

The funeral service was held in a Roman Catholic church close to the family's home, the church packed, the atmosphere stifling – Resnick, who because of some strange divisions in his own, largely Jewish family, had been brought up as a Catholic, falling automatically into the ritual of signs and observances, prayers and obeisances. The temperature inside and outside the church was close to thirty Celsius.

On the previous evening, Andreea's parents, brushing his protestations aside, had insisted on taking him to dinner in the old casino, a handsome, almost baroque building with an arched entrance and huge arched windows, which stood on a promenade overlooking the sea. Black-suited waiters with white aprons tied at the waist brought a succession of dishes in solemn procession: fish soup, carp roe salad, and then – shepherd's sirloin, according to the translation on the menu – pork stuffed with ham, then covered with cheese and a sauce of mayonnaise, cucumber and herbs. The wine, Andreea's father assured him, was the best in Romania, Fetească Neagră, with a rich redness that was close to purple, almost black. A dessert of crisp pastry soaked in syrup and filled with whipped cream was, in every sense, too much.

Head reeling and stomach rolling, when they had left the restaurant – the sky a vivid midnight blue pricked with stars, the moon floating in the darkness of the water – Resnick's only thoughts had been of falling back into bed, but his hosts had insisted on his accompanying them to a piano bar for a glass or two of rachiu, Romanian grape brandy. To settle the stomach, Andreea's father had suggested with appropriate gestures.

The bar was below ground, a couple of small smoke-filled rooms, neither of them, as far as Resnick could see, containing a piano. The music, piped through overhead speakers, had been, in the main, piano music, however; jazz of a sort, an extended free-form extemporising with Monkish overtones, which Resnick decided, in different surroundings, could be rewarding.

His head throbbed and his eyes stung.

Harry Tavitian, he was told when he enquired, that was the pianist's name. From there, in Constanta. Famous everywhere. All over the world. Resnick nodded, never having heard of him before.

Finally, he had stumbled up the steps and out into the

471

air. It was still warm and the sweet sweat of his body made him nauseous.

Here inside the church, the incense was close to overpowering. The congregation was standing to sing a hymn and Resnick stood with them, mouth open, no words forthcoming. He had had enough of funerals, enough of death, enough dying. He closed his eyes and ignored the tears and waited for it all to end.

Packed and ready, there was an hour still before leaving to catch his plane and there were things he could see. He had read the leaflet in four languages at the hotel. He could go to the top of the minaret above the Mahmudiye Mosque for a panoramic view of the town and harbour, or to the Museum of the Romanian Navy with its photographs of the Russian battleship *Potemkin* arriving unexpectedly with its crew of mutinous sailors. Instead he walked down through the central square of the old part of the town, named after the poet Ovid, who was exiled there from Rome by the Emperor Augustus for writing *The Art of Love*, which had somehow offended the emperor's sensibilities.

Poor bastard, Resnick thought, looking up at the statue that was daubed in pigeon droppings and eroded by the weather. Doomed to live out a lonely life in a country that was not his own. There were a few lines of his poetry reprinted in the leaflet, miserable as sin. And cold. As if all the time he was there he could never get warm, the snow drifting in off the sea.

Resnick walked on down for a final look at the water.

At the airport, Andreea's mother hugged him and held him close, murmuring her thanks; her father shook his hand as heartily as before and wished him well. Monica hid behind her grandmother's skirt and only came out at the last moment to stand, wide eyed, and wave, her teddy bear clasped tight against her chest.

They were lovely people, Resnick thought, warm and caring. Hurting, too. Fifteen minutes later, his plane was in the air.

Though it had only been days, the house seemed unlived in, felt alien, cold. That again: cold. As he'd turned his keys in the door, the cats had come running, the familiar sound signalling food, a Pavlovian response, though he guessed the neighbour he entrusted them to would have overfed them as usual.

There were several messages on the answerphone, one from Karen Shields that said simply, Call me. When he did, she asked if he wanted to come into the station, or whether he'd prefer for her to come to him.

'I'm knackered,' Resnick said, 'why don't you come out here? Just give me time to shower and change.'

Twenty minutes later she was there. White vest, red skirt, flat shoes.

'Hot as hell,' she said.

'There's water in the fridge. Juice.'

'Water would be fine.'

The rear of the house was in the shade and that was where they sat.

'How did it go?' Karen asked.

'All right, I suppose. I was glad I went.'

'I'm sure they were too.'

Resnick nodded.

'I'm just about through here,' Karen said. 'I've only been coming up for odd days and now there's no need for even that. Anil can handle anything else that crops up before the trial.'

'You did a good job.'

'I did bugger all.'

Resnick smiled.

'You know,' Karen said, 'we found the shoe? The Adidas trainers? Marcus had sold them. A friend of a friend. It helps fill the picture.'

Resnick nodded. 'How about our pal Daines?'

'Still stonewalling,' Karen said. Lazic had testified that the SOCA man had been in the Zoukas brothers' pockets, evidenced by the fact that both had successfully slipped out of the country avoiding arrest, Viktor using a false passport. He had also provided a blurred video which showed – or seemed to show, Daines's lawyers were strongly disputing it – Daines taking part in a three-way sex session involving, at various times, a riding crop, a large strapped-on dildo and a woman stretched out on a bed and tied hand and foot.

'He's claiming,' Karen said, 'any involvement was justified in terms of the information it allowed him to obtain. And the information he passed on was pretty damn useful, there's no getting around that.'

'You think he's going to walk away?'

'Who knows? Right now, he's suspended on full pay, while SOCA's Professional Standards Department carry out an investigation. I reckon he'll be lucky if they don't turn it over to an outside force.'

Whatever was decided, Resnick thought, it looked as if Lynn's instincts had been right all along.

'How about you?' Karen asked.

'How about me?'

'You know what I mean.'

One of the other messages on the answerphone had been from the police surgeon, wanting to know when Resnick, who had cancelled two appointments in the past month, felt able to come in and see him for a check-up and an all-clear to go back to work. The truth was, he was unsure if he wanted to go back at all.

'I've got my thirty years in,' Resnick said. 'I could retire.'

'And do what?' Karen said incredulously. 'Take an allotment, grow your own fruit and veg?'

'Why not?'

Karen laughed. 'You'd go crazy.'

Resnick shrugged. Maybe she was right, maybe he would. But he wasn't sure if he had the taste for it any more. Not after all that had happened. And besides, maybe an allotment wasn't all that ridiculous an idea. Plus, he could read all those books he had never found time for, visit those places he had never been. And how many jazz festivals were there? Wigan, Brecon, Appleby, North Sea. And those were just for starters. He could even go and see his pal, Ben Riley, who'd

475

moved out to the States more years ago than either of them cared to remember, and who had almost tired of inviting him to come and stay.

He shook his head; he didn't know.

'You'll sort something out,' Karen said. 'Maybe you just need a little more time.'

Reaching down into her bag, she took out the box set of CDs she'd borrowed, back when it had all started.

'Thanks,' she said. 'Now I'll have to get my own.'

He walked with her to the door.

'Watch out for that Catherine Njoroge,' Karen said with a wink. 'She'll have her eye on you now you're single.'

'You are joking?'

'Probably.' She tapped a fist against his shoulder. 'Though you never know.'

When Karen had gone, he went into the kitchen and stood for a moment staring into an almost empty cupboard. Time to restock. The smallest cat nudged against him and he picked it up and felt the soft fur of its head against his neck, the quick beat of its heart against his hand.

What would Lynn say, he wondered? Jack it in or carry on?

He thought about poor bloody Ovid, mired now in bird shit, stranded and alone.

Later that evening, curtains partly drawn, glass of good Scotch at his side, he put the first of the Bessie Smith CDs on to play, Bessie's voice full and raw and strengthened, it seemed, by adversity. 'After You've

476

Gone', 'Empty Bed Blues' and Resnick's especial favourite, 'Cold in Hand', the young Louis Armstrong's muted cornet shadowing her phrase for phrase and note for note.

Cold in hand.

How had Ovid put it? Freezing his balls off in Constanta. Something about the snow?

One drift succeeds another here.
The north wind hardens it, making it eternal;
It spreads in drifts through all the bitter year.

Bitter. That wasn't going to be him. Old and bitter. He smiled. Lynn would never forgive him for that.

ACKNOWLEDGEMENTS

Much-needed editorial help aside, the biggest debt of gratitude I owe is to Peter Coles, formerly a detective superintendent with the Nottinghamshire police, who has done his utmost to keep me to the straight and narrow as I falteringly navigated the changes in current police nomenclature and procedure. All failings, it should go without saying, are down to me alone.

Romania I visited under the auspices of the British Council, and I am grateful to them and, especially, to the people I met in Constanta – teachers and students – for their kindness and hospitality. Anyone wishing to explore the avant-garde world of jazz pianist Harry Tavitian should begin at www.harrytavitian.ro.

And for those seeking a more salubrious side of the fair city of Nottingham than the one presented in these pages, any of the following would be a good place to begin:

www.visitnottingham.com

www.nottinghamcity.gov.uk

or www.bbc.co.uk/nottingham

And, of course, www.nottscountyfc.co.uk. Come on, you Pies!

Will Grayson hated mornings like this: this time of the year. Not so dark that when the alarm went he could guiltlessly ignore its call and steal, as long as the kids remained asleep next door, ten, fifteen minutes more, but just light enough, the sky beginning to break at the far horizon, to prise him from his bed.

Alongside him, Lorraine stirred and for a moment he turned back towards her warmth, her hand reaching sleepily for his as he kissed the smooth skin of her shoulder then rolled away.

Downstairs, he pulled on his running gear and laced up his shoes, Susie's first cry reaching him as he slipped the bolt on the door and stepped outside. A few stretching exercises and he set off along the narrow road towards the end of the village, the path that would take him between the fields towards the fen.

Though there were times when he would deny it, disclaim responsibility, it was Will's decision that had finally brought them here to this small, strung-out village in the sparsely populated north of the county, where everything beneath the widening sky seemed to be water, sometimes even the land.

Lorraine, it was true, had been prodding them, even before their eldest, Jake, had been born: wanting them to move out of the city, away from the small, terraced house, with its pinch-sized garden and damp walls. Somewhere in the country where they could find more space and room, fresh air, somewhere healthy for the kids – she had always talked of two, at least – to grow. And Will had half-agreed but hung back, uncertain, valuing the push and flurry of Cambridge proper, the proximity, if not of friends, at least of people they knew, and dreading the long commute into work, the backed-up lines of barely moving traffic. Maybe they should stick fast, stay where they were, extend upwards if she liked, a loft conversion, plenty enough of those. But then, driving east from Ely, having looked at something in the town – no bigger than where they already were and close to twice the price – they had been attracted by a For Sale sign pointing away from the main road, not an estate agent's board, but one the owner had put up himself; a builder with an eye for design who had bought the land two years before and built this place – simple, clean lines, pale wood and glass – as a dream house for his wife. His dream, as it had turned out, not hers.

Will liked the wooden porch than ran the length of the building at the rear, the comfortable feel of the rooms, the high, broad windows with views out towards Ely cathedral and the slow-setting sun.

'So what do you think?' he'd asked Lorraine, and read the answer happily in her eyes.

Once the novelty had worn off they were certain they had made a mistake. The drive to the police station where Will was based, close to Cambridge city centre on Parkside, took even longer some days – most days – than he had reckoned, and in the long hours that he was away, Lorraine, marooned with only a barely crawling child for company, felt as if she were going slowly out of her mind. Sometimes not so slowly at all.

'Okay,' Will said. 'Sell up. Cut our losses. Find somewhere else.'

They'd stayed. Gradually, almost grudgingly, Lorraine found other women in the village, other mothers, with whom she had common cause; Will's move, as detective inspector, into the Major Investigation Team was confirmed, taking Helen Walker with him as his DS, a working relationship that had sparked and flourished now for close on five years. How much longer Will could hang on to her before she was heading a squad of her own, he wasn't sure.

Something had been itching at Helen lately, he'd noticed, making both tongue and temper sharper than ever, and maybe that's what it was. A lack of recognition: too long spent trailing in his wake.

Forty minutes after setting out on his run, Will was back at the house, muscles aching, head clear, vest sweated to his skin; a quick shower and a brisk towelling and then into the kitchen for breakfast, Jake spooning Rice Krispies into his mouth as if there were no tomorrow, Susie managing to get more of the glop from her bowl into her hair than anywhere else.

Will poured himself a second cup of coffee and spread marmalade on his last piece of toast; Lorraine was upstairs putting the finishing touches to her face. Three days a week she worked in the admissions office at King's College and on those days she dropped Susie off with the registered child minder, before taking Jake to the local primary from where the child minder would collect him at the end of the day.

At first, Will had been against the idea of Lorraine going back to work before Susie had started at nursery, but now he'd be the first to admit they were all better off for it – even though, financially, once the childcare had been paid for, it made little positive difference.

He swallowed down the remainder of his coffee and rinsed the mug at the sink; stooped to give Jake a quick hug and kissed the top of his head. 'Have a good day at school, okay? Work hard.'

'Okay.'

Susie put her arms out towards him and he managed to kiss her cheek without getting cereal from her sticky fingers all over his shirt.

'Dad?' Jake's voice stopped Will at the door. 'This evening, when you get home, can we play football?'

'Sure.'

Leaving the kitchen and living-room curtains open

would give them all the floodlighting they would need. Jake would be Manchester United, varying between Ronaldo and Rooney, while Will, no longer Arsenal, was doomed to be Cambridge United. A lopsided contest at best.

When Will stepped out into the lobby, Lorraine was almost at the bottom of the stairs.

'You off?' she said.

'Better be.'

'Home late?'

'No more than usual.'

She slid inside his arms and when he bent his head towards her she kissed him lightly on the lips and stepped away. 'Later, okay?'

Will laughed. 'On a promise then, am I?'

'You wish!'

Still laughing, he pulled his topcoat from the rack and headed out the door.

As often, Helen was there before him, leaning against the roof of her blue VW, enjoying her last cigarette before entering the building.

In the past few years she had tried patches, hypnosis, Nicorettes, even acupuncture, but the longest she had been able to abstain had been three months: one more particularly grisly case, one more set of early mornings and late, late nights and she had tumbled off the wagon and back onto the nicotine.

She straightened as Will approached, squinting slightly against the light, surprisingly bright for so early in the day, so early in the year – Helen, wearing black trousers over red ankle boots, a grey sweater under a blue wool coat, her newly lightened hair pulled back – and Will thought, not for the first time, what a good-looking woman she was and wondered why men – if that was her preference, which it seemed to be – were not forever beating a path to her door.

Perhaps they were.

One sour and oddly possessive relationship aside, she had rarely, if ever, confided in Will about the vicissitudes of her private life – and only then because she had been hospitalised and feeling especially low.

'Hi,' Helen said cheerily now.

'Hi yourself.'

'Kids okay?'

'Fine.'

'Lorraine?'

'Likewise.'

Helen grinned. 'Got it made, haven't you?'

'Have I?'

'Beautiful wife, lovely kids, clear up rate second to none.'

Will frowned. 'Is there a point to this? Or is it just your normal common or garden goading for a Monday morning?'

Helen tilted her head sideways. 'There's a point.'

'Because if it's about your promotion, I've told you I'll support . . .'

'It's not my promotion, long-overdue as that might be.'

'Then what?'

'Mitchell Roberts.'

'What about him?'

'He's being released.'

'When?'

'End of the week.'

'Jesus!'

'Supervision order, but . . .' Helen shrugged.

'Jesus!' Will said again. 'Jesus fuck!'

Helen ground her cigarette butt beneath her heel and followed him between the cars towards the entrance to the building . . .

Gone to Ground

John Harvey

'Stylish writing, cunning plotting, sharp characterisation, thrills, chills, and lime-sharp twists.'
Reginald Hill

Will's first thought when he saw the man's face: it was like a glove that had been pulled inside out . . .

Stephen Bryan, a gay academic, is found brutally murdered in his bathroom. Will Grayson and Helen Walker, police detectives investigating the case, at first assume that his death is the result of an ill-judged sexual encounter: rough trade gone wrong.

But doubts are soon raised. Bryan's laptop has gone missing – could the murder be connected to a biography he was writing on the life and mysterious death of fifties screen legend, Stella Leonard?

Convinced there's a link, Bryan's sister Lesley sets out to prove that Bryan had uncovered a dangerous truth, and that – desperate to keep it hidden – Stella Leonard's rich and influential family have silenced him.

But soon both Lesley and Helen Walker find themselves victims of the violence that swirls around them, as gradually the investigation uncovers the secrets of a family corrupted by lust, wealth and power . . .

'Harvey is a master craftsman . . . this is classic stuff.'
Guardian

arrow books